Kandy Shepherd swapped a career as a magazine editor for a life writing romance. She lives on a small farm in the Blue Mountains near Sydney, Australia, with her husband, daughter, and lots of pets. She believes in love at first sight and real-life romance—they worked for her! Kandy loves to hear from her readers. Visit her at kandyshepherd.com.

Ruby Basu lives in the beautiful Chilterns with her husband, two children, and the cutest dog in the world. She worked for many years as a lawyer and policy lead in the Civil Service. As the second of four children, Ruby connected strongly with *Little Women*'s Jo March, and was scribbling down stories from a young age. She loves creating new characters and worlds.

SECOND CHANCE WITH HIS CINDERELLA

KANDY SHEPHERD

BABY SURPRISE FOR THE MILLIONAIRE

RUBY BASU

MILLS & BOON

First Published in Great Britain 2022
by Mills & Boon, an imprint of HarperCollins*Publishers* Ltd,
1 London Bridge Street, London, SE1 9GF

www.harpercollins.co.uk

HarperCollins*Publishers*
1st Floor, Watermarque Building,
Ringsend Road, Dublin 4, Ireland

Second Chance with His Cinderella © 2022 Kandy Shepherd

Baby Surprise for the Millionaire © 2022 Ruby Basu

ISBN: 978-0-263-30212-7

SECOND CHANCE WITH HIS CINDERELLA

KANDY SHEPHERD

MILLS & BOON

To Julie O'Loughlin and Lynne Bartlett,
who so expertly and cheerfully packed up
my possessions for me when I moved house—
and gave me insight and inspiration for this story.

CHAPTER ONE

SEBASTIAN DELFONT STOOD still and silent on the balcony of his Docklands penthouse as he gazed for the last time at the early-morning mist rising from the Thames and shrouding his view of the London skyline. His fists curled over the top of the cold metal railing so tightly it hurt him. But he scarcely noticed. He could no longer evade his duty to the name he bore. He had to leave here and say goodbye to his independence, his freedom to live his life on his terms. Death had swept through his family and now it was his time to step up.

He heaved a deep profound sigh, knowing there was no one nearby to hear him. How could he possibly feel sorry for himself? Immense wealth. Privilege. A place in the highest echelons of society. All came with the inheritance. Yet the family history was scarred by tragedy and loss. He felt trapped by that story. But he could not walk away from it. He was a Delfont and with that came responsibility and duty, no matter how unwelcome.

The women he'd engaged to pack up the apartment would soon be here. PWP had come highly recommended as specialist packers giving discretion, skill and care. He could only have the best professionals handling his possessions. Of his books, artworks and collectibles some were valuable, others valuable only to him. All were important. In some way they cocooned him with the security he had longed for while growing up. Many of the items would have to go into storage as they wouldn't suit the period house on Cheyne Walk. Like he himself didn't suit, had never suited.

Once the packers arrived, his home here would be dismantled until it would no longer be his own; he had already let it for a hefty rent. He could only ever regard the house he was moving to as his grandfather's, no matter what the deeds of ownership might say. And he had never spent a happy moment there.

It was shaping up to be a typical October day in London, unable to make up its mind whether to be crisp and autumnal or cloudy and drizzly. As Sebastian started to turn and go back inside, a shaft of sunlight pierced the grey clouds. He watched for a long moment as its brilliance illuminated the sky and the water below. His Spanish mother had been superstitious, and a part of him could not help hoping that this was an omen for the times to come.

Kitty Clements never felt nervous at the start of a new assignment. Why would she? Launching their company PWP—People Who Pack—two years ago with her friend Claudia had been an excellent way for her to make a new start. Packing prized possessions for clients moving house was straightforward, interesting—who could resist a peek into other people's lives?—and gave her the under-the-radar anonymity she craved.

But today her hand wasn't quite steady as she keyed in the code to admit her to the private elevator that would shoot her up to the ninth floor and the Docklands penthouse that their client, Sebastian Delfont, was vacating. She'd been warned the client might be 'difficult' and she wasn't quite sure what that could mean. She had cause to distrust difficult men. But this was a client. And the job was the most lucrative they'd contracted in their two years of business. Everything here had to go without a hitch. Their business relied heavily on recommendation and word of mouth. Who knew where a testimonial from a wealthy client like Sebastian Delfont could lead?

The elevator deposited her in the starkly elegant marble foyer of the penthouse. Her nervousness dissipated at the reassuring sight of folded flat packing boxes propped against a wall, along with bales of wrapping paper and boxes of sealing tape that had been delivered the evening before by a member of their team. The tools of her new trade. She would find more placed in each of the rooms. This was a substantial job and she and Claudia would be here for several days. As soon as she was inside, she would put in her earbuds, switch on some get-those-boxes-packed music and get going. She knew what she was doing. There was nothing to worry about.

As the double doors to the penthouse opened Kitty looked up. She caught her breath. *Difficult* wasn't the thought that came to mind at her first sight of Sebastian Delfont. *Outrageously handsome* was more to the point. And young, thirtyish she guessed. Why hadn't Claudia told her? Claudia was the one who did the initial negotiating with clients; surely she hadn't failed to notice he was hot, if a touch forbidding? *Hotter than hot.*

Tall, broad-shouldered, with black hair that looked as if it was past time for a cut and a lean, chiselled face with more than a morning's dark stubble, he was dressed in black jeans and black turtleneck sweater that made no secret of a strong athletic body. Not that she should be noticing. *How could she not notice?*

'Mr D... Delfont,' she managed to stammer out. 'Kitty Clements from PWP.'

Dark brows furrowed. 'I was expecting Claudia.' His voice was deep, resonant and very posh.

Kitty felt a quick flash of the self-doubt she still battled to overcome. Of course he would be disappointed. Claudia was tall, red-haired, glamorous in her own understated way. Kitty was shorter and curvier, more cute than couture. Not, perhaps, to be taken as seriously as her friend. How had that horrid red-top tabloid headlined her? *Pretty, Plump and Predatory.* She shuddered at the very thought of it. The man who'd lost her a promising career in public relations had been the predator, not her. But no one had believed her.

She forced a bright professional smile. 'Claudia is caught up in traffic; a lorry overturned on the motorway. She'll be here as soon as she can. In the meantime, I'm ready to start packing if you'd like to point me in the right direction.'

'I'll show you exactly what I require,' he said.

'Of course,' she said. It wasn't in her nature to be subservient but in this business the client's needs ruled.

Kitty followed him into the apartment, taking care to keep a good distance apart. She couldn't help a heartfelt silent 'wow'. PWP had packed up flats, suburban houses, country manor houses, even a houseboat. But nothing as spectacular as this. The enormous apartment was all stainless steel and glass and stark designer furniture. She looked through walls of glass doors to a spectacular view of the Thames.

'Very impressive,' she said.

'Yes, it is,' he said. 'I'll be sorry to leave here.'

I would be too, she almost said. But her own feelings and thoughts didn't come into this job. Sometimes clients didn't even bother to remember her name. And that anonymity suited her very well.

Kitty knew this client was moving to an even more impressive house on Cheyne Walk, Chelsea, one of the most prestigious and expensive addresses in London. PWP had been employed to unpack there. But it was not her place to chit-chat about his move. She was just here to pack up what her grandfather called 'goods and chattels' as quickly and safely as possible. It was PWP policy that packers didn't get personal with clients.

Sebastian Delfont picked up a small black digital camera from the console and handed it to her. 'Before you start to pack, I want you to photograph everything so it can be placed in exactly the same way in the new house. The library is particularly important.'

It was an unusual request, but nothing she couldn't handle. 'I can do that,' she said.

'I'll take you to the library first,' he said.

Kitty followed him through the living areas and past the kitchen. The rooms were all furnished in the same modern style, shades of grey and metallics a foil for a collection of contemporary paintings and sculptures. It was very masculine. Was there a Mrs Delfont? There was certainly no feminine touch here.

The library was a surprise; it was lined with bookshelves crammed with books from top to bottom. The limited wall space was covered in brightly coloured paintings that jarred with the sombre tones of the rest of the apartment. Claudia had warned her there'd be a lot of books. They'd had to order more of the smaller book boxes than ever before. Paper was heavy and a bigger box packed with books would be too heavy to handle, both for the packer and the mover who would transport them. Thankfully, there was a library ladder that would help her access the top levels. Still, it was a daunting task.

'That's a lot of books,' she said. 'I'd better get started.'

Her client put up his hand in a halt sign. A masculine hand yet somehow elegant, long fingers with well-kept nails. The man had the looks to be an actor or a model. But she had never heard of him. And that accent didn't come from lessons at drama school.

'Not just yet,' he said. 'First, I want you to photograph each row of books. They have to be placed in exactly the same order on the bookshelves in the other house. There mustn't be one book out of place.'

Kitty swallowed hard. So this was what Claudia meant by saying their client might be difficult. Obsessive, it seemed. Would he be standing over her shoulder, directing her every move? She gritted her teeth at the thought. But that was okay. He was the client. His demands were nothing she couldn't handle, although she would have to tread carefully. As long as he didn't get too physically close to her. She couldn't deal with that.

'I understand,' she said very seriously. 'I think I might also record the order of the rows in a notebook as an extra working document and then label each box with a code.'

'Good,' he said as he nodded. And she saw what she could only interpret as a flash of gratitude in his slate-grey eyes.

Sebastian went to turn on his heel to leave the room but then paused, arrested by the way Kitty Clements's hair, loosely tied behind her head, glowed golden in that sole shaft of sunlight that filtered through the window.

She was very pretty. He fought for a less clichéd word to describe her. Blonde hair, a heart-shaped face, blue eyes—what else could he think but pretty? Pretty, cute, curvaceous. They all worked. Her black leggings and a long baggy black T-shirt with a bright pink PWP logo emblazoned across her chest did nothing to hide her shape.

But it was more than her pretty face and shapely figure that made him look twice. He'd seen warmth and kindness in those blue eyes, understanding without condescension. She hadn't questioned his requests, just thoughtfully suggested further ways of making sure she did what he needed. His doctor had reassured him he did not have obsessive compulsive disorder, but he knew his desire for control over certain aspects of his personal environment wasn't everyday behaviour and it sometimes made people uncomfortable around him.

Not, so it seemed, Kitty Clements. After all he'd been through with Lavinia, his former fiancée, who had fought to turn him into what she wanted and ruthlessly mocked his need for orderliness in his library, he was grateful for Kitty's quiet understanding. Even though she was just a woman he had engaged to pack up his possessions.

He knew he should leave the library and let her get on with it—after all, he was paying her by the hour—but he found himself compelled to stay.

'What made you go into packing as a job?' he asked. The PWP website had listed both her and her business partner Claudia Eaton as directors.

'I wanted to be my own boss.'

'Understandable. Why packing?' He noticed how sleekly muscled Kitty's arms were; her workday was probably equivalent to a weightlifting session at a gym.

'I had to pack up my flat in a hurry, had no time to pack for myself and wasn't in the slightest bit happy with the way the movers did it.'

No explanation of why she'd had to pack up in such a hurry. Sebastian felt he was on the receiving end of a practised spiel she no doubt gave to any client who showed interest. It did nothing to deflect his interest; rather it made him intrigued about what story lay behind those guileless blue eyes.

'I see,' he said.

'Claudia had a similar experience. We knew we could do better. Much better. At first we worked freelance with a big removals company then set up on our own. We found there was a demand for women packers. People believe we take more care with their possessions, and some people feel more comfortable with women in their house.' Her smile was like a practised punctuation to her story. Yet it lit her eyes and seemed to up the wattage of the sunbeam that danced through her hair.

'Why PWP?' he asked. The small specialist company had come highly recommended for honesty and discretion.

'People Who Pack,' she said. 'We started with Ladies Who Pack. After all, our earlier clients referred to us as "those ladies who pack".' Her smile dimmed and she gave a small, almost imperceptible shudder. 'But it brought us the wrong kind of attention. We were also accused of being discriminatory. So we amended the name and went from there. It keeps us fit and we enjoy it. Now we have a team of women working for us.'

She looked pointedly at her watch. 'And, talking of working, I have a lot of books to pack.'

'And you want me out of here,' he said.

'Please. I know what I have to do, and I don't need you to direct me. I'll call you if I need any clarification.' Her words were lightly said and delivered with another smile, but it was a definite dismissal.

To his surprise, Sebastian was okay with that. He felt reassured his books would be packed—and unpacked— just the way he wanted them to be. His spirits—subdued since he'd awoken this morning, aware that it was the last day of his life as a lone wolf—lifted with the knowledge. There could be no doubt he was in good hands with PWP—and Kitty Clements.

'I'll leave you to it,' he said as he somewhat reluctantly left the room.

Kitty was fascinated by the contents of Sebastian's bookshelves. The titles ranged from leather-bound first editions and histories of London to the latest bestsellers. She had to force herself not to get too distracted by them. She was here to pack, not to browse. While the books were mainly in English, there were titles in Spanish too. Surprisingly, there was an entire row of paperback romances all by one author, Marisol Matthew. Kitty held a title in her hand for a moment too long before she carefully placed it in the box with the others—in strict order of publication. Memories came flooding back.

After her parents had died when she was fourteen years old, Kitty had been brought up by her maternal grandparents. Her beloved grandmother had been an avid reader of romance novels and Marisol Matthew one of her favourite authors. Towards the end of her battle with cancer, Gran had become too weak to read or hold a book. The last story Kitty had read out loud to her, as she'd sat by her bedside, was by Marisol Matthew—a rousing tale with a gorgeous Spanish hero. Gran had loved it.

Sebastian Delfont didn't seem to be the type to be a romance reader, but she had learned the hard way not to judge people by appearances. There was also a shelf packed with the latest thrillers. One thing was for sure, she wouldn't ask him. Part of the PWP code of conduct was to keep up the illusion of privacy by never commenting on the client's belongings. No matter the sometimes startling and strange things they might come across.

Kitty was well into the rhythm of packing books, taking notes and coding boxes when Claudia arrived. Her best friend and business partner rushed to her side.

'I'm so sorry to leave you alone with a new client, a man. But it couldn't be helped. The fuel tanker blocking the way was in danger of exploding. We actually had to turn around and go back on the wrong side of the road until we could get onto a diversion. Are you okay?'

Kitty brushed aside her friend's apologies. Claudia had been there for her through the entire unpleasant time she'd reported the director of the big public relations firm where she'd worked for attempted sexual assault. She hadn't been believed and the incident had been turned against her.

'I'm fine. Seriously. Sebastian Delfont is okay. I feel safe with him.'

'Good. I liked him too. Although I thought he might be difficult about the way he wanted things packed.'

Kitty shook her head. 'He's exacting. But not difficult. Nothing we can't handle.'

'I'm glad to hear that.'

Kitty turned to her friend. 'But you might have warned me about how good-looking he is. We've never packed for such a hot client. It's quite distracting. I... I didn't know where to look at first.'

Claudia smirked. 'Does it matter? As you haven't dated for the last two years, in fact have sworn off dating for ever, I didn't think you'd notice.'

But Kitty had noticed, was intensely aware of Sebastian Delfont. Even though there was a strict rule against establishing personal relationships with PWP clients. Even though it was true she'd sworn off dating.

She'd made that vow not just because of what had happened with the director, not because she'd lost her job and her reputation as a rising star in the PR world, but because her boyfriend had publicly doubted her word. To stand by her had meant he would be standing against his manager. He'd decided not to risk his own career in the company.

His betrayal had hurt her more than anything else—the doubts cast on her honesty, the slurs on her character, even the lurid headlines in the tabloids. All those fervent words of love, their plans for a future together, had been destroyed by the fever of her ex's ambition. How could she ever allow herself to trust in love again?

CHAPTER TWO

SEBASTIAN'S NEW HOME, the detached four-storey period mansion on Cheyne Walk, was magnificent. With a prime position on the Chelsea Embankment on the northern bank of the River Thames, it was worth untold millions. The building had come into Sebastian's family's hands as their townhouse more than one hundred and eighty years ago. But could he ever consider it home?

He stood in the new library, a former bedroom he'd had gutted to accommodate the custom-made bookshelves. Despite the changes, his grandfather's presence seemed to be embedded in the walls. The grandfather who had seemed to despise Sebastian's very being because his father had married against his wishes. Sebastian's beautiful, loving Spanish mother had been persona non grata and so, by extension, had been her son.

He had never felt welcome in this house. Both sets of grandparents had been against his parents' youthful marriage. His Spanish family had thawed somewhat when baby Sebastian was born. Not so his English grandparents.

His father had been on a gap year in Spain after he'd finished university when he'd met his mother, an art student who had been working as a barmaid. They'd married in a hurry when they'd discovered Sebastian was on the way. The day his parents had exchanged vows, his wealthy

English grandfather had revoked his second son's trust fund. The birth of his grandson hadn't softened his stance.

Money had been very tight for the young couple, who'd existed on seasonal work that dropped dramatically at the end of each tourist season. In the hope of getting financial help, Sebastian's father had taken his baby son back to London, staying in this house. Even as a toddler Sebastian had sensed the hostility from his grandfather and a puzzling lack of affection from his grandmother. Weren't older ladies meant to swoop him up and smother him with kisses and cuddles?

By all accounts, the early years of his parents' marriage had been stressful, lack of money being a major issue, his father's homesickness and alienation from his family another. Several times, his father had taken him to London to try and forge a connection between his son and his grandparents, to seek help.

When he was nine years old his father had brought him here from their home in Barcelona to live for four months, the longest of any visit either before or after. The deal, brokered by his grandparents, had been that they would pay his father's tuition fees for him to study for a postgraduate teaching qualification, if Sebastian attended a private boys' school. His mother had stayed in Spain, working to help keep their little family afloat.

That had meant four months of seeing his mother only once at half-term break. Four months of his grandfather's harsh rules that had made him tiptoe around this house, terrified of angering the tyrannical old man. He simply hadn't been able to fit into the rigid mould his grandfather had tried to force him into—then or later.

In defiance of those expectations, he'd done very well treading his own path in the world of finance. He was independently wealthy. He'd never had to ask his grandfather for a penny. All the family obligations had fallen on the shoulders of his uncle, the first-born son, and his father, the 'spare' second son. The tragedy of both their premature deaths had established Sebastian as the reluctant heir. Although he had still been no closer to the grandfather who, it had seemed, would live for ever. Yet his grandfather had died six months ago—felled by a virus—and had left everything to Sebastian, his only living heir.

Sebastian's first thought had been that the inheritance was a hateful burden. He'd wanted to sell the house and put the memories it held behind him. And yet it was his heritage. Duty to his name, to his blood, reined in his impulse to shed them. He felt he owed it to his father and his uncle, whom he'd loved, to carry on the family traditions that had been so important to them both—despite the way his father had been treated. And he'd felt a link to the ancestors who had lived here since way back when his great-great-multiple times-great-grandfather had made his initial fortune in railways and textiles. Not all his ancestors had been the mean tyrant his grandfather was—he was proud to share their name.

'Knock-knock.' A sweet feminine voice interrupted his bitter memories of the past. Kitty Clements stood at the carved wooden doorway into the room. In her leggings and sturdy trainers, her cheeks flushed from exertion, she looked far from glamorous. But he couldn't remember when he'd last seen a lovelier woman.

'I wanted to check if you're happy with the way we stacked the bookshelves,' she said. 'Because if—'

The move to his late grandfather's house was proving to be not as traumatic as Sebastian had anticipated. He put that happy circumstance down to the cheerful, matter-of-fact presence of Kitty and Claudia from PWP over the last two days. Especially Kitty. Her golden hair and bright eyes seemed to bring sunshine to the darkest corners of the house and the sound of her laughter banished

memories of angry shouted words. He realised his interactions with her were not about checking the accuracy of
her work but about simply enjoying her presence.

'You've done a wonderful job,' he said. 'Perfect, in
fact. Every book is in its correct place, exactly as planned.
Thank you.'

She smiled. 'I'm glad. I knew how important it was to
you to have everything just so.' Again, he had that feeling
of an unstated but real understanding. She seemed kind.
Not a quality he'd often found in the women he'd dated.
'It was a challenge, but satisfying. The work we did at the
other end paid off.'

'I appreciate that,' he said. He also appreciated the way
she behaved as if there was nothing unusual about his request. There would be a generous bonus going PWP's way.

Sebastian couldn't imagine that unpacking boxes and
crates would be much fun, but Kitty gave every appearance of enjoying it. He'd like to ask her about her career
before she'd become a person who packed but it would be
inappropriate; she was what his grandfather would have
called 'hired help'. He'd like to know her personal status
too—she didn't wear a wedding or engagement ring but
that didn't necessarily mean anything. She and her business partner, while pleasant and courteous, were careful to
maintain a professional distance. But surely it must have
been a job where she'd dealt with people, as Kitty was
so warm and engaging. Retail? Hospitality? Health care?

'Thank you,' she said. 'We're on track to finish this afternoon. Let me know if there's anything else we can do
for you before we leave.'

Kitty was leaving. Of course she was. He'd employed
her to do a job and she'd fulfilled the terms of the contract
most efficiently. He didn't know why he railed at the idea
of saying goodbye to her, but he did. He tried to think of
something that could delay her departure.

She glanced down at her watch. 'I would particularly like to leave on time today.'

Who did she go home to? A husband? Kids? A woman this appealing would surely not be single. Whoever held Kitty's heart would be a lucky man.

Sebastian felt saddened by the fact that, unless he decided to move house, he would never see Kitty Clements again. He didn't like that idea at all.

The light would go out when she left this house and he would be left to face the shadows on his own.

During her two years of business with PWP, Kitty had noticed the difference in people's attitudes towards the stages of a house move.

Packing up to leave was often tinged with sadness, especially if it was a move prompted by circumstances such as divorce or a landlord's whim. Even in the wake of a much-anticipated move there was angst about what to pack and what to discard. Countless times she'd had to unseal a taped box to accommodate an impulsive inclusion of something rescued from the give-to-charity pile.

Unpacking at the new dwelling, on the other hand, was sometimes a resigned acceptance of changed circumstances but more often a time of excitement at new beginnings. Of people rushing about oohing and aahing as they fitted belongings from an old life into an exciting new one.

Not so with Sebastian Delfont. His new home on Cheyne Walk was, hands down, the most amazing house she'd ever seen. And in her former life in public relations she'd seen inside more than a few grand residences, used for location shoots and product launches. Sebastian's house was four storeys of traditional luxury, high ceilings, ornate staircases and spacious rooms furnished with priceless antiques. It faced the Thames, glorying in a part of London that boasted the millionaire postcode of SW3.

Yet in the two days she'd spent there unpacking, her client had showed little excitement at his change of circumstances. His attitude seemed decidedly glum. Kitty couldn't understand why. Did he have no idea how the other half lived? How fortunate he was? Her entire rented flat where she'd lived in Camberwell would have fitted into one of the reception rooms.

Since the day she'd first met him she'd seethed with curiosity about this gorgeous man. Spoiled rich boy, so used to this level of privilege and wealth it simply didn't make an impression? Perhaps. That would go with the posh accent. Yet he struck her as being more down-to-earth. For one thing, he'd organised coffee and tea for her and Claudia in the vast old-fashioned kitchen, which was not something all clients thought to do.

She stood facing him in his refurbished library, the only newly decorated room in the house, having passed his inspection of the books placed in their correct order.

'What next?' she asked. 'I believe you have the people we recommended coming to hang your pictures tomorrow. We've stacked them against the walls in the same places they were hung in your Docklands apartment. We've also sent them the photos of how they looked there.'

'Well done. I'd put them up myself but hanging pictures is an art form in itself.'

'That's a good way of putting it.'

Kitty paused, knowing she shouldn't be chatting with him, but unable to stop herself. There was something about this man that interested her. Okay, be honest, attracted her. She couldn't deny that he'd occupied rather too much space in her thoughts than a client should. But she'd never see him again after today. She didn't move in the same elite circles as people who lived in Cheyne Walk.

She indicated the paintings in this room, lined up along the wall. 'I love those pictures. They bring a splash of

Mediterranean colour into gloomy old London. Where are they from?'

'The island of Mallorca.'

'Gorgeous,' she said.

'I think so,' he said.

There was another question she ached to know the answer to and this was her last chance. 'I notice you have a lot of books here by Marisol Matthew. My grandmother loved romance novels and was a real fan of hers. I also loved them. With all those books on the shelf, you must be a fan too.'

'You could say that,' he said.

His tone was oddly neutral but still Kitty ploughed on; if she didn't, she would always wonder about the presence of those books on this man's shelves.

'When my gran was ill, she got me to read her favourite books out loud to her. Her very favourites were by Marisol Matthew; they were a great distraction in her... in her last days.'

She cursed under her breath. What had possessed her to say something so personal? Claudia would want to fire her. She wanted to fire herself. Personal details unwisely shared could be used as ammunition; she knew that only too well.

'She would have liked that.'

Kitty looked up at him. 'You knew her?'

'Marisol Matthew was my mother,' he said.

Kitty was so taken aback she struggled to find words. 'Your mother?' was all she was able to stammer out. 'I... I had no idea.'

'Why would you?' He politely didn't state the obvious: that she knew nothing about him either. 'Her true identity was a well-kept secret.'

Kitty knew the author had died some years ago; her

grandmother had mourned the fact there would be no new books.

'Really and truly? Marisol Matthew was your mother?'

He smiled. Kitty realised it was the first time she'd seen him smile. It was the merest lifting of the corners of his mouth, but it lit his grey eyes and lightened his expression. He was even more handsome than the handsomest of the heroes in his mother's books. She caught her breath as awareness tingled through her.

'Really,' he said. 'I'm very proud of her. Of both of them. Not many people knew, but she worked with my father on her books. She came up with the stories and the characters and he helped her with the English as it wasn't her first language. Her name was Maria and his was Matthew. Marisol is a combination of Maria and the Spanish word for sun.'

'Was she Spanish? I only ask that as she wrote about such wonderful Spanish heroes.' But none so utterly gorgeous as her son. The thought intruded, despite Kitty's insistent jumping down on it.

'She was very Spanish.' His smile deepened.

'And your father was English?' She paused. 'Of course he must have been.'

He nodded. 'Matthew Delfont.'

She should leave it at that; she'd overstepped the boundaries already. But Kitty felt an urgent desire to grab as much knowledge about this intriguing man as she could while the clock ticked down to her departure.

'Did your parents live here?'

'No. But my father grew up in this house.'

'And you?'

He scowled. 'Only briefly.'

'Oh,' she said, realising that she might have strayed into a story where she had no right to be. But she couldn't help but register that he looked even more handsome in an intense, brooding way when his dark brows drew together in that forbidding scowl. She wondered whether he always wore black, because it certainly suited him.

'This was my grandfather's house. He died six months ago and I inherited.'

'I see,' she said, not at all certain she did or even wanted to.

'He and I did not see eye to eye,' he said. 'He was somewhat of a tyrant.'

A *tyrant*. Her own grandfather was kind and thoughtful. She couldn't imagine having a tyrant for a grandfather and she itched to know more about Sebastian Delfont's fascinating family. But Claudia would be here any moment for their final wrap-up of this job. Enthralling as she found this discussion, she had to quickly change the subject. The conversation had definitely strayed way too far into the personal.

She took a deep breath and forced herself to sound practical and professional. 'This beautiful old house will need a lot of maintenance,' she said. 'Have you got all your household staff in place?' Imagine having a place where you needed household staff. It was a world she was getting an outsider's glimpse into.

'Not yet. There was a mass exodus after my grandfather died.'

'They were loyal to him? To someone his own grandson calls a tyrant?'

'Whatever his other faults, his staff were loyal. They wanted to retire. The live-in housekeeper was here for as long as I can remember. She was practically fossilised.'

A housekeeper. Kitty's imagination sketched images of a stern lady dressed all in black with the keys to the household kept on a chain around her waist, or someone round and jolly but with a firm hand, presiding over a 'downstairs' domain. She had no real-life experience of a housekeeper. Friends with busy careers had household help, but no one she knew had an actual live-in housekeeper.

'Your grandfather must have paid them fairly.' She knew only too well that loyalty could be bought.

'The salaries seemed above board, and they each retired with a good pension.'

In that case, if the staff were looked after properly, perhaps she could help. It wasn't the first time a client had moved into a new home and felt overwhelmed at the thought of getting it in shape. 'I can recommend Maids in Chelsea if you're looking for staff. They're an excellent agency. Quality people, credentials all checked.'

'Thank you,' he said. 'I'll note that.'

She glanced down at her watch. 'If there's nothing else, I'll finish up.' She paused, knowing there was no scope for a personal goodbye. 'Thank you for giving PWP the business. It's been a great assignment for us.' She wouldn't forget Sebastian Delfont in a hurry.

'You've exceeded all expectations,' he said.

She looked up at him, and for a long moment she met his steady grey gaze. Was there a hint of interest in her there, echoing her own interest in him? She felt overwhelmed by a pang of melancholy for something she could never explore, not with this man.

Flustered, she dropped her gaze, risked another personal comment, talking too fast, tripping over her words. 'I'm going to go home and reread my gran's Marisol Matthew books. She would have been thrilled to know I've met the author's son.'

'As my mother would have been thrilled to have such an avid fan. You have your grandmother's books at home?'

'I actually live with my grandfather and all her books are still there.' It was only a year since Gran had died and neither she nor Gramps could bear to change anything that would eradicate her presence.

'You're not married?'

Kitty choked on her surprise. 'Er...no.' And not likely to be any time soon. This was the first time she'd experienced even a twinge of attraction to a man since the disaster with Neil.

'Children?'

'I'll say no to that too.' She was twenty-eight; there was time for that yet. If she ever got the man right, if she ever trusted someone enough to commit. 'What about you? Are you married?' There had been no evidence of a wife or children in either of his residences, but you never knew.

'No,' he said. 'No ties.'

Again Sebastian held her gaze. A tremor of excitement rippled through her. Was he going to ask her out? She'd say no. Of course she would. It was impossible. He was a client. They came from different worlds. But he was *so* attractive. Surely rules were meant to be bent? Especially when she'd been the one to impose them.

'The reason I ask—' That voice! So deep and, well, yes, sexy.

Kitty felt herself swaying towards him in anticipation. She held her breath, was conscious of her heart beating so fast he could surely hear it. 'Yes?'

'—is I'm in dire need of an excellent housekeeper I can trust, and I think you'd be perfect. I'd like to offer you the job.'

CHAPTER THREE

SEBASTIAN THOUGHT HIS off-the-cuff idea to offer Kitty Clements the housekeeper's job had been an excellent one. Not only had he realised he needed help with this house, the idea had been a spur-of-the-moment brainwave to ensure he would see her again. However, as soon as the words left his mouth, he realised he might have made a very big mistake. In fact she might have taken his well-intentioned offer as an insult.

Kitty's blue eyes widened as she stared up at him for a long moment. 'Me? A housekeeper? Are you kidding?' Her tone was more abrupt than he might have expected. 'I'm not known for my housewifely skills.'

He frowned. 'But you're brilliant at packing.'

'Different skill set altogether.' She started to say something then stopped. 'You really don't want to know about the fuzzy things growing in my refrigerator. Or the fact I've been known to go out and buy underwear because I'm so behind on my laundry. Or—' She smiled but it seemed forced. 'I'll leave it there.'

Sebastian was glad she had. He didn't want to think about Kitty in her underwear. More to the point, if he let his thoughts stray that way he might think about Kitty without her underwear. Specifically, about him slowly peeling off said underwear, exploring the curves teasingly concealed by that long, baggy T-shirt.

'What exactly is the skill set required for a house-keeper?' he asked.

Kitty shrugged. 'I haven't a clue. I've never been fortunate enough to have one.'

'Neither have I,' he said.

'Really?' Her eyebrows rose in obvious disbelief. 'What about the housekeeper here who retired?'

'My grandfather's housekeeper. Employed by my late grandmother heaven knows how long ago. The only thing I needed to know about Mrs Danvers—that was my father's name for her—was how to stay out of her way. I visited this house on and off through my childhood, actually lived here for a while when I was nine years old. She didn't appreciate having an active little boy underfoot. I found her terrifying.' When he thought back to his time here, the house had been full of scary old people. No wonder he'd hated it.

'What about your parents?'

'Never. For one thing, they couldn't afford a house-keeper. My parents married very young, against my grandfather's wishes. Her family weren't happy about the marriage either. They struggled in their early years.'

'I see,' Kitty said.

Of course she couldn't possibly understand. Like others, she would see the trappings of his wealth, both earned and inherited, and make assumptions. But he'd shared enough of his family history. 'For another, my mother would have seen employing one as an affront to her housekeeping skills. And she made certain my father and I pulled our weight with household chores.'

'Just like an ordinary family,' Kitty said. 'I mean a family who doesn't live in a house like this.' She indicated the grandeur around her with a sweep of her hand. 'You could hardly call this ordinary.'

'But not mine,' he said. 'At least not until recently.'

Her eyes narrowed. Suspicion looked cute on her. 'What about your fabulous apartment in Docklands?'

'Mine, yes.'

'I didn't see so much as a spot of dust when we were packing. Did you do the housework yourself?'

'A team of commercial cleaners once a week. Efficient and anonymous.'

'The kitchen was pristine. The plastic wrapping was still on the oven door.'

'Why bother to cook when I was surrounded by restaurants and food delivery services?'

'Same in Chelsea,' she said. 'Restaurants galore.'

'Yes,' he said. 'But my life will be different here. More obligations. I'll be expected to entertain, to live a more public life.' A life he had never sought, but had promised his grandmother, practically on her deathbed, that he would take up. 'And the house needs to be brought up to date.'

'I know what you mean about the house.' She looked around her. 'It's beautiful but a touch...not outmoded— that's not the right word—not gloomy, that's not the right word either.'

'An old person's house?'

'Not that either, although I know what you mean. But the rooms I've seen are so elegant and spacious, the antique furniture so timeless, maybe it simply needs to be lightened up.'

'What would you do with the house?'

'Me?' She looked startled. 'I'm no interior designer.'

'But you must see inside a lot of houses in your line of work.'

'To be honest, your house is one of the most beautiful I've been in. You wouldn't want to ruin its character by modernising it too much. Perhaps change the curtains from heavy dark velvet to linen or silk. Replace some of the wallpapers. Swap out the dark carpets for something fresher. That would make an immediate difference.'

'How would I go about that?'

He honestly didn't know. The Docklands apartment had been brand-new when he'd moved in. All he'd had to do was order the furnishings and make sure there was a place for his cherished possessions. He'd easily replicated that library here by giving measurements and photos to a decorator recommended by his father's lawyer, who'd been unimaginative but good at following orders.

He'd never allowed himself to get attached to places, or people for that matter. Too often as a child, as his parents followed seasonal work, he'd been torn away from rooms he'd settled into, a school where he'd made friends, a neighbour's dog he'd grown to love. As an adult he'd had more control over his life and this library, in some form, had gone with him—to his room at his uncle's house when he'd moved for university, to the rented apartments where he'd lived until he'd bought in Docklands. His obsession with keeping it just so had been a source of cruel amusement for Lavinia—which had only made him more obsessive about it, about his other possessions that had significance.

'Employ an excellent interior designer who would respect the history of the house,' Kitty said. 'You should get them to update the kitchen and bathrooms too.'

He nodded. 'You mean put my own stamp on the house?'

'Rid it of your tyrant grandfather.' Again that understanding from Kitty that he didn't expect.

'There is a lingering sense of his presence,' he conceded. The Spanish side of him felt something the pragmatic English side of him couldn't really acknowledge.

Kitty paused. 'I haven't got a psychic bone in my body and don't feel any kind of presence. Except that feeling of the lives who have gone before us you find in any old house.'

'That's reassuring,' he said, not sure whether to take her seriously or not.

'But, just in case, you could have a smoking ceremony. I believe you burn sage and wave it around to dispel lurking malevolent spirits.'

A grin tugged at the corners of his mouth. 'He was ghastly, but I don't know that I'd describe my grandfather as lurking and malevolent.'

'But you want to banish him just the same. While at the same time preserving the heritage of the house.'

'Exactly.'

'Think about the sage,' she said with a half-smile.

She glanced down at her watch and Sebastian felt a stab of panic. It was vital he did something to convince her to work with him. Of course he could just ask her out to dinner, but that would take interaction with her to a level he wasn't yet prepared for. His attraction to Kitty had come from nowhere. His mother had made a career out of instant attraction in her heroes and heroines. That was okay in books, not in real life.

Sebastian had grown more cynical when it came to relationships. In real life he had to be more considered. He'd learned his lesson with Lavinia. Uncle Olly had been quite the party animal and when Sebastian had moved to London for university he had always included his nephew when he'd been entertaining. The gorgeous brunette had been part of Uncle Olly's social set, two years older than Sebastian, seductive and sophisticated. He'd been instantly besotted—and he'd completely misjudged her motives. If he'd been more cautious he wouldn't have found himself trapped in an engagement he hadn't really wanted.

He didn't trust the sudden attraction to Kitty. He needed

to test this feeling. Give it time. Get to know her. Be certain. And see if she felt it too.

'On second thoughts, I believe it isn't a housekeeper I need,' he said. 'It's more of a household manager.'

'Not someone to scrub the bathrooms and cook your meals? I warn you, I'm not great at housework.'

'No,' he said dismissively. 'A person who could oversee what needs to be done, find the people to do it.'

'So hire the bathroom scrubber and the cook?'

'And the gardener too. Most importantly, the interior designer you suggest I need. And work with me to make sure it happens.'

She crinkled up her nose in a way he found delightful. 'And you seriously think that person could be me?'

'You've proved yourself to be formidably organised and efficient. And those ideas you've just outlined make sense.'

'But I know absolutely nothing about your needs.'

'My needs?' Needs of a kind that had nothing to do furniture or wallpaper and everything to do with this lovely woman came immediately to mind. The sudden flush high on her cheekbones made him aware her thoughts might have followed a similar path. *Interesting.*

'I… I mean your preferences, your likes and dislikes when it comes to furnishing and decorating and food too, I guess. But it's a moot point. I have my own business. I don't need to be your household manager, or anyone else's for that matter.'

Sebastian had a convincing argument right on the tip of his tongue. He really wanted Kitty to work with him. And not just because he found her so attractive. So why did Claudia have to breeze in at that moment? He smothered a curse word. There was an exchange of glances between the two women that he didn't understand. What did that little nod on Kitty's part mean?

Claudia looked from him to Kitty and back again. 'Did I just hear you offering my business partner a job?'

'No,' Kitty said.

'Yes,' he said. 'I need a household manager and I believe Kitty has just the right skill set for it. I'm prepared to pay more than the going rate, whatever that might be. What do you think?'

Kitty looked a touch bewildered at the speed his idea was progressing. He didn't mean to steamroller her. But the more he thought about it, the more he realised how much he needed her in that role, wanted her in that role. Because, although he'd only known her for a few days, instinctively he trusted her. And trust didn't come easily to him.

Kitty looked up at Sebastian as she considered her reply. Thank heaven she had somehow managed to conceal her utter embarrassment and searing disappointment at mistaking his intentions. There she'd been, entertaining a crazy idea that he was going to ask her out. Instead, he had placed her squarely in the 'downstairs' part of the 'upstairs/downstairs' equation. Weren't people of his class notorious for doing that? Not that she liked to believe such a thing as class existed these days, but his accent and obvious extreme wealth seemed to place him in a different strata from her.

The role of a housekeeper—even when cleverly worded as 'household manager'—brought with it certain implications. The main one being a deeply ingrained imbalance of power—more so even than the office scenario of which she'd fallen foul. Her attacker had taken full advantage of the fact he'd been in a position of power over her. She couldn't get caught in that terrifying trap again. That was the joy of being her own boss. She and Claudia had agreed when they started working together that if one of them felt uncomfortable with a client—male or female—they would not work with them. An instant out was guaranteed.

Not that she felt uncomfortable with Sebastian. Far from it. Not only did she find him almost insanely attractive, but she liked him. Liked him more than she could have imagined liking someone on such a short and limited acquaintanceship. But she didn't want to be at his beck and call.

'I'm flattered. The job interests me. I would love to help give this house a facelift and help you, as you say, put your stamp on it. But I like being my own boss. I'm not looking to be employed ever again. And I wouldn't let Claudia down by leaving our company.'

'Let me try a different tack. I hired you to pack for me on a contract. What if I were to offer you a contract to be my household manager?'

'You mean contract for Kitty's services through PWP?' said Claudia.

'Exactly. A short-term contract. Say six weeks, with an extension to be negotiable.'

He named a fee that made Kitty gasp. She had to disguise the gasp as a cough, so she didn't show her hand in a possible contract negotiation. Her hand being a need for extra money. Gramps was in a rehab hospital after having fallen and broken his leg. She was working with the health service to make his house safer and more old-person-friendly for when he got home. But she was paying to remodel his dated bathroom for safer shower access. That extra money would really help.

'I think we could spare you for six weeks,' Claudia said. 'We've got some good freelance packers in place to handle the rush of people wanting to move before Christmas.'

'That's true,' Kitty said.

She couldn't help but feel excited at the prospect of working for six weeks on something more creative than packing boxes. And she would still be able to stay under

the radar. Who would expect the so-called notorious se-
ducer and accuser of an innocent married man, Kathryn
Clements, to be working as a household manager in one
of the poshest parts of London?

Despite the hideous headlines and the hostility from
her former employer, there were people who believed her
about the assault. She firmly believed she would be vindi-
cated one day. Living and working anonymously in central
London would make it easier for her to keep in touch with
those people and continue her discreet search for other
victims of Edmund Blaine. He'd be exposed one day for
the monster he was. She had to believe that.

She turned to Sebastian. 'If—and it's a big *if*—I took
the job, would I be able to work after hours on admin for
PWP with Claudia?'

'We're talking normal working hours,' he said. 'If you
want to work on your business in your own time, I don't
see a problem.'

'Do you intend this to be a live-in position for Kitty?'
Claudia asked in her best client-interviewing tone.

'There is the housekeeper's apartment on the top floor
or a downstairs guest room with her own bathroom at her
disposal if she wants it,' he said.

Claudia turned to her. 'Great idea, Kitty. You told me
there will be dust and disruption when you start renovations on your grandfather's house. Isn't the builder about
to tear the bathroom out so you can get it all done by the
time he's out of rehab?'

Six weeks living rent-free on Cheyne Walk, one of the
most desirable addresses in London? She should jump
at the chance. Six weeks working shoulder to shoulder
with a man as attractive as Sebastian Delfont? Dangerous, perhaps. Not when she was attracted to him and he
saw her as staff.

'Let me think about it overnight,' she said.

CHAPTER FOUR

Next morning, Kitty made her way through the security gate and up the hedge-bordered pathway to stand at the top of the marble steps outside the glossy black front door of Sebastian's house. Her breath clouded in the chill of the late October morning and she stamped her feet in their fine leather boots. She had spent a sleepless night thinking about Sebastian's offer and wanted to give him her decision today. She nodded to the courier standing by his bike, also waiting for the door to open. 'Can I take the parcel in for you?' she asked.

'Thanks, but no,' he said. 'Legal documents here. They have to be signed for by the recipient.' He looked at the address. 'Sir Sebastian Delfont.'

Kitty's mouth went dry. '*Sir* Sebastian?'

'Lot of sirs and ladies living around here. Dukes and duchesses too. You waiting to see him?'

'Uh, job interview,' she said, still reeling from the revelation of Sebastian's title.

'Good luck,' he said.

The door opened to frame Sebastian—*Sir* Sebastian. He was in black again, superbly cut trousers, a linen shirt that emphasised his broad shoulders, clean-shaven, even more handsome. Her heart thudded a warning: *danger*. She should not acknowledge her attraction to this man, even to herself. It could go nowhere.

He nodded at Kitty with a slow smile that sent a shiver of awareness through her. 'Glad you could make it.' He turned to the courier. 'I need to sign for that.' The courier handed him a large envelope and waited for Sebastian— *Sir* Sebastian—to sign. Kitty watched Sebastian give him a generous tip. The courier waved her a cheerful goodbye as he rode off.

She shivered. Perhaps from the cold, perhaps from trepidation.

'Come in; it's freezing out there,' he said.

Warm air enveloped her as she stepped into the marble tiled foyer. The beautiful old house seemed to be somehow welcoming; she had no feeling she wouldn't fit in there. In a downstairs role, she reminded herself, not as Sebastian's guest. No lingering malevolent spirits had haunted her while she'd been unpacking Sebastian's possessions. She still occasionally dreamed of her parents, taken from her by a drunk driver on the wrong side of the road when she'd been fourteen, but they were a loving presence and she woke from those realistic dreams feeling comforted and happy. It seemed Sebastian's grandfather had been more the stuff of nightmares.

Sebastian went to help her as she shrugged out of her coat. Kitty gave into a little shudder of pleasure as his hands brushed her shoulders. Thankfully, he mistook it for a shiver of coldness.

'You'll warm up quickly; the central heating seems to operate as it should.'

'It's lovely and toasty, thank you, Sir Sebastian.'

He paused, her navy coat over his arm; her favourite red one had been banished to the back of her wardrobe— red drew too much attention.

'It seems strange to hear you call me that,' he said. 'I'm still getting used to it.'

'Really?' Kitty wondered why he hadn't mentioned his

title in his dealings with her and Claudia. She had mixed feelings about it. It deepened the social chasm between them. At the same time, a reference for PWP from Sir Sebastian Delfont rather than Mr Delfont would hold greater sway in the competitive London market.

He hung her coat in the coat cupboard and turned back to face her.

'My grandfather was Sir Cyril. The title should have gone to my uncle, the first born, or my father, the younger brother. They both died too early to ever be Sir Oliver or Sir Matthew and their…their deaths brought the title to me.' He paused in an obvious effort to keep his voice on an even keel. 'It's my birthright, going back to my ancestor who made a fortune from the railways and had a baronetcy conferred on him for his loyal support of parliament.'

So Sebastian was a hereditary baronet. Her training in public relations had taught her how to address people from all walks of life, and the British honours system could be tricky to navigate. To her understanding, a baronet ranked below a baron but above a knighthood.

'That is a long history,' she said slowly. He'd been born into such privilege. Her history was peopled with hardworking everyday folk; her parents had met at university, each the first of their families to get a degree. 'I noticed the round blue plaque on the house honouring John Delfont, the nineteenth century artist who lived here. He was famous for his London landscapes, wasn't he?'

Sebastian nodded. 'There appear to be two streams of talent running through my father's side of the family. The majority of the Delfonts have displayed a remarkable skill for making money. But every generation also kicks up creatives like John Delfont, my great-great-aunt Betty, who was a star of musical theatre in the nineteen-fifties, actors, opera singers, writers, and my father, of course, with the Marisol Matthew duo.'

'And you?' Kitty asked. 'What stream of the family talent do you swim in?'

'Hands down the money-making. Thankfully, I excel at that.' His mouth twisted. 'I never want to be poor again, like I was as a kid, or dependent on the good graces of a tyrant like my grandfather.'

He waved his hand to encompass the ornately framed paintings on the walls of the foyer, the enormous crystal chandelier that made Kitty shudder at the thought of cleaning it. 'And now I step into all this, my heritage going back so many years.' He paused. 'But sometimes I feel like an imposter.'

'You don't look like an imposter.' The words slipped from her mouth before she could stop them.

'What do you mean?' he said.

'You look…born to the part,' she said. She was going to say he was handsome and very well dressed, every inch the aristocrat, but feared that might sound flirtatious and she couldn't be perceived to be flirting with him. What she thought of as being friendly had been construed as a sexually charged come-on, according to her attacker's lawyers.

'I was and I wasn't. There was an heir and a spare; I was third in line. If my uncle Oliver had had children I would have been pushed further down the line.'

'I'm sorry,' she said. 'That you lost your father and your uncle and…and your grandfather.' And Marisol Matthew had died too. 'So much…so much loss.' She didn't feel she could ask for details.

'I wasn't prepared for all this,' he said with a sweep of his hand. 'Uncle Olly was the one schooled in the duties and responsibilities that come with it. That's why I need help. It's why I need you, Kitty. Have you thought about my job offer?'

There was a vulnerability in Sebastian's eyes that tugged at her heart, frozen hard and impenetrable since the day the man she'd loved, and thought she'd spend her life with, had told her he actually believed her boss had assaulted her but couldn't stand by her and put his career at risk.

She wanted to help Sebastian, who seemed to have so much and yet had lost so much, but she had to be careful to keep her head, and above all to protect her vulnerable heart.

Kitty stood just footsteps into the room, as if she wasn't certain she wanted to be there. Sebastian found it difficult not to stare at her in admiration. In a wrap dress and high-heeled boots, businesslike-Kitty looked so very different from person-who-packed-Kitty. Subtle make-up enhanced the blue of her eyes and the lushness of her mouth. Her hair was up in a tousled bun and for a crazy moment he ached to tug it away from its pins and let it tumble around her shoulders.

'I've thought a lot about your job offer,' she said very seriously.

'And?' He held his breath for her answer, not knowing quite why it was so important to him.

'It interests me. But, before we discuss it further, there's something you need to know about me.'

'Something terrible?' he joked, thinking it would be impossible to believe anything terrible about Kitty Clements.

She looked up at him, the blue of her eyes intensified by the blue dress she wore.

'Yes,' she said.

That wasn't the answer he'd expected, and Sebastian wasn't sure how to respond. If it was something truly terrible, he didn't want to hear what she'd done. And yet if he was to employ her, he had to know.

'You'd better talk about it,' he finally managed to get out.

'I need to,' she said firmly.

He showed her to the small living room that led off the foyer. It was a feminine room and he remembered it had been his grandmother's favourite place in the house when he'd lived there. He'd desperately missed his mother, but he'd only had rare crumbs of affection from his grandmother, Lady Enid—she was too much in thrall to her husband, who hadn't wanted 'the boy' mollycoddled. Nonetheless she'd sometimes slipped him a few pounds in an envelope when Sir Cyril wasn't around and had always sent him a card at birthdays and Christmas with some crisp notes in it. Once, when he was twenty years old and living with his uncle Oliver, Lady Enid had showed up at one of his parties. Sebastian had been stunned at the witty, vivacious woman his grandmother was when she was away from her husband's sphere. He had laughed with her, even danced with her, felt sad for her that she'd allowed herself to be so stifled.

Then he hadn't seen her one-on-one for years, until his uncle's funeral. She'd been devastated by the deaths of both her sons and later had reached out to Sebastian, just weeks before she'd been felled by a massive stroke.

Kitty sat down on the blue and yellow chintz-covered sofa and Sebastian took the opposite sofa, a coffee table between them. An empty crystal vase sat on the side table, and he remembered how his grandmother had always filled this room with flowers as his grandfather hadn't cared for them elsewhere in the house. Now the scent in the room was from Kitty's perfume, sweet and floral and alluring.

Kitty tugged her dress over her knees as she leaned forward towards him. The dress was high-necked and long-sleeved, as if to cover as much of Kitty as possible. But it did nothing to disguise her curves.

'Tell me about the terrible thing you did,' he said stiffly. Had he been fooled by her open face and honest manner?

'It wasn't so much what I did, except be a naïve young

woman, but about what was done to me.' She sighed. 'Have you looked me up online?'

'Only when I was researching packing companies. Your reviews were outstanding.'

'Then you wouldn't know that, before we started PWP, I worked for Blaine and Ball Communications.'

'The public relations company?'

She nodded. 'I wasn't Kitty then; no one called me that childhood name but my family. I went by my full name, Kathryn—with a K—and I much preferred it. More grown-up and professional.'

But not as cute, he thought.

'I started there as an intern after I graduated from university. At the end of the internship I was offered a job as a trainee account executive.'

'Well done,' he said.

'I was beyond thrilled. It was awesome to be part of a prestigious company. I worked with brand names with deep pockets for public relations as well as boutique start-ups where we had to be really creative with limited funds.'

'Sounds challenging.'

'Challenging, but I loved the work and met so many interesting people. I thought I'd found my lifetime career.' She paused, and he could see she was struggling to find the right words. 'After a few years slowly climbing the ranks, I was promoted into a role that brought me into the orbit of one of the directors, Edmund Blaine. Charismatic, a PR guru. I was flattered when he took an interest in me and became my mentor, which involved quite a lot of one-on-one time with him. I...' Her voice wobbled and she had to take a deep breath to steady it. 'I couldn't believe how lucky I was to have caught his attention.'

Sebastian's hands fisted tight. Now he had a strong suspicion of where this was leading. 'He was a predator?'

She nodded. 'I didn't realise that, but I started to feel

nervous around him. His comments got personal, laden with sexual innuendo in a joking way that I didn't find funny. But I was still relatively junior and he held all the power.'

'Did you complain?'

Her hands were trembling and she gripped them so tightly together her knuckles showed white. 'To him? I felt too intimidated. I spoke to my direct manager as I thought she'd be understanding. But no. I can still remember Hilary's exact words. "That's just Edmund being Edmund. Be nice to him. Laugh it off. He can make or break your career".'

Sebastian cursed. 'Did you take her advice?'

'I tried to avoid him but it was almost impossible.' The colour had drained from her face. 'Then one evening I was working. Too late I realised he and I were the only ones on the floor. He called me into his office on some pretext, pulled me down to his lap and…and let me know what he wanted.' She shuddered and paused to take a deep breath. 'I was shocked frozen for a moment but then I protested and tried to get away. But he held me so tightly I couldn't free myself. He told me he knew I wanted it, when I was very definite I did not. Then he tried to…to sexually assault me.'

Sebastian uttered a vicious curse.

'I didn't give consent to anything, let alone what he was trying to do. There was no one around to hear me as I screamed and struggled. He clamped one hand over my mouth to shut me up and…and attacked me with the other hand. He was so much bigger and stronger than me, I couldn't stop him. But there was a second when he let go of me to…to fumble with his zip and I found the strength to kick him hard in the shin and free myself. As I ran, he called after me that no one would believe me.' Her voice faltered. 'He was right. They didn't.'

'I'm sorry,' Sebastian said, knowing how inadequate the words were. Her pain, her disbelief, her *horror* at what had happened was etched on her face, in the way she'd bowed her head and hunched her body. His instinct was to reach out and lay a comforting hand on her arm. But unwarranted contact with a man she didn't know well would be totally out of order. 'I believe you.'

She looked up at him. Her brow pleated together in a frown. 'You do?'

'Why would you make up something like that?'

'I wish other people thought like you do.' Her voice was underscored with bitterness and the light in her eyes had dimmed. 'Next day I reported the assault. Nobody at the company believed me. My version of events was totally discredited. It came down to a "she said, he said" scenario. What the older, powerful man said was believed. No proof, you see, except my word and my torn skirt that they said could have been caught on a nail.'

'Terrible is the right word for what happened to you,' Sebastian said. 'Why did you think you needed to tell me?'

'Because it got worse. The story was leaked to the media. I was labelled a troublemaker who had tried to seduce a happily married man then badmouthed him when he rejected me. I lost my job. My reputation. Doors slammed closed to me in every PR company in the country. If you search Kathryn Clements online you'll find the most horrible headlines. You…you might think twice about letting the person they portrayed into your house.'

'You seriously think I would let the gutter press influence my decision? If I'd seen those stories I would have asked you for your side of the story.'

She looked up, her eyes huge. 'You wouldn't judge me?'

Sebastian seethed with suppressed anger. He couldn't let her sense that anger in case she felt it was directed towards her, instead of the man who'd taken advantage of his power over her, and the company that had let her down.

'I've made my judgement. You were treated atrociously.' He'd seen this happen at the investment company he'd worked for after he'd graduated from university. The new female graduates were seen as fair game by some of the senior managers. 'I would have sought revenge,' he said.

She laughed a mirthless laugh. 'I didn't have the resources for revenge. I was twenty-six years old and the man paid my salary. There was no proof; the police told me I had no case.' She paused. 'But I can't believe I was the first girl this guy attacked. Or the last. I'm watching and waiting for the opportunity to clear my name.'

He leaned towards her. 'If you decide to accept my job offer, you have my word you will be safe in this house. I will never step over the line of what is appropriate between employer and employee. And I'll make damn sure anyone else working here does the same.'

She unclenched her hands. Her tentative smile was enough to restore the light to her eyes. 'Thank you. In that case, I accept your offer.'

A wave of relief swept over him. He hadn't realised just how much he'd wanted her to say yes.

'Excellent,' he said. 'When can you start?'

CHAPTER FIVE

'I CAN CARRY my own bags, really I can.' On Monday Kitty was back in Cheyne Walk after a weekend at her grandfather's house in Kent, getting things ready for the builders. She glared up at Sebastian, determined to start this first morning in his employ the way she meant to continue. 'These small suitcases are nothing compared to the boxes I haul around for PWP.'

'It goes against the grain to see you carrying heavy bags,' Sebastian said, glaring back. 'My father would never let my mother carry anything heavy. No gentleman would, he used to say.'

Kitty's glare softened. 'And you were brought up to be a gentleman, I can see that,' she said. 'My grandfather is the same. It grates on him that he's in his eighties and I want to take the burden off him rather than the other way round.'

'So you'll let me carry your bags?' Sebastian said with that hint of a grin she found so appealing.

'No, I won't,' she replied with her own smile.

'Then I won't insist,' he said quietly, and she knew he had in mind the story she had shared with him the week before.

'Thank you,' she said. For a long moment their gazes met and, as before, she was uplifted by the compassion she saw in his eyes. She averted her eyes to hide the rush of emotion it triggered—if only Neil had showed even a fraction of this stranger's understanding—and reached down to pick up the two compact suitcases she'd packed for her six-week stay. 'As I understand, I only have to carry these to the elevator that will shoot us up to the apartment where I'll be staying.'

'Follow me,' he said.

The elevator was small, installed no doubt at some much later stage after the building's construction. Kitty found even with her suitcases between them she was still too close to Sebastian for comfort. Not that she didn't feel safe with him in such confined quarters, it wasn't that at all, but rather that she felt so intensely aware of him. Of how tall he was, although in heels she didn't feel so diminutive beside him, how broad his shoulders, how heady his spicy scent, how determined he appeared to be to keep a respectful distance from her.

It was impossible to pretend away her attraction to him. But denying it was made easier because she was under contract as his employee. That fact put a barrier between them so formidable it could be a high wire fence topped with broken shards of glass.

The elevator took them to the top floor of the house and the one-bedroom apartment the previous housekeeper had lived in for years.

'It's lovely,' Kitty said, looking around the surprisingly roomy living room. The Arts and Crafts willow leaves wallpaper, ivory curtains, white woodwork and simple furniture made it cosy but elegant. Her grandmother would have loved it. The window framed a view over the streets of Chelsea.

'Are you surprised? The apartment was redecorated not so long ago. I told you my grandfather, for all his faults, treated his staff well.'

Just not his grandson, Kitty thought.

'I wasn't exactly expecting bare boards, an iron bedstead and a view of a sooty chimney, but it's very nice indeed for staff quarters.'

'I'm glad you approve,' he said drily.

The bedroom was restful in a soft blue, the bathroom more than adequate. The kitchenette had everything she needed to make a simple meal.

'I'll be very comfortable here, thank you.' More than comfortable. She could never in a million years afford to live in prestigious Chelsea. She'd have weekends off for the next six weeks. Visiting her grandfather would take up some of her spare time but otherwise she'd have a once-in-a-lifetime opportunity to explore this exclusive part of London. 'Thank you,' she said again, before realising such profuse thanks was overkill. She was here to work.

'There's an office for you on the ground floor.' He looked at his watch. 'Why don't you come down in thirty minutes?'

'Why not now?' she said. 'I can unpack this evening. If I'm going to help you put your stamp on the house, we might as well jump straight into it.'

Sebastian—*Sir* Sebastian—seemed disconcerted by her enthusiasm. Kitty remembered his obsessive placement of the books in his library. Did he like to work to a rigid timetable? Would any kind of spontaneity be a problem? Was he going to be *difficult?*

After what seemed like an overly long pause, he spoke. 'I like your attitude.'

'I only have six weeks,' she said by way of explanation. 'Within that time frame I'll only be able to start projects, not see anything substantial through to completion.'

'So we should get started.' He headed towards the elevator.

Kitty went to follow, then stopped. 'Wait. I'll get my laptop. Never too soon to start taking notes.'

The room Sebastian had designated as Kitty's office

had been his grandmother's study. There was none of the dark stuffiness of some of the other rooms. Kitty admired the classic desk and bookshelves, duck egg blue walls, framed botanical art, oriental rugs in pastel tones. She itched to park her behind in the upholstered desk chair and start working from such a delightful base.

'What a beautiful room; I wouldn't change a thing in here,' she said. 'What did your grandmother—?'

'Lady Enid.'

'What did Lady Enid do here?'

'I have no idea. Household management, I suppose. Then there was her charity work; I've only recently discovered how involved she was. Remember I told you how the money-making stream and the creative stream run through the family? Lady Enid swam in a money-spending stream—not in a particularly extravagant way but in a generous way. It appears her life was pretty much devoted to the charities she supported through the family foundation named after her. She was an heiress in her own right from her wealthy family.'

'That's admirable,' Kitty said. Donations which no doubt resulted in considerable tax deductions for her husband, a cynical part of her whispered.

'Since she died a year ago there hasn't been a Delfont actively involved with the foundation. Now I have to take over her mantle and work with the board of trustees. I made a promise.'

Kitty looked up at him. 'Sounds like a big job.'

'But a worthy one and I'm committed to it. I've inherited other roles too. My grandfather sat on a number of commercial company boards and I'll need to decide which ones interest me.'

Again, Kitty wondered why he didn't show more enthusiasm for his inheritance. But, curious as she was, it was none of her business.

'You have your work cut out for you,' she said brightly. 'Let's get started on the part where I can help you.'

'One more thing before we start,' he said.

'Yes?'

'I looked up the sage smoking ceremony. It's called smudging. I could be open to it.'

Kitty stared at him for a long moment before she spoke. 'Seriously?'

He nodded.

'To banish any lingering tyrannical presence?'

'Exactly,' he said.

She wasn't sure quite how serious he was.

Sebastian was deadly serious about the smoking ceremony. At his mother's funeral, her distraught mother, his *abuela,* had said there must be a curse on the Delfonts. Why had his parents died so young? his grandmother had wailed. Why had they only been able to have one child?

His father had died in a boating accident. He'd been fishing with friends off the rugged coastline near Port Soller, the closest port to their farmhouse in Mallorca, when the boat's engine had exploded. There were no survivors. His mother had been inconsolable. Sebastian, at twenty-seven, had been devastated. More so when his mother, still in her forties, had donned traditional black mourning and withdrawn from life. She'd died six months later of a heart attack. His *abuela* swore she had died of a broken heart from the loss of the man she had adored since she was eighteen.

What about me? Sebastian had silently screamed. Wasn't he enough to keep his mother alive? Irrationally, he'd seen her death as another abandonment. For the four months he'd lived in this hellish house, all he'd had of his *mamá* had been phone calls and postcards and that one half-term trip back to Spain. At nine years old, he couldn't understand why the feud with his grandfather had kept her from her son. *Hadn't he been lovable enough?*

When Uncle Oliver died eighteen months ago, buried by an avalanche while skiing in Switzerland, followed by Lady Enid's fatal stroke, then Sir Cyril had been felled by a virus—like dominos falling—Sebastian had started to believe in the possibility of a curse. And the source of any possible malevolence had been his grandfather.

'I'll organise the logistics of holding a smudging ceremony,' Kitty said, straight-faced, he was pleased to notice. 'In the meantime let's do something more practical about erasing your grandfather's presence from the house by redecorating.'

'I'll take you to the dining room first. Lady Enid held an annual dinner party at this time of year for the trustees of the foundation and their partners. I'd like to revive the tradition.'

The last time he'd seen his grandmother she had urged him to get involved with her foundation, which disbursed funds to charities involved with childhood illnesses. She'd been unwell, but not critically so, and had expressed concern that it would be in trouble without her at the helm. With his grandfather still alive that couldn't happen; Sir Cyril had barely spoken a civil word to him at Uncle Oliver's funeral, even though Sebastian had been his heir. Now, with both grandparents gone, it was his duty to take it over and be a steady hand on the tiller.

He already knew Kitty well enough to know that she showed her emotions on her face. Excitement danced across her features as she surveyed the grand room with the carved rosewood furniture, crystal chandeliers, ornate swagged velvet curtains and deep red walls. When the curtains were open the windows overlooked the formal city garden with its clipped hedges and central fountain.

'What an utterly splendid room for your dinner party,' she said.

'Splendid, yes, but I find it oppressive,' he said. Overbearing, like his grandfather. Sebastian shuddered at the memory of Sir Cyril sitting at the head of this table and picking at a nine-year-old's table manners in his haughty, bordering on cruel manner.

'The colours are too strong for today's tastes, aren't they?' she said. 'Change them and I suspect the room would be as impressive but have a very different feel.'

'You could be right,' he said.

'As I said earlier, I'm no interior designer. But I do know someone who I think would be perfect for your house. Evelyn Lim has worked with some of the best high-end design companies, both traditional and contemporary, and has just struck out on her own. Shall I make contact and see if she's interested and, more importantly, available?'

'Please do,' he said.

'Because I'm guessing you want to hold this dinner party sooner rather than later?'

'I want to hold it in two weeks' time so it will have to be in this room the way it is now.'

'Not necessarily,' Kitty said. 'If you have enough resources, and enough money to fund those resources, you might be surprised what you can achieve in terms of transformation.'

'How do you know all this?' he asked. She seemed so competent and knowledgeable.

She shrugged. 'Working in public relations, you meet all sorts of people. I first met Evelyn when I was working with a paint and wallpaper client.'

Under that heading of 'all sorts of people' was also a predator who had effectively destroyed the career she'd loved. Sebastian renewed his determination to never cause Kitty more grief by stepping over the line between employer and employee. He would wait out the six weeks getting to know her and then make a decision about where to take it from there. One thing he'd already realised—Kitty wasn't looking for a short-term fling. *Neither was he.*

Kitty typed out a few notes on her laptop and turned back to him. 'Perhaps we should look at the kitchen next?'

One of the few people in this house who'd been kind to Sebastian when he was a child had been the cook. After his interminable days at the private boys' day school where his grandfather had enrolled him, he would sneak down here knowing the kind woman would always have a treat for him. Not the almond and anise *carquinyolis* his mother baked which he'd missed so much, but buttery shortbread or chocolate chip cookies which were nearly as good.

The large Victorian room hadn't changed: the black-and-white-chequered flagstone floor, the imposing fireplace, the big black range, the scrubbed wooden table where he'd sat, well-used cooking implements hanging from a rack. There were no bitter memories here.

Kitty critically examined everything in the room. 'The appliances are all relatively new; in fact everything is in excellent condition. Much better than I thought when I first glimpsed it last week.'

'I like this room just the way it is,' he said.

'Me too; it's wonderfully Victorian and cosy. I can just imagine the delicious meals that have been cooked here over the years your family has lived here.' She paused. 'Which brings me to ask about your thoughts on a cook. Do you want someone to live in? Or a daily cook? Or no cook at all and use caterers for the functions you say you'll be expected to host?'

'Let me think about that,' he said. 'There's more staff accommodation on this floor. But there will only be me living here. And you for the next six weeks.'

'You don't need to count me in for meals,' she said

hastily. 'There's a perfectly adequate kitchenette in the apartment.'

'Of course,' he said. 'However, there might be occasions when you want to share a meal with me.' He would make sure of it.

'Er...that would be nice,' she said, flushing high on her cheekbones, dropping her gaze. 'In the meantime I'll talk to Maids in Chelsea about your cook situation. As well as the other staff you need, of course. If they can't help me, they'll know who can.'

Sebastian paused. He knew whichever way his words came out, they could be misinterpreted.

'We should continue your tour of the public rooms but, before you talk to the interior designer, I want to show you my bedroom. I mean the master bedroom. I mean a room that needs total refurbishment.'

Inwardly, he groaned. To even put the words *bedroom* and *Kitty* in the same thought led him somewhere he would not—*could* not—go.

CHAPTER SIX

KITTY FOUND HERSELF mesmerised by the sight of the carved wooden four-poster bed that dominated the overly elaborate Victorian splendour of the master bedroom. *Sebastian's bedroom.* He stood slightly behind her, yet her mind recklessly conjured up images of him in the bed, lying naked between heavy linen sheets that rumpled around his hips, his chest bare, that lazy grin she liked so much playing around his mouth, *beckoning her.* The fantasy was so strong she took a step towards the bed, intent on joining him, then recoiled as she realised what she had done.

What was happening here? Her libido had been firmly disconnected since Neil's betrayal, frozen in the 'off' position. No man had aroused the slightest interest. Now desire came rushing back through every erogenous zone she possessed. Sebastian had given her no cause for these crazy imaginings. He hadn't even touched her. There had been not a touch nor a kiss, no hint of mutual attraction to ignite the fuse.

Abruptly, she turned around—to put out of sight the bed that triggered such powerful yearnings for a man she couldn't have—and bumped straight into him. For a moment her hand was on his chest, her gasp of surprise not just from the unexpectedness of it but also from the intimate proximity to his strong body, his intoxicating scent.

'Sorry,' she said, her cheeks flaming hot as she stumbled back. 'Sorry.' She was shaking and had to take a deep breath to steady herself. Dear heaven, she hoped none of the desire for him her fantasy had aroused showed in her eyes.

'Sorry,' he said, also taking a step back.

Awkward. Excruciatingly awkward.

He was her boss—on a temporary contract to be sure—but it meant they would always be on an unequal footing. Then there was the inescapable fact they were from different worlds—the chasm between the mansion on Cheyne Walk and her grandfather's semi-detached two-up, two-down in the Kent village of Widefield was so deep she could never see it being crossed. Not to mention that Kathryn Clements still needed to fly under the radar. Having any kind of relationship—even a casual sexual fling—with a man who must surely be one of the most eligible bachelors in London could put her back in the unendurable glare of a hostile media spotlight.

A casual sexual fling? Where had that idea come from? *Get a grip, Kitty.*

She took another step back from him, tried to gather her thoughts, make her voice sound normal.

'I don't care as much for this room as some of the others.' She remembered the word Sebastian had used to describe the dining room. 'It's oppressive with these deep colours and dark furniture.'

'I agree. I think it would give me nightmares, which is why I haven't slept in here.'

Her flush became hotter. 'You haven't?' Her voice came out like a squeak. So much for her vivid imaginings. She cleared her throat. 'I... I thought it was your bedroom.'

'Not until it's completely remodelled. This room will be first cab off the rank for the smudging ceremony, along with my grandfather's study. It was Sir Cyril's bedroom.'

Kitty looked around her, at the dark ebony wood

dressing table, the heavily textured wallpaper. 'It looks like it might have been your grandfather's *grandfather's* bedroom.'

'Like a museum,' he said, again with a hint of that grin she found so toe-curling. 'But it's such a great space and has a huge dressing room and a bathroom. And just look at that view over the Thames. It interconnects with what was my grandmother's room, which is beautifully done. I think she must have had it decorated when she did her study.'

'It's awesome when you think of the continuity, generation after generation of your family living here. But I guess there might be a feeling of all those shadowy figures with their eyes on you.'

'It sounds creepy when you say that, but I like to think most of my ancestors would be benevolent. My father and uncle grew up here and...and I loved them dearly. I know my father didn't care much for this room either.'

'We'll get it exactly how you want. I promise you. If I can get Evelyn Lim on board, she'll talk to you in detail about your taste in colours and styles to ensure that.'

Please don't let him want to turn this fabulous—if dated—room into a stark grey space like his apartment in Docklands. That look worked brilliantly there, but would not here.

He paused. 'Should I not be speaking to you about my likes and dislikes so you can brief possible contractors or staff?'

Her mind segued immediately to wondering about his other likes and dislikes that had nothing to do with paint colour or fabric patterns. She had to shake her head to clear her thoughts. Was she still in a sensual stupor from her hallucination about Sebastian lying on the bed where he hadn't ever slept?

'Er...yes, of course. Can we set some time aside for that?'

'This afternoon, three o'clock, my office,' he said.

His office was also his library, the one where she'd so painstakingly shelved his books into the correct order. He'd said he could never use the room that had been his grandfather's study. The more snippets of information he revealed about his family, the more intrigued she became.

'Right. That's a date.' She paused. 'Not a date. I...er... didn't mean that. I meant that's an appointment. In my diary.'

'I know what you meant, Kitty,' he said, and she had a horrid feeling he was trying not to laugh.

'Back to work then,' she said. 'I mean, I'm not telling you to get back to work. It's me who has to get to work. You know, calls to make and all that.'

'I'll see you at three,' he said and this time he grinned.

When Claudia called Kitty at lunchtime to ask how her first day of the contract with Sir Sebastian was going she could only say, 'So far, so good.' She couldn't confess even to her best friend she'd been having erotic fantasies starring Sir Sebastian starkers and how very disconcerting she found it.

Her awoken libido was nothing to do with her attraction to Sebastian, she firmly told herself. It was more likely her body was screaming at her that two years had been too long without a man. To be in close contact with someone as good-looking as her temporary boss had obviously awoken desires that had been too deeply buried for too long. If she had told Claudia, Kitty knew what her friend would have said: she needed to get dating again; by cutting herself off from men she was letting Neil win, letting despicable Edmund Blaine win.

When the six-week contract was over, she'd dip a cautious toe into the dating pool by signing up to some online dating apps. She'd never used one before, had never needed to. Her first boyfriend, Owen, she'd met in high school. That had ended when she'd set off to university in Nottingham. Dating disasters of the common student kind had followed. Until she'd fancied herself in love with an exchange student from Australia. The relationship lasted all the way through second year, at the end of which he'd gone home to Sydney. They'd vowed to make it work, but absence hadn't let their hearts grow fonder and her long-distance romance had dwindled away to nothing. She only wished him well and vice versa.

She'd met Neil on her first day of her internship with Blaine and Ball. There had been just the two of them in the intake and they were often in each other's company. He'd been fiercely competitive but a lot of fun, with the handsome, sporty kind of blond good looks she'd always found appealing. In retrospect, she sometimes wondered if he'd pursued her so relentlessly because other guys at work had shown interest and Neil couldn't bear to be perceived as a loser.

She'd let herself be picked up by his whirlwind of networking and partying and, before she knew it, they were exclusive. When her flatmate moved out, it had seemed the right thing for him to move in. Not just by default. He'd seemed as in love with her as she'd been with him. They used to have long discussions about what their future children might look like; baby names had been debated. It was understood that living together would lead to an engagement. She had never doubted him, even though he could be an outrageous flirt when he'd thought it might get him somewhere. He swore he'd never cheated on her and she'd believed him. But his ambition had come between them and when that whirlwind had changed direction she'd crashed out of it to land on her own, heartbroken, bruised and betrayed.

Yes, it might be time to release herself from her dating sabbatical and look at those apps. Although the insidious thought crept into her mind that there wouldn't be any men like Sir Sebastian Delfont around and it was he who had brought her libido to such a roaring awakening. What other man could possibly come close to him?

At three o'clock she sat opposite him at his desk in the room surrounded by his strictly ordered books and the beautiful paintings of a Mallorcan farmhouse and a citrus grove. She was glad of the distance the desk put between her and him. Glad that it emphasised her position as employee. It was safer that way. Not safe from him, rather safe from her newly activated hormones.

'I've got some positive news to report,' she said, forcing herself to sound totally businesslike. 'First, Evelyn Lim is both interested and available. We're lucky. She was about to start on a major design job but the couple decided to divorce and sell the house, so Evelyn is unexpectedly free. If you want to move quickly on the dining room for your dinner party, she can meet with you tomorrow morning. Does that suit?'

'Perfectly,' he said. 'Only I want you in on that meeting.'

She nodded. 'Regarding your cook situation, I've thought somewhat outside the box.'

'Fire away.'

'I've found two well-trained chefs with impeccable references who are friends. Both have young children and would like to job share. I set up a conference call with them both. I liked them and think the job share could work.'

'How does working evenings tally with the cooks having kids?'

'It's up to them to sort out their childcare. In my experience, people who job share are keen to make it work. These two women know the role here entails lunch and dinner—if you remember, you said you'd get your own breakfast.

And sometimes entertaining might call for working later into the evening. When would you like to meet them?'

'No need for me to interview the potential cooks. I'll leave it to you.'

Again, there was that indifference she was coming to expect from him. Again, she felt like shaking him. If she had the opportunity to have a cook prepare all her meals she'd be dancing on air.

'I appreciate your confidence in me.' She smiled her thanks. 'But when it comes to food, I really think you should be involved. Why don't we ask each of them to cook lunch here and see how you like what they come up with? Alisa can do tomorrow, Josie the day after. Does that suit?'

'I'll leave it in your capable hands.'

Capable hands. He'd meant it as a compliment but how boring it made her sound. Was that how he saw her? How very different from her fantasies about him.

'Finding a housekeeper might take longer, but I've got Maids in Chelsea and another very reputable domestic staff agency on the hunt for us. Once we've got a housekeeper, they can work with us on the other household staff.'

'As long as they're of the same calibre as my household manager. You've achieved so much in one day.'

'Thank you,' she said, unable to help from basking in the warmth of his praise.

'Thank *you*,' he said. 'You've exceeded all expectations already.'

'I'm pleased to hear that,' she said, not sure what else she could say. She felt suddenly shy with him and covered it up with a businesslike briskness. 'Moving outside the house to the garden. I've got some names from an agency specialising in gardeners and horticulturists, but I haven't interviewed them yet. To be honest, I know very little about gardening.'

'It's not my forte either.'

She sighed. 'I wish I could have my grandfather help me interview the potential gardeners and put them through their paces.'

'Your grandfather is a gardener?'

'He loves his garden and spends even more time in it since my grandmother died. He also has an allotment where he grows fruit and vegetables.'

Kitty wondered if someone as posh as Sebastian would know what an allotment was—a small plot of land leased from the council for a nominal fee for the express purpose of growing plants.

'Why not get your grandfather up to London to help you?'

'It's not as easy as that. Gramps refuses to admit he's in his eighties and has to slow down. He insisted no one but him could prune his favourite climbing rose, fell off the ladder he shouldn't have been up, fractured his leg in several places and is now in a rehab hospital.'

'I'm sorry; that sounds very painful.'

'As he puts it, his pride got a worse battering. He's working his way towards being able to go back home and live independently.'

'I hope all goes well for him,' Sebastian said politely. He paused. 'I would suggest getting help from the man who kept this garden in order for many years, as well as the country estate in Dorset. But he retired after my grandmother died and moved up north.'

There was an estate in Dorset? Of course there was.

'Was his name Albert?' Kitty asked. 'If so, he left a handwritten workbook, where he recorded the seasonal work done in the garden. It even has sketches. I found it in Lady Enid's office, surprising really as I thought it should belong in the potting shed. I'll refer to that when I interview gardeners.'

'My grandmother thought highly of Albert and left him a substantial legacy in her will,' Sebastian said.

'Really?' Kitty's imagination raced. 'You think they were friends?' More than friends?

Sebastian frowned, a stormy look that put Kitty back in her place. 'Delfonts don't make friends with staff. My grandfather would never have sanctioned that.'

Okay, make that *firmly* put back in her place.

'I understand,' she said, tight-lipped. *Only too well.*

Immediately, Sebastian realised he'd got it wrong— again—with Kitty. She was obviously offended by his pronouncements about Delfonts and their staff. Already he could read so clearly the emotions that skittered across her face.

'I was, of course, referring to my grandfather's generation of Delfonts. Not mine.' He pushed his fingers through his hair in frustration. 'It's taking me some time to get used to the fact I am now the sole Delfont—and my grandfather is certainly not my role model.'

In deciding to shoulder all his inheritance entailed, Sebastian had vowed he would be a different kind of baronet from his grandfather—one with morals and compassion, a baronet who would make his uncle Olly and his father proud, someone who could make a difference through his grandmother's foundation and the ethical way he did business.

'I understand,' she said, her mouth still turned down.

But could she? He would have to share an awful lot about his past and his toxic family interactions before she could begin to understand. And he wasn't prepared to do that. Not when it would reveal so much about himself.

No woman will ever want to live with you, his former fiancée, Lavinia, had shouted at him, after he had broken off their engagement.

According to the woman who had hidden her despicable hidden agenda, he was obsessive, too focused on work and stingy in that he'd refused to finance her excessive, extravagant spending sprees in the designer boutiques of Bond Street.

'You certainly know the value of a penny,' she'd sneered at him.

Actually, he did. He'd grown up in a family where, as a child, every *peseta* had counted, where he'd known what it was not to have the essentials. To crown her litany of complaints, Lavinia had accused him of being unlovable and unable to love. Ironic, as she'd been happy enough to pretend to love him, when really she'd been in love with the idea of one day becoming a Lady, with the Delfont fortune at her disposal.

But was he being fair to Kitty? She hadn't blinked at his compulsive need to have his bookshelves in order, in fact had reacted with rare understanding. She might understand how that boy who'd lived in poky rooms as the son of the seasonal caretakers in a block of Spanish holiday flats felt such a fraud as Sir Sebastian. There was no doubt that she brought light into the shadowy corners of his house. Could she do the same with his life? Dare he even let himself hope for such a thing? *Was he worthy of her?*

He leaned across the desk towards her. 'I actually don't think of you as "staff". You're an independent contractor helping me out. If we end up friends after all this, I'll be happy.'

One thing was sure, when she'd tripped in the master bedroom and bumped into him, friendship hadn't been his initial thought. She'd felt so good—her warmth, her curves—it had taken all his determination not to be that man who took advantage. For the moment she'd taken to steady herself, all he'd been aware of was how lovely she was and how much he wanted to pull her into his arms.

'Er...me too,' she said, although she didn't sound convinced.

Unwittingly, she'd hit a sensitive spot. His grandmother had summoned him after Uncle Olly's funeral to the Dorset estate where she'd been living. She'd been full of regrets that her grandson was virtually a stranger to her. It had been the start of a tentative reconciliation, when she had discussed her concerns about the Lady Enid foundation. The time had been poignantly precious as he hadn't seen his grandmother again.

Kitty had picked up on something he had suspected when he'd seen Lady Enid and her head gardener Albert together. There had been something there, definitely friendship, perhaps something more. His grandmother had told him she and Sir Cyril had led independent lives for a long time—or as independent as life could be married to such a domineering man. It had become obvious to him that his grandfather had been emotionally ill-equipped to manage close relationships of any kind—his wife, his sons, certainly his grandson. His grandmother had hinted that Sir Cyril's own father had been cruel, borderline abusive.

Had Lavinia been right? Had he inherited some kind of emotional inability to love? Because the disaster with Lavinia had made him realise he had never been in love. Not the kind of 'in love' that led to commitment and happy ever after. Was it even possible for him?

'As for your question about my grandmother, yes, I think she saw Albert as a good friend. Her marriage to my grandfather wasn't a happy one. Good for her if she found comfort with a man those in her social circle would deem totally unacceptable.' Like his family had found his mother unacceptable. 'Perhaps it was more than friendship; I don't know. I might be the son of Marisol Matthew but I'm not good at picking up on romance.'

Kitty's eyes widened. 'Perhaps it was a real-life romance.

The more I hear about your family, the more fascinated I become. Maybe you could write a novel about them.'

'Huh,' he snorted. 'No one would believe it.'

He had written a novel. Two, in fact. Not about the possibly cursed lives of his wealthy family, but dark thrillers with a tortured detective hero. The manuscripts were sitting in a drawer. He'd written them in the sad time after both his parents had died and he was living with Uncle Oliver. There was no time for writing stories now, with his new duties to fill the days.

His phone buzzed with a message. 'Excuse me. I need to read this.'

'Of course,' she said.

Sebastian read the message with some relief. He looked over to Kitty. 'The executive assistant I approached has agreed to come on board. Guy Perrint worked with my uncle Oliver and is just the person I need.'

'That's good; I wondered if you would need an assistant.'

'And you're glad you didn't have to recruit him too?'

Her smile lit up her beautiful blue eyes. 'I didn't say that, but yes. I'm glad I can concentrate on getting your household in order.'

'That said, I need to spend some time on a call with him.'

'Now?'

'Yes.'

'But Evelyn Lim is coming in the morning and we'd scheduled to discuss the changes you want done to the house.'

'Can we do it over dinner instead?' He voiced the invitation without thinking about it, forgetting she might be averse to having anything to do with an employer outside of work hours.

It was the first time he'd seen her flustered. 'I…er… I'm not sure…'

'Not a good idea? I thought, as it's your first night living in the house, you might welcome a meal out. But of course I shouldn't be demanding overtime so quickly.'

'Overtime? I wouldn't see it as overtime.'

'There are some excellent restaurants within walking distance.'

She bit down on her lower lip. 'That's the thing. I can't risk being seen in a restaurant with you.' She flushed high on her cheekbones. 'I need to keep a low profile. It seems you're considered one of the most eligible bachelors not only in London but the whole of Great Britain. If you're noticed, so might I be.'

'I hadn't thought of myself like that,' he said, frowning.

'Handsome, wealthy, a title. I'm afraid you won't be able to escape media interest.'

'Which I most certainly don't want.'

'But you will need to court it if you want to move forward with Lady Enid's foundation. I'm speaking with my PR hat on here.'

'But not scandalous speculation about my private life.'

'Or mine,' she said.

Her eyes were downcast and her full lower lip trembled. With good reason. Since their last conversation about what had happened at Blaine and Ball, he'd looked up some of the truly hideous stories about Kathryn Clements that had been splashed across the tabloids.

'I don't want to risk subjecting you to that again,' he said.

'Thank you,' she said in a very small voice.

'Perhaps a meal from one of those good restaurants delivered here and eaten in privacy might be a better idea?'

She paused and he thought she might refuse that idea too. But she nodded. 'A much better thought.'

'And now it's my turn to quiz you about your likes and…uh…dislikes.'

A sudden flash of what it might be like to explore her likes and dislikes in bed caused his voice to hitch. She was wearing a smart navy trouser suit cut in a masculine style, but it only served to emphasise her femininity and sensuality. Images of him slowly peeling off that suit, the shirt, the underwear beneath it to reveal pale skin flushed with arousal and blonde hair tumbling around her breasts tormented him.

Startled, she looked up at him. 'Me? Why?'

He banished the images, cleared his throat. 'About food,' he said hastily. 'Italian? French? Indian? Vegetarian? Vegan? For dinner, I mean.'

'Let me think,' she said.

Was there something in her eyes to indicate she'd known exactly what he'd been thinking? And that perhaps the very same thoughts had crossed her mind regarding him?

He could only guess. That line between employee and employer he'd promised never to cross lay stark and strong between them.

CHAPTER SEVEN

KITTY WAS GLAD that Sebastian had suggested eating dinner in the basement kitchen rather than the elegant breakfast room, where the family had traditionally eaten casual meals, or in that grand, imposing dining room. The kitchen was altogether a more pleasant and welcoming space. Or was that because she felt more comfortable 'downstairs' rather than with the grandeur of 'upstairs'?

The kitchen was grand in its own way, with its size and the venerable age it wore with such dignity. She sat opposite him across the scrubbed oak table. She and Sebastian had laid the table together, searching through drawers for the blue and white checked tablecloth and the heavy china plates and serviceable cutlery intended for staff use over the years. Such an everyday activity had gone some way to break the ice between them—after all, she'd only known him for a week.

Even so, she had to pinch herself—here she was sharing a meal delivered from a fashionable restaurant in Chelsea with Sir Sebastian Delfont. Surreptitiously, she darted a glance up at his lean, handsome face, shadowed with the sexiest trace of evening stubble, and her heart seemed to skip a beat. He had a sensuous mouth, full lips but not too full, the top lip narrower than the bottom—wonderful to kiss, she would imagine. He'd said he wasn't married. Did he have a girlfriend—lucky woman—or a string of girlfriends? She mentally shook herself out of that thought. She had to fight to keep her guard up, to remember this wasn't a date. *And to keep her erotic fantasies about this man at bay.*

It had been a unanimous decision to order Italian, although Indian had come a close second. Sebastian had said he would never eat Spanish food from a restaurant, as it could never compare with his *abuela's*—his grandmother's—cooking. Kitty had understood exactly where he was coming from. No one cooked roast beef and Yorkshire pudding the way her gran had, she'd told him. One thing, at least, they had in common, although it was a tenuous connection. She would struggle to find points of connection with Sebastian, their worlds were so very different, even beyond the upstairs/downstairs thing.

They enjoyed a minor battle of wills as Sebastian insisted Kitty have the last of the delicious antipasto selection they had ordered, while she thought he should have it. But she didn't need much persuasion to lay claim to the remaining bite-sized crostini topped with artfully placed Parma ham, Stracciatella cheese, rocket and pine nuts.

'This looks deceptively easy to put together, for something so delicious,' she said, eyeing it critically.

'Are you planning to replicate it?'

'Maybe. I might organise a little party for Gramps when he gets home from hospital. He's quite adventurous with food considering his age. Not that I'm anything but an everyday kind of cook.'

Everything she'd learned about cooking she'd learned from her gran. When she'd arrived to live with her and Gramps, the family were in deep shock and grief, Kitty from the loss of her parents, her grandparents at the loss of their daughter. Her uncle, their son, had come from Canada for the funerals but he had his own life there and had soon returned home. She hadn't been particularly close to her father's family in Norfolk; there'd been no question of her going to live with them.

Kitty had had to adjust to a very different life. Her beloved grandparents had become her parents too. Gran had nurtured her with home cooking, supplemented by the bounty from Gramps's allotment. Her grandmother had cemented their new bond by keeping her granddaughter close in the kitchen.

'Why do you live with your grandfather?' Sebastian asked.

Surprised, Kitty paused with the crostini halfway to her mouth. She put it back down on her plate. 'Why do you ask?' she said.

'It's common among my family in Spain for the different generations to live close by, but not so much here. You're a very attractive woman and I'm surprised you—'

'Don't live with a man?' she said.

'Yes,' he said.

'I've lived with a man and have no intention of repeating the experience any time soon.' She could hear the bitterness in her voice that rose like a poison whenever she thought about Neil in any context. Sebastian nodded in acknowledgment of what she'd said. He seemed unsettled by her change of demeanour, perhaps unsure about what to say in reply.

'I see,' he finally said.

She took a sip from her glass of mineral water in an effort to regain her composure.

A very attractive woman, he'd said. Were they just throwaway words, or did he really mean them? She certainly thought he was an attractive man. Exceedingly so.

She forced a more neutral tone to her voice. 'My grandparents brought me up after my parents died when I was fourteen.'

'I'm sorry,' he said, as people always did when she told

them about her childhood tragedy. She used the phrase herself, though sometimes wondered why she was saying sorry for something that had been quite out of her control.

She took another sip of her water. 'After the scandal erupted, I was left without a job and unable to pay the rent on my flat.' Neil had moved out, leaving her with the entire rent burden and the gutter press on her doorstep. 'I went home. And found not only did I need my grandparents, but they needed me. That's why I live with my grandfather.'

She picked up the crostini again. 'And I think Gramps would very much enjoy something like this.' There had been more than enough talk about her personal life and she hoped Sebastian would pick up on the change of subject.

'I'm sure he would enjoy it,' he said. 'I certainly did.'

'Why is Italian antipasto so extraordinarily good? I could eat an entire meal just from the antipasto table.'

He smiled. 'But then you'd be cheating yourself of the main meal, wouldn't you?'

When he smiled like that, it was impossible not to smile back—her smile tinged with relief that he hadn't further questioned her about her private life. The ending of her relationship with Neil had left her broken and with that had come an immense sense of failure—she'd meant so little to him that he'd chosen his job over her. If he'd ever loved her, how could he interact with her abuser every day?

'Our next course looks good too,' Sebastian said as he eyed the *ragu alla Bolognese* made with handmade tagliatelle. Kitty could see just by looking at it that the dish bore no resemblance to the humble spaghetti Bolognese she made and the smell of it was making her mouth water.

'We haven't done a lot of talking about your preferences for the meeting with the interior designer,' she said, daring to tease him a little without stepping over the formidable boundaries between them.

'Perhaps not for the interior designer, but certainly for the two cooks,' he said, looking longingly at the *ragu*.

'True,' she said with a smile. 'I've certainly garnered some clues about what you like in food. Italian, Indian, Greek, Thai, Spanish—but only when it's homemade—French, Chinese—'

'In short, any good food that I don't have to cook myself.'

'And plenty of it, I notice,' she added.

He was lean but strong and firmly muscled. She hadn't failed to notice that when she'd stumbled against him that morning. He either exercised a lot or was one of those people who ran hot and burned up energy. She had to tear her mind away from imagining how he'd look in nothing but sleek tight-fitting athletic gear.

'Exactly,' he said. 'What about you?'

'Does it matter what I like?' she asked, surprised.

'I hope this won't be the only dinner I share with you.' Kitty tried to hide her surprise, successfully she thought, as Sebastian continued without hesitation, 'And when our two cooks are on board—if we approve of them—I will expect them to make lunch each day, not just for me but for anyone working in the house, including you and my new assistant, Guy.'

So it wasn't personal, the sharing dinner thing. Just a benefit for the staff. She had no cause to feel disappointed.

'That's kind, but I don't expect—'

'You won't have to eat the meal if you don't want to, but it will be there if you do.'

He was generous and thoughtful and, not for the first time, Kitty wondered why Sir Sebastian wasn't married. There must be eligible women lined up along Cheyne Walk all the way to Battersea Bridge. But she wouldn't have this job or be here eating in his kitchen if he was married, she reminded herself. A wife wouldn't have hired the notorious Kathryn Clements to work with her husband.

'Okay, let's start on that *ragu* and the tomato and basil salad,' she said. 'But we really need to be prepared for the meeting with Evelyn Lim, especially if you want the dining room transformed in time for your foundation board dinner.'

'I need no second invitation,' he said. He started to serve her a generous helping of the wide-cut tagliatelle, coated with a rich, slow-cooked sauce.

She put up her hand. 'Whoa, that's more than enough for me.'

'Are you sure?'

'Absolutely,' she said.

It was an automatic response. Once she'd left home and her grandmother's home cooking to go to university, she'd enjoyed the freedom to eat what she wanted. That had meant too many convenience and fast foods, not to mention nights out at the pub with her friends. And she'd been more inclined to join drama and music societies than sports clubs. She'd stacked on the weight and it had been very hard to shift. That *Pretty, Plump and Predatory* headline had really stung, and not just for the predatory part. After the incident with Edmund Blaine she'd thrown herself into intense self-defence training. That, coupled with the appetite-destroying misery she had sunk into after her public humiliation, had seen her back at a more comfortable weight. But she was still vigilant with what she ate.

'All the more for me then,' he said with mock greed, which made her laugh as it was something Gramps would say. Who would have thought Sebastian, who had seemed so forbidding at first, would make her laugh?

The *ragu* was every bit as delicious as it looked and they only exchanged exclamations of appreciation as they ate. She put down her cutlery at the same moment Sebastian did and they both smiled. He was handsome whichever way she looked at him, but when he smiled his grey eyes warmed his serious expression and made him appear not just extraordinarily good-looking but also more approachable.

'You seem more relaxed down here in the kitchen,' she ventured.

His dark eyebrows rose, and for a moment she regretted her temerity in taking the conversation to something perhaps more personal than was warranted. The slow tick of the big farm-style clock above them on the wall dominated the sudden silence.

'Perhaps because it was the only room in this house I ever felt happy in,' he said finally. 'That was thanks to the cook. Fran. Her name was Fran. She was kind to a homesick young boy.'

'And other people in the house weren't?' Kitty said tentatively. 'Like…like the tyrant grandfather?'

'And the grandmother who didn't dare go against his wishes,' he said, his voice sombre, seemingly lost in memories that were less than pleasant.

Kitty held her breath. She was so curious about his story, but she didn't want to seem to be prying. Of course she'd looked him up on the internet but he wasn't on social media and there was virtually nothing, apart from a story about the death of his uncle in a skiing accident.

Finally, she decided to ask the questions. He didn't have to reply. 'You mentioned you lived in this house only briefly. Was that when you were nine years old?'

He nodded. 'For four months while my father was studying in London for his postgraduate teaching qualification. I had to go to school here. My mother stayed behind in Barcelona with her parents.'

'Your mother stayed behind? That must have been tough for you.'

His eyes darkened with, she thought, remembered pain. 'It was. For my parents too. But it wasn't the first time. Circumstances meant we were quite often separated as a family when I was a child.'

Kitty didn't say anything, hoping he would elaborate. She had a feeling he didn't talk much about his past; an ill-timed comment from her might pull him out of his memories.

'It wasn't just the need for them to go where the work was,' he said. He took a sip from his glass of wine, put it slowly down as if he were deliberating whether or not to answer her. 'My mother's health was uncertain. She had several miscarriages but no more babies. At times she had to have bed rest, and I was shunted around various Spanish relatives while my father had to work away. At the time, all I was really aware of was that I never got my promised baby brother or sister.'

Kitty's heart went out to him. 'I... I have some idea of how that must have felt. I'm an only child too. I longed for a brother or sister, but I was told it wasn't "meant to be".' She'd sometimes thought dealing with the death of her parents might have been less traumatic if she'd had a sibling.

'My *mamá* used to say I got all her love.'

Kitty smiled. 'I think I remember my mum saying the same thing.' She dared another question. 'Was your mother's health the reason she couldn't come to live here too with you and your father for that four months?'

'Not that time. My father needed to gain qualifications to get better paid jobs. My mother needed to work to help support our little family; she had a job in an art gallery she didn't want to lose. Besides, she wasn't welcome here, had never been welcomed here. That's why we lived in Spain.'

'Why was that?'

'My father married against my grandfather's wishes. My father was on a gap year in Spain after he finished uni. My mother was an art student working as a barmaid in Barcelona. They were very young. She always said she could write truthfully about love at first sight in her books because that was how it was for them.'

'How lovely,' Kitty said. The fan girl in her appreciated this was Marisol Matthew's own love story. It seemed surreal she should be hearing it from her son.

'Unfortunately, not everyone thought that. Both sets of parents disapproved. My mother was nineteen when she had me; her parents weren't happy she didn't finish her degree. But they rallied round when I was born.'

'And your English grandparents?'

'My grandfather barely tolerated me, and he loathed my mother.'

'Why?' Kitty couldn't resist asking.

'Who knows? Because she wasn't English? Because she and my father defied him and got married? Because she was beautiful and loving? Because she bore a child with black hair instead of the Delfont blond?'

Kitty's heart ached for Sebastian as a little boy. She could just see him sitting here in the kitchen with his dark hair, his serious expression. He must have been very cute. 'But why take it out on you? You were just a child.'

'Not a good enough child to bear the name of Delfont, apparently. Grandfather was determined to turn me into a "proper English schoolboy".'

'How did he do that?'

'There were strings attached to any help from my grandfather. Back then, Grandfather paid the first term of my father's university tuition—which would lead to a better job—on the proviso I came with him for the four months. Discipline at home and a private boys' day school, where I was miserable, was his tactic. He would have sent me away to boarding school, only my father refused to allow it.'

Kitty struggled to see why a grandfather would do that to a nine-year-old. 'I suppose you were in line to the title?'

'Third in line. I doubt at that stage he knew that my uncle Oliver was gay and had no intention of having children. Or if he did know, he refused to acknowledge it.'

'Your family story is…complicated.'

'You could say that, yes,' he said with a wry twist of his mouth.

'These are painful memories to revisit,' she said slowly, regretting that she had brought up the subject with her questions.

'Being back in this house has brought back memories. It seems like yesterday that I sat at this table—in this very chair—and snacked on treats Fran baked especially for me.'

'Did you see your mother during that four months?'

His face tightened. 'Only at half-term. But there were regular phone calls. A postcard every day. She painted each of them with a different little scene from her parents' house, where she was living. It was the only place I'd known that seemed like home.'

'But a poor substitute for your mum.'

'Yes,' he said tersely. He paused.

Kitty wanted to reach over the table and grip his hand hard. But she couldn't. It wouldn't be appropriate. The remembered bewilderment etched on his adult features was heart-wrenching. It brought back the agony of losing her parents when she'd been only fourteen and she couldn't bear to trigger it further, mixing it up with the more recent loss of her grandmother, the loss of the future she'd been so sure she'd have with Neil.

'I'm sorry,' she said, knowing how inadequate the words sounded, knowing there was worse to come in his personal story, with two generations of his family gone.

'It didn't last for ever. My grandfather's demands became unacceptable, as they always did. We went back home after I finished the term at school and my father his term at university. Life back in Spain went on much as before, only my father went back and forth to London to finish his teaching qualification. When I was eleven, an elderly uncle of my mother's died and the family allowed us to live in his run-down farmhouse and citrus orchard in Mallorca. My father got a position teaching in an English school for expats outside of Palma and I started school there. Later, they were able to buy the farmhouse.'

'The paintings in your library; are they—?'

'Of our farmhouse.'

'Painted by your mother?'

'In Mallorca, we lived not far from some popular tourist hotspots. She painted the local area because she loved it, but her art proved to be very appealing to tourists wanting to take home a tasteful souvenir. It became a steady income stream.'

'She was very talented.'

'In many ways. She painted those pictures in my library just for me. Mamá wanted me to never forget where I came from when I moved to London for university and to live with my uncle Oliver.'

'Yet you came from here too. Chelsea, I mean.'

'I never found it a conflict, until I ended up the heir.'

Kitty sensed there was a lot more underlying the flat statement than he had chosen to share. She ached to know more about this man, yet this wasn't the time to question him further.

'I can't begin to understand, and I'm sad if I've stirred up painful memories from a long time ago,' she said.

She felt utterly out of her depth with him. If the conversation swung around to the subsequent death of his parents and his uncle, she wouldn't know what to say, how to comfort him, if indeed he needed comforting, rather than stumbling into platitudes.

'You didn't stir up memories.' He indicated the room around them with a wave of his hand. 'The house did. But this room has only happy memories. And tonight has layered more on top of them.' He leaned towards her over the table. 'You're a wonderful listener, Kitty, and you don't judge. I don't know you very well at all, but it seems to me that you take people for who they are, and that's rare.'

She flushed, pleased by the compliment, not certain how to react. 'Thank you,' she said after a beat too long. 'But I've made some bad misjudgements of character along the way.'

He frowned. 'Don't blame yourself in any way for what happened with your boss. You expected him to behave as a manager working with young staff should and he broke that trust in a terrible way.'

'I only blame the people in that company who failed to protect me,' she said, looking down to avoid his too perceptive gaze.

'So you should,' he said. His voice hardened. 'And you know I believe you should have your revenge.'

'Vindication is what I want, not necessarily hardcore revenge,' she said.

And then there was Neil. But Kitty had no intention of sharing the story of that massive misjudgement with Sebastian. How could she have been so stupid as to trust in a future with Neil? The episode with the man she'd thought had loved her had scarred her. She could never again trust her judgement when it came to a man.

She got up from the table to clear the plates, putting up her hand to stop him from helping. 'Now we really need to get down to business.'

'Agreed,' he said with, she thought, a degree of reluctance.

She returned to the table with a takeaway box, which she placed between them, alongside two pretty china plates.

'There's a *torta caprese* waiting for us in there,' she said.

'What exactly is a *torta caprese?*' he said. 'You chose it.'

Kitty quoted in a theatrical style from the delivery description on the elegantly boxed dessert. 'Flourless chocolate almond cake, dusted with powdered sugar and served with macerated strawberries and mascarpone.'

'Sounds very good to me,' he said. 'What about we have the *torta* then get down to business?'

'Because before you get to taste dessert I'm going to torture you,' she said.

'Torture?' he said, humour and not one trace of alarm in his grey eyes.

'No cake until you've answered the first five questions on my list to help me brief Evelyn Lim tomorrow morning. I sense you've been avoiding this, even though it's the reason we're having dinner together.'

'Not fair,' he said. 'Totally unfair.'

'But necessary, yes?'

'Cake first would be better,' he grumbled.

Sebastian grumbled about the cake, but secretly he was tickled at how Kitty took charge to push forward his interests. Her chin was set at a stubborn tilt and yet she was charming in the way she manoeuvred him. He could see she would have been very good in her PR role.

'Okay,' he said, dragging out the word with mock reluctance.

'Question one: what colours do you like?' she said. 'If you opened your wardrobe door, what colours would you see?'

'I think you might know me well enough by now to know the answer to that,' he said. 'Want to hazard a guess?'

She tilted her head to one side and pretended to think. 'Let me see—how about black, black and black, charcoal, grey and perhaps a touch of white?'

'Close,' he said. 'It's easier for a man to get dressed if he doesn't have to worry about what goes with what.'

He wasn't being completely honest with her: wearing sombre colours suited his mood. There was colour in his wardrobe; he just hadn't chosen to wear it since his father's death had formed the first link in the chain of loss in his life.

'Shades of black and grey pretty much sum up the colours in your Dockside apartment. They worked well there.'

'But not here,' he said.

The undisguised look of relief on her face amused him. Had she seriously thought he would try to bring the minimalism of his apartment here?

'I'm glad you think so,' she said. 'Which brings me to my next question: what colours do you like for the house?'

'I don't like gloomy, but I don't mind dramatic.'

'A good answer for a designer, I would think. Any colour you particularly like?'

'Blue.' The colours of the sea and the sky in Mallorca, the mellow stone walls of the farmhouse, the citrus yellow of the lemons hanging from dark green leaves in the orchard. Those were the colours he loved but they were unique to his Spanish home. 'Muted tones of blue.'

'Any colour you don't like?'

'Mustard.' It was the first thing he thought of, to please Kitty with an answer. If the designer presented him with colours he didn't like, he would certainly let her know.

'How do you want the redesigned space to feel?' she asked. She wasn't taking notes, but he could see her mentally keeping track of his answers.

'Maintain the history of the house but make the rooms more welcoming.'

'Any rooms you particularly like or dislike the look of?'

'I don't actually dislike any room, just aspects of their décor. And I don't want my library changed at all. It's exactly how I want it.'

'Would it be safe to say the rooms where Lady Enid's influence is stronger are preferable to—'

'—the darker touch of my grandfather and possibly his grandfather? That's a given.' He looked at her across the table. 'And those are your five questions answered.'

'Please, just one more question,' she said, hands together in a gesture of mock pleading. 'It's an important one.'

How could he resist her?

'One more. Then cake,' he said darkly.

It wasn't that he was excessively hungry for dessert, but he was uncomfortable with answers about his private life that would be transmitted to a third person. He'd opened up to Kitty about his personal history because he trusted her and, for the first time, he wanted to share thoughts he had never shared with anyone else. She had a gift of making him feel comfortable with her, so much so he was starting to feel more at ease with himself and the forces that had shaped the last few years of his life.

'Final question,' she said. 'What's your budget for the designer?'

He made a dismissive gesture with his hands. 'Whatever she needs to spend to make the changes as quickly as possible.'

'I'll get Evelyn to give me a ballpark quote and you can look at that.'

'I'll authorise what you ask me to,' he said. 'But only the best quality.'

In truth, whatever the refurbishment cost, he could

more than afford it. The penny-pinching days of his youth were long gone. He had independently amassed his own fortune, thanks to shrewd investments in biotech companies before they'd gone gangbusters, inheriting first from his father and then from his mother, including all ongoing royalties. Uncle Oliver had made him his heir, and his grandmother had left money from the trust fund she'd had from her wealthy family. Now the Delfont fortune and estates were in his hands, and with them the responsibility to maintain and improve them.

'I'll ask the designer to justify the costs,' said Kitty. 'Not that I think Evelyn would take advantage, but I think people work better within parameters.'

'You're the household manager,' he said.

'I'll always do my best for you, keep your interests first; you know that, don't you?' There was such honesty and sincerity in her blue eyes—blue was his favourite colour—he felt moved, grateful and humbled. She was an exceptional person in every way and he felt most fortunate to have her in his life, even if only temporarily.

'I do, and I'm grateful,' he said.

'And I'll bet you'll be even more grateful if I relent and serve the *torta*, with an extra helping of strawberries?'

'So you can read my mind now?'

'When it comes to dessert, it's not difficult to read you,' she said teasingly.

Could she also read that his interest in her was not just as a member of staff or a platonic friend? Or that he was finding it increasingly difficult to mask it?

CHAPTER EIGHT

THE FOLLOWING MORNING, the meeting with the interior designer went quite differently to what Kitty had expected. She'd been both surprised and disconcerted to see a very different Sebastian from the one with whom she'd shared confidences in the cosiness of the kitchen.

He'd greeted Evelyn Lim, a warm, confident woman in her mid-thirties, with polite professionalism but none of the enthusiasm that Kitty had expected from him for stage one of putting his stamp on the house. He'd reverted to that reticent, somewhat forbidding person she'd first encountered at the Docklands apartment and Kitty couldn't help but feel more than a touch intimidated.

He'd accompanied her and Evelyn on a perfunctory tour of the house, letting Kitty do most of the talking. At the end, he'd thanked Evelyn and told her that further communication should go through Kitty.

Kitty had taken Evelyn to Lady Enid's office, where they'd discussed terms and timelines for Evelyn to present proposed schedules and Computer Assisted Design images. The first, most urgent priority was the dining room. Could Evelyn give it a new look by the time of the foundation dinner?

Kitty had apologised for Sebastian's aloofness. Evelyn had laughed off her concerns. According to the designer, Sir Sebastian was a mere two on a scale of ten for client grumpiness. 'I'm excited to be working with you again, Kitty, and on such a wonderful house,' she had said as they'd parted. Evelyn, more a work acquaintance than a friend, had stood by Kitty through the scandal, unfailing in her support.

Sebastian was tied up for the rest of the morning in meetings with his executive assistant, Guy. It wasn't until after the successful trial lunch with Alisa, one of the proposed job-share cooks, that Kitty was able to pin him down in his library.

The door was half open. 'Knock-knock,' she called out. Sebastian looked up from his desk, frowning at the interruption. She hesitated, not sure which Sebastian she was going to encounter. His frown turned to a welcoming smile and he stood up. 'Kitty. Come in.'

She realised she had been holding her breath and she let it out on a sigh of relief and an answering heartfelt smile. This was *her* Sebastian. She pulled herself up quickly. He wasn't her Sebastian; in fact he didn't appear to be anyone's Sebastian. What she meant was this was the more relaxed Sebastian she had got used to. Not the distant Sebastian that Evelyn had met.

He gestured to the visitor's chair opposite his desk and sank back into his chair as Kitty took her place, putting the parcel she'd brought in with her on the floor by her side. She liked this room, with all the books and those beautiful paintings evocative of a happy time in a sunny climate. Now she knew their significance in Sebastian's life—and that they'd been painted by the person she knew as Marisol Matthew—she ached to look more closely at them. However, this room was not one she could just casually stroll in and out of. It was sacrosanct for Sebastian. She would have to brief whatever housekeeper they appointed on the importance of keeping his books and possessions exactly as he placed them. Hearing about his childhood yesterday made her appreciate his need for consistency and certainty—even if it could make people like her initially think he was being *difficult*.

'To what do I owe this pleasure?' he said.

'Good news. Evelyn has already come back to me with a few ideas for the dining room. She wants to know if you like the idea of switching out the heavy red for smoky blue which, in her designer's terminology, is "evocative and moody" while at the same time "serene". And she says it will work beautifully with the wood tones of the antique furniture and highlight the contrasting rich reds in that magnificent Persian carpet.'

'What do you think?' he asked.

Kitty appreciated the way he valued her opinion. Her confidence had taken a battering at Blaine and Ball.

'It sounds lovely to me,' she said. 'If you agree to the colour, Evelyn will send preliminary designs in the morning. Because she had a team of trades people ready to go on the other house, as soon as you approve her plans they can start on preparation. She says it's a blessing the room is painted, not wallpapered so they don't have to strip it and that the plasterwork is in such excellent condition.'

'Do it,' he said. 'I liked Evelyn, liked the examples of her work she showed us. Smoky blue sounds good to me and I know her CAD images will show me exactly how the room will look. I intend to be more involved with the master bedroom because that will be my personal space.'

'You didn't have many questions for Evelyn this morning,' Kitty said, making it an observation, not an accusation.

'I'm not good on things like that, especially with people I don't know. It's why I have you to organise them for me.'

'Yes, of course,' she said, biting down on a *yes but*. This renovation would take a lot longer than the six weeks she was contracted to work here. Who would provide the continuity?

He leaned towards her over the desk. 'Remember, you had the information about my preferences that you extracted under torture.'

He said it so seriously that she couldn't help but laugh. 'The torture of withholding *torta caprese*?' she managed to get out between splutters of laughter.

'You called it torture and the pain was very real,' he said deadpan. He cast a stern look at her. Then spoiled the effect by laughing too. His laugh was deep and rich and very engaging.

Laughing with her boss. This was nice. *Too nice.*

Laughter brightened his grey eyes, erased the tension from his face, magnified the power of his smile a thousandfold. Sebastian laughing was a different person yet again. She couldn't keep her eyes off him. It was as if his laughter had blown open a set of formidably high gates to reveal tantalising pathways she had never imagined: exciting, crazy—but still impossible.

The danger to her was that his laughter stirred not only desire but affection. It would be too easy to grow to care for Sir Sebastian Delfont. But nothing had changed to allow her to entertain the thought of anything that extended, even slightly, into a kind of friendship she doubted would outlast her six-week contract.

'I make no apology for my very effective method of torture,' she said. She willed her imagination to cease with the forbidden thoughts of other ways she would like to tease and tantalise him.

Sebastian sobered and Kitty took a deep breath to force herself back into business mode.

'Seriously, Kitty, your methods work,' he said. 'Briefing Evelyn Lim to get the dining room refurbishment started, organising that excellent lunch served by the first half of the job share team—you've again exceeded my expectations. You're quite the miracle-worker with all you've achieved already here.'

'No miracles involved,' she said with a shrug. 'It's amazing what a great address and a generous budget can do.'

'I think you underestimate your powers,' he said. Their gazes met for a long moment. She couldn't be sure what she read there—gratitude for sure, admiration too, and something else that evaded her. It flustered her and consequently she spoke too quickly, determined to change the subject.

'Speaking of powers, I'm not so sure about this one but we won't know until we try it,' she said. She reached down for the package and put it on the desk in front of her. 'This is the fun part of the day's agenda.'

'What's in there?' he asked.

'A smudging kit. I ordered it online and it just arrived.'

'You need a kit? I thought you burned a bunch of sage from the supermarket and waved it around the room.'

'I thought that too, but apparently not,' she said. 'Smudging is a serious business, apparently not to be undertaken on the spur of the moment. It seems you have to weave the leaves into a tight bunch and let them dry out for at least a week. If we want to smudge before we start the renovations, we don't have time for that.'

'Good point,' he said. He had surprised her with his willingness to try the ritual and she watched him closely for signs he might be making fun of her. But he seemed genuinely involved.

'Traditionally you also need an abalone shell and a large feather,' she said. 'Heaven knows where I'd find those myself. It seemed easier to buy a kit that included everything. The kit also includes instructions on how to conduct the smudging ceremony. There are an awful lot of reminders not to set the house on fire.'

'That's another good point. Should I be concerned about safety?' he asked. 'I don't want to risk burning the house down.'

Sebastian watched Kitty as she sought the right answer, her brow pleated in a slight frown. He liked the way she took this seriously, her sincere belief she was helping him to banish shadows from the past.

'No need for concern if we use care and common sense,' she said, rather primly he thought. Prim looked cute on her. Hell, any expression looked cute on her.

'You know I'm not so sure where common sense comes in when it comes to a smudging ceremony,' he said ruefully.

'Perhaps more a suspension of disbelief is required?' she said.

'That sounds about right,' he said.

'From what I read, smudging rituals originated in indigenous cultures around the world. If people have believed for a very long time that the ceremony banishes bad energy, maybe there's something to it. Even if it's just superstition it's worth a try. That is, if you can live with superstition.'

Sebastian snorted. 'Superstition was part of my life growing up with my Spanish family. My great-grandmother had a potted cactus on every entrance to her house to ward off evil. And no one would ever dare take off their hat and put it on a bed as that brought bad luck.' He thought about sharing with Kitty his *abuela*'s theory about a curse on the family and decided that would be going too far.

'Really? My grandfather blames his broken leg on the fact he absentmindedly walked under the ladder before he climbed it. And he would never open an umbrella inside the house.' Kitty rolled her eyes as she said it, which made Sebastian smile.

'And we're about to perform a smudging ceremony,' he said. 'I wonder what your grandfather would say about that.'

'I think he'd say it was very un-British,' she said. 'But each to his own, as my gran used to say. When do you want to start?'

'No time like the present, as my father used to say.'

'I'm okay with that,' she said. 'What about Guy? Do you want to involve him?'

'Absolutely not,' he said. 'Guy is out for the rest of the day.' He suspected his executive assistant would ridicule the idea, and therefore Kitty, and he couldn't allow that.

'It's just us then,' she said.

'Yes,' he agreed.

He liked it being just the two of them, knowing he could be himself with her. When the house was up and running, filled with staff, it would be very different. His spirits plummeted when he realised that by the time the staff were in place, Kitty would be back working in her own business. But that was five and a half weeks away and that was surely enough time to get to know Kitty, to see if his attraction to her had staying power, and to gauge if she had any interest in him.

'So we're smudging conspirators, and we won't let anyone else into our secret circle,' she said, her eyes dancing with mischief.

'That's us,' he replied, surprised at how much the idea of a secret circle with just him and Kitty in it appealed.

She stood up. 'I'm dying to see what's inside the kit.'

Sebastian walked around to her side of his desk to join her. Considering her history, he stayed a respectful distance from her, although he was very aware of her sweet floral scent. He watched, bemused, as she opened the package with all the excitement of it being a gift.

She tore away the brown paper wrapping to reveal a brown cardboard box filled with a ten-centimetre bundle of dried leaves tied with white string, an iridescent abalone shell and a large feather in shades of brown.

'Interesting,' he said. 'Not quite what I expected.'

'Me neither. I think of sage leaves as green. This is white sage.'

Kitty pulled out a printed instruction sheet. 'We need to light the smudge stick then waft the smoke around the room with the feather. The resulting smoke is said to banish malignant energy from the house and invite good energy in. That means opening a window wide to avoid a traffic jam of conflicting energies.' She smiled. 'Who knew?'

She was delightful, and Sebastian found himself getting totally caught up in the game.

'Malignant energy? That's one way of describing my grandfather.' He glanced at his watch. 'Shall we get started?'

'First stop Sir Cyril's study?'

'Yes,' he said, keen to get on with it, surprised she knew that was the room most imbued with his grandfather's presence.

He followed Kitty down the stairs to the ground floor, admiring her back view, the sway of her hips in narrow-legged black trousers and a fitted jacket. Every time he saw her, he was struck again by how lovely she was. And each meeting left him both liking and admiring her more.

He stood outside the closed door, his hand poised above the handle. Kitty turned to him. 'You're having to brace yourself to go in, aren't you?'

He nodded, unable to speak, to admit even to himself that, after all these years, he still felt the fear. But Kitty understood; he knew she did without any words being exchanged. He wanted to reach out and hold her hand but he couldn't—and not just because she was holding the smudging kit.

'I used to feel physically ill when I got the summons to come to this study.'

'Let me go in first,' she said.

'No. I have to do it,' he replied as he reluctantly turned the handle and pushed open the door.

It was just a room, empty of the glowering figure of his grandfather, who had summoned him there on so many occasions to berate and lecture him, not just as a child but on those occasions he'd been obliged to see him as a teenager and as an adult. And yet a shiver ran down his spine at the memories that assaulted him.

Without a word, Kitty put the smudging kit down on the big traditional walnut desk. She went over to the windows and pulled the heavy ruby-coloured velvet curtains aside so light streamed into the room, dust motes dancing in a sunbeam. She pushed up one of the windows, enough for fresh air to come in. It ruffled the papers stacked on the desk and lifted the hair away from Kitty's face in fine blonde strands.

She turned back to him. Her eyes warm with compassion—and not a trace of the pity he would have hated—she put her hand on his arm. It was the first time she had touched him.

'When you were a little boy, was there physical abuse?'

He shook his head. 'Not…not sexual. No. Not physical either. He couldn't have hidden that from my father. More than once he told me how he'd like to take his belt to me, but the worst he did was what he called a "clip around the ears" which was basically hitting me on the side of the head.'

'What's that if not abuse?' Kitty flushed with outrage on his behalf.

'I suppose he did it to keep my father and uncle in line, so perhaps it was seen as normal in this family.'

'Normal,' she muttered. 'I don't think so.'

'Relentless mental abuse was Sir Cyril's thing, about how useless I was, how stupid I was—because sometimes I forgot and spoke in Spanish—how I had to obey him in everything or my parents would suffer.'

'How would they suffer?'

'Probably withdrawal of funds. But at nine years old I didn't question what would happen to them as a result of my misbehaviour. I just wanted to protect them.'

Kitty cursed. 'I'm just so furious on your behalf. He sounds like a monster. How dare that man use his power and his money to intimidate a child?' She stopped. 'I'm sorry. It's not my place to—'

'Say anything you want. I appreciate your indignation.'

'Now I think I know why…' Her voice trickled away.

'Why what?'

'No. I shouldn't say—'

'Please say it.'

'Well, the reason you're not delirious with joy at inheriting all this. And…and the title. I… I'd wondered.'

He sighed. 'And yet it seems so ungrateful. Now you know what I mean when I say I feel like an imposter.'

'How can you say that? I mean apart from the obvious, that you…well, you look and act the part. But you're going to continue to do good, stepping into the shoes of Lady Enid.'

'As she had a fondness for teetering high heels, perhaps not literally.'

She looked up at him and his heart swelled at the compassion and understanding he saw there. 'I don't know you well, but I believe you're a good man doing your best to honour your legacy and to fulfil the wishes of your grandmother.'

'Thank you,' he choked out. There was a very long beat of silence as he looked into her face, so close, already so familiar. 'Your faith in me means a lot.' She bowed her head in acknowledgement and he wondered if he had given too much away about how he felt about his household manager.

Kitty dropped her hand from his arm and he felt immediately bereft of its warmth. She took a step back.

'Let's start the smudging,' she said briskly. 'We'll give your grandfather—or the memories of him—a proverbial clip around the ear and send his presence packing from this room.'

'I like the way you put that.' Sebastian picked up the smudging stick and held it out in front of him. He could imagine the horror with which his ultra-conservative grandfather would have viewed such a ritual taking place in his traditional study.

'Let me light it,' Kitty said, pulling a lighter from her pocket. 'I found this in Lady Enid's desk. The sage stick is not meant to flame, just smoulder. When ash forms, we knock it into the shell. To get things happening, we wave the stick in an anti-clockwise direction and chant a mantra.'

'A mantra? You didn't prepare me for that.'

'I only just read it in the instructions,' she said. 'They give an example: "cleanse my home of negativity". But I think we can do better than that.' She looked up at him. 'Why not say to your grandfather what you were too scared, and under his thumb, to say when you were nine years old and powerless?'

'I don't think that will be difficult,' he said. He started to wave the smudging stick around in the requisite clockwise direction. It was a large room and it took a few waves of the stick for the pungent smoke to be noticed.

Kitty sneezed.

'Shall I stop?' he asked.

'No, I'm fine. Just getting used to the smoke. Start with your mantra.'

'Banish Sir Cyril's cruel words that linger in this room,' he intoned.

Kitty repeated his words very solemnly then paused. 'That's good. But I'm not sure it's what a nine-year-old would say.'

'How about goodbye, Grandfather?' he said.

'Grandfather begone,' Kitty intoned dramatically.

Sebastian emulated her theatrical tone. 'Get lost, Grandfather. Good riddance, Grandfather.'

'I like that,' she said.

He stopped himself. 'I'd better leave it at that before I embellish my mantra with words my nine-year-old self most certainly didn't know.' But he silently uttered those curse words under his breath, giving a private vent to his anger against the man who had caused so much heartache for his family.

Kitty looked up at him and he could see she was struggling not to laugh. 'I'm not laughing at you but at the thought of you as a sweet little boy standing up to your horrid grandfather and telling him where to go, with him unable to do anything about it.'

Sebastian joined in with her laughter. 'Sir Cyril would have absolutely hated this. He'd be incandescent with rage. I'm a naughty, defiant little boy, giving him the finger.'

'Like you never dared to do before. How does that feel?'

'Wonderful. Cathartic. Healing.' He placed the still smouldering stick carefully onto the shell. 'So much so I don't see the need to smudge any other rooms.'

'I'm so glad to hear that,' she said. 'Not about the

smudging—I'm prepared to do every room if it helps—but that you feel so good about what we've done.'

Was it their combined laughter that made the atmosphere in the room seem to lighten? The symbolism of the smudging ceremony? The catharsis of chanting the mantras? The actual smoke itself?

It was Kitty. Her kindness, her belief in him, her sunshine banishing the shadows. *Kitty.*

'I really think he's gone from this room,' he said. 'And it's all thanks to you.' Without thinking about it, he swept her into a hug. Initially stiff with surprise, she then relaxed into his arms.

She felt so good there and for a moment he allowed himself to enjoy the comfort of her closeness, her warmth, the sweet scent of her perfume. Until he remembered the promise he'd made to her: *I will never step over the line of what is appropriate between employer and employee.*

Abruptly, he let her go, took a step back. 'I'm sorry. That shouldn't have happened.'

She looked up at him, her eyes wide. 'It's fine. Really.'

Tension hummed between them and he cursed himself for stepping over that line and changing the easy camaraderie they'd shared.

Until she sneezed again—once, twice, three times, little sneezes as cute and feminine as she was. She looked up at him, dismayed. 'I think I'm allergic to smudging.' She laughed again and after a moment's hesitation he joined in with her laughter.

He realised he hadn't laughed as much in years.

CHAPTER NINE

'KITTY, I'D LIKE you to act as my hostess for the Lady Enid foundation dinner party next Saturday night.' Sebastian's request came quite out of the blue. Kitty stared at him, totally taken aback.

She and Sebastian had just finished a gourmet lunch cooked by Josie, the second cook in the job share, and served to them in the breakfast room with its olive-green wallpaper and ornate carved sideboard. Sebastian's assistant, Guy, had been with them, but had just headed back upstairs. The crew working on the redecoration of the dining room had stopped for lunch too, downstairs in the kitchen, so it was a rare quiet moment on the ground floor.

'What exactly do you mean?' Kitty asked. But she didn't wait for an answer, rather launched into a list of what she'd arranged for the dinner. 'I've already organised everything. The menu has been chosen—and approved by you. Both the cooks, Alisa and Josie, will be on board for the evening. We raided your grandfather's cellar and found some remarkable wine. Waiters have been hired. Guy has had acceptances from all on the guest list and we've worked together on your speech. I've got Evelyn involved in the table decoration. We discovered a treasure trove of china, silver and crystal, not to mention antique table linen—your ancestors had fabulous taste. The most fashionable florist in London is on board. It was short notice, but I managed to pull strings as I used to work on their PR account. The room will be breathtaking.' Kitty knew she was blabbering on to the point of feeling breathless, but she didn't want to have to face answering his question.

Until she had to.

When her words finally petered out, Sebastian spoke in a low but firm voice from the other side of the table. 'By acting as my hostess, I meant for you to be by my side while greeting the guests and during the meal. There will be five people who were appointed by my grandparents to the board of the foundation and their spouses. They know nothing about me. I doubt they even knew Lady Enid and Sir Cyril had a grandson or, if they did know, I wasn't to be mentioned. There won't be one familiar face. My grandmother was concerned her foundation would struggle without her and these people hold the key to discovering if that's happened.' He paused. 'I'm dreading it. Please, Kitty, be there for me.'

Again Kitty was struck by that vulnerability behind his good looks and title. Her immediate instinct was to help him. Now that she knew something of his background, she was beginning to understand him. She'd felt so close to him during the smudging ceremony. But that didn't mean she wanted to expose her own vulnerabilities, still raw after two years.

'Why me?'

'Because I'll feel comfortable having you by my side. I'm not great with people I don't know, nor the social chit-chat this kind of gathering requires.'

She had fantasised about him asking her out on a date and he'd asked her to be his housekeeper. Where was this request leading to?

'Don't you know someone else who could act as hostess for you? A date, I mean.'

'No. I haven't dated anyone since I broke off my engagement two years ago.'

'You were engaged?'

'It didn't work out,' he said shortly.

Despite her resolve, Kitty's heart did a flip at the confirmation he was single. She didn't realise how possessive she had become about him until she imagined him with another woman. She wondered what was behind the broken engagement, had to bite her tongue to stop her from asking for the details.

'Could you ask a friend to act as hostess?' she said.

Sebastian shook his head. 'I don't want to give anyone the wrong idea that I want to get serious with them.'

How did she fit into that scenario? Kitty wondered. The *downstairs* being elevated to the *upstairs* for one night? Wasn't there a story about a girl like that? What was her name? Something beginning with 'C'. Got it—Cinderella.

'I honestly don't know what I can bring to the table for you, so to speak,' she said.

'You're warm, open, smart; you'll charm everyone.'

'That's nice of you to say so.'

Kitty couldn't help but feel flattered by his comment. However, she was a lot less warm and open than she used to be—she'd had to become more cautious, wary of other people. She'd been stung by those who'd appeared to have her interests at heart. And she wasn't at all sure that appearing as Sir Sebastian Delfont's hostess at a dinner party was a wise move.

'There's also the fact you're a PR professional,' he said. 'I feel confident you'll know exactly what to say.'

So not quite Cinderella, she thought. Not anything resembling a date, more along the lines of her being capable and useful—which was why she was here, she reminded herself. No need to feel disappointed that there wasn't something more personal behind his request.

'If—and I'm only saying *if*—I were to agree, I'd be putting myself in the spotlight again by sitting alongside Sir Sebastian Delfont as his hostess at a private dinner party. What if someone recognises me?'

'You've seen the guest list. Is there anyone on it you know?'

'Not one.'

'If it's any consolation, I don't know them either,' he said with a wry twist of his mouth. 'But they're all well acquainted with each other.'

For a long moment her gaze met his as they shared a moment of connection. He was shy, she realised. Even though he was born into the elite strata of people who existed way above the A-list.

'Do you think they'll be like your grandfather, judging you, watching for you to put a foot wrong?'

'Something like that,' he said.

'You've got the power, you know. You've got the title, the wealth, the property that puts you, fair and square, on their level—even a step up from their level.' Not to mention the extraordinary good looks of a hero from one of his mother's books.

Sebastian got up from the table. Paced back and forth before stopping opposite her. 'Do you think I care about that? To be judged for what I own, rather than who I am?'

He towered above her and she got up from her chair to face him on a more equal footing. Not that he intimidated her. In fact she felt safe with him, never more so than in that brief, awkward hug they'd shared on the day of the smudging ceremony. She'd relived that hug several times in her mind and that feeling of safety seemed just as memorable as the soaring excitement of being so close to him.

'I haven't known you for long, but you don't seem to care about that at all,' she said. 'But, no matter who these people are, they've come into your orbit because they're actively working for charity by being on the board of your grandmother's foundation. That's a point in their favour, if you ask me. I suggest you give them the benefit of the doubt before you meet them.'

Sebastian looked at her for a long moment. He nodded and she could almost see the trepidation about the dinner lift from his face. 'Perfectly put, Kitty Clements. Of course you're right And that's why I need you by my side.'

'I couldn't bear any more media attention,' she said. She realised she was wringing her hands and put them behind her back. 'It was a nightmare in so many ways. What if the press got hold of it and decided to make more of it than your household manager helping you out for the evening?'

Her critics had accused her of 'punching above her weight' with regard to her much older boss and her so-called infatuation with him. The scorn they'd pour on her for 'aspiring' to a man with a title, even more 'out of her league' didn't bear thinking about.

'The dinner is in the privacy of my home, and the guests are unlikely to be seeking out scandal. Besides, you look different from the press photos. Your hair is much longer. And you're Kitty, not Kathryn. Do you have a second name?'

'Rose—my middle name is Rose.'

'I could introduce you as Kitty Rose, without having to lie.'

'How would you explain my presence? I can assure you people will be curious about any woman seen by your side.'

'I'd say you were a friend. We're heading that way, aren't we?'

She paused. There had been a relaxing of limitations since the smudging ceremony three days ago, although she didn't let herself think beyond that and had steered clear of any cosy dinners for two in the kitchen. 'Yes.'

'I'm asking you as a friend as well as an employee.'

Still she wavered. 'I'm not sure.'

'You're the only person I trust to be there for me,' he said stubbornly.

She sighed. 'How can I say no, when you ask me in that way?'

He didn't try to mask the relief in his eyes. 'Kitty. Thank you. Perhaps I can start to look forward to my debut entertaining event if I know you'll be there with me. There's a lot riding on it in terms of the future of my grandmother's foundation.'

'I've agreed to be your hostess, but let me make it clear I'm still not sure it's a good idea.'

For him perhaps, but not for her. She was way too attracted to him to be able to kid herself she wanted to be 'just friends' even if that were a real possibility. She didn't have erotic fantasies about men who were 'just friends'. Nor did her heart skip a beat when they smiled at her.

And that was apart from the risk of putting herself in the public eye again. But she had advised Sebastian to think positively; perhaps she needed to do so herself. Knowing the parameters, that being his hostess meant no more than an extension of her household manager role, she should let herself look forward to the dinner. After all, she'd organised the whole event and it was promising to be an exceptional evening.

Now there was just one more item to organise for the dinner party: something for her to wear. She was planning to meet Claudia the next day, Saturday. It could become a shopping day in Chelsea.

The Kings Road was lined with shops, even more in the Duke of York Square and heading up Sloane Street all the way up to Knightsbridge, home to Harrods and Selfridges. Some of the boutiques were press-her-nose-to-the-window only, the prices were so stratospheric. But there were also branches of popular fashion chains that were more in line with her budget, not to mention the Peter Jones department store in Sloane Square.

She planned to spend time on Sunday with Gramps in the rehab hospital and could swing by his house to pick up shoes and accessories on her visit to Gramps's house. It was a long time since she'd had the occasion to dress up. *To dress up for Sebastian.* She forced the insidious thought from her mind. Why would he care what she looked like?

CHAPTER TEN

ON THE EVENING of the dinner party, Sebastian thought it looked as if a magic wand had been waved around the dining room and completely transformed it. Evelyn and her team had indeed performed a kind of magic to get it looking like this in two weeks, all thanks to Kitty.

Gone was the deep red he had found so oppressive, replaced by smoky blue in varying tones with ivory highlights. The room still looked opulent and traditional but in a softer, more inviting way. The new curtains had formal swags and tails but in two shades of smoky blue in a lustrous silk, rather than the dark red velvet with tarnished gold fringing they had replaced. Lush flower arrangements, formal yet not stiff, were artfully placed as centrepieces on the table, the marble mantelpiece and on the pedestals that had always stood empty in his grandfather's day. The table was laid with vintage linen, white porcelain rimmed with silver, heirloom crystal and antique silver cutlery engraved with the Delfont crest. The silver and crystal glittered and gleamed under the light of the chandeliers.

There was a definite feminine touch present, yet it was a room where he felt immediately comfortable. For the first time he felt as though this grand old house could become his home.

Sebastian took a deep sigh of relief mingled with anticipation. The room was like a stage set, awaiting the actors to bring it to life. No one would do that better than Kitty.

He glanced down at his watch. Kitty should be here by now. He'd asked her to come downstairs in plenty of time before the guests arrived. Perhaps he should go up and escort her down on his arm, start the evening the way he intended to continue, with Kitty by his side.

He knocked on her door. 'Kitty, it's Sebastian,' he called, after he didn't get an immediate response. Still no answer. He was surprised, as Kitty was usually so punctual. He knocked again. Slowly the door opened.

'Sebastian, I… I didn't expect to see you. Aren't you meant to be downstairs waiting for your guests?'

'Aren't you meant to be downstairs waiting with me?'

Kitty was wearing a silky wrap in the style of a Japanese kimono, in a soft pastel aqua patterned with flowers. Not that Sebastian was overly noticing the pattern; his eyes were drawn to the way it gaped at the neck to reveal the edge of a lacy blue bra and the swell of creamy breasts. Kitty clutched the edges together to bunch the fabric and protect her modesty. He noticed her hands weren't steady. Why wasn't she dressed?

The silence between them became uncomfortable, until she raised her eyes to his. 'I… I can't do this, Sebastian. I was about to call you. I'm sorry.' Her eyes were huge, her mouth trembled.

'Do what? I'm not sure what you mean.' Could she not work for him any longer? Fear clawed him at the thought.

'The dinner. I thought I could be your hostess, but I can't. I… I'm too scared to face those people. I'm not just terrified of being exposed but also… I don't want to…to see you drawn into my scandal. This dinner event is important to you, and I don't want to ruin it.'

Sebastian was disappointed. Deeply disappointed. The thought of having Kitty by his side had made the prospect of meeting the trustees and their spouses so much less confronting. But at the same time he was stunned to see confident, capable Kitty reduced to this because of him. He knew she'd had doubts about the dinner but he'd still talked her into it. Because he needed someone to help him face up to his own fears. But that shouldn't be at a cost to her.

'Kitty, I'm sorry. I should never have asked you to step so far out of your comfort zone.'

She shook her head. 'No need to apologise. It made sense to ask me to hostess. It…it's just me—my fears, my doubts. Letting panic get the better of me. I didn't sleep last night for worrying. I'm the one who should be apologising for letting you down.'

She was wearing more make-up than usual, the dark shadowing around her eyes and the deep pink lipstick making her appear more sophisticated, and her hair fell to her shoulders in sleek waves, perhaps as a result of a visit to a hairdresser. It told him that at some point quite recently she had been committed to the evening.

He drew a deep breath, conscious he had to say the right thing and not make her feel worse, aware he was responsible for throwing her into the situation that was causing her this angst. 'You wouldn't be letting me down,' he said.

She started to protest but he put up his hand to stop her. 'I won't lie and say I'm not disappointed, but I understand. What the press did to you was appalling and even though I rate at practically zero the chance of them finding out about your presence at this dinner tonight, I totally get why you don't want to risk it. But don't worry about my reputation. The media have no power over me whatsoever.'

With his birthright and his fortune as protection, it would be difficult for the gutter press to come up with anything to attack him that would wound. But hurting Kitty was another matter altogether. He'd been sickened about some of their speculations about her motives. Her fears were well founded. Much as he wanted her at the dinner, he wouldn't try and guilt her into it.

'You're so kind,' she said, a tremor in her voice. 'Thank you for being so understanding.'

'I won't say you won't be missed, because you will. But I owe you my thanks for the incredible job you've done in pulling everything together to make sure the dinner will be a success. I predict the guests will be talking about how different it is now from my grandparents' day—and it's all because of you.'

'Thank you,' she said. 'Event planning is part of what I do...what I did.' She fanned her hand in front of her face. 'Don't be so nice that you make me cry; it will ruin my make-up.'

'I don't want you to cry because I don't want you to be unhappy. But if you want to cry, go ahead and open the floodgates, because if you're up here by yourself watching television it probably doesn't matter if your make-up is ruined.'

She blinked, bewildered. 'No, I don't suppose it matters at all.' She smiled, a shaky smile that didn't reach the corners of her mouth. 'How silly of me.' She started to laugh but it was tinged with hysteria. 'How very silly of me.' Big tears welled up in her lovely blue eyes. 'I... I'm sorry, I...' Her face crumpled as she choked on a sob.

Sebastian only hesitated for a second before he pulled her close. If she resisted, he would immediately let her go. But as his arms went around her she relaxed against him. He held her tight, murmured a litany of soothing words, told her she was wonderful and how much he valued her and that it didn't matter if she wasn't at the dinner—well, it did because he would miss her—but he'd be okay on his own and he was sorry if he'd pushed her into something she wasn't ready for. He wanted to comfort her, soothe her, protect her—never allow anyone to hurt her. A rush of emotion swept through him. No woman had ever made him care like this.

When her sobs shuddered to a stop, he gently released her.

'Sebastian, I'm so s—'

'There is absolutely no need to say you're sorry. I pushed you too hard. End of story.'

He gently wiped a smear of dark make-up from under her eye with his thumb, before realising he had no right to perform such an intimate action and taking a step back in case she misinterpreted it.

'Oh, my gosh, my make-up.' Her hands flew to her face. 'Is it smeared all over your tuxedo?'

She checked the fabric of the bespoke jacket he'd had made for him at Uncle Olly's Savile Row tailor. Her action brought her close to him again, her scent sweet and heady, and he felt intoxicated by it, entranced by the light touch of her hands on the lapels of his jacket. He had to fight the urge to take her in his arms again, to suggest he also skip the dinner and stay up here with her.

'No lipstick or mascara seem to have migrated to your jacket, thank heaven,' she said. 'That would have been awkward to explain to your guests.'

'I'm sure they'd be too polite to mention it if they noticed.'

She fell silent for a long moment, her face woebegone. 'What will you tell them about why I'm not at the dinner?' she asked in a very small voice.

'That you fell ill and had to send your apologies.' He glanced down at his watch. 'And, speaking of guests, I need to head back downstairs for when they arrive. Will you be okay?'

'Yes, of course. Embarrassed about the way I behaved, but okay.'

'I'll instruct the cooks to send up some dinner for you.'

'That won't be necessary,' she protested.

'Of course it will,' he said. 'After all your planning of the menu, I expect you'd like to taste it.'

As he headed for the elevator he was aware of Kitty's gaze on him from her doorway and he kept his shoulders straight, his step determined. It was only when he was in the privacy of the elevator that he let himself slump. He'd made such a mistake with Kitty. Not in asking her to be his hostess, but by not asking her out on a straightforward date in the first place. This whole subterfuge about having her work for him as his household manager had blown up in his face. He wanted her by his side without having to spin stories and half lies.

He hadn't trusted the instant attraction portrayed in his mother's romance novels for the basis of a relationship. Especially not after the disaster of his infatuation with Lavinia. But these two weeks in Kitty's company had proved that the attraction he felt for her was real. Getting to know her had only made him like her more, *want her more*. However, instead of making it easier to establish a relationship, he had made it more difficult. Imagine how much simpler it would have been if he could have introduced Kitty as his girlfriend to his guests tonight? And if the press had got hold of their connection he would be there to protect and defend her.

But it was useless to castigate himself with a barrage of 'what ifs'. Because without Kitty's amazing organisational skills and her gold standard contacts book, the dinner tonight wouldn't be anywhere near as successful as it promised to be. Left to his own devices, he would have held the event in the untouched dining room, dark with memories of his grandfather's cruelty, ordered catering from heaven knew where, not given flowers or anything like that a thought. And if Kitty wasn't working here she'd be working all hours with PWP, and he might have only seen her for a few dates—that was if she'd agreed at all.

Still, he couldn't stop the old gloom from descending on him—he realised how few his dark moods had become since Kitty had brought her own brand of sunshine to Cheyne Walk.

The way it was panning out, the dinner would be a success and launch him into his new role as Sir Sebastian Delfont, upholder of the family traditions. But it would be a hollow triumph without Kitty by his side.

The guests would start arriving soon. He headed to the reception room where they would gather before going in to dinner. With no Kitty, he had to face up to the ordeal of enduring the evening on his own, although all she'd done in preparation would make it easier—she'd even put her PR skills to use for his speech.

Evelyn, the interior designer, had done her best in the limited time to make a few welcome changes to the reception room. Sebastian sat there in the lull before the guests would arrive to be greeted with cocktails, and went through the list on his phone. He'd compiled notes on all ten guests—including photos—with details on their family situations, personal history and role as a trustee of the foundation so he'd have some basis for conversation. He was just checking on the name of the third wife of a titan of business when there was a quiet knock on the door. He quickly switched off his phone and slid it into his inside jacket pocket. Someone must have arrived early and was being ushered through by the staff hired for the evening.

He rose from his chair and pasted a polite smile on his face. Only to have it freeze as he heard Kitty's familiar, 'Knock-knock.'

'Come in,' he said hoarsely.

Kitty. Kitty in an elegant navy dress that was long-sleeved and modest but hugged her shapely body and teased with discreet hints of creamy skin through dark lace that sparkled with tiny crystals around the neckline. Kitty walking towards him, tentative in high-heeled silver shoes that strapped around her ankles. Or perhaps her tentative steps had more to do with trepidation about what kind of reception she might receive.

'I wonder if you're still in need of a hostess,' she said, her voice not quite steady.

'Only one in particular,' he said, unable to keep his eyes off her, fisting his hands so he didn't reach out and touch her. Her hair was pulled back on one side from her face with a glittering comb, her make-up perfect again with no trace of tears. She looked absolutely beautiful.

'Kitty Rose, reporting for duty,' she said, a tremulous smile dancing around the corners of her mouth.

'Why?' he said.

'I realised I'd not only be letting you down, but also letting myself down if I didn't stand by my word.'

Relief and elation lifted him right out of his gloom. Kitty was here—all was well.

'I'm grateful you came to that decision.' There was so much more he wanted to say but he couldn't find the words.

She stood very close, looking up at him. He saw something in her eyes he didn't recognise. She swayed towards him—was it the heels making her unsteady or an invitation? As she parted her lips, he lowered his head to kiss her, but his mouth had barely grazed hers when there was a discreet cough at the door.

'Your guests are arriving, sir.'

Sebastian cursed quietly under his breath at the interruption.

Kitty smiled ruefully and reached up to kiss him lightly on the cheek. 'Shall we go and face them?' she said, placing her hand in the crook of his elbow and taking her place by his side.

CHAPTER ELEVEN

KITTY SAT AT Sebastian's right hand throughout the dinner. This time it was her turn to feel like an imposter. She was acting as hostess under entirely false pretences. That was the place for the guest of honour. The rules of etiquette dictated that she, as hostess, sat at the opposite end of the table. But Sebastian had told her in no uncertain terms what he thought of the 'rules' as they applied to him, and had insisted she be placed next to him.

She was so very glad he had done so. If she'd been at the far end of the table from him, she would have been second-guessing every word she said. His presence so close by, the knowledge he was watching out for her, helped her relax and she found the guests weren't as intimidating as she'd feared. In fact, she was surprised to find how much she was enjoying the evening. Not to mention how incredibly pleased she was at how flawlessly the meal service went and how well received the menu.

Before the main course was served, Sebastian stood to give his speech. He welcomed everyone to the first annual dinner without his grandmother and explained how he intended to take over her role as chairperson of the foundation that bore her name and continue her high standard of ethics. He asked the trustees to be frank with him about any troubles they might have encountered. Throughout his speech, he was confident and charming, with touches of dry humour. Kitty's heart swelled with pride. How could he ever consider himself a fraud?

He took his seat beside her to a smattering of applause. 'Well done, Sir Sebastian,' she murmured.

He took her hand and squeezed it in silent thanks. *Sebastian was holding her hand.* He was coming down from the high of a well-received speech, and probably didn't even notice he had held onto her hand for longer than required, but she noticed. Every nerve-ending in her body noticed the contact, innocent though it was. Did it mean anything? Did that almost kiss in the reception room mean anything? She honestly didn't know what to think.

He was still the one holding all the power. Tonight she really was in Cinderella territory. On Monday she'd be back hunting for prospective housekeepers and cleaners and gardeners. In another month she'd be back packing boxes for clients' house moves. While she loved PWP, and the self-employment opportunity it had given her and Claudia, Sebastian had given her different opportunities here.

He'd given her the chance to try out her management skills and to prove she was still every bit as good at event management as she'd been back in that former life when she'd been a rising star in the public relations world. It made her realise how much she'd missed the work that she'd believed to be her lifetime career.

And her attraction to him? It wasn't just sexual attraction she felt for Sebastian; the last two weeks had seen her liking him more each day. More than liking. But Sebastian was a man she couldn't have. They still came from very different worlds—nothing had changed there.

The more he took on the mantle of the Delfont title and fortune, the more he might become Sir Sebastian, the millionaire—or perhaps even billionaire for all she knew—welcomed by that top strata of society, and less the guy who would enjoy a meal in the kitchen with his household manager or laugh his way through a smudging ceremony. He said he didn't care if she dragged him into a scandal, but the more he became involved with the foundation, the less he might welcome adverse attention from the tabloids—and there was always the risk she would attract that, until she could clear her name.

She slipped her hand from Sebastian's as she answered a question from the woman sitting next to him about the interior designer who had transformed the dining room. She wasn't the first person this evening she'd shared Evelyn's contact details with, and she was glad her amazing work here might lead to new commissions for her.

The trustees varied from middle-aged to elderly and all appeared pleased that Sebastian would be stepping into Lady Enid's shoes. So far, no one seemed to make any connection between Sebastian's friend Kitty Rose and the scandalous Kathryn Clements. They were too polite to grill her about her friendship with him and seemed happy to accept the explanation that they had met through work. Sebastian freely acknowledged her part in planning the dinner and she graciously accepted their praise, finding it just the teeniest bit difficult to keep a straight face. She'd planned functions like this before but she'd never attended as a guest, let alone as the hostess to a handsome man with a title. It all seemed surreal.

Sitting on her other side was a charming retired judge and his erudite professor wife. They confided that they had been close to Lady Enid—although not, it seemed, Sir Cyril. They'd become tight-lipped at any reference to Lady Enid's husband, without actually saying anything critical. The judge hinted that he wanted to retire from his role as trustee as he and his wife wanted to move permanently to their house in Portugal. That would give Sebastian the opportunity to appoint his own people to the board. Kitty would share that information with Sebastian at the end of the evening. It might be the first step to putting his stamp on another aspect of his inheritance. And a move further away from her.

After all the frantic planning to get the dinner organised it was over all too soon. After the farewells were made, Kitty stood facing Sebastian in the hallway after the last of his guests had left.

Behind closed doors, the dining room and kitchen were still a flurry of activity as the temporary staff cleared up. They'd be back in the morning to complete such tasks as polishing silver and putting everything away in pristine condition. One of the joys of being wealthy must surely be having someone to do all that for you, Kitty thought. Small scale dinner parties at her flat used to leave her facing a mess of unwashed dishes to clean up in the morning while—now she thought of it—Neil slept it off. Recently she'd heard he had announced his engagement. She'd waited for the rush of jealousy and pain, but it hadn't come. By his betrayal, her ex had killed all feeling she'd ever had for him. She couldn't find it in herself to wish him well, just felt a pang of pity for his fiancée.

Sebastian turned to face her. 'Thank you, Kitty. Thank you for everything you did to make the evening such a success.'

'It did go well, didn't it? I'm pleased. You could reasonably expect something would go wrong, but nothing actually did. And didn't the room look beautiful? I kept looking around, hardly able to believe it was the same room we looked at just two weeks ago. The smoky blue made such a difference with the silver instead of the red and the gold.'

'As a strategy it also worked,' he said. 'It marked significant change.'

'You mean out with the old and in with the new?'

'Something like that. You certainly did me a favour finding Evelyn Lim.'

'I can't wait to see what she does with the rest of the rooms.'

Only Kitty probably wouldn't ever get to see those rooms finished. The master bedroom required major refurbishments and so did the bathrooms. That would take time, and her time here in Cheyne Walk was limited. She felt inexplicably sad about that, perhaps like Cinderella had felt at the prospect of returning to the ashes and dust of her downstairs life. She didn't want to face the thought that, like Cinderella, she would be mourning the loss of not the prince in her life but her baronet.

'Me too,' he said.

'It's getting late,' she said. 'I'll head upstairs.'

'I'm not tired. I'm still buzzing from the evening and not ready to turn in.'

'Me neither.' After the emotional ups and downs of the day, and then being 'on' all evening, she was wide awake.

'Would you like to come for a walk with me?' he asked. 'Get some fresh air.'

'Now?'

'Why not?'

'Because I'm not used to walking the streets at night. I don't feel safe.' She didn't like to admit it; however, that was the way it was.

'You'd be with me. Would you feel safe then?'

She didn't hesitate. 'Yes.' On more than one level, she felt safe with Sebastian.

'It will be chilly out; I'll get your coat from the cupboard,' he said.

Kitty glanced down at her gorgeous new silver stilettoes. 'I'll pop upstairs and change into boots.'

Five minutes later, she caught her breath at the November chill as she stepped out of the front door and into the night.

'Cold?' Sebastian asked.

She wrapped her arms around herself. 'A little; it was so warm inside.' She needed to collect her warmer coat when she went home the next day.

'Here,' he said as he removed the cashmere scarf he was wearing. 'Wear this.'

'Oh, no, I couldn't—'

'Please, I don't need the scarf.'

He looped the soft grey scarf around her neck. His fingers, in their fine leather gloves, brushed her neck and sent shivers of awareness down her spine. He was close. Kissing distance close. They'd come so close to kissing earlier in the evening. Or had that just been relief on both their parts that she'd overcome her panic attack?

'Better?' he said. All the better for being so close to him. She wanted to reach up and bring his face down to hers, to finish the kiss that had been cut short before.

'Much better,' she said. She nestled into his scarf. It was warm and soft and carried a hint of his scent. 'You might not get it back,' she teased.

'It's yours,' he said.

'Oh, no, I didn't mean… I couldn't possibly accept it.'

'The scarf looks so much better on you than on me,' he said. 'I've got others.'

Of course she couldn't keep his scarf. But she was certainly going to enjoy wearing it tonight, and the heady sense of connection to him it gave her. She pulled it up higher over her ears.

'Where are we walking?'

'I usually cut through over there past the statue of St Thomas More to take us to Chelsea Embankment.'

'Then a walk by moonlight along the Thames,' she said. She nearly added, *How romantic*, but stopped herself just in time. She couldn't let herself think there was anything romantic about a man and his household manager taking a stroll to wind down after an event that had been gruelling for both of them. *Except there had been that nearly kiss.*

It was quiet as they walked along the paved Embankment pathway, softly lit by a progression of traditional London lampposts placed along the river wall. There were trees still hanging onto some of their autumn leaves on the left, on their right the river at high tide, the occasional wash from passing boats surging against the wall. The night was crisp and clear with a full moon hanging in the sky. There weren't many people about, even though it was Saturday night, and not much traffic on the road or the river. It felt as if they had London all to themselves.

'It's magic,' she said. 'Even better than it is during the day. I've walked up here a few times, thinking I'd like to see the Chelsea Physic Garden.'

'I run here most mornings,' he said. 'Along the riverside pavement, across Chelsea Bridge to Battersea Park, then over the Albert Bridge and back home.'

What an incredible part of London to live in. She wondered if he would become complacent about the privilege; she doubted she ever would. Not for the first time she thanked her lucky stars for giving her the chance to stay here for six weeks, the opportunity of a lifetime.

'Impressive,' she said.

'Not really; it's less than two miles. But it wakes me up for the day.'

She could think of better ways to wake him up, she thought, glad he couldn't see her blush in the semi-darkness at another of those erotic fantasies about him that continued to plague her. It was entirely inappropriate, she knew, but she wanted him. Wanted him so badly he was beginning to invade her dreams. When she really thought about it—which she tried not to—she had wanted him from the day she'd first met him.

'You must get up very early.' He'd always been around, dressed for work, when she'd come downstairs at nine.

'I like the mornings,' he said.

She shuddered. 'I'm a night owl through and through. I can stay up all hours, but I hate getting up early in the morning. Like I'll have to do tomorrow.'

'Do you have something special planned for your day off?' he asked.

'Visiting my grandfather in the rehab hospital.' That really made her sound like a social butterfly, didn't it? 'He has friends from the village who visit but he needs to see me and…and I need to see him.'

'Of course you do. How do you get down to Kent as you don't have a car here?'

'The parking is way too expensive around here. I catch the train when I go back home. My car is parked there.'

'Can I drive you tomorrow?'

Kitty was too flabbergasted to answer. 'You mean to visit my grandfather? Why would you want to do that?'

'To help you out. To enjoy a day out of London. To meet your grandfather and talk to him about gardening. Have lunch together somewhere.'

'But why? I still don't get it.'

She scarcely noticed they'd stopped walking and stood near the river wall, facing each other.

'Because I want to get to know you better, Kitty.'

'But you already know me. I—'

He put his hands on her shoulders and looked into her face. Kitty stilled, uncertain of what was happening.

'I know you as an employee. I want to get to know you outside of a work situation.' His face was in shadow and she couldn't read his eyes. 'Would it be an intrusion for me to spend your day off with you tomorrow?'

'Oh,' was all she could manage to squeeze out with a voice that felt too constricted to form a proper word.

'Is that a yes or a no?'

There was an edge to his voice that made her realise that her answer was important to him.

'It's a *no*. I mean *no* to it being an intrusion, *yes* to spending the day with you.'

She sensed him relax at her answer. 'Good,' he said gruffly. 'I understand why you're reluctant to be seen in public with me in London.'

His hands still rested lightly on her shoulders, which brought him close and gave a certain intimacy to the conversation.

'Visiting Gramps isn't going to be very exciting,' she said.

'The company is sure to be good. You, for a start, and I like the sound of your grandfather.'

'Are you serious? You really want to visit my grandfather? It's a small community hospital so isn't too grim, but it's still a hospital.'

'I'd be meeting someone who is important to you.'

'He certainly is that,' she said with a catch in her voice.

'I can wait outside while you visit, if you'd prefer,' Sebastian said.

'No, Gramps would want to meet you. He's heard about the work I'm doing for you and fascinated by me living in what he calls millionaires' row. He says it doesn't sound like you're too la-di-da about being a Sir and all that. He's very down-to-earth, my gramps.'

'I like the sound of him. And I'll try not to be too la-di-da.'

She smiled. Never had he sounded more posh.

'He's a good man,' she said. 'I think you'll like him.'

'If he's anything like you, I'm sure I will,' Sebastian

said. 'You know you're a very good woman, don't you, Kitty Clements?'

'I…er…well, I try.'

'You're kind, you're understanding and you're not judgemental. Do you know how rare that is?'

'Thank you,' was all she could manage to choke out in her surprise. She'd had no idea he'd been so observant of her. His words warmed her, but she didn't think she was rare at all. There must have been people in his life who had made him believe that, as well as his tyrant grandfather. But, for all the horrible people at Blaine and Ball, and the media people who had shredded her reputation, she firmly believed there were more good people than bad in the world. She was fortunate to have friends and family who had never doubted her.

'You've made what could have been a very difficult time for me less difficult,' he said. 'Not just the dinner tonight, which would have been far more of an ordeal without you, but the way you've smoothed my path ever since I moved into my grandfather's house.'

'Do you think you'll ever start to think of it as your own house?' she asked.

'I believe so, thanks entirely to you.'

'I'm flattered,' she said. 'And glad.'

She remembered how she'd feared he might be difficult, and instead it had turned out he wasn't difficult at all, and how much she enjoyed working with him. How some nights she lay awake in her bed on the top floor of the house and thought about him sleeping alone below, in the bedroom that had been his father's as a boy, and tried to keep at bay her fantasies of creeping down the stairs and knocking on his door.

'After we've visited your grandfather, we could have lunch in a pub or somewhere off the beaten track where there'd be little chance of you being recognised, or me for that matter,' he said.

'That rules out the one pub in Widefield, as all the locals know me. We'd be besieged. We'll have to go further afield.'

'I'm sure we'll find somewhere,' he said.

'There's a nice gastro-pub not too far from the hospital, on the river, good food. I could book online for lunch when we get back inside.'

'You're a marvel of efficiency as usual,' he said.

Efficient, capable, understanding. Was that the only way he saw her? For a painful moment she longed for him to see her as beautiful, exciting, sexy—the way she saw him in her fantasies.

She looked up at him, willing him to see her as something beyond his household manager, beyond a make-believe friend to act as his hostess. In the half-light his face was in shadow and his grey eyes seemed dark and unreadable. But there was a glimpse of something there that made her heart thump and her breath become shallow. Her gaze held his for a long moment. Then he lowered his head to hers. In silent assent, she raised her face to meet him then sighed into the pleasure of his kiss.

She wound her arms around his neck to bring him closer; he slid his hands to her waist. Even through her coat she could feel his warmth and strength. His kiss was gentle and she kissed him back, enjoying the tender touch of his mouth against hers, the slight rasp of his beard shadow against her face, pleasurable rather than painful.

Sir Sebastian was kissing her and she was kissing him back.

It was such a sweet kiss and she was loving it, but it wasn't enough and she ached for more. The signal would have to come from her. Aware of her history, he would be respectful of her and she appreciated that. She slipped her tongue between his lips in unspoken communication that she was happy to deepen the kiss.

He needed no urging. Lips and tongues became more demanding as the kiss quickly whooshed into something passionate and intense and urgent. She was stunned it escalated so fast from a tender exploratory kiss to something that had her pressing her body close to his, cursing their coats, their gloves, wishing she was alone in a bedroom—any room—with him instead of in a public place. Somewhere, anywhere where she could—

Bewildered, she broke away from Sebastian's kiss. A kiss that was so much more than something physically exciting and arousing. There was something deeper, more profound to it that stirred up emotions she had no right to be feeling. Emotions she couldn't handle right now.

He staggered and she had to put out her hand to steady him, glad of the contact, having felt bereft of his touch when she'd stepped back from him to break the kiss.

'That…that was a surprise,' he said.

'I… I wasn't expecting that,' she said at the same time, her hand still on his arm.

They stared at each other and even in the shadowed light she could see the same bewilderment and uncertainty on his face that he must surely see on hers.

'Wow,' he said.

'Double wow,' she said.

Then she started to laugh, with exhilaration and incredulity and a big dash of joy that she was still capable of feeling something so visceral and real.

Still looking dazed, he joined in her laughter. 'I… I had no idea.'

'It was just a kiss,' she said, spluttering with the remnants of her laughter.

Slowly, he shook his head. 'Oh, no, it was so much more than that.'

'Perhaps we've unleashed something that needs to be put on the back burner until after we stop working together,' she said, forcing the tremor from her voice. It was the only way she could quickly put into words her sudden urgent desire for distance and space so she could process what had just happened.

He put his arm around her. 'You could be right,' he said. 'C'mon, let's get home.'

His ancestral home—*her* temporary residence in the servants' quarters. She mustn't forget that. His arm rested companionably around her shoulder as they made their way back to the house on Cheyne Walk.

CHAPTER TWELVE

SEBASTIAN LOOKED AROUND the small, attractively furnished living room of Kitty's grandfather's house while Kitty was upstairs packing some clothes for both herself and her grandfather. He was hungry for details of her life and this room was rich with them.

Framed photos were everywhere: on the bookshelves, the mantelpiece, the coffee table. They tracked Kitty from a tiny baby, held proudly in the arms of beaming young parents, to a triumphant, laughing toddler walking on chubby legs towards her doting mother, to a posed professional group photo of Kitty with her parents and an older couple who must be the grandparents, the resemblance was so strong. In pride of place, hanging over the fireplace, was a large photo of Kitty at her university graduation, in cap and gown. There were pictures of her in school uniform through primary school to high school, with her arms around some girls in a netball team, snuggled with a golden Labrador, in a long gown beside an obviously besotted teenage boy at a school formal. And always Kitty with her parents, until they disappeared from the photos and there was a young teenage Kitty with sad eyes, obviously struggling to smile.

Sebastian's heart turned over for her. He had suffered loss, but he hadn't lost his parents until he was an adult. He looked more closely at the photos, saw the resemblance between Kitty, her mother—who hadn't been given the chance to grow old—and her grandmother, all attractive women with blonde hair and blue eyes, and variations of that same open warm smile. A beautiful family, struck by tragedy and yet uplifted by family loyalty and love.

On the bookshelves he noticed a row of Marisol Matthew books, picked one up and put it down again. He still missed her too much to open it and read his mother's words. Yet he marvelled at the legacy she'd left behind, a legacy that reached as far as this suburban living room and was a link to Kitty.

What would be his legacy? Increasing the already huge Delfont fortune? An image of a laughing little girl with dark hair and blue eyes running towards him flashed through his mind. A daughter? Since his broken engagement, he hadn't let himself think as far forward as having children. One day, perhaps, maybe. If ever he met the right woman, if ever she believed him to be the right man.

Lavinia had pressed for the idea of having a child as soon as they were married. But even before he'd become totally disillusioned with her, he'd realised she'd had an ulterior motive. His former fiancée had been aware that his uncle Oliver didn't want children and that ultimately Sebastian would inherit. Any children Lavinia might have borne him would have been in line to inherit the Delmont fortune, although only a son could inherit the title. Her interest in having children with him had been about securing her stake.

Her words still haunted him: *No woman will ever want to live with you.* Yet Kitty didn't seem to find his company too objectionable, and right from the get-go she'd been aware of his obsessive need to have his things in order that Lavinia had deemed so unacceptable.

Kitty. That kiss had changed everything. It had made him realise what might be, if he could overcome his lack of trust not just in others, but in himself. If he could let genuine feelings develop instead of constantly slamming the brakes on them. Looking at her family photos today had brought home the painful empty truth of his own life—the people closest to him whom he had loved and who had loved him had all died. He was fearful that if he dragged out from the depths of his heart the courage to love again, he would lose that love—and he didn't know if he could cope with more loss. Was that the curse his *abuela* feared?

He walked over to the glass doors that opened out to the narrow back garden. As with the front, it was immaculate. He didn't know what the plants were but there were masses of flowers in bloom, a small tree bright with autumnal orange leaves, a winding path of crazy paving leading right to a gate in the back fence. There was real talent in creating a garden as harmonious as this.

He sensed Kitty coming into the room—her footfall, her scent—before he turned to see her. He caught his breath at how lovely she looked, dressed casually in blue jeans, a fluffy powder blue sweater, short boots, her hair a golden mass around her shoulders. But when did she ever look less than lovely? She joined him at the doorway.

'Delightful, isn't it?' she said. 'Gramps is never happier than when he's pottering around in his garden. And there's more natural beauty behind the fence. The gate leads out to open fields. It's a wonderful place to walk, and it's covered in wildflowers in the summer. Birdwatchers like it too.'

'This was a good place for you to live.'

'When my parents were alive we lived in Bromley, which isn't very far away…they were both schoolteachers. We visited my grandparents often, so it wasn't unfamiliar when I…when I had to move here to live with them.'

She turned away, hiding, he thought, remembered grief. The pain of losing beloved parents always stayed raw around the edges. She'd lost her grandmother recently too. And had also suffered a different kind of loss with her career, her lifestyle. She must have felt rudderless until she and Claudia had the initiative to set up their own business.

Kitty sneezed, that cute little sneeze that made him smile.

'Have you been smudging?' he asked.

She smiled. 'No need for that here. No malevolent spirits casting their shadows. The house was a new-build when my grandparents moved in. It's the dust from the bathroom renovation upstairs that's making me sneeze.'

'Let's get you outside, shall we?' he said, following her to the front door. 'Here, let me take that bag.'

'Gramps asked me to bring his best tweed jacket to wear for his meeting with you.'

'I'm honoured.'

'You should be. He was always a snazzy dresser, but hasn't bothered so much since Gran died. He said he only ever wanted to look his best for her.' Her voice was tinged with sadness.

'They were happily married?'

'Very much so. Gramps and Gran adored each other. They met each other at a dance when they were eighteen and that was it.' She paused. 'Somewhat like your parents, really.'

'No wonder your grandmother liked reading my mother's books.'

'I liked reading them too, although I sometimes wonder if they gave me unrealistic expectations.'

'Expectations?'

'About romantic love and honourable men.' Her mouth turned down in a bitter twist.

'You say that with a distinct air of disillusionment,' he said.

'Disillusionment? You could say that.'

'Who made you feel that way?'

'You don't want to know,' she said. 'He doesn't deserve airtime.'

Sebastian looked down into her face. 'But I do want to know; I want to know so much more about you. Last night. It seemed like it could be the start of something... something deeper between us.'

She looked up at him. 'Did you feel that too?'

He paused, not wanting to frighten her off by revealing the intensity of his feelings. 'To be put on hold, as you say.'

'Until we can meet each other as equals, not employer and employee.' She swept her hand around to indicate the house. 'Although my home is somewhat more humble than yours.'

He snorted. 'Humble? Your grandfather's house is a palace compared to our farmhouse in Mallorca when we first started living there. The old uncle, who had been there on his own, had let it practically fall down around his ears. He had chickens living in the house. I remember they were scratching around in the kitchen when we arrived. I was enchanted at the idea of them becoming my pets, maybe even sleeping in my room. My mother, needless to say, had no intention of allowing any such thing.'

'Seriously?'

'It's true. I didn't notice all that was wrong with the place. I just loved it that at last we had our own home.'

'What happened to the chickens?'

'The way my father told it, his first job at the new place was to build a chicken coop. In the meantime, the chickens roamed around outside during the day and slept in the decrepit laundry room, along with the goat.'

She laughed. 'It must have been heaven for a young boy.'

'Not so heavenly for my parents at first, but over the

years they worked hard to turn it into the beautiful home it is today.'

'You must share that story with my grandfather; I think it would give him a good laugh,' Kitty said as they walked out of the door.

It wasn't until they were in his car and heading for the rehabilitation hospital that Sebastian realised Kitty hadn't told him anything about the man who had put such a bitter expression on her face.

Of all the places Kitty thought she'd see Sir Sebastian Delfont looking relaxed and happy, it wasn't the communal living room at the hospital where patients met their visiting family and friends.

After a brief initial awkwardness, Sebastian and Gramps had hit it off. So much so that she sat to the side as they talked, Sebastian with his tall frame folded onto a small plastic chair, Gramps with his left leg in a brace stretched out in front of him, his crutches resting against his larger, more comfortable chair. The leg had had to undergo surgery and a plate and pins inserted, and there was a lot of physical therapy still ahead of him. But Gramps wasn't talking about his injury. Rather he was telling Sebastian the story of how as a little boy he had been evacuated during World War Two from London to Widefield, where it was considered to be safer and less likely to be bombed.

Kitty never tired of hearing her grandfather's tale of how he—barely six years old—and his brother had been sent on a steam train to Widefield, with a small bag of possessions each and brown paper labels around their necks to identify them. How they'd been lined up with the other evacuee children to be billeted with a host family. He and his brother were one of the last to be chosen, fortunately by a kind older couple who'd welcomed them into their home for the duration of the war.

'Why did your parents allow that?' Sebastian asked Gramps. 'It must have been distressing for all of you.'

'To keep us safe from the bombing in London. The government called the mass evacuation of London's children Operation Pied Piper. My mother visited us as often as she could; my father was fighting in the Middle East. After the war ended, we'd come down here for holidays with my host family, who became like real family. When I grew up and could choose where I lived, I came back to Widefield and have never moved from here since.'

Sebastian turned to Kitty. 'Our generation has had it so easy by comparison.'

'You young people have your own stresses,' Gramps said. Sebastian's mobile phone rang. Gramps chuckled. 'Such as being at the beck and call of electronic devices.'

Sebastian excused himself and headed outside to take his call, which he said was important. Kitty watched him as he strode towards the door, admiring his rear view in black jeans with a hopeless kind of yearning.

'He's a good bloke, love,' Gramps said. 'You could do worse.'

'We're just friends,' Kitty protested. 'Not even that, really. He's my temporary boss.'

'Rubbish. I might be old but thankfully I'm not blind. I saw the way he looked at you, and you at him.'

There was something there, that extraordinary kiss had proved that, but it was too new and fragile to admit it to anyone—it was difficult enough to admit it to herself.

'I won't always be around to look after you, you know,' Gramps said.

Her heart chilled at the thought of losing her beloved grandfather. But they'd had this conversation before. 'I don't need a man to look after me, Gramps.'

'Yes, you do, and he needs someone to look after him. That's what it's all about, to look out for each other, be each other's best friend, be loyal and—above all—always be kind to one another.'

'That's your secret recipe for happiness?' she asked.

'It's not so secret. Your mother and father loved each other like that too.'

Why was she talking about commitment as if it were something possible with Sebastian? Because she wanted it. Wanted *him*. Not as her boss. Not as a friend. Not as a fling.

'But, Gramps, we come from such different worlds. You should see his house in London. He's wealthy almost beyond comprehension. He downplays it but he's a baronet. *Sir* Sebastian.'

'And you're a smart, well-educated young woman the equal of anyone in Britain. For all his wealth and status, your Sebastian is just a man like the rest of us. To me he seems in need of someone loving and kind-hearted like you; there's a sadness at the core of him.'

'Do you think so?' Her grandfather sometimes astounded her with his shrewd insights.

'If you like him, don't let pride or self-doubt stand in your way. He's twice the man of *that* Neil.' Gramps hadn't liked Neil and always called him *that* Neil. Maybe she should listen to her grandfather when it came to Sebastian. Take the first step towards him. *If she dared.*

When Sebastian joined them again he tried to convince Gramps to come with him and Kitty to the riverside pub she'd booked for lunch, but he was adamant that his leg wasn't fit enough to be taken on an outing.

'Next time,' Sebastian said as he shook her grandfather's hand in farewell.

Next time?

'Talk about a tale of two grandfathers; how different

could mine and yours possibly be?' Sebastian said, after they were settled back into his car. It wasn't the latest model of European sportscar, as she might have expected, but rather a meticulously restored British classic. He made no move to drive away and she welcomed the opportunity to talk with him.

'I really liked Stan,' he said.

'I could tell,' she said. She swallowed hard. *Take that first step.* 'Seeing you with him, listening to the way you talked about Mallorca, made me realise we have more in common than I ever could have anticipated.'

'Apart from the fact we both have books by Marisol Matthew on our bookshelves?'

'That too.'

'I told you I didn't always live in a mansion on Cheyne Walk, nor did I have aspirations to it.'

'The apartment in Docklands. That looked like a different kind of upscale lifestyle altogether.'

'The home of a man intent on making as much money as he could, as quickly as he could,' he said. 'A driven man.'

'A lonely man? It seemed, despite your artworks, to be an empty kind of place.'

'Perhaps it was, although to me it symbolised independence and freedom.'

'Tell me about your fiancée.'

'*Ex*-fiancée,' he corrected her. He paused. She noticed his fists were clenched. 'This is very difficult for me to talk about.'

'I appreciate that,' Kitty said. 'But I've been told I'm a good listener. And someone recently told me I wasn't judgemental.' That earned her a smile from him.

'Lavinia was bad news from the start, although I didn't realise that at the time.'

'We never do,' Kitty said.

'My uncle Oliver was very sociable and had a circle of friends who were always at his parties or at the theatre or a concert. I sometimes went along; his young nephew was somewhat of a novelty.'

His extremely handsome young nephew, Kitty thought.

'Lavinia was on the edge of the circle. She was older than me, gorgeous, very glamorous. She hooked me without too much trouble.'

His cynical tone surprised her. 'Hooked you?'

'I was what they called "a good catch". Everyone knew my uncle had made me his heir, and I wasn't exactly hard up in my own right. I fell hard for her. She supposedly fell for me. What I didn't know was that she was the long-term mistress of a married man who was never going to leave his wealthy wife. So she went after me, although she had no intention of ever giving up her lover. Uncle Oliver thought I was just having some fun with her but when we announced our engagement—she threatened she'd leave me if I didn't marry her—he quickly revealed the ugly truth about her.'

Kitty's hand flew to her mouth. 'That's terrible. What a shock for you.'

'It wasn't a total shock. I was already having serious doubts about her, one reason being she became so critical of me. When I broke off with her she flew at me, screaming.' He shuddered. 'She was hateful and vindictive as she saw her meal ticket fly out the window. I had a very lucky escape.'

'Don't tell me—she made sure she got to keep the engagement ring.'

'I didn't care what she kept or how much it cost just so long as I didn't have to see her again. Needless to say, she was swiftly excluded from Uncle Olly's social circle. I felt like such a fool for having been taken in by her.'

'She sounds horrible,' Kitty said vehemently. 'And

not very clever for treating a wonderful man like you in that way.'

'I'm glad you think I'm a wonderful man,' he said.

His words, the look in his eyes flustered her. 'Well, of course I do. Wonderful, yes. I… I wouldn't be working for you if I didn't think you were a wonderful man…person.'

'I happen to think you're a wonderful woman,' he said with his lazy grin.

'You do?'

'An exceedingly wonderful woman.'

'Are you teasing me?'

He sobered. 'Not at all. After my experience with Lavinia, I didn't let myself believe that wonderful women like you existed.'

'And now?'

'I'm here with you and feeling happier than I have for a long time.'

'Really?'

They were close in the confines of the car, with its polished walnut dash and leather upholstery that gave it a scent of luxury and wealth. He leaned over to kiss her, a warm tender kiss that said more than words could. She pressed her mouth to his to keep him there, not wanting the contact to end, barely able to believe this was happening.

'I'm happy to be with you too,' she murmured against his lips. She broke the kiss but stayed close, looking up into his eyes. 'The hospital car park is perhaps not the best place for this.'

'Perhaps not,' he said. 'But before I drive out of here I'd like you to tell me about that guy who doesn't deserve airtime.'

She sighed and drew back from him. 'I warn you, the story of me and Neil is nothing as interesting as you and Lavinia.'

'I'm not sure the drama of my story is anything to be proud of,' he said with a wry twist of his mouth.

'I met Neil at work when we both started at Blaine and Ball as interns. I don't remember ever consciously deciding I wanted a future with him; he just swept me along and we were having so much fun I let it happen.'

'Was it serious?'

'We lived together, had a future planned. I believed we were in love. It wasn't an angsty kind of relationship, if you know what I mean. We were a normal couple with our ups and downs, but nothing to indicate the way it would end.'

'I don't think I've ever had a non-angsty relationship, but I think I know what you mean.'

'Then came the assault.' She paused. Still the ugly memories came, Edmund Blaine's disgusting wet mouth on hers, his fingers that had hurt like claws, her feeling of powerlessness. 'I… I find this distressing to talk about, but I want you to hear, so bear with me.'

Sebastian took her hand, which comforted her. 'Take your time.'

'The night it happened, I staggered home in distress, expecting comfort, a hug. But he held me at arm's length because another man had touched me, as if I were tainted.'

Sebastian cursed in Spanish.

'That was the thing that brought my future with Neil unstuck—he believed me that I had been assaulted; however, no one else of any consequence in the company did. He wasn't going to be the lone dissenting voice—not when his career would suffer. When he made my pain all about him, that I selfishly wanted to ruin his career by forcing him to take sides, I told him to get out and he did. Essentially, he chose his job over me. End of story.' She had collapsed on the living room floor of their flat and cried until she had run out of tears.

Sebastian expressed his opinion of what kind of man Neil was in no uncertain terms.

'I was devastated at the time; we were on the point of getting engaged,' she said. 'On top of the assault, the nightmare media coverage, losing my job, the thought that someone I believed in—who was supposed to love me— could be so disloyal really…really wounded me. It left me with such trust issues I haven't dated since.'

He squeezed her hand. 'Last night?'

'The first time I've let anyone close since then.'

There was a long beat of silence between them before Sebastian leaned over to kiss her again. A swift touch that didn't demand or expect anything.

'He didn't deserve you,' he said gruffly.

'He most definitely did not. And for a long time I wondered what I'd done wrong to deserve him. But I got over missing him so quickly it made me wonder if I had ever really loved him enough to build a life with him. There had never been fireworks.' Not like the fireworks that had exploded when Sebastian had kissed her, not like that instant buzz of attraction when she'd first met him at his Docklands apartment.

'The breakup was why you had to use packers to get you quickly out of your home.'

'You remembered that?'

'I remember everything you've told me about you.'

'And…and me you.'

She didn't care that she was in a public car park, when Sebastian kissed her again nothing else mattered as she let herself enjoy the sensations of being close to him.

Finally, when the windows were beginning to fog up, she broke away from the second most wonderful kiss she had ever experienced, her body pulsing with desire. The first had been the night before. Whatever happened to them in the future, she would always cherish her first kiss with Sebastian, which had unleashed possibilities she had never allowed herself to dream of.

'What do we do now?' she asked, her breath still coming a little short, her heart beating in double time.

His voice wasn't steady. 'I know what I'd like us to do right now but, as you said, we're in a public car park.' He pressed a short fierce kiss on her mouth. 'However, I don't think that's what you meant. I suggest we keep our private lives private.'

'So things will be the same back in Chelsea? I would prefer that,' she said. 'In public, employee and boss—'

'Temporary boss,' he said.

'Temporary boss,' she amended. 'In private—'

'Whichever way we choose to take it,' he said.

'Whichever way we choose to take it...' she echoed.

They shared smiles for a long moment and Kitty felt something fundamental shift into place between them, on the edge of something that could be momentous and life-changing.

'Today at lunch can we be cautious? I'm still anxious about being seen—'

'Strictly business,' he said. He started the engine, coaxed it into a luxurious purr and put it into gear. 'To lunch, Ms Clements.'

'To lunch, Sir Sebastian,' she said.

They traded a warm, convivial laugh of shared secrets, possibilities and anticipation.

CHAPTER THIRTEEN

KITTY ENJOYED THE meetings she had with Sebastian and his executive assistant, Guy. Guy was older than both her and Sebastian, whip-smart, super organised, seemed to know everyone who was everyone, and had a marvellous ability to mimic them that often had her in stitches. He'd previously worked with Sebastian's uncle Oliver and had confessed to Kitty he'd had a huge crush on his boss that hadn't been in any way reciprocated. He'd been devastated when Oliver Delfont had died, and delighted when Sebastian had recently headhunted him from his last role to bring him back into the family.

Kitty tried to avoid any gossip about Sebastian, especially as she suspected eagle-eyed Guy would jump on any sign of her, Kitty, having a crush on her boss. Which she most definitely did. However, any crumb of information that would help her understand Sebastian better was welcome. According to Guy, Oliver Delfont had cared deeply for his nephew and had done his best to shield him from Sir Cyril's malice. Now Guy was committed to helping Sebastian shoulder the responsibilities of his new life as he had a wealth of useful knowledge from when he had worked with Oliver, anticipating the day he would have taken over from Sir Cyril.

On the Monday afternoon after the visit to Gramps, Kitty and Guy sat opposite Sebastian across his desk in his office. 'The dinner party for the trustees on Saturday was so successful I'm emboldened to think we should have a party to follow up. Perhaps in another two weeks. What do you think, Kitty?' He'd put forward this thought to her at their 'strictly business' lunch at the riverside pub the day before.

'If you think two weeks is notice enough for your guests,' she said.

Guy replied, 'I've put out a few feelers; it would work for most of the people we want here.'

'In that case, if we can get the same hospitality team together, I'm confident they will pull out all the stops for another successful party,' said Kitty. 'Although I'm not sure Evelyn Lim could perform the same miracle when it came to transforming rooms as quickly as she did for the dining room.'

'Even the small improvements she made to the reception rooms made a difference,' Sebastian said. 'If she could make a few more such changes, that would be good but not essential.'

'I'm speaking in confidence, as you know.' Sebastian leaned towards her and Guy as he spoke. 'Some of the trustees gave me disquieting news about how the Lady Enid foundation was managed after she died. It was rumoured Sir Cyril intended to dissolve it. Donations dropped off, and confidence in the foundation's viability is at an all-time low. I want to restore that confidence and lift the level of donations.'

'A cocktail party for about fifty people,' said Guy. 'Company directors, high-flying entrepreneurs, C-level executives—you know, where the C stands for Chief in their work title.'

Fifty high-ranking business people, all involved in some way or another with the Delfont enterprises and investments. Kitty quailed. That kind of number upped the chance of someone recognising her. All her old fears flooded back.

'Do you have the guest list handy?' she asked, forcing her voice to sound even and professional.

Guy passed a sheet of paper to her. She quickly scanned it. Yes. There were names she recognised there, people who might in turn recognise her. People she'd worked with on their PR campaigns but who had cut her dead after she'd 'falsely accused a good man'.

'An impressive list,' she said.

She would make it clear to Sebastian from the start she wouldn't be in attendance on the night. Make a fuss about it now in front of Guy and he might get suspicious of her motives. He knew she was Kathryn Clements, there had been no point in hiding it from him, but he didn't know her whole story—nor did he need to.

She pasted a smile on her face. 'Do you want to set a theme for the party?'

'No.' The vehement answer from Sebastian was so definitive that it made Kitty and Guy laugh and she immediately felt less on edge.

Sebastian continued. 'I want the party to be relaxed and quite different from the stuffy parties I know my grandfather used to host.'

'To mark a change in direction from the new Delfont on the block,' Kitty said.

'Exactly,' he said.

'The cool new baronet on the block,' said Guy. 'Your uncle Oliver would be proud of the way you're handling this.'

'Uncle Olly certainly was one for a good party,' said Sebastian, but Kitty could see the remembered pain in the rigid set of his jaw.

She swung right back into event planner mode. 'So, a cocktail party on the agenda for the Saturday after next,' she said. 'I'm confident that our two cooks Alisa and Josie can create food that's fashionable yet delicious.'

'Can we have crostini on the menu?' Sebastian asked. Kitty's eyes met his across the desk.

'Of course,' she said with an inner secret smile, dropping her gaze in case she gave away the game to Guy. She didn't miss his speculative glance between her and Sebastian. They would have to be careful if they wanted to keep their changed relationship private. Until they knew where it might take them.

She continued, 'And we need to secure some really good bar staff specialising in cocktails—some call them mixologists. The drinks as well as the food need to be outstanding to get some buzz happening.'

Sebastian smiled. 'A party totally unlike anything my grandfather would have planned.'

'Indeed,' said Guy.

'One other thing we need to consider—music,' said Sebastian. 'Friends of mine from uni play in a soft jazz quartet. I'd like to book them.'

'Done,' said Guy. 'Just shoot me their details.'

How little she knew about Sebastian, Kitty thought, as he and Guy chatted. Yet what she did know about him pleased her very much. That chasm between them no longer seemed as deep as she might have imagined. Did she have the courage to take a leap over it?

Guy got up to go. Kitty did likewise.

'Kitty, can you stay behind, please,' Sebastian said. 'I'd like to talk about the food for the party in more detail.'

Guy left, closing the door behind him, making an elaborate show of closing it properly. *He knew.*

Sebastian immediately strode around the desk to Kitty.

'I'll talk to the cooks about the food and—' she started.

Sebastian made a dismissive gesture with his hand. 'I don't give a flying fig about the food.' He pulled her into his arms. 'During that entire meeting I just wanted to do this. I don't even remember what Guy said about the strategic importance of inviting two company directors with a known history of animosity towards my grandfather.'

Kitty looked up at him, his lean, handsome face already so familiar. 'Is it ridiculous to say I missed you, even though we've seen each other several times today?' she said. They'd talked, together with Evelyn Lim, about bathroom designs, bumped into each other as Kitty was leading housekeeper candidates into her office. But, until now, not for a second had they been alone.

'I've missed you too,' he said hoarsely.

The night before, after returning from Widefield, it had seemed an unspoken understanding that, while they'd kissed each other goodnight, they had each gone alone to their own rooms. It would have been too soon.

Kitty nestled in against his shoulder with a sigh of pleasure. For a long moment she was content to just be close to him in the circle of his arms. It was the first time they hadn't had coats as a barrier between them. Kitty was wearing her blue wrap dress, Sebastian black trousers and charcoal shirt. It would be so easy to unbutton his shirt and slide her hand through to find warm, bare skin. It seemed the natural next step, but surely it was too soon for that. She was super aware of how strong he was, the firmness of his muscles, the solid comfort of him. Then that comforting closeness was no longer enough. With a murmur of impatience she wound her arms around his neck, pressed her body closer to his—close, closer, as close as she could get with the pesky barrier of their clothes. She couldn't wait any longer to feel his mouth on hers and she reached up and kissed him.

Their first kiss in private, behind a solid door that no one would dare open without Sebastian's say so. The kiss was immediate, urgent, snatched from their everyday life in the house where she was his household employee. It wasn't a kiss that started with gentle questing lips and slowly built up in increments of passion. It started hot and proceeded to flaming in just seconds flat. Urgent. Demanding. Greedy. Her nipples pebbled and she was melting with want as she pressed her body closer to him. She scoped out the room. There was a desk, there was a leather Chesterfield sofa…heck, there was the floor or the wall. Kitty whimpered her need for him and heard the same need in his deep moan. She was lost in one of her own fantasies of seducing her boss.

The tie of her wrap dress had loosened and he slid his hand through where the top gaped open to cup her breast and thumb her hard nipple so she gasped her pleasure and need.

Then a knock on the door. They stilled, then sprang apart. Sebastian cursed under his breath, as did Kitty. She rearranged her dress. The knock came again. Josie, today's cook, called through the door, 'Excuse me, Sir Sebastian, is Kitty still with you? I urgently need to talk to her about tonight's dinner menu.'

Kitty signalled with her eyes for his help. He cleared his throat. 'Yes, she's still in a meeting with me. I'll send her down to the kitchen when we're finished.' His voice sounded remarkably normal.

'Thank you,' Josie said, and Kitty listened until the cook's footsteps receded.

Kitty looked up at him, her lips curved in a teasing smile. 'Finish what, I might ask?' she murmured.

'Not what we were starting,' he said in his deep posh voice.

Kitty felt overwhelmed by the urge to laugh at the ridiculousness of it, a thirty-two-year-old baronet and owner of this grand house and her twenty-eight-year-old self compromised like a pair of hormone-crazed teenagers. She ached with the effort to suppress her giggles. What made it worse was that Sebastian was trying not to laugh too and they were setting each other off. They held each other as they both shook and spluttered until finally she was able to control her breathing and his voice returned to normal.

She stepped back from him, tugged her dress into place, pushed her hair back from her face where Sebastian had raked his fingers through it. She probably didn't have a scrap of lipstick left. 'Do you think Josie guessed?'

'I doubt it; we often have meetings in this room.' He paused. 'Perhaps it was fortuitous Josie came along when she did.' He drew her close to him. 'I don't want our first time to be rushed and uncomfortable.'

She followed his gaze to the wooden desk, the carved wooden chair. He smiled and she smiled back. Could he tell how thrilled she was at his words? *Our first time.* It sounded romantic, sexy and thoughtful—all of which augured well for, well, their first time.

He kissed her slowly and thoroughly. The fire of arousal that had been so abruptly doused by that knock on the door still smouldered, and little flames of desire started flickering through her. Reluctantly she pulled away.

'I don't think we'd get away with it a second time,' she said. 'I think Guy suspects something.'

'Perhaps,' said Sebastian. 'But he would be too discreet to gossip about it, I can assure you. He was loyal to my uncle and is loyal to me. I trust him as I've come to trust you.'

She kissed him briefly on the mouth. She, of all people, knew how easily trust was lost and how hard it was to earn. 'I'm honoured,' she said.

She reached for her laptop case. In an inside pocket she kept a comb and a lipstick. Sebastian watched as she did a quick repair job. 'I've never seen a woman put on lipstick without a mirror,' he said.

'A trick I learned years ago from a friend.' She turned to go. 'I won't kiss you again as it would mess up my lipstick and I don't want to walk down to that kitchen looking like I've just been kissed.'

'Even though you have been kissed and you'll be thoroughly kissed again the second I get the opportunity.'

'I'll look forward to that,' she said. She trailed her fingers over his cheek in lieu of the kiss she ached to plant there, thrilling at the intimacy of the contact. But she didn't want people gossiping about her, especially in the run-up to the cocktail party.

She turned to go. Sebastian put his hand on her arm. 'Wait.' She turned back to face him.

'Dinner tonight?' he said.

'I'm not sure I—'

'Not at a restaurant. In the kitchen. Just you and me.'

There wouldn't be anyone else in the house. The cook would prepare the dinner and go home. Guy would go home to his husband.

'I'd love that,' she said.

That evening, Sebastian worked alongside Kitty in the kitchen as they heated up the chicken poached in coconut milk and Thai herbs Josie had prepared for dinner. The room was filled with warm spicy aromas that should send his mouth watering. But thoughts of Kitty overwhelmed every other sense. His hunger wasn't for the dinner, it was for her.

That blue dress, although it was long-sleeved and high-necked, did nothing to hide her luscious curves, or the way she moved with such grace and sensuality. All it did was emphasise how incredibly sexy she was and make him want to peel the dress off her to discover and explore those curves for himself.

Her grandfather Stan—in a moment when Kitty had

been chatting with a nurse—had warned Sebastian not to let his granddaughter's prettiness and sweetness blind him into thinking she was anything less than very smart and very talented. Sebastian had known all that from the get-go—it was part of her appeal. Along the way, he'd learned that she was kind and funny and perceptive. It wasn't just her looks that attracted him, but right now they were top of mind. She was beautiful and alluring and all he could think about was how much he wanted her.

Kitty turned from the stovetop and caught him in full, heavy-lidded appraisal of her shapely behind. She knew immediately what he was doing and smiled a slow, lascivious smile as she let her eyes, in turn, roam over him. And succeeded in arousing him to fever pitch.

She put down the spoon she was holding. 'I don't think you're hungry at all.'

'Not for dinner, no, delicious as it undoubtedly would be,' he answered honestly.

'Me neither,' she said, switching off the gas burner and taking a step towards him. The invitation in her blue eyes was unmistakable and his body responded accordingly. 'This kitchen would be no more comfortable than your study,' she said.

'I imagine it would be exceedingly uncomfortable,' he said. 'Not to mention inappropriate for so many reasons.'

'A bed—vanilla as that might seem—comes to mind as the ideal place for our purposes,' she said in a silky, sensuous voice.

'It has a long-standing reputation as such,' he said, scarcely able to choke out the words.

'There is a very comfortable bed in my apartment, just a short elevator ride away,' she said.

He shuddered as politely as one could shudder. 'A room where Mrs Danvers once resided does not appeal.' An image of the bad-tempered old housekeeper flashing into his mind could put him off his stroke.

Kitty climbed her fingers up his arm. 'Can you nominate somewhere you believe to be more appropriate?'

'A beautifully appointed guest bedroom in this very house where I can personally attest to the comfort of the bed.'

'Shall we assess it for possibilities?' she murmured, sliding her arms around his neck and pressing her mouth to his. She flicked her tongue along the seam of his mouth. He moaned his want and opened his mouth to her. They kissed for a long, arousing moment before he disengaged from the kiss. He had to take a deep breath to steady his voice. 'Before we go any further, I have to ask you—are you sure this is what you want?'

Consent was essential from anyone, but particularly so from Kitty, who had suffered a heinous assault from someone she should have been able to trust. Kitty was important to him, and growing more important every day, until he was at the point where he couldn't imagine his life without her in it. He had to get this right.

'You absolutely have my consent, wonderful Sebastian.' To his stunned delight she then proceeded to whisper in his ear the intimate acts to which she was giving her wholehearted consent and how she would like to both receive and give them.

Sebastian growled his assent to anything she wanted, swung her up into his arms and headed for the stairs.

How many fantasies had Kitty had of making love with Sebastian since she'd come to live in his house? Even her most fervent and erotic dreams had nothing on the reality of being carried by Sebastian up the stairs and towards his bedroom. It was like a scene from one of his mother's books—only way sexier.

The journey from kitchen to Sebastian's bedroom was punctuated by laughter, kissing, stumbling as they tried to walk to the elevator while kissing, and a display of extreme impatience with the elevator. She felt giddy, not from the one glass of wine she'd had in the kitchen, but from desire, racing hormones and excitement. Over all the emotions she was feeling bubbled joy. She was falling for this man and enjoying every step of the journey. It was all so different and exciting because of him. Sebastian.

She didn't notice the details of the bedroom when they reached it, except that it was elegant in a Lady Enid style of way. But she didn't want to pause for breath to admire the room when all she wanted to do was to make love with Sebastian. Fortunately, he seemed as eager to make love with her.

They kissed, deeply, hungrily as if they could never get enough of each other. She unbuttoned his shirt to splay her hands against a hard wall of muscle. In her eagerness to undo the buttons one tore off and bounced to the floor. She gasped and went to pick it up. 'Leave it,' he said. She gladly complied. She didn't want to think about anything but him.

'How do you get this wrap thing undone?' Sebastian grumbled as he played with the ties that secured her dress at the waist.

'How about I stand still and let you undress me,' she said, loving the look of eager impatience on his face.

'Great idea,' he said hoarsely.

It felt intensely erotic to put herself into his hands and stand still as he undid the ties of her dress, as he pushed it off her shoulders, as he touched her anywhere he felt so inclined. Every such touch sent urgent messages through her body to all those erogenous zones he'd unlocked simply by being him.

Her dress pooled on the floor and she stepped out of it to stand just in her underwear and high-heeled shoes.

'Wow,' he breathed. He stood back and looked over her, every glance a caress as real as if he were actually touching her. 'You have the most beautiful body,' he said.

Kitty had to swallow the response that had been automatic until she'd fought to suppress it. *I just need to lose a few pounds.* He thought she was beautiful just the way she was and she should accept that unconditionally. 'Thank you,' she said instead.

'Now you,' she ordered. She started to undo the rest of the buttons on his shirt, button by button, but her fingers fumbled in her haste. 'Darn it, I just want this shirt off you.' She struggled with his belt. 'And your trousers.'

He laughed, shrugged off his shirt, kicked off his shoes and stepped out of his trousers, leaving him in only black boxers that made no secret of how ready he was for her.

'Oh, my,' she sighed at the sight of his broad shoulders, powerful chest and six-pack belly. 'When it comes to beautiful bodies...' She took a deep breath. 'I just want to kiss you all over.'

'Please don't hesitate to start,' he said, flinging his arms wide in invitation.

As she kissed first his mouth then down his jawline, tasting him, stroking him with her tongue, down the strong column of his throat, across his shoulders, he was caressing her breasts, removing her bra, sliding his hand down her waist to cup her bottom and caress inside her panties.

She looked up at him, whimpered. 'Enough of the slow burn. I can't wait any longer. Please.' They were on the bed in seconds, with all remaining underwear discarded and tossed aside.

She stilled. 'Protection. I didn't think...'

'I did,' he said, reaching for the bedside drawer. No fantasy could match the sensation as he pushed inside her, filling her, thrilling her, taking her rapidly to orgasm. But it was more than sexual pleasure—it was a sensation on a different level that urged her to believe they were meant to be lovers.

Their first time was urgent, hungry and utterly perfect. Their second time was slow and thorough as they explored each other's bodies. It was also utterly perfect. To Kitty it seemed as if they had been waiting for each other, and that everything in her life had built up to this moment. Him. Sebastian. The man she had fallen in love with without really realising it had happened. She should be panicking because she had only known him for less than a month, but at a deep soul level she believed he felt the same way.

She woke very early the next morning to find herself lying with his arm slung possessively over her chest. He looked so beautiful when he was asleep. His black hair was ruffled from when she'd run her fingers through it, his face relaxed, dark stubble shadowing his jaw. The linen sheet was rucked up around his hips and she took a long moment to admire his body, his smooth olive skin, his muscled chest with just the right amount of dark hair, his powerful shoulders. She shivered with remembered pleasure of their lovemaking and felt boneless with desire.

Regretfully, she went to slide out of the bed so as not to awaken him. She had to get up and back to the apartment on the next floor before anyone arrived at the house: the daily cleaners she had engaged, Alisa the cook whose day it was on the job share, Guy, Evelyn's team of builders and decorators.

But a strong arm shot out and clamped her to the bed. 'Don't go,' Sebastian commanded. Remarkably, she didn't feel self-conscious or uncomfortable at finding herself naked in Sir Sebastian's bed. The easy repartee they'd established had translated well into lovemaking. They had quickly discovered each other's needs with anticipation of more to be learned.

'I thought you were asleep,' she murmured. 'I have to go, so no one sees me leaving your bedroom to take the walk of shame up to my apartment.'

'Why can't you stay? There's absolutely nothing to be ashamed of.' He pushed himself up on one elbow. The sheet slid away to reveal the full glory of his body. 'This is my house. We're both single, not hurting anyone by being together. I'm not really your boss, you're a contractor so we're not bending any employment laws.'

Kitty screwed up her face. 'I'd just be happy to not have the change in our relationship subject to scrutiny. Not…not just yet.'

She wanted to hug to themselves this wondrous thing that had flowered between them. Gossip and innuendo, the revival of her scandalous past, would only sully something that was beautiful and new and so very special. She tried to explain that to him.

'I understand,' he said. 'For now.'

'Thank you,' she said. 'I'm not ashamed, just cautious.' She kissed him.

'Are you sure you want to leave?' He slid a hand down her shoulder and cupped her breast.

'I find it impossible to resist you, Sir Sebastian,' she said, falling back into his arms until they were skin to skin.

CHAPTER FOURTEEN

NINE DAYS LATER, on the Thursday before the party, Sebastian was getting fed up with skulking around with Kitty in his own home. She spent each night in his bed. There were snatched kisses and surreptitious hugs whenever they had a private moment during the day. They went for long evening walks holding hands, along the Thames and around Chelsea, wearing hats and scarves up around their faces so they couldn't be recognised. But in front of anyone else it was no touching, no kissing and business as usual.

It wasn't enough. He wanted more, so much more. When he'd woken up the morning after the night they'd first made love and seen Kitty's blonde head next to him on the pillow, he'd known he was in love with her. In the past, he'd questioned if he had ever truly been in love. Now he knew he hadn't. He had never felt this depth of emotion for a woman before and he fell more in love with her every day. So much for Lavinia's cruel words: he *was* able to love. He'd loved his parents and his uncle. He loved his Spanish *abuela*. He just hadn't loved Lavinia.

Although no one had exactly come out and said they knew about the change in his relationship with Kitty, Sebastian suspected the people working in the house were aware. Guy almost certainly knew, but he was too much the professional to say anything. The cooks had guessed; it wouldn't have been difficult for them to know he and

Kitty ate dinner together. He suspected Evelyn Lim knew too. But he got the distinct feeling they were all happy for him and Kitty, and okay with pretending they didn't know if that was what was required of them. Claudia knew—apparently she'd guessed Kitty's secret the second she'd seen Kitty the day after they'd first made love.

Sebastian wanted to tell her grandfather, Stan, that he and Kitty were a couple. He wanted to tell his *abuela* he had a lovely English girlfriend, as she worried that he wasn't married at thirty-two. He wanted to go public with the woman he loved. Not that he'd told her he loved her. It seemed too soon to actually put it into words.

When Kitty next popped into his office with a query about the arrangements for Saturday's party, he shut the door, took her in his arms for a swift hug and faced her. 'I want to talk to you about something really important to me.'

'Fire away,' she said.

'I want you to act as hostess at the party on Saturday. I know you said you wouldn't do it again—'

'Under any circumstances, if I recall my words correctly,' she said.

'But this would be very different to the last time. I don't want to fib about us being "just friends" when you mean so much more to me than that. I want you by my side as my girlfriend.'

She smiled. 'So I'm your official girlfriend now.'

'Something like that. If you prefer not to put a label on what we have together, I'm okay. My woman, perhaps, although that does sound rather beating-on-the-chest caveman stuff.'

'I'm fine with girlfriend. However, *boyfriend* doesn't seem dignified enough for you. But I can't really call you my lover; it seems way too intimate.'

'Probably not,' he said. 'Though feel free to say it in private.'

'Partner?' she said.

'Seems like a business partner. You already have one of those.'

'Gentleman friend?'

'A hundred years out of date, perhaps?'

'My guy?'

'Too casual.'

'Okay. Boyfriend it is. I'll try to think of something better. In the meantime, maybe I'll call you Sir Boyfriend.'

He groaned. 'Please, no. But does that mean you'll come to the party?'

'There will be people there who knew me in another life, who believed I—'

'Do you honestly think that people who owe a substantial part of their livelihood to the Delfont dominated companies would dare to criticise my girlfriend?'

'Perhaps not,' she conceded.

'I'm not like your jerk of an ex, Neil.'

'You're certainly not like him in any way.'

'I'm one hundred per cent on your side. I know how fiercely independent you are, and how you'll tell me you don't want my protection, but I want you to know you've got it.'

'Whether I like it or not?' she said.

'I wouldn't put it quite like that,' he said.

'Yes, you would,' she said with a smile. 'And I'll surprise you by saying I will accept your protection.'

'Seriously?' he said. 'Why the change of mind?'

'Something Gramps said about looking after each other.'

'He's a wise man, your grandfather.'

'He is, and I haven't always listened to him.' She paused. 'There's something else. Something that might tip me back into the media glare I hate so much, no matter how I try to hide from it.'

He frowned. 'What could that be?'

'Can we sit down?' she said.

He led her to the chesterfield sofa that Uncle Olly used to have in his study. He and Kitty had taken to sitting next to each other, rather than across the desk.

He took her hand in his. 'I'm intrigued.'

'Do you remember me telling you about my direct manager at Blaine and Ball, a woman named Hilary?'

'The one who told you to grin and bear it when the director started acting out of line?'

'That's the one. She contacted me yesterday and we met this morning for coffee on the King's Road.'

'Why did she want to see you? To apologise?'

'Oddly enough, yes. She confessed that she too was a victim of Edmund Blaine, and that there had been others.'

'What? And she did nothing to protect you?'

'Difficult to understand, isn't it? But she told me she was a single mum and he held the threat of losing her job over her.'

Sebastian frowned. 'I still don't like what she let happen to you when she could have protected you. Surely that makes her complicit.'

'I have mixed feelings about that too. I could barely look her in the eye, to tell you the truth. But what she said proved what I'd always suspected: that I couldn't have been the first and wouldn't be the last. What Hilary wanted to talk to me about was his latest victim. Edmund didn't realise when he tried to assault a pretty young intern that she was a martial arts expert and fought back. Not only that, she recorded the incident on her phone, then went home and showed it to her lawyer father.'

'In other words, he's in trouble.'

'Not necessarily. His defence is that it was a one-off incident brought on by stress. Hilary wants his other victims to come forward to say "me too", and establish a pattern of similar previous assaults.'

'Including you.'

'Including me, yes.'

'Will you do it?' he said.

'If others come forward, I will too. It's the only chance I have to fight back and clear my name.'

'Are you sure you want to put yourself through all that again?'

'I don't want to, of course not. But if it means that horrible man gets what he deserves it will be worth it. It could be my only chance to restore my reputation.'

Sebastian felt a fierce urge to protect Kitty. He held her close. 'Whatever happens, I'm there for you.'

'Thank you. And I want to be there for you. I'll come to the party, as your girlfriend.' Her voice softened. 'I'll be proud to.'

Kitty headed back to her office. In truth, the party was shaping up to be so good she had found herself wishing she could be there to enjoy it, instead of sitting the evening out in the kitchen.

But was it a step too far to use the event as the official 'outing' of her as Sebastian's girlfriend? She had to take the plunge some time. It was getting harder to hide the fact they were a couple, to keep it secret from everyone but Claudia. There was also the fact she didn't want to hide it any more; she wanted to be with him all the time. She had never felt happier with a man—although she was still intent on protecting her heart. It was early days yet— fireworks and flames could fizzle out as quickly as they flared.

But she wanted the freedom to pursue her relationship with him out in the open. Sebastian was giving her that opportunity by asking her to be by his side at the party. He masked it well, but she knew he was shy and must be secretly dreading meeting all those people. She knew she could help ease the way by being there. He wouldn't say it because he wouldn't want to pressure her, but he needed her.

She still dreaded the idea of encountering people who believed she had attempted to seduce an older married man and then when he'd refused her advances had reported him for assault as payback. But now there was a very good chance that man would soon be exposed for the monster he was. Surely that would generate better headlines than raking up her old so-called scandal.

CHAPTER FIFTEEN

SEBASTIAN'S HOUSE WAS filled with music, the rise and fall chatter of people having a good time and the occasional burst of laughter. In other words, Kitty thought—not without a sense of pride—all the signs of a successful party in full swing.

While she was a guest—being Sebastian's girlfriend had elevated her status—she was also the event planner who had worked hard to get all this running so smoothly. In a moment she'd pop down to the kitchen, just to check there would be no interruptions to the so far seamless flow of silver trays filled with delicious cocktail snacks circulating around the guests, borne by charming 'resting' actors who moonlighted as waiters between gigs.

She and Sebastian had started the evening standing resolutely side by side to greet the guests. He'd introduced her as Kitty Clements, after all they were dating now, and she couldn't hide behind Kitty Rose. As he'd predicted, no one looked at her askance or said anything untoward and she'd begun to relax. The dinner party had passed without incident; why shouldn't the party be the same?

She was glad she'd invested in a credit-card-bruising new dress for the occasion—a flattering aqua silk sheath overlaid with a silver-threaded lace that gave a subtle touch of bling. It had a modest vee neckline, elbow-length sleeves and came to just a few inches above her knees.

That afternoon, she'd visited the hairdresser to have her hair done up in a messy bun, and she wore her favourite turquoise and silver earrings. She'd had a manicure and taken extra care with her make-up. All in all, she was confident she looked less housekeeper and more Cinderella as Sir Sebastian's date for the evening. Sebastian looked devastatingly handsome in a dark suit. But then Sebastian looked devastatingly handsome in anything he wore, and even more handsome in nothing at all, as she'd been recently privileged to discover.

But while she and Sebastian had chatted with guests— the renovation of Sir Cyril's house was a popular topic— they'd somehow spun away from each other. He was now several groups of people away from her and, at the realisation, Kitty felt a flutter of panic. She couldn't do this on her own. He was her anchor in a sea of unknown faces. She managed to catch his eye and indicated she was going to head down to the kitchen. He nodded and gave her his special smile that reassured her, even across the room, he had her back. If her heart showed in her eyes when she smiled back at him, she didn't care. There was a gratifying freedom in not having to pretend otherwise.

She left the room and headed down the short corridor that led to the kitchen stairs, her thoughts turning to the food. Several people had asked her for the name of the excellent caterers, and she'd been happy to tell them it was Sebastian's own staff. She wanted to tell Alisa and Josie; they'd be pleased at the compliment.

Someone grabbed her roughly by the top of her arm and spun her around to face them. 'Hey! Let go of—' she started, but the words stopped on her tongue. Edmund Blaine glared down at her, face red, eyes bulging, his alcohol-tinged breath nauseating her. Like a nightmare come to life. His grip on her left arm was so hard it hurt. All the remembered terror of the night he'd assaulted her rushed back like a black fog smothering her brain. She froze, as if her feet were glued to the floor.

'Well, well, look who's weaselled her way into somewhere she doesn't belong,' he sneered.

But she did belong here. His words pierced her terror, deflating it. She was a different person from that girl he'd assaulted, and no longer his victim. Using moves she'd learned in her self-defence classes, she chopped at his hand that gripped her arm and kicked hard at his kneecap with her silver stiletto shoe. Taken by surprise, he stumbled back from her, uttering a string of foul expletives.

'You're the one who doesn't belong here. Your name isn't on the guest list.' She could not let him know she was shaking inside.

'I was close to Sir Cyril. On the boards of his companies.'

His hateful name on the guest list would have shone out as if neon lit. Had it been added later? She could not, would not, believe Sebastian had knowingly invited this man to his home.

'This is Sir Sebastian's party.'

'Your *boyfriend.*' The way he sneered the word made it sound like something dirty. 'Wouldn't he like to know the truth about you.'

'He knows the truth about *you*,' Kitty retorted before she realised it was pointless engaging in any kind of conversation with this loathsome man.

'He'll believe my version of what happened over yours,' he said. 'Then we'll see who'll flounce around boasting about her rich boyfriend. Watch for the headlines when I leak an update on what I discovered about you tonight to my favourite news editor.'

Kitty clenched her teeth. Nausea and fury roiled inside her. She could not show her fear and revulsion—this man thrived on it. Nor could she tell him he'd be getting his comeuppance very soon when the women he'd hurt spoke out against him. They were keeping that confidential until their numbers were finalised.

'Get out,' she said.

'Yeah. I'll find your boyfriend and let him know exactly what kind of little hussy he's got himself mixed up with.'

He limped away—quite a bad limp, Kitty was pleased to note. If she'd broken his kneecap, she'd be glad.

An elegantly dressed woman—not his wife—rushed to him, giving Kitty a haughty, disapproving stare. It was meant to put her in her place, the 'hired help' place, and Kitty cringed from it. She'd told Edmund she belonged here, but did she?

She wanted to push past Edmund and find Sebastian before he did, but she knew her shaky legs wouldn't carry her that far and she was in danger of collapse. She staggered to the guest bathroom and locked the door. As the room spun, she fought the nausea but she feared she was about to faint. She sank down onto the chair, braced her head between her hands and lowered it to her knees. Gradually she started to feel better, and she slowly got up from the chair. Steadier now on her feet, she took a few deep breaths then splashed cold water on her face. She fixed the resulting mascara run with a tissue and took more deep breaths to compose herself.

By the time she got back to the party, Sebastian should have shown Edmund the door. But, to her shock, Edmund was still there, in the middle of the room and engaged in conversation with Sebastian. Was her boyfriend booting the older man out? It didn't appear so. In fact their conversation appeared to be downright convivial.

Kitty couldn't believe it when she saw Sebastian lay a hand on Edmund's arm. Then he laughed—Sebastian actually laughed at something Edmund had said. Edmund had told her Sebastian would believe his version of what had gone down between the two of them years ago. Were they laughing at her? And what was Edmund doing here in the first place? No way would she have agreed to be at this party if she'd had any inkling he'd be here too. By schmoozing with Edmund—knowing full well what he'd done to her—Sebastian was as bad as Neil. He was so engrossed in the discussion that he didn't see her. But Edmund did, and shot her a look of malevolent triumph.

Kitty felt her heart shrivel up until it was a dried-out husk. Again that social chasm loomed between her and Sir Sebastian. How could she have optimistically imagined it could be ignored? As she stood watching her lover in conversation with her abuser, it seemed as if the priceless Persian carpet on the floor between them tore in half and the floorboards cracked and opened up a dark black sink hole that ran beneath London—particularly this part of London.

Edmund came from the same kind of family as Sebastian had—not the Spanish side, but the Delfont side—public school, Oxbridge, gentlemen's clubs, the arrogant privileges one could only be born into. That upper echelon that she had joked went way beyond the A-list. So very different from her background. How could she imagine that anything more could develop between her and Sebastian?

He cared for her, she was sure he did, although he had never actually said he loved her. And she loved him. But there could be no tomorrow for them. Sebastian would probably reach that way of thinking himself, perhaps when it was time to produce an heir. But it was Kitty who would end it—right now. Because she could not live with a man who was talking and laughing so jovially with the person who had caused her so much trauma. A man who knew how that encounter and the betrayals that followed had wounded her. It was a searing pain that cut right through her and she couldn't imagine she would ever recover from it.

No guest rushed to talk to her, standing there alone on the fringe of other people's conversations. All her old insecurities came rushing back. She was worthy of attention from these people only when she was part of the Sebastian/Kitty act—not for herself. Perhaps she hadn't played her role well enough. She was the downstairs girl allowed upstairs to join in the party, the downstairs girl who had had the temerity to move upstairs to the master's bed.

She had to leave this house. Now. For good. She had one more week on the contract, but she couldn't endure being here for a moment longer.

Kitty straightened her back, pasted a socially acceptable smile on her face, turned her back on the unbearable sight of the man she had grown to love in conversation with the man who had assaulted her then blackened her name and ended her career, and headed towards the elevator that would take her up to the housekeeper's apartment.

Sebastian had just delivered the news to Edmund Blaine that he was fired from his directorships of the Delfont companies, and that if he didn't leave the house this second he would call his security guards and have him charged with trespassing, when he looked over to see Kitty heading away from the main throng of party guests. Her back was unnaturally rigid, her footsteps too carefully placed, as if she feared falling. *Why?*

With a firm grip on the older man's elbow, he steered Blaine to the door and told him in a threatening undertone exactly what he could expect if he had anything to do with him or his girlfriend again. And that he would sue him to kingdom come if any damaging stories about Kitty appeared in any media, conventional or online. If he could have booted Blaine in the rear end to send him tumbling head over heels down the marble stairs he would have done so, but that would have placed him in the wrong. And the man was not worth being charged with assault.

Now he needed to find Kitty. There was something about the way she'd held herself that had worried him. As he headed towards where he had last seen her, one of his guests caught his arm and it was all he could do not to shake her off. By the time he'd exchanged pleasantries, Kitty was gone.

He didn't want to make it obvious he was looking for her; she would hate having attention drawn to her. But a subtle search showed she wasn't with any of the guests in the party area or the kitchen. Guy, walking by with two colourful cocktails in hand, told him he'd seen Kitty on her way to the elevator.

To touch up her make-up and do girly things? That couldn't be right. Eminently practical Kitty could do those things without the aid of a mirror. Sebastian headed for the elevator.

There was no light coming from under the door to the housekeeper's flat. He knocked on the door. No answer. He knocked again. 'Kitty,' he called softly. His voice hung still in the hallway. He tried the handle of the door, was surprised when it opened under his hand. 'Are you okay?' he called. But his words echoed back at him. As he pushed the door open, he was overwhelmed by a sense of foreboding.

Kitty was gone.

There was a coldness to the rooms that had nothing to do with the time of year and everything to do with her absence. Empty clothes hangers hung in the wardrobe. The bathroom shelf was bare, and nothing out of place in the kitchenette. His grey cashmere scarf lay folded neatly on an arm of the sofa—a gift resoundingly rejected. The rooms were empty, yet her floral fragrance lingered on the air, taunting him. He felt as if he'd been hurtled into some alternate reality where everything had turned upside down.

Where was she?

Something shiny glinted from under the sofa and he

bent to retrieve it. One glittering silver high-heeled shoe, discarded after the party, missed in what must have been a hasty packing. He looked at the shoe for a long time.

Kitty had been so bright and vivacious at the party in her shimmering dress, these sexy shoes and her knock-out smile. She'd known exactly what to say to make him look good and endear herself to some of the crustiest of characters. She'd charmed several on-the-spot promises of donations to the foundation out of the most unlikely of people. He was so proud of her. What the hell had happened?

Then he saw the note. A page torn from a notebook, propped up against the bookshelf, the words hastily scrawled. His hand shook as he picked it up, dreading what he might read.

Sebastian,
I can't do this. It's not going to work for us and I can't face living here. How could you have welcomed the man who attacked me into this house, a place where I felt so safe?
Please consider this the termination of my contract. I'm sorry if I've let you down, but the staff I've put in place all know what they're doing. You don't need me.
Kitty

The words hit him like a punch to the gut. *You don't need me.*

How wrong could she be? A rush of anguish swept over him, so powerful he had to hold onto the back of the sofa. He needed her more than he'd ever needed anyone. He needed her, wanted her, *loved* her. Regret smote him like a sledgehammer. *Yet he hadn't told her he loved her.*

Her leaving shouldn't surprise him. This party had been a huge deal for her. Not just the organising of it, but accompanying him as his girlfriend. She must have faced down the same fear and trepidations she had for the foundation dinner party—worse, as she'd known there could be people here who knew her. He should never have strayed from her side. Her worst nightmare come true would have been the presence of Edmund Blaine.

She obviously hadn't seen him kick the odious guy out of the house. He had to find her, had to explain.

But he still had a houseful of guests downstairs. If he disappeared now it would cause a ripple of gossip that would widen to include Kitty. He knew she would hate that. And it would negate all the good work she had done here.

Where would she have gone? To Claudia? Sebastian realised he didn't know where Kitty's friend and business partner lived. Or would she have gone home to her grandfather's house? That was more likely.

He would go back to the party now, then in the morning find out where Kitty had gone, tell her all the things he should have told her before this—and hope she would forgive him. He wanted a second chance with Kitty.

Kitty got out of the cab at Victoria Station. It wasn't yet nine p.m. There were still trains for Widefield to take her to the security of home. As she wheeled her two small suitcases to the platform, the enormity of what she had done hit her. She started to shake, had to stop and pull her coat around her.

She'd left Sebastian without saying goodbye. Sneaked quietly out of the house while the party went on around her. Had he noticed she'd gone? This morning she'd woken up entwined in his arms, feeling happy and safe and, yes, in love. Safe no longer. In love no longer. The flames of her shock and anger at the sight of him being so chummy with Edmund Blaine still smouldered. She could think of no worse betrayal on Sebastian's part than welcoming that heinous man into his house. It was as if he had rejected her and all they'd shared.

CHAPTER SIXTEEN

SEBASTIAN HAD BARELY slept for thinking about Kitty and how badly things had gone wrong. He'd beaten himself up for the whole stupid idea of employing her instead of following his instinct and being honest with both her and himself about his attraction to her. Instead of telling her exactly how he felt.

But now he faced the morning with determination. He would fix this. He would win her back. He would do whatever he had to do. Even if he had to grovel. But to do so, he might need an ally. And he knew just the person to enlist.

He was up early enough to book a suite for himself at a luxury boutique hotel not far from Widefield and be on the road to Kent. He would not return to Cheyne Walk without fighting for a second chance with Kitty.

He was convinced Kitty would have gone to her grandfather's house, not least because she had told him before the party that she would be heading down to the rehab hospital the next morning. He had offered to drive her; she had accepted. Now he could only assume she would visit her grandfather under her own steam. He'd been looking forward to seeing Stan again; he'd liked the older man a lot. Now he might have to enlist his help.

Kitty woke up in the bedroom that had been hers since she was fourteen years old. A feeble sun was filtering through the daisy-patterned curtains she'd never let Gran update; they represented continuity and security to her. She'd always thought of this house as her haven. Now, for the first time, she didn't feel at home here. And she felt so very alone without Sebastian by her side.

What had she done?

The right thing. She reminded herself of the terror and loathing that had overwhelmed her when Edmund Blaine had grabbed her, and then again at his look of malicious gloating over Sebastian's shoulder when he'd noticed her staring at them.

He'll believe my version of what happened over yours, he'd boasted.

Was that why Sebastian had been so convivial with her attacker? Had he believed him? In her heart of hearts, Kitty couldn't believe that. And yet he had had his hand on Edmund's arm like an old friend.

Had Sebastian perhaps not realised to whom he was speaking in such a friendly manner? Not possible. Edmund would have made it very clear who he was before he'd starting spilling poison about her.

The fact was, Edmund came from Sebastian's world and she didn't. She'd been foolish to imagine she could fit in.

But she didn't feel as though she fitted in this world any more either.

The night before, when she'd arrived by train at Widefield, she'd started off on the well-lit and well-trod way to Gramps's house, only to be stopped by her high school boyfriend, Owen, who'd just dropped a friend at the station for the London train. Owen, as good-looking and nice as ever, had insisted on driving her home and checking all was okay at the house. She'd been in no mood for chatting, but had forced herself to be polite. He'd suggested they meet up for a drink. For a moment she'd been tempted. He was smart and funny and single and felt utterly familiar.

But he wasn't Sebastian.

And she didn't want to be with any other man but him.
Ever.

She forced herself up and out of bed. The bathroom
wasn't quite finished but she could have a shower and get
ready to go visit Gramps. She'd probably burst into tears
at his first kind word, but she knew he would always be
on her side.

An hour and a half later, Kitty wasn't so sure about that.
She'd arrived at the rehab hospital to visit Gramps, only
to be stopped in her tracks at the sight of her grandfather
deep in conversation with Sebastian. She gasped, speech-
less, as she was swept by a feeling of déjà vu—Sebastian
in the small chair next to Gramps in the larger one, his
leg in a surgical boot, his crutches nearby.

'Kitty.' Gramps smiled at her, sheepishly she thought.

Sebastian immediately rose from his chair to greet her.
She was wearing flat boots, jeans, a plain white shirt and
a navy-blue hooded parka she'd had since high school,
and felt at a distinct disadvantage. In his black jeans and
superbly cut charcoal jacket he looked just like a baronet
visiting someone else's grandfather should look. But his
eyes were shadowed and wary.

'Kitty,' he said, his gaze never leaving her face. 'You
had me worried. Are you okay?'

'Perfectly fine,' she said stiffly. 'I caught the train
home.'

'I was looking forward to seeing Stan so I—'

'Came on your own,' she said tartly, glaring at him.

'Yes,' he said.

Gramps looked from Kitty to Sebastian and back again.
'I can see you're not happy, love, but there are always two
sides to every story. Sebastian has told me his side of what
happened last night. I know he wants to tell it to you.' She

went to protest but Gramps put up his hand. 'I think you'll want to hear it.'

'I feel I've been hijacked,' she said, swallowing a sob. How could Gramps do this to her?

'Blame me for that,' Sebastian said gruffly. 'This was the only way I thought I could get you to see me. I've been calling you all morning.'

'I've had my phone switched off,' she said in a tone as offhand as she could make it.

'Come on, love,' said Gramps. 'You don't want to be the entertainment here for the other old folks.'

'I'll go,' said Sebastian. He turned away from her, but not before she'd seen his expression of utter devastation.

'No. Wait. I… I'll hear you out. But not here.' Gramps was right; eyes were turning in their direction.

'Don't worry about me,' said Gramps. 'I've got a card game going with a few mates I've made here.'

She had to do this. Let Sebastian know how much he'd wounded her. It wouldn't make any difference to her decision to go. But at least she'd get the chance to say goodbye.

She followed Sebastian out to where his car was parked. 'I don't want to talk in your car,' she said, remembering the passionate kisses she had shared with him the last time she'd been here.

'I'm booked into a hotel not far from here.' The only hotel nearby was a very swish boutique hotel in a converted Georgian mansion. 'We could go there to talk if that suits.'

They were speaking to each other like strangers. Not lovers who had joyously explored each other's bodies. It was heartbreaking.

He got out his car keys.

'No,' she said. 'Er, not *no* to the hotel but no to going in your car. I'll follow you in mine.' No way would she let herself get trapped.

He shrugged. 'If that's what you want, Kitty.'

Of course it wasn't what she wanted. She wanted to be laughing with him with the old ease they'd felt from the get-go, to be swept into his arms and hugged close.

This was a nightmare.

'It's what I want,' she said, clamping down on any hint of her tumultuous emotions creeping into her voice.

In her somewhat battered small hatchback, she drove behind him for the ten minutes it took to reach the circular gravel drive of the hotel, swallowing hard against the persistent sob that seemed determined to break out, blinking away tears she refused to let him see.

She parked the car next to his, thinking bleakly that the difference in their situations was blatant even in the cars they drove.

Inside, the hotel was exquisitely decorated in a subdued elegance with a nod to the building's history and a deference to modern expectations of comfort. But she barely noticed it.

'I'll order lunch to be sent up to my suite,' he said.

She'd been alone with him so many times, why did this feel so awkward?

'I couldn't eat a thing,' she muttered.

In the elevator she stood as far away as she could in silence. And then they were in his suite, a stylish living area with two fat, overstuffed sofas placed opposite each other, the bedroom dominated by a modern version of a four-poster bed. She refused to let her eyes be drawn to the bed.

Sebastian had never seen Kitty look so uncomfortable. She stood apart from him as if dreading any inadvertent touch. Her face was drawn and wan as if all the light had gone out of her. Had he extinguished that sunshine that had always spilled onto him?

'Why did you leave Cheyne Walk?'

Why did you leave me?

'Didn't you read my note?' Her voice was laced with sadness so profound his heart clenched.

'I did and it puzzled me. I thought things were working out well for us. You were brilliant last night. I was so proud of you. So happy you were by my side.'

'So why were you schmoozing with Edmund Blaine? What was he doing there in the first place?' Her blue eyes were dark with accusation and pain. He hated to see her like that. He wanted to take her in his arms and comfort her, but she'd thrown up a barrier around herself, invisible but impenetrable.

'Schmoozing? You seriously think I was *schmoozing* with that man?'

'That's what it looked like. What was he doing there? Of all places, I thought I was safe from him in your house. Yet when I left to check on things in the kitchen, he came up behind me, accosted me, threatened me, *frightened* me, told me he was going to spin more lies about me, this time to you. Did you notice he was limping? That was because of me. I had to kick him in the knee to stop him from touching me.'

'Kitty. No. I'm so sorry.' He should have thrown that monster down the stairs.

'I came to warn you about him but he beat me to it. And I saw you chatting with him as if he were an honoured guest, laughing, even putting your hand on his arm.' Her face crumpled and she shuddered in revulsion. 'How could you? When you knew his history with me?'

'I'm horrified you should think that. You have to believe me. My encounter with Blaine wasn't like that at all.'

'It wasn't?' Her eyes narrowed suspiciously.

'For one thing, he wasn't an honoured guest. He was a gate-crasher.'

'What do you mean?'

'Odd to apply that term to a middle-aged man, but there it is. He was limping when he approached me, so it must have been just after his encounter with you. I couldn't put a name to most of the guests, as you know, and had no idea who he was. He wanted to reminisce about Sir Cyril, of whom he was a great admirer. Needless to say, that didn't go down well with me. I was about to make my excuses and circulate when he introduced himself. I recognised the name straight away. He must have seen something in my face as he made a joke of not having received an invitation, told me it must have been an oversight on my part.'

'He really had the gall to come to your party uninvited?'

'As if it were his due. I didn't say anything. I could tell he thought he had me fooled.'

'Had totally underestimated you, you mean.' At last a warming of the coldness in her eyes.

'I played him like I'd seen Sir Cyril play a trout at the end of his line when he'd dragged me and my father in our time of exile up to a cousin's Scottish estate.'

'Tell me,' she said.

'He reminded me he sat on the boards of two Delfont companies—both of which I knew were particularly well remunerated—in a public relations advisory capacity. There was a lot of blah-blah-blah about how Sir Cyril had valued him. And the underlying, terribly polite insinuation I could never be the man my grandfather was. He's like one of the loathsome boys who bullied me so mercilessly at that private school when I was nine.'

'Yet he can be charming,' she said.

'As the worst bullies can be,' he said. 'That's when I started looking around for you, then remembered you'd gone down to the kitchen.'

'Me? Surely you couldn't believe I wanted to meet him?'

'Of course not. But I thought you might enjoy being with me when I fired him from his directorships.'

'You fired him? But you were being so chummy with him. You even had your hand on his arm, like you were best buddies.'

'I wasn't being chummy. What you must have seen was me laughing at his preposterous suggestion he was the innocent party in the scandal two years ago. The hand on his arm was me restraining him and telling him, with a pleasant expression on my face so I didn't alert the party guests to what was happening, that if he didn't leave right then I'd call our security guards and have him arrested for trespassing.'

'But you don't have security guards.'

'He didn't know that. But even then he continued to slander you. So I fired him, told him what I would do to him if he did or said anything that could harm you, and personally escorted him from the house.'

'You did? But I didn't see…' She paused. 'Because I was so upset by seeing you with him I'd turned away.'

'I hope the next time you see him will be in court, along with your fellow accusers.'

Kitty went very quiet. 'I completely misread the situation. No wonder Gramps told me I needed to hear your side of the story.'

'He gives wise counsel, your gramps.'

'I overreacted big time. And badly misjudged you when I should have known better. I… I think I was still in shock after the way he grabbed me and was then so vile. Can you forgive me?'

'There's absolutely nothing to forgive. He should never have been allowed in the door. Next party, we really will have security guards.'

'I've been wanting to ask you. That party. Is mixing

with that kind of people what you want to do for the rest of your life? A lot of them were really boring.'

'You mean the pompous windbags?' he said.

'And the droning narcissists. The trustees of the foundation were so much nicer.'

'Agree. Hand-picked by Lady Enid and not Sir Cyril as these people were. Although they're not all bad, you must admit. Some of them were fun.'

'But is upholding the money-making stream of the Delfont family really all you want to do with your life? Your friends in the band told me you like to jam with them on trumpet and you're really talented.'

'A hobby only.' He paused. 'Before I inherited, when I had no idea I was going to end up with the title, I thought I'd like to write a novel.'

'Like your mother?'

He shook his head. 'A crime novel. A dark story with a damaged detective hero and lots of twists and turns in the plot.'

'Where revenge is delivered and justice prevails in the end?'

'Something like that. I wrote two novels, planned a series with my damaged hero.'

'What happened to them?'

'They're under the bed, never to see the light of day.'

'I'd like to read them.'

'One day, perhaps.' Or he might burn them, wipe them from his computer.

She paused. 'Talking of your mother, I'm sorry I said she'd given me unrealistic expectations about men.'

He frowned. 'Did you say that?'

'You know I did. Now I realise reading her books set me up for meeting you. Down with my gran in Widefield, I read so many of them.'

'What do you mean?' He had no idea what she was getting at.

'You're one of her honourable Spanish heroes stepped right off the pages. It's like I was programmed to fall for you—to recognise you when I met you.'

'Isn't that a bit fanciful?' he said.

'Perhaps. It's just a strong feeling.'

'Have you fallen for me?' he said slowly.

She hesitated. 'Head over heels, just like in a Marisol Matthew novel.' She looked up at him. 'Only...only I love you in real life.'

Never had those words resonated with him so strongly. Happiness surged through him. 'I love you too, Kitty. Love at first sight, just like in one of her books. I didn't believe it could happen. But I fell for you the first day I met you. I just didn't realise because I didn't recognise what it was to fall in love.'

'Me too. Fell for you straight away. I complained to Claudia that she hadn't warned me about how hot you were. You were very distracting.'

'And you brought sunshine into what was shaping up to be a rather gloomy life.'

He cradled her face in his hand and kissed her long and slow and tenderly.

Kitty felt flooded with emotions, not the least of which was relief that the incident with Edmund Blaine had been a misunderstanding and that Sebastian had defended her and exacted revenge on the horrible man. There was joy that he had followed her down here, had gained the respect of her grandfather and had fought for her. But, most of all, there was the exquisite happiness of knowing he loved her.

She kissed him back, hoping she transmitted the joy and love she felt. This was how it was meant to be. She never wanted to be parted from him again.

She broke away from his kiss. 'We have some catching up to do,' she murmured against his mouth.

'We do,' he said. 'So much we need to tell each other.'

'That too,' she said. 'But it's not what I meant. We wasted an entire night and morning when we could have been together. That was my fault. I need to make it up to you.'

'And just how do you intend to do that?' he said, his voice husky, his eyes narrowed.

'Did you realise there's a rather wonderful bed in this room?'

'It hadn't escaped my notice,' he said.

'And the room is rather warm,' she said. 'I think we're wearing far too many clothes.'

'It is indeed heating up,' he said as he pushed her parka from her shoulders and threw it on the sofa. She kicked off her boots; he did the same with his. He started to undo the buttons on her shirt, his hands brushing against her already aroused nipples.

'My turn first,' she said, her breath coming short. She rid him of his jacket then his fine knit sweater. She slid her hands over the hard muscles of his chest, the smoothness of his olive skin, his broad shoulders, as she revelled in the sense of possession the knowledge that he loved her gave her. He was hers and she wanted to brand him with her touch.

'Strangely enough, I'm not cooling down,' he said as his hands slid inside her shirt to undo her bra.

'Me neither,' she said. 'Quite the opposite, in fact.' She gasped as he tugged off her shirt and her bra, cupping her breasts, rolling her nipples between his fingers. She could quite happily take him now, she ached for him, but she wanted to prolong the exquisite torture of desire.

She let him help her with his belt but then pushed his hand away. 'This is my pleasure,' she said.

'Mine too,' he gasped, gripping her shoulders.

She made the act of removing his trousers an extended

caress, more so as she took off his boxers. She took him in her hand, admiring his strength and virility and rejoicing in the power she had to arouse him.

'No more,' he groaned. 'I want to come with you.'

Impatiently, he picked her up and carried her to the bed.

'I love it when you hold me like this,' she murmured from the security of his strong arms. 'I'm afraid I'll never be able to return the favour.'

'There are other favours you can return,' he said huskily, lying her on the bed. 'Just not right now.' He kissed her, then broke away to kiss each breast in turn, then down to the edge of her jeans. Impatient for his intimate touch, she wiggled out of her jeans, leaving her just in her pink lace panties. He pulled them off with his teeth, slid them down her thighs, then made love to her with his tongue and mouth to bring her to a climax so intense she felt light-headed.

When she'd got her breath back, she urged him towards her. 'I want you inside me, now,' she moaned.

He needed no further urging and entered her. His rhythm soon had her climbing for the peak again and she came with him, their cries of ecstasy mingling in the privacy of the room.

'You really are amazing in every way, Sir Boyfriend,' she murmured as she snuggled against him and slid into a satisfied sleep.

She woke to find Sebastian sitting on the bed next to her, dressed in the hotel's luxurious black robe, looking impossibly handsome.

'How thoughtful of the hotel to have a robe in your favourite colour,' she said as she sat up, clutching the sheet to her breasts.

He pushed the sheet away from her. 'Don't cover yourself,' he said. 'You have no idea how lovely you look, with your hair all wild around your shoulders. I could never have enough of you.'

'You say the nicest things,' she said. And he did. He made her feel good about herself in every way. How could she have doubted him?

'I've called for lunch. It should be here soon.'

'Good,' she said.

He took her hand. 'Before it arrives, there's something I want to say to you.'

He looked into her face and she was stunned at the unmasked love that shone from his grey eyes. 'I'm asking you to marry me, Kitty. I love you and want to make you my wife.'

Kitty swallowed hard against a lump of emotion. For all her fantasies of him, she had never envisaged this moment, never dared dream that far ahead.

'Yes. I say yes to becoming your wife. I love you, Sebastian.'

He reached for the pocket of his robe, pulled out a small Tiffany blue box. 'After you agreed to come to the party on Thursday, I went shopping. I wanted to be ready. Just in case.'

Just in case he happened to propose. Wasn't that just Sebastian? How she loved him for it.

He handed the box to her. 'Before I put it on your finger, I want to make sure you like it.'

'I'll like whatever you chose,' she said.

'Just to be sure,' he said.

Of course he'd want to be absolutely sure. That was Sebastian and another of the reasons she loved him.

With fingers that weren't quite steady, she opened the box, fumbling a little with the lid. Inside was a diamond ring nestled in dark velvet, a very large classic solitaire on a fine platinum band.

'It's...it's perfect,' she said, her voice breaking. 'Simple and elegant. I love it.' She held out her left hand, fingers splayed. She couldn't help but be glad she'd had that manicure the day before.

Sebastian looked delighted as he slid the ring onto the third finger of her left hand. It fitted perfectly.

'I wanted to ask you to marry me in a more romantic location,' he said.

'What could be more romantic than this gorgeous country house hotel? It's perfect. I do have a request for our honeymoon though,' she said.

'Anywhere in the world you want,' he said.

'I'd like it to be a certain farmhouse in Mallorca,' she said. There she would find more clues to what made Sir Sebastian tick, so she could better understand him. Not to mention escaping the English weather to the milder climate of the Balearic Isles.

Her answer pleased him, she could tell.

'I promise no chickens in the kitchen,' he said.

She laughed 'Or goats in the laundry room.'

'If we're talking honeymoons already, I'd like to get married as soon as we can. I want you living with me as my wife, and mistress of the house you've helped bring to life. And perhaps wielding your PR skills for the Lady Enid foundation.'

'I'd like that very much,' she said. She and Claudia would have to sort out how her commitment to PWP would pan out; she wouldn't let her friend down. Perhaps she could still keep a stake in the business, while not actually packing boxes.

Kitty held her hand up to the light and little rainbows danced around the room. 'I absolutely love this ring.' She paused. 'Do you mind if after lunch we go back to the rehab hospital to show Gramps?'

'I was going to suggest that myself,' he said. 'Then perhaps we can have a video call with my *abuela*. She'll be very happy with our news.'

She admired the ring again, then looked back up at him. 'Does this mean I can call you Sir Fiancé?'

'Why not?' he said as he swept her into his arms.

CHAPTER SEVENTEEN

Four weeks later, St Swithun's Church, Widefield, Kent

SEBASTIAN STOOD AT the altar of the small thirteenth-century stone church in the village where Kitty had lived with her grandparents since she was fourteen. Her grandparents had been married in this church, so had her parents; Kitty herself had been christened here. Her grandmother had done the altar flowers for many years and her grandfather still helped tend the grounds. There had been no other choice for their marriage ceremony. Sebastian appreciated the feeling of continuity and community he had been welcomed into.

At Kitty's request, the wedding was small and low-key, just family and close friends. And the staff from Cheyne Walk, of course.

It was the week before Christmas and the church was decorated with masses of magnificent blooms organised by Kitty's florist. But there was also a nativity scene set up near the sanctuary, which somehow added an extra layer of celebration. Christmas had never been a big deal for him, but Kitty loved Christmas and loved the idea that their wedding anniversary and Christmas would be so close.

Now he waited alongside the minister, flanked by his groomsmen: his two best friends from university and his favourite Spanish cousin. Kitty and her bridesmaids—

Claudia and two university friends—were fashionably late by ten minutes.

In the front row sat his *abuela* and other Spanish family. His *abuela* had told him she had a feeling in her bones that this marriage would break the curse and she looked forward to many English great-grandchildren. Sebastian hadn't passed that one by Kitty yet, although they'd agreed they wanted children, sooner rather than later.

Thoughtful Kitty had set up a small table with framed photos of the people who couldn't be there to celebrate with them: her uncle and cousins in Canada, friends living in Australia and also the family who had passed away— her parents and grandmother, his parents, Uncle Olly, even Sir Cyril and Lady Enid. Somehow Kitty's beloved childhood dog, a golden Labrador named Peter, also had his photo there. Sebastian had carefully placed Peter in front of Sir Cyril, to mask his cruel face with a sweet doggy smile.

Just as he was again checking his watch, the organ struck up the wedding march. There were murmurings of anticipation among the congregation and heads turned towards the entrance of the church. Who would be the first to spot the bride?

Sebastian's heart started to thud. First the bridesmaids glided up the aisle, each in the same gown but in different pastel shades: pink, lavender and a soft blue.

Then Kitty was there, starting her journey up the aisle towards him. Surely she was the most beautiful bride ever, in a floor-length white gown with long tight lace sleeves, and little white boots peeping out from under the skirt. She wore a halo of white flowers on her head and her hair fell in soft waves around her face and over her shoulders.

Hers was a slow procession as her grandfather was still on crutches, but Kitty had insisted that no one else could be there for her and Stan had refused the option of being pushed in a wheelchair.

It was a cold, grey December day. But when Kitty and Gramps were halfway up the aisle the sun came out from behind a cloud and a shaft of sunlight shone through the ancient stained-glass window like a spotlight on Kitty, lighting her hair to a shimmering gold. The effect was so striking, everyone gasped. But Sebastian was not surprised. From the morning he had first met her, Kitty had brought sunshine to his life—and he knew she would continue to do so.

Kitty took small steps to keep up with Gramps's slow progress on crutches. She cherished every minute with her beloved grandfather. Sebastian had invited him to come and make his home with them in Cheyne Walk but Gramps was determined to stay in the village he had always loved.

As they neared the altar, Kitty looked up to see Sebastian. She didn't see the smiling faces of her family and friends, scarcely noticed the familiar beauty of the church. She only had eyes for Sebastian, his eyes full of love and anticipation and joy.

She knew they weren't supposed to kiss at the start of the ceremony, but she couldn't resist a kiss of love and affirmation on his lips when she took her place at his side, to the happy sighs of the congregation.

All too soon the timeless traditional ceremony was over, their rings had been exchanged and they had pledged their lives to each other. The minister pronounced them man and wife, Sebastian and Kitty, Sir Sebastian and Lady Kathryn Delfont. It seemed surreal that she now had a title; it would take some getting used to. But the most important title she had was *wife* to the man she loved. 'You may now kiss the bride,' the minister intoned.

Their kiss was long and heartfelt and their friends

started to clap. Flushed and laughing, she broke away from the kiss. 'I suppose I can call you Sir Husband now,' she murmured.

'I like the sound of that, Lady Wife,' he said as he took her hand to walk down the aisle and celebrate their new life with the people who loved them.

* * * * *

BABY SURPRISE FOR THE MILLIONAIRE

RUBY BASU

MILLS & BOON

To Gareth, it must be love.

CHAPTER ONE

'I SEE THE prodigal best friend has returned.'

Saira Dey straightened her shoulders. The rich deep timbre of the voice behind her was unmistakable.

Nathan Haynes.

It was inevitable she would see him again at his sister Miranda's engagement party, but in her imagination she was calm and poised, not being jostled for service at an open bar.

Was there any chance she could pretend she couldn't hear him?

Finally getting her Sauvignon, she took a gulp of liquid courage before turning to face him with a bright smile pasted across her face.

'Nathan, how absolutely delightful to see you again. It's been too, too long. How have you been? How is everything?' she said.

He frowned. 'Are you okay? Why are you speaking like that? I thought you'd come back with a broad Texas accent, not received pronunciation.'

'I'm fine.' She laughed self-consciously and spoke in her normal accent. She tended to slip into a 'posh' British accent when she was unusually nervous, but she hadn't expect him to notice. Not after all this time.

She took a couple of centring breaths. This was Nathan Haynes. She'd known him for years. Nothing to be nervous about.

'You look well,' she said.

A complete understatement. He looked amazing. The years had treated him well. Not a single strand of grey was apparent in his lush wavy brown hair. He wore it much shorter now, clipped straight along his nape, more in keeping with the quintessential businessman he was. She missed the overlong, slightly shaggy hairstyle he'd had when they were younger. His hairstyle wasn't the only thing she missed. Always a handsome man, his face had matured. His jaw had narrowed, and his tanned skin was moulded over chiselled cheekbones, emphasising deep-set intelligent blue eyes. But there was a serious expression there now. Gone was the carefree laughter and welcoming demeanour of his youth.

She lifted her hand to his shoulder to help her balance as she stood on tiptoe to give him an air kiss. Her hand tightened briefly, as she admired the breadth of his shoulders. It evoked a fleeting memory of burying her head against his chest, being held in his arms.

The warmth of his hand on her elbow as he steered her away from the bar towards the side of the roof terrace triggered nerve-endings she'd thought were half-dead.

Careful, Saira, she cautioned herself, *you can't go there again.*

But avoiding all conversation was unrealistic. It would be better to get the initial discomfort out of the way.

'Miranda mentioned you've moved back to England,' Nathan said, once they were able to hear themselves better.

'Yes. A few weeks ago now.'

'I'm sorry to hear about your husband. Miranda told me what happened.'

She nodded in acknowledgement, taking a sip of her drink to avoid replying. It had been two years since her husband's accident, but she never knew how to respond to condolences. One of the benefits of returning to England was that hardly anyone knew her history. They'd never met her husband, which meant she didn't have to deal with the sympathetic looks or, worse, the awkward avoidance of eye contact from people who didn't know what to say to a young widow.

'This is a beautiful venue, Nathan,' she said, deliberately changing the subject, gazing round the roof terrace instead.

The view of the River Thames, still visible in the red hues of the setting sun, was magnificent. Dim lights were strewn across the glass balustrades, reflecting in the water of the roof pool. Blankets had been placed on chairs and couches for when the evening cooled, although the heat lamps would make them unnecessary. They'd thought of everything to make the event perfect.

'Isn't this your flagship hotel?'

Nathan raised his eyebrows. 'I'm surprised you remember. You didn't show much interest when I was buying it.'

'Of course I was interested, Nathan,' she said in surprise. It was the only thing he'd talked about nine years ago. She always tried to support his dreams, even when they'd been taking him away from her. 'I'm sorry if I made you think otherwise.'

She sensed him staring in her direction but purposely concentrated on the view—as if the London skyline had her completely enthralled. It was strange seeing Nathan again after so many years. Part of her looked forward to it, wanting to know whether the man she'd once been close to had changed, but a larger part of her dreaded it. This inevitable tension—the tension from a shared past—was exactly the reason why.

Saira glanced skyward with a small smile of relief when

some other guests came up to them, hoping to take the chance to speak to Nathan.

She had to admit Nathan's accusation she hadn't shown much interest wasn't completely unfair. She'd been an engineering student—business and eco-tourism were different languages to her.

Being at university, and free from parental rules for the first time in her life, she'd been too immature to understand the true nature of what Nathan was dealing with. Leaving the financial sector to move into the hospitality industry had been a huge risk for him. It had meant turning his back on his family wealth and the role he'd been born into, for which he was raised, with the expectation that he would take over. Not many twenty-two-year-olds would have been prepared to take those steps.

It was no surprise Nathan had built the Haynes Group into a huge multi-billion-pound enterprise. The hotels and resorts were only a small part of the conglomerate. According to the financial news, Nathan had an almost uncanny ability to forecast consumer desires to exploit the market.

She watched him for a few minutes. People were constantly coming up to speak to him. It wasn't simply his imposing height and tall, athletic frame, accentuated by the perfect tailoring of his tuxedo, which allowed him to command the room.

He was the consummate host, engaging and engaged. Charismatic and debonair. It was like being in the pull of a strong magnet. Hopefully, eight years and her marriage would serve to dull the attractive force which always simmered between them. A resurgence of their sexual attraction was the last thing she needed right now.

Any kind of relationship wasn't on the agenda. She'd been married and, although she'd been incredibly happy, it was safer to put all thoughts of love and marriage behind her. Losing someone she loved had been devastating. It wasn't something she ever wanted to experience again.

She was an independent single woman in charge of her own destiny.

But she had to admit it was more difficult than she expected, being in the same room as Nathan again. Living an ocean away, in the States, she'd been able to put her feelings away. Now that locked box was at risk of opening.

She pressed her hand against the flutters in her stomach. Not wanting to risk Nathan catching her scrutiny, she tore herself away from his dynamic presence. It would be safer to make her way inside, where it was quieter and where Nathan was unlikely to go while most of the guests remained outside, making the most of the warm early September evening.

She went to search for Miranda, not yet having seen her best friend since she'd arrived. She finally came across her on the way to the bathroom.

They shared a long hug, both unable to speak at first, emotion overwhelming them. Their friendship had been instantaneous the moment they'd met as five-year-olds on their first day at primary school and had lasted despite their going to different secondary schools, different universities and Saira moving to the US. It had been two years since they'd seen each other in person, the last occasion being when Miranda had flown out to support Saira at Dilip's funeral.

Miranda said, 'I can't believe you're here. This is the best thing that's happened in ages.'

'Ahem!' Her new fiancé Steve coughed in mock affront.

Laughing, Miranda made the introductions. 'We have loads to catch up on. Let's grab some food and eat together. You haven't eaten yet, have you?' Miranda asked.

'No, I haven't been here that long.'

They walked arm in arm to the extensive buffet, sensibly laid out inside, where the wind wouldn't cool the food too quickly.

'Are you really back in London for good?' Miranda asked once they were seated.

'For the next few months at least, but I need to find a job soon.'

'Are you staying at your parents' flat?'

Saira grimaced. 'For now, but I'll be moving out soon. My parents left for India a few weeks ago. It's their six months there.'

'Ah, of course. I've always envied how your parents get to follow the sun,' Miranda said. 'Why won't you stay on at the flat, then?'

'Ravi's there, and I don't think it's the best idea for us to share space. He's always been so overprotective—even more protective than Ajay. It's almost like they forget I'm twenty-eight now and don't need to be looked after. Not that I ever did. But I'll always be their baby sister.'

Miranda laughed. 'Believe me, I know what you mean,' she said with a wink.

'Anyway, I decided it would be easier if I stay at a bed and breakfast instead. It's only for a few weeks until I can find a short-term rental.'

'Way to go, Saira. You've come back a whole new woman,' Miranda said, patting her on the back affectionately.

'What do you mean?'

'You were always such a dutiful daughter, doing whatever your family told you to. It's nice to see you standing up for what you want.'

'Thanks, Miranda. I appreciate you noticing,' she replied in an amused tone. Same old Miranda, still speaking her mind with brutal honesty. It was wonderful. 'I'm not sure moving into a B&B is quite enough to warrant my being considered a new woman.'

'But you don't need to stay at a B&B. I'm sure we can find a room in one of the Haynes Hotels. Where is Nathan? Have you seen him yet? He'll be happy you're here. I know he'll help,' she said, turning towards the roof terrace.

'Oh, no, please. That's not necessary. I'm happy with the place I've chosen. Anyway, I want to hear more about what's been happening with you and I need all the details about your engagement.' Saira smiled at Steve. 'I'm sure I remember you saying you would never marry unless a prince came and swept you off your feet.'

'I think this is my cue to mingle,' Steve said, standing and giving Miranda a quick kiss. 'I'll try and waylay anyone coming in your direction. That way, you and Saira can have a proper catch-up.'

The joy shining out of her friend's eyes as she watched her fiancé walk away warmed Saira's heart. 'I'm so happy for you,' she said, blinking away unexpected tears.

Miranda beamed at her. 'I'm happy too. My parents' divorce pulled the rug out from under me. I didn't realise how much until I met Steve. I almost lost him because I was convinced love didn't exist.'

Saira reached out a hand. 'It sounds wonderfully romantic. Start at the beginning.'

Nathan loved his sister, but at times like this he could wring her neck. She was living in a fantasy world of blissful happiness and wanted everyone to join her in her bubble. Naturally, he would do what he could to make his sister happy, and it was simple enough for him to arrange a place to stay for Saira. But his preference would have been to keep his interactions with Saira brief and impersonal.

He'd done his duty when he welcomed Saira to the party. The only reason he made his way directly to her the moment he spotted her was that it was always best to get difficult situations over and done with. The abrupt end to their conversation was for the best, and he didn't have any inclination to speak to her again. If the tension in his jaw was any indication, he was still annoyed about the way things had ended, even if it had been eight years ago.

Life was good. His family were content. He had female companionship when he wanted it without any strings to tie him down. His business was more successful than ever and, if he were able to complete this latest project before Christmas, the Haynes Group would be the biggest developer of luxury eco-resorts in the world.

Saira was the only small blot on his horizon.

He'd contacted his executive assistant to book out a suite for her at his Haynes Mayfair, London hotel. Now he needed to seek her out to let her know. He supposed he could pass the information on via Miranda, but it would probably be easier if he did it directly.

He sensed the moment she came back out onto the terrace, his gaze automatically going to her. She was beautiful, framed by the lights strewn across the trellis. Tiny tendrils escaped from the mass of raven hair she'd swept into a knot, framing her oval face. Even from a distance he could see the skilfully applied make-up shadowing her features, emphasising her cheekbones. Had she had her make-up done professionally? The girl he had known never wore any, her fresh-faced complexion not needing it. But that was years ago.

The cocktail dress she wore draped over her curves, showing off her trim waist. For a petite person she had surprisingly long legs, their slim length displayed by the above-the-knee hemline of her dress. Red had always been her colour, the perfect complement to her golden-brown complexion.

She stood alone near the doorway, biting her lip and glancing around, not trying to make eye contact. 'Shy' wasn't a word he would use to describe her. She'd never had any problem voicing her opinions to him. But when they were younger she'd taken her time and let the conversation happen around her, observing people before she participated, and she probably didn't know many people at the party, which could explain her uncertainty.

He grabbed two flutes of champagne from a passing waiter and made his way over. Holding out a flute, he said, 'I've organised a room for you at our Mayfair hotel. You can move in whenever you're ready.'

'What do you mean?' she asked, gazing at him with curiosity in her large brown eyes.

'Miranda asked me to arrange a room at a Haynes Hotel. It's been booked for you,' he replied, checking his watch, then glancing around the room.

Saira sighed. 'Your sister doesn't know how to give up. I honestly didn't ask her to interfere. Thank you for going to all this trouble, but I already have a place to stay.'

'She said you aren't staying at your parents' flat.'

Saira nodded and explained her living situation.

'Are your parents still going out to Kolkata in time for Durga Puja, then?' he asked.

Her mouth broke into a wide, friendly smile. 'You remember?'

'I found it interesting you celebrate Durga Puja, not Diwali. I must have retained the fact.'

Her smile faded as she lowered her head. Was she disappointed by his factual response? She must know what they'd had was in the past, long buried.

'About the room,' he said, trying to end their conversation. 'It's all organised now. You may as well take it.'

'I don't need it.' Saira sighed again. 'I am grateful to you and Miranda, but it isn't necessary.'

His temple started to throb with irritation. He briefly squeezed his eyes shut and pinched his nose, then, giving her the tight but courteous smile he used during difficult business negotiations he said, 'Miranda asked me to do her a favour and I did. Maybe you should try convincing her you don't need it.'

Saira threw him an amused glance. 'Have you met your sister? You can't convince her of anything.'

His lips twitched involuntarily. 'Exactly, so you may as well give in gracefully and accept the room.'

'The path of least resistance?' She nodded. 'I see your point.'

'It would make her happy,' he added.

If Saira was at all like the person she used to be, she wouldn't want to disappoint her friend. He could tell she was weighing up her options. What would she decide, and why did he even care?

'In that case, I accept your offer of a place to stay. Thank you,' she said finally.

His smile was warmer as he handed her a business card. 'Call this number. My assistant will give you all the details.'

They stood next to each other for a few moments, not saying anything, avoiding each other's eyes. He glanced down—she was resolutely staring ahead. He followed the direction of her gaze to where his sister was laughing with a group of people, her fiancé next to her with his arm around her.

'They look so happy, don't they?' Saira said a little wistfully.

'Yes. Steve's a great guy. Still, I am surprised Miranda thinks she wants to get married.'

Saira expelled an exasperated-sounding breath. 'Well, of course you would be. I still remember your views on marriage. It doesn't sound like they've changed over the years.'

'No, they haven't,' he replied, his voice cold and exact. 'And Miranda used to share my views.'

'Perhaps Miranda's views have matured a bit since she was twenty,' Saira said.

She glared up at him, a glimmer of annoyance sparking fire in her deep, dark eyes. A brief smile touched his lips—it hadn't taken long for her to drop her polite veneer and let her acerbic tongue reappear.

'If you ask me, it's hope triumphing over experience,' he replied.

'Experience?' She gave a loud, disbelieving laugh. 'You mean your parents?'

'Not only them. I'm sure I don't have to tell you about the statistics for unsuccessful marriages.'

She narrowed her eyes. 'I'm guessing you haven't shared your opinions with Miranda? I mean, she still seems to be talking to you.'

'Of course I haven't.'

He couldn't and wouldn't say anything to convince Miranda not to get married. After the break-up of their parents' marriage they'd become disillusioned with the idea of happily-ever-after. Something had changed, and Miranda seemed happy now, but it had taken her a long time to find personal happiness. They didn't have any role models for a good lasting marriage, but perhaps Miranda and Steve would work at their relationship. All he could do was support her decisions and be there for her when it fell apart. The way he had been there for his mother each time his father had left.

He formed an image of his mother the first time his father had walked out. Nathan had been twelve. He'd returned home from school to find her lying in bed, unable even to get changed. He never considered his mother to be weak or dependent—her depressive state had come as a shock. He tried to protect Miranda from seeing their mother that way, making meals and helping with her homework until his mother slowly started trying to get back to normality—only for his father to waltz back into their lives as if nothing had happened.

That had started a pattern which would last for another ten years. His father would come home, only to leave when he inevitably got bored again. Each time Nathan not only had to pick up his mother but Miranda, and two younger sisters had also been relying on him, crying on his shoulder. He'd even decided to study at Oxford so he could be within a reasonable distance of his family.

The final time his father had left, emigrating to Australia with his latest girlfriend, Nathan had been in his twenties. It had been almost a relief when his mother had received the divorce papers—at least he wouldn't be back in their lives.

After seeing first-hand the damage his father's actions had inflicted on his mother, on his family, Nathan would never put himself—or anyone else—in that situation. He ensured his relationships were short-term, moving on before there was any emotional involvement. There was no promise of love. No fiction of happily-ever-after.

'Well, I'm pleased you're managing to hide your pessimism so well,' Saira said, interrupting his thoughts.

'I would never do anything to upset Miranda. I would do anything for my sisters.'

'I know. And you always go above and beyond. You gave her this engagement party,' she said, gesturing round the room. 'It really is amazing.'

And suddenly he watched the fight go out of her. She was once again a polite stranger, turning back to stare around the room, anywhere but at him.

He pressed his lips together. This chilly atmosphere between them wasn't ideal. Miranda hadn't set a wedding date yet, but Nathan had offered to pay for everything, which meant he would probably have some involvement with the arrangements. Now Saira was back in London,

Miranda would want her best friend to be part of the wedding preparations. Avoiding her wasn't a realistic or practical option, even though it would be his preference.

He closed his eyes briefly in resignation. He would do anything to ensure nothing spoiled his sister's happiness.

'Saira, with Miranda's wedding coming up, I'm sure we're going to see each other occasionally. Perhaps we should have coffee some time to talk…try to find a way to get past our issues.'

She looked up at him in surprise. 'You think we have issues left to resolve?'

'No, I think this awkwardness is perfectly normal for two people who pretty much grew up with each other.'

Saira raised her eyebrows at the clear sarcasm. Nathan had been polite and distant during most of their conversation. She'd assumed he felt nothing for her, but it sounded as if he was angry. That was crazy. If anyone had the right to be angry it was her. Clearly he was right—they did have issues to resolve.

They were interrupted by Miranda, who flung her arms round them both. 'Two of my favourite people right here. Together. Nathan, can you believe we have our Saira back?'

'Yes, it's great,' he replied. The lack of enthusiasm in his voice belied his words. 'Are you a bit tipsy?'

'No!' Miranda laughed. 'I'm so, so incredibly happy. I'm going to marry the best man in the world. I have the best brother, and my best friend is back in London. Could anything make this more perfect? I wish we had more chance to talk.'

'That's the problem with being the popular one,' Saira said, putting her arm round Miranda's waist. 'But don't worry. I'm going to be around for a while. We can catch up soon.'

'Not soon enough. Day after tomorrow, we're going to be away for ages,' Miranda said with a pout.

'Okay then, let's arrange a date for as soon as you get back.'

'No, I don't want to wait,' Miranda replied.

'There's nothing you can do about it,' Nathan said.

Miranda gave a moue of disappointment, then a bright smile crossed her face. 'Yes, I can,' she said. 'Saira can come with us.'

'I am not going on a romantic holiday with you and Steve,' Saira said, her voice rising in horror.

'It's not a romantic holiday. At least not for the first few days. We're going to one of Nathan's new resorts, with him and his uni buddies. It's a diving holiday. You should come along.'

Nathan's grimace was a clear indication he wasn't happy with his sister's suggestion. 'I still can't gate-crash,' Saira said. 'It's obviously been arranged for a long time. Besides, I don't know how to dive.'

'Neither do I,' Miranda replied. 'This is even more perfect. Now I don't have to be bored while the others do their dives. They go on holiday every year in September. It's not a special one-off event. And I need someone I can chat to properly. Some of the other girlfriends who go…well, the nicest way to say it is we don't have much in common. You'll be doing me a favour. We can catch up over cocktails at the beach and spend time in the spa getting mani-pedis or massages.'

'That sounds lovely, but it must be too late to get flights and rooms.' Saira silently appealed to Nathan for support.

'The hotel is booked up and all the huts we're staying at are already taken,' Nathan confirmed.

'Then Saira can stay on the pull-out bed in my hut.'

'I am not staying with you and Steve!' Saira protested,

laughing at Miranda's insistence. Her friend didn't know when to quit.

Miranda was quiet for a moment. 'Then she can stay with you,' she said to Nathan. 'You're between girlfriends, aren't you? You're not bringing anyone on this trip.'

Saira and Nathan exchanged glances.

'Please, Nathan,' Miranda implored.

'I suppose Saira could stay in my hut,' he said after a long pause, surprising Saira with his easy capitulation to his sister's request. 'I'll speak to one of the others, see whether I can bunk with them. We're only there for four nights anyway.'

'Then it's all settled,' Miranda said with satisfaction. 'I'm going to tell Steve the wonderful news.'

Saira watched as Miranda walked away. She turned to Nathan. 'Wow, your sister's still a bulldozer, I see.'

'Miranda likes being in control.'

'Really?' Saira smiled. 'Thanks for the information, pot.'

'What's that supposed to mean?'

'Being in control is a Haynes family trait.'

'I don't think that's a completely fair assessment.'

Saira sighed. She'd offended him. Would they ever be able to have a normal conversation? It was a good job she wasn't really going on holiday with them, even if it were practically possible.

'What are the chances of Miranda forgetting about this holiday?'

'None. You may as well start packing.'

Saira laughed. 'You're going away the day after tomorrow—surely there's no way I could get a plane ticket.'

'That's not a problem. I presume you have a valid passport?'

'Of course.'

'Then reconcile yourself to coming on this holiday.

When you contact my assistant, he can give you the full details of the flights and anything you need to know.'

Saira shook her head. 'I don't know if it's a good idea. Particularly if you're single. Miranda is so loved up she probably thinks we should be together.'

'Perhaps. But that's because she doesn't know.'

'Know what?'

'We've already tried that and failed. Twice.'

CHAPTER TWO

A HUT!

Saira couldn't believe Nathan had referred to this accommodation as a hut. The only similarity between her definition of a hut and the bungalow suites at the Haynes Malta Beach Resort was their construction material.

It was the kind of place that didn't need 'luxury' in its title. Even without the Haynes branding, the resort was a piece of paradise sprawled across a private island close to Gozo. Their accommodation, the Beach Huts, was a group of six bungalows set apart from the main hotel with their own private facilities.

It felt surreal that she was there. Life really did fall into place when you had almost unlimited wealth. Plane tickets weren't a problem when you owned a private jet.

Inside the bungalow there was a large bedroom with an en suite bathroom. The living area was spacious, with a comfortable-looking sofa and armchair, a small dining table and a fully stocked bar and kitchen area with a fridge, microwave and tea-making facilities. She walked towards the trifold windows at the back of the living space, which led to a deck with seating, a hot tub and plunge pool.

She exhaled, her shoulders loosening as she envisaged spending her time by the pool, sipping a glass of wine while gazing at the sparkling turquoise waters of the Mediterranean.

'I presume you expect me to be a gentleman and offer you the bed, don't you?'

Nathan's voice interrupted her inspection. Her shoulders tightened again immediately. The only slight cloud over this holiday was having to share the bungalow with Nathan. Unfortunately, since his friends had all brought their current partners, and neither she nor Nathan wanted to impose on the couples, they'd agreed to share his suite.

She'd tried to back out of the holiday, tried to persuade Miranda it was a bad idea. She'd caved under Miranda's insistence on wanting to spend time reconnecting with her friend—according to Miranda she would only be happy on holiday if Saira were there too.

If Saira was honest with herself, she was curious to discover how much Nathan had changed from the young man she'd known. It was for less than five days, after all. At least the sofa in the lounge pulled out into a bed, so there was no risk they'd have to share.

'No, I expect nothing from you, Nathan,' she replied, rolling her eyes before turning from the windows to give him a sweet, clearly false smile. 'I'm happy to take the pull-out. You're offering me a holiday, after all.'

'That was Miranda's idea.'

'I know, but you agreed. You didn't have to.'

Nathan probably didn't realise how kind he'd been—arranging somewhere for her to stay in London, letting her come on the holiday in the first place, even sharing his bungalow with her. Miranda had asked him so, as always, he'd gone out of his way to make his sister happy.

'I'm sure I could have stayed at the hotel,' Saira said.

'The hotel is a ten-minute drive from here and the facilities are completely separate, although we can use them. It's more convenient for everyone if you to stay here.'

She sank into the couch, then stretched her legs in front of her. Nathan was still standing near the entrance to the guesthouse, stiff and uncomfortable. She closed her eyes. She should have insisted she stay somewhere else. But it would have been difficult to refuse to share with Nathan without giving a good excuse to Miranda, who didn't know about their past relationship.

Saira bit her lip. 'I'm sorry, Nate. You won't be able to relax if we're sharing. I don't want to spoil your holiday with your friends. Perhaps I should stay at the hotel.'

There was an almost imperceptible sigh before he walked over to sit in an adjoining armchair.

'The hotel is at capacity. I guess we can make the best of a difficult situation,' he said in clipped tones.

'Ah, I forgot how much of a charmer you are.' She smiled brightly as he briefly pursed his lips, barely able to conceal his irritation.

'Well, pardon me for finding it awkward sharing a room with my ex-girlfriend.'

'Ex-girlfriend? Is that how you think of me?'

'I've barely thought of you since you ran away to America.'

Saira frowned. Ran away? That was a surprising choice of words. Did he honestly see what had happened as running away? She'd always been going to study in the States as part of her degree. Perhaps she had travelled abroad a little earlier than planned, when he told her there was no long-term future for them, but it had been the best thing for her to do.

'That was lifetimes ago,' she said simply, rather than indulging her curiosity by asking him to explain himself.

But he'd brought up their awkward situation again. And it was true. It *was* awkward, because nobody, including Miranda, knew about their previous relationship—or Saira was sure Miranda would never have suggested they share. There was history between them. They couldn't get away from it.

'Look, you mentioned we should chat, clear the air. Perhaps we should do that now.'

'Now?' he asked.

'It seems as good a time as any.'

'If you want.'

She closed her eyes and counted to ten, then counted to ten again. The entire time she'd known him it had never been about what *she* wanted. She expelled a deep breath.

'Saira,' Nathan said, breaking into her thoughts, 'this doesn't need huge introspection. We don't have to rehash every detail of our past. I meant we should acknowledge it, draw a line under it and move on.'

'"Past is prologue,"' she murmured.

'I don't think Shakespeare's relevant here. My priority is Miranda. She's been through a lot and I don't want anything to spoil her wedding plans. Let's be realistic. Miranda will want you involved with her wedding, probably in the wedding party. That means we need to get along somehow.'

'I agree. Miranda is our priority. But we can't pretend the past didn't happen. We were young, but we were together for a while, and neither of us can pretend it ended well. You even said at the party we had issues we need to resolve.'

'I didn't mean doing a forensic analysis going into excruciating detail. It's not necessary.'

She threw her hands up in exaggerated despair. 'Why am I surprised? It has to be your way, doesn't it?'

Nathan frowned. 'It's not about that. Tell me what purpose dredging through the past will serve.' He barely glanced in her direction.

'Well, how else do we resolve our issues?'

'Draw a line under them.'

'How do you suggest we do that if we don't talk about them?' She could hear herself almost whining in frustration.

'It's quite simple. We agree that the past is in the past. It has no bearing on what we need to do for Miranda's sake. Anything more is unnecessary. There's no need to blow this out of proportion.'

She was about to insist that discussing their past was a proportional response, then changed her mind. He wasn't going to listen. What was the point?

He continued, 'It was over between us a long time ago. You've been married since then.'

'And you've had a revolving door of relationships,' she bit out.

They locked eyes, neither willing to be the first to break the contact, not quite at war but in a battle for dominance. That was the only reason her breath was coming a little faster. Nothing to do with the sensation of drowning in deep blue eyes with hues rivalling the Mediterranean.

They were interrupted by Nathan's mobile. Glancing at the number, he apologised before turning his back on her to take the call.

'Sorry,' he said again a few moments later. 'There's something urgent I have to deal with. Can we talk about this later?'

'Sure.' It wasn't as if she had a choice.

He ran his hands through his hair, the only visible indication their exchange had affected him at all. 'I'm going to be working until lunch. My friends and I prefer to eat meals together when we're on holiday, because we've carved out this time especially to spend it together. After that I may need to do some more work, but I will make some time to talk later.'

Saira shrugged. She admired his dedication to maintaining his friendships but was still slightly disappointed he wouldn't stop working. He used to complain about his father never spending time with his family on holiday.

Besides, if Nathan refused to discuss the past fully what

was there left to talk about? But this wasn't the right time to go into it.

'Fine,' she said. 'Until we've had a chance to talk let's try to be on friendlier terms, particularly in front of Miranda. We don't want her to worry about us. Deal?' She extended her hand.

He glanced at her hand. His upper lip twitched, then he reached out to shake. 'Deal.'

Her hand was enveloped by his larger one, strong and firm. His nails were neatly manicured. She had always loved his hands. His fingers were long and shapely, almost artistic. She remembered his fingers running over the piano keyboard as he played a piece he'd composed. Those same fingers strumming her body, easily finding all the right notes.

Nathan tugged his hand. She released it immediately. How mortifying to hold on longer than necessary.

She stood and walked over to the windows, opened the trifold doors and stepped onto the deck. The warmth of the Maltese afternoon hit her strongly after the air-conditioned room, matching the heat in her cheeks.

She needed to avoid spending much time alone with Nathan. She was already staring at him far too often and he'd notice if she wasn't careful. He probably wouldn't understand that she was only searching for remnants of the young man she'd once known. This cool, detached man he presented to her, and to the world, was mostly a stranger.

She held a hand to her heart reflexively, experiencing a momentary pang for a lost love. It would be too easy to confuse the present with her memories of being nineteen again, experiencing the thrill of falling intellectually and passionately in love for the first time.

This wouldn't do. If she was beginning to relive emotions from a love affair that had ended eight years ago, it would be safer for her if Nathan remained a stranger.

Nostalgia wasn't welcome—for either of them. Too much water and all that.

He was right. There was no point raking over the frozen coals of their past. They never had a shared future.

She'd already decided to be independent. To focus on her career. Romance wasn't part of that. She'd returned to England so she could move on with her life. That life didn't include Nathan—not then and not now.

She stepped back inside as their cases were delivered. Nathan was working on his laptop when she took her case through to the bedroom to change. The flight had only taken three hours and, because they had flown in a private plane, they were able to land directly on the island's airstrip rather than flying into Malta then taking the ferry to Gozo and another boat to the island.

She still wanted to get out of the clothes she'd travelled in, which were better suited to the late-summer weather in England than the glorious temperature of the Mediterranean.

Checking her watch, she picked out a bikini and a simple sundress. There was still an hour before she'd agreed to meet Miranda for lunch. She would take her e-reader and sit by the pool, perhaps have a swim.

Nathan was still working, barking orders at someone down the phone, and didn't notice when she left.

She chose a lounger and started to arrange her things before being interrupted almost immediately by an attendant, who set up her sun lounger, laid out towels, adjusted the parasol and showed her a fridge with water and soft drinks. He handed her a cocktail and snacks menu before leaving her with a pager.

She wasn't sure if the high level of attention was because she was the only one out there. She had to admit she was looking forward to getting to know Nathan's friends—the people Nathan chose to have in his life. She had seen them on the plane but hadn't had the chance to talk to them.

Nathan and his friends were all exceptionally handsome men in their early thirties. The five of them were also wealthy and unmarried, so naturally they'd caught the attention of the press. A tabloid had noticed the five bachelors met regularly—once in September, for a holiday, and again in March for the Talbot family's Spring Ball. Their meet-ups gained interest because they were always with a new partner at each semi-annual event. Because of this, the media had dubbed them 'The Six-Month Men'.

Saira couldn't imagine starting a relationship with someone when you knew it was likely to end within six months. Either the partners foolishly thought they could change their man, or they were also only after something short term.

She'd never had a fling. She'd gone from her relationship with Nathan to her marriage. Perhaps she should add a fling to her list, now she was in control of her own decisions, no longer needing to account to anyone else.

She scrunched her nose. There was a lot to do to get her life on track—having a fling could stay off the list.

Nathan glanced at his watch. Four o'clock. Work had taken longer to deal with than he expected. Usually he enjoyed the intellectual challenge, finding solutions to intractable problems. But today it had been more frustrating than invigorating.

His satisfied gaze went around the fully serviced business suite he'd been using since after lunch. Nathan wanted his resorts to be primarily family-friendly places, to relax and unwind, but he ensured each one had a business centre for people to keep on top of work if they needed.

Nathan might not believe in love or want a family—he'd been told often enough he was too much like his father to take that risk—but his vision was to have resorts where all facilities were available. That way work would never be an excuse to stop anyone coming on holiday and spending time with the people they cared about. Unlike his own father, who had always managed to be dealing with a work crisis whenever they were due to go away. By the time Nathan's younger sisters had been born there hadn't even been any pretence his father would join them on their family holidays.

He grimaced. This annual holiday with his friends was a testament to the fact that people could make time if it was important enough. They all knew the pressures and burdens of running large organisations, but none of them wanted to be the kind of person who let his friendships fade because of work or success. So far none of them had failed to turn up for their annual September holiday.

He left the business centre and took a buggy back to the bungalows. The unexpected sight of Saira on a lounger by the poolside, surrounded by his friends, stopped him in his tracks.

He should have expected this. He didn't regret giving in to Miranda's request for Saira to join them, even if it meant sharing his accommodation. His sister's happiness at having her best friend around was evident—any uncomfortable moments he might feel were worth it for that alone. But he hadn't fully considered the interest Saira's presence would create. Of course his friends would remember her name from eight years ago, even though they'd never met her before today.

He stood at the side for a few minutes, observing the group. He barely noticed his friends' partners around the pool, his gaze invariably going to Saira. The shadows moving across her face threw her cheekbones into stark relief, emphasising her delicate beauty.

She laughed. His breath caught.

He remembered that laugh—would recognise it any-where…could pick it out in a crowd. It was deep, throaty, full-hearted. Over lunch he'd heard her quieter laugh, the one she used when she was amused but didn't want to bring attention to herself. But, although he listened out, he hadn't heard her other kinds of laughter. Like her in-fectious giggles when something punny tickled her, or her gravelly laugh, bordering on evil, when something was a bit naughty or risqué.

Was it possible to miss someone's laugh? He would go out of his way to hear all her different laughs. Which was ridiculous. Whatever they'd meant to each other was in the past and she meant nothing to him now. He always needed to remember that.

It didn't surprise him that she'd managed to captivate his friends. These men were like brothers to him. They supported each other and were always there for each other. He would trust them with his life.

But that didn't mean he wanted them interrogating Saira.

He walked over to the group. Almost immediately the others moved away, giving them privacy. Nathan frowned. He didn't want anyone reading into his relationship with her. Surely lunch had proved there was nothing between them—that she was nothing more than his sister's best friend, practically a stranger.

The only seat available for him at the table had been opposite her, but they'd barely interacted. She'd spent most of her time speaking with Miranda, answering questions from the others, not even glancing in his direction, and never making eye contact. Unfortunately, judging by his knowing smile his friend, Bastien Talbot, who had sat next to her, had caught Nathan staring at her.

'Is everything all right?' Nathan asked now, sitting

on the side of the lounger next to her so he could face her directly.

'Yes, it's been perfect. Really relaxing,' she replied.

He stared, transfixed, as she stretched. Her sundress was moulded to her body, damp from when she'd gone for a swim.

'How about you? Did you get your work done?'

He glanced away quickly. Had she noticed his appraisal? 'Yes, for now,' he replied. 'I'm hoping to finalise a few deals today, which means I won't be disturbed while we're diving. I'll probably have to work before and after dinner, though. Where are Miranda and Steve?' he asked, not seeing them round the pool.

'They went for a walk round the resort. I think they wanted to be alone.'

She gave him the barest hint of a wink, but the humour in her expression brought back memories of the way she'd looked when they were younger.

He smiled at her, not anticipating his visceral, yet familiar reaction when she beamed a smile in return. She was still a beautiful woman—he was having the normal reaction of a healthy straight male. That didn't mean there were any residual feelings between them.

For his sister's sake, and their own, they needed to find a way to put the past behind them—to make sure there wasn't any awkwardness between them when they were around other people. Only then would they be able to treat each other as casual acquaintances, the same way he treated all of his sisters' other friends. Forget they had ever been more to each other.

But that conversation wasn't going to be an enjoyable experience when Saira gave him the impression she wanted to dredge up and analyse their past in detail. As if she had no understanding of what her leaving him had done.

No. Rehashing their former relationship wouldn't help either of them. Some things were better left unsaid.

His lips twitched as he recalled her quoting Shakespeare. His mother loved her for sharing the same passion for the Bard as she did. Luckily Saira had promised never to copy his mother in naming her daughters after characters from the plays...

He mentally gave himself a shake. The names of her future children were of no concern to him.

'Are you all right?'

Her voice interrupted his thoughts. Her quizzical expression made it clear he'd been quiet for a while.

'Yes, I'm fine. We still need to find time to have that talk.'

'I've been thinking about this, and you're right.'

He raised his eyebrows at that unexpected response. 'You never think I'm right.'

'That's because you rarely are,' she replied with a smirk.

'What am I right about this time?'

'Our talk. I'm overcomplicating things.' She frowned. 'It's not like either of us has any lurking resentment about the past. We've both moved on so, unless there's something you want to bring up about our relationship, we can simply draw a line under it like you suggest.'

He stayed silent. He wasn't convinced she was accurate in her assertion that he didn't have any 'lurking resentment', but she was right—they had both moved on.

'Agreed.' He grimaced at the terseness in his tone. 'We're both adults and can be civil in each other's company.'

'Civil?' She sounded amused. 'We used to get on well. I was hoping we could at least try to be friends by the end of the holiday.'

Friends? He briefly considered whether a friendship with Saira was possible. Instinctively he knew it would be difficult. He was still experiencing some kind of attraction, but whether it was to the person she was now or a residue from their past he wasn't sure. And there wasn't any point delving into it. She was a marriage kind of person and he steered clear of long-term commitment. There had never been any future for them and friendship might cause lines to blur.

'Are you hungry?' he asked. 'I can arrange a light afternoon tea... I'll be honest, Saira. I don't know if we can ever be friends, but I don't want us to be enemies. A walk on the beach and something to eat while we have a quick chat will be a good way to start.'

Saira's furrowed her brow. She opened her mouth, closed it, then sighed. 'Sure. Give me a moment to change. I'm still damp.'

Her words drew his attention back to the lush curves of her figure in the sundress. His mouth went dry.

'Nathan?' Saira said in a confused tone.

He cleared his throat, prevented from saying anything when Bastien came over to let them know about a beach volleyball game being arranged.

'Saira and I are going for a walk,' Nathan said. 'I'll organise for some afternoon tea to be served on the beach for all of us and we'll meet you for that.'

'I'll join you in a bit,' Saira said, still giving him confused glances.

He watched after her as she walked away.

'So that's the elusive Saira,' Bastien said.

'Hardly elusive,' Nathan scoffed.

'You talked about her all the time but never introduced us.'

'We weren't together until after I left uni, so there was no opportunity to introduce you.' He glanced at his friend. 'And I didn't talk about her *all* the time.'

'Sure you didn't,' Bastien replied with humour in his tone.

'It doesn't matter—it's all in the past.' Where it had to stay.

'Really? Because the rest of us assumed she was out of bounds. But if she's not...'

Despite being fully aware his friend was goading him, he turned to stare at him. 'Don't you have a girlfriend?' he asked, raising an eyebrow.

'For now,' Bastien agreed. 'But who knows what the future holds?'

Nathan narrowed his eyes. 'Well, whatever the future holds, consider her out of bounds. For all of you.'

He walked off, sensing Bastien was grinning after him. He shook his head. It wasn't jealousy that caused his reaction. Saira was his sister's age. He was being protective over her. That was it. He had no other feelings for Saira. He never could.

CHAPTER THREE

WALKING ALONG THE beach with the sun starting to set and the waves crashing over her bare feet should have been incredibly romantic. Instead Saira was tense and uncomfortable. She glanced at the others playing volleyball in the distance, wishing she were with them instead.

She'd agreed to Nathan's suggestion expecting that drawing a line under their past relationship would put an end to the awkwardness. He was right. What good would bringing up the past do? She certainly had no desire to relive that embarrassment and heartbreak.

Apart from occasionally seeing each other for Miranda's wedding arrangements, they wouldn't need to be in each other's company. From his brief mention of her running away, she imagined their memory of what happened was at odds. Rehashing it would only make those occasions they did have to meet more uncomfortable.

Miranda had looked surprised and curious when they told her they were going for a walk on the beach. With hindsight, it did sound like a couple's thing to do. She didn't want anyone to get the wrong impression or speculate there was more to her relationship with Nathan.

While she had been lying by the pool earlier, Bastien had teased her about noticing some sexual tension between her and Nathan over lunch, commenting on their charged looks. Which made no sense. During the meal, whenever she'd looked in Nathan's direction—which had been more often than she cared to admit—he'd been talking to his friends or their partners. He hadn't looked in her direction. Not once. There had been no accidental meeting of the eyes, no longing looks.

There wasn't any sexual tension between Nathan and her. Tension, perhaps, but sexual? No way. Just because she found him incredibly attractive, and her eyes zoomed in on him even among a group of handsome men like his friends, it wasn't enough to create sexual desire.

She turned to look at Nathan, striding beside her in board trunks and a tight T-shirt which accentuated his chiselled biceps. Her heart accelerated. Her skin felt as if it was too tight for her body. She expelled a breath.

She was having a basic physical reaction to the presence of a gorgeous man. She should be relieved she could still experience that kind of reaction. She thought it had died when her husband did.

Attractive didn't equate to *attracted to* in her book. And Nathan definitely didn't have the kind of personality she was attracted to any more.

Nathan was the kind of person who couldn't help taking control. At lunch she'd watched as Nathan took charge of ordering the meals and organising the stay. Even among a group of alpha males he was dominant, the others happily deferring to him, although perhaps that was because they were staying at his resort.

She didn't want that.

Nathan was her past—from when she'd been young and shallow and cared about looks. As she matured, her preference had been for someone she had things in common with. Someone easy-going. Someone who considered her an equal—making plans with her, sharing decision-making. Someone like Dilip.

She stopped to gaze out over the ocean. It had been

two years since Dil had passed away. She missed him. But the pain was a little less sharp with each passing day. She needed to move on with her life. She was ready to move on.

Her first step had been returning to England. Now she wanted to be independent. She *needed* to be independent.

There was no time—no inclination—for a relationship. How could she allow anyone else in? Losing love was devasting and she'd experienced it twice. She didn't have the strength to risk her heart again.

She had no interest in any kind of relationship at all—not with alpha, beta or even omega males.

All she had to do was keep her body under control.

Despite their intention to deal quickly with their former relationship, they hadn't spoken much since they'd started walking. One of them needed to make the first move.

'You said a quick chat would be a good idea?' she began, not intending it to sound like a question.

'Yes. It sounds as though we're both on the same page, which makes it easier. Our priority is Miranda.'

She nodded.

'Few people know we were together. Nobody else needs to know. It was a long time ago and we were both much younger. It wasn't a big deal. I see no need to rehash what happened and the whys and the wherefores.'

Not a big deal? Wasn't that part of the problem—their past relationship might have been insignificant to him, but it had been a big deal to her.

'I see,' she replied. 'I've already said I agree with you. I don't see the point of this talk.'

Nathan took a deep breath. 'You may have said it, but you're still tense in my company and that's going to make the others uncomfortable.'

'I'm not,' she lied. 'Why would I be? As you say, it was years ago. I'm over it. I've been married since then. I think that makes it obvious it's in the past. And I was just one in a long line of women for you. Why would that make me tense?'

Nathan came to an abrupt halt and turned her towards him. Sensations ran through her body from the points on her upper arm where his fingers touched her.

'That kind of remark is what I mean. You make digs about my relationships. It suggests you're bothered.'

She laughed. 'I couldn't care less. Come on—it's not as if I'm the only person who comments on the longevity of your girlfriends. You and your friends are well known as the Six-Month Men.'

It had been easier to talk when they were side by side. Face to face it was harder to hide her feelings. She made sure to maintain a blank expression.

'I promise you, Nathan, we're on the same page. I may not be happy with the way we ended things, but I'm absolutely fine we did end.'

He narrowed his eyes. 'Are you sure?'

She laughed. 'Of course I'm sure. If you don't like me teasing you about the six-month thing then I won't. Past may be prologue, but it's still the past. Whatever happened between us then, now you're just my best friend's brother. Nothing more.'

He searched her face. She met his gaze unflinchingly. He gave a brief nod and they turned forward to continue their walk.

'Good,' he said. 'That's all settled, then.'

She breathed out. Her arms still felt the imprint of his hands. Was that normal when you felt nothing for a person?

Worried about the direction her thoughts were taking, she searched for a neutral topic. 'This is a beautiful place,' she said, before segueing into questions about his other resorts.

'What you're doing is amazing,' she said, after he'd described his new projects.

Although he'd spoken in brief, concise statements, she had sensed his underlying passion. She'd always admired his strong work ethic, his determination to succeed on his own terms, but she hadn't realised what a visionary he was, with his emphasis on ensuring his hotels were ecologically sustainable and researching carbon-neutral travel.

'Your family must be exceedingly proud of you,' she said without thinking.

He frowned, as if the thought never occurred to him. 'Only Miranda has visited any of the Haynes Hotels outside England. Mum won't travel, and Beatrice and Juliet prefer to go on holiday with their friends. I've offered them free accommodation for their friends too, but they like to be independent.'

She smiled at the contradiction he presented. He might be a hard-headed businessman, but he was also still the big-hearted, family-orientated person she'd once loved.

Miranda had told her that their mother was still somewhat of a recluse after her husband had abandoned her the final time, even though it had been over eight years ago. It was a shame she was missing out on experiencing her son's accomplishments.

Instinctively, Saira reached out to give him a sympathetic pat, but her hand had a mind of its own, coming to rest on the warmth of his hard biceps.

'What?' Nathan asked, his eyes boring down at her hand.

'Oh, nothing. Sorry.' She hurriedly removed it.

Turning too quickly, to avoid the intensity in Nathan's gaze, Saira tripped and face-planted into the sand. Warm hands on her shoulder and waist gently turned her onto her side, then her back, their touch heating her skin more than the sun. She blinked as his head blocked the sun.

'Are you okay? Nothing broken?' he asked, moving her hair behind her ears.

She would swear he was trying not to laugh.

She nodded. 'Fine.' She grabbed his arms for balance as she slowly sat up rubbing her forehead. 'I'm fine.'

'You should rest for a few minutes,' Nathan said. 'I'll help you back to a sun lounger.'

Their walk had brought them close to where their friends were playing volleyball. Near them was a seating area where the afternoon tea Nathan had ordered had been laid out.

Carefully he supported her to stand. Enjoying the secure and protected sensation of his arm round her shoulder, she resisted the urge to bury herself in his chest.

After he'd set her down on a lounger, Nathan brought over some drinks and a fruit platter. 'How are you feeling?' he asked. 'Still shook up?'

She shook her head. 'I'm okay. Not too bruised, apart from my dignity.'

His mouth quirked. 'Still not an athlete, I see.'

She laughed. 'No. I must have two left feet.'

'I wouldn't say that.'

'No?' she asked, tilting her head up at him.

'I've seen you dance.'

Heat filled her cheeks as her mind burned with the memory of the last time they'd danced. It had been her second year of university. They'd been back together for a couple of months. He'd completed an important deal and wanted to celebrate with an outing to an exclusive club. The kind of place Saira would never have got the chance to go in her ordinary life.

The sensuality of the music and their movements had swept them up in a maelstrom of passion which lasted throughout their journey back to his flat, leading them almost inevitably to the bedroom, where they'd made love for the first time.

Was he remembering too?

To dispel the memories she said, 'I haven't danced in years.'

'That's a shame. There's a nightclub that's part of the hotel. It's fairly popular. We should go.'

Saira cleared her throat. That probably wasn't a good idea. 'You have great friends,' she said, to change the subject.

'I do.'

'Not many people I know are still in regular contact with uni friends,' she observed. She'd lost touch with most of her friends when she'd emigrated to the States.

'Bastien makes sure of it. And I think it's important to spend time with people if you care about them.'

For a brief moment Saira wondered whether he was thinking about his father. He'd often complained that his father hadn't spent time with them, even before his parents' divorce. But this thaw in the frost between her and Nathan was still tentative. She didn't want to risk saying anything to ruin that.

'Are you still in touch with any of your gang from school?' she asked, instead.

'Of course. Most of them.'

'How are they doing?'

Saira was soon laughing as Nathan updated her, sharing amusing anecdotes and wry observations. This man, with his teasing wit and ready smile, was the one she remembered, the man she'd fallen in love with. His relaxed countenance was a refreshing and welcome change after his previous antagonism and, worse, polite detachment.

When they'd first met he'd been only eight and she had barely registered his existence. As she grew older, and her visits to Miranda's house became less frequent because of their different schools, he had been nothing more to her than Miranda's aloof brother. It wasn't until she was sixteen and he was eighteen, when one of her friends had started going out with one of his, that she started to see him in a different light. Then she had got to spend time with him in a more casual setting, with the two groups of friends hanging out together often. In experiencing his intellect, his humour and charm first-hand, she had lost her heart.

Watching him interact with his university friends on the flight, over lunch and round the pool, she kept catching glimpses of that carefree young man from years ago. These men were good for him. They brought him out of his head and into a happier frame of mind. She suspected they had a mutual effect on each other.

She had a momentary regret for what the two of them lost as a consequence of trying to be a couple.

After he'd told her they had no future together she'd needed a clean break. Across the ocean, it had been easy enough for her to keep in contact with Miranda while cutting ties with him. Perhaps that had been a mistake. With their shared sense of humour and similar outlook on the world perhaps they were meant to be good friends.

She sighed softly. There was no point thinking about what might have been. They'd already agreed to leave the past where it belonged and concentrate on how they would act in the future.

Easier said than done when her feelings were threatening to resurface—physical feelings of attraction. Not romantic feelings. Those were definitely in the past. Romance led to heartache, and she'd had enough heartache for one lifetime.

But it was strange to be so comfortable sitting next to someone, to be relaxed in their company but at the same time intensely aware of their slightest movement. And hadn't he checked her out when they'd all been talking by the pool?

There was silence between them now.

'I've organised some jet skis,' he said, breaking the quiet. 'They should be available soon. Have you been on one before?'

She shook her head.

'Do you want to try?' he asked.

'I would love to, but it may not be the safest activity for me to risk.' She laughed self-deprecatingly.

'I'm sure you'll be fine. But if you're worried you can ride behind me.'

She took a sharp intake of breath as she imagined sitting behind Nathan, his hard body between her legs, her arms wrapped securely round his waist.

To cool her thoughts, she took a sip from her drink and winced. 'Oh, brain freeze.' She rubbed her forehead where she'd hit the sand. 'Am I going to get a bruise here?' she asked, turning her face up to his.

'I don't think so.' He brushed a kiss against her forehead. 'To make it feel better.'

Her mouth fell open. It had been the lightest of touches but her heart started pounding. She took a couple of shaky breaths, tried to speak, but couldn't get words out. If she read his wide eyes and absolute stillness correctly, he was as shocked as she was by his action.

Before either of them spoke he was hailed by his friends to join them for a volleyball game.

'Are you okay if I go?' he asked, standing.

'Of course. I'm fine now.'

She watched him as he played, every motion precise and economical, but with a caged energy. Her eyes moved from his broad shoulders to the rippling muscles displayed when he spiked the ball. The fabric of his shorts did nothing to hide his taut backside.

Her body had moved into a heightened state of arousal. So she tore her gaze away from the volleyball game and stood up. A cooling dip in the Mediterranean was needed.

Alone in their suite after dinner, Nathan poured them both a soft drink. As Housekeeping had already converted the sofa into a bed, they took their glasses out on the deck.

It had been a surprisingly good day. After their rocky start, Saira was more comfortable in his company. Their agreement to be on friendly terms for Miranda was working and they'd gradually fallen back into their old mellow ways.

There had been nothing to hint at their former romantic relationship.

Apart from his brief, impulsive kiss on her forehead earlier.

He still couldn't explain what had caused him to do that—an unwelcome throwback to their past, maybe? By silent mutual consent, neither of them acknowledged it had happened.

Dinner had been a raucous occasion, full of laughter, when the conversation flowed easily and the topics had been diverse, causing some heated debates. Initially, as at lunch, Saira hadn't said much, but after a while she was happy to join in.

She'd been particularly eager to participate when his friends started gently ribbing him. Like theirs, Saira's teasing had been good-natured and she always took as well as she gave.

It was her teasing wit which had first drawn his attention when they were teenagers. In a large group she had never been one to make herself the centre of attention, but once he'd heard a few of her pithy observations he found himself listening out for her input, purposely drawing her into conversations when he could.

Without even trying, she'd always known exactly how to make him laugh, their sense of humour meshing perfectly.

She hadn't changed that much. Still cynical, sarcastic. Adorable.

He pressed his lips together. They'd agreed to draw a line under the past, but that would be hard to do if small actions were going to bring back memories.

Saira yawned, stretching her mouth wide. His lips quirked. She couldn't make it clearer she had no romantic interest in him. Apart from his sisters, no other woman he knew would yawn so inelegantly in front of him. But now his attention was focused on her mouth, on the tempting pout of her naturally full lips.

'I'm shattered,' she said, resting her head against the back of the seat. 'I could probably sleep for a week. But my mind is buzzing. I can't remember the last time I enjoyed dinner conversation like tonight.' Her eyes were dark and languorous. 'I know you have an early start for the dive tomorrow. Don't stay up on my account.'

He shook his head. 'It's only ten. I should probably check my emails before I go to sleep, but that can wait a few minutes. You should take the main bed tonight.' He held up a hand to stop her protests. 'It's easier for me if I work in the lounge and I don't want to disturb you.' Seeing she was still not convinced, he said, 'Or I could go to the business suite to work, if you prefer.'

She dipped her head in acknowledgement. 'If you're sure.'

He raised his eyebrows. 'That was easy.'

She twitched her nose impishly. 'I'm not going to fight too hard when someone offers me a comfy bed.'

'So your protests were only for show, then?' His lips quirked.

She shrugged.

They both smiled, their eyes meeting for a few moments before she glanced away.

Interesting. Why couldn't she maintain eye contact?

He stretched his legs in front of him, feeling more relaxed and content than he had in ages. Usually on these holidays he would work late into the night, even on the rare occasions when he brought a girlfriend with him. This time he would finalise a few details, then trust his team to deal with most issues—they could contact him if something urgent requiring his attention came up.

'Do you have any plans for tomorrow while we're diving?' he asked.

'Honestly, my plan is to do absolutely nothing while I'm here. I may book a massage or a treatment of some kind. The last few months have been quite hectic. Truth be told, even though your sister can be a steamroller sometimes, I'm grateful to her for inviting me on this holiday or I'd be rushing straight into job hunting.'

'Are you looking for an engineering job?'

'I don't know. I've only been on the outskirts of engineering work recently.'

'I can speak to Kent,' he offered. 'One of his companies is Calthorpe Engineering. His father runs it at the moment, but Kent's taking control soon, bringing it under his Calthorpe Enterprises umbrella. He may be able to help you with some leads.'

She said nothing for a few moments, her expression shuttered. Then, 'Thanks. I'll think about speaking to him.'

He narrowed his eyes. Why did he have the impression he'd offended her somehow? For every step forward they were taking, in many ways they were still on a knife-edge, and any wrong sentence could ruin the growing warmth between them.

To keep things light, he didn't delve into what caused

the shift in her demeanour. 'Why do you say you've only worked on the outskirts?' he asked.

'After we got married, Dilip wanted me to work for Shah Toys—his family's company. I joined the design and production teams, and did some consumer product engineering, but the work was quite different from my electrical engineering expertise, so I took a back seat. Besides, it's not like I could come up with new product ideas myself. I can create the necessary components, but what do I know about what games children like?'

There was some sadness in her voice when she mentioned children. Part of him wanted to ask more, but he didn't want to upset her—and, if he was honest with himself, he didn't want to hear about her marriage to another man.

'Anyway, enough about work,' Saira said. 'How did you get into diving and where are your favourite spots?'

He answered her, trying to make eye contact, but she continued to avoid looking at him directly even as she asked questions. He couldn't tell whether she genuinely wanted to know about diving or if she was trying to distract herself.

Did she feel the attraction he did?

It didn't matter if she did. They couldn't act on it. Shouldn't. Nothing had changed since they'd broken up all those years ago. He still couldn't offer her a long-term commitment and she was unlikely to agree to anything less. Any attempt to rekindle their affair would risk hurting her. Hurting them both. Again.

He openly studied Saira's profile as she sat in the moonlight, the reflected light glimmering off her delicately carved facial bones. Maturity had heightened her beauty. He'd always loved her face, but it was its expressive nature and the intelligence clearly on display which captivated him, not its bone structure.

Saira sighed deeply, looking over the faint lights to the horizon, reflected in the dark waters. 'This is the most beautiful view.'

'Yes, it is,' he replied, his eyes fixed on her.

CHAPTER FOUR

THE DAY HAD passed by in a haze of blissful relaxation by the pool. Now, after dinner, Saira went to her room, sorting through the borrowed clothes on her bed, trying to choose something to wear for dancing.

Dancing!

Apparently, the hotel nightclub was quite glamorous—the smart trousers and blouse she'd worn at dinner wouldn't be up to scratch. Not that the other women in the group had said so that blatantly. But they'd been quick in offering her the spare dresses they'd brought with them.

Who even brought spare posh frocks for a five-day diving holiday?

She grimaced. She was being uncharitable. All the women were kind and generous, and now she was spoiled for choice.

She picked up one of the dresses at random to try it on.

It wasn't the outfit. It was the idea of dancing. And Nathan. Mostly Nathan.

So far she hadn't seen much of him. She'd been asleep when he'd left for diving. More accurately, she'd stayed in the bedroom until she heard him leave.

By the time the group had returned from their dive she'd been waiting with Miranda at the bar, to make sure there was no chance she would be in the bungalow alone with him. Over dinner she'd taken a seat as far away from him as she could, short of eating at a different table. She'd stared in his direction more than she would like to admit, but any time he'd caught her eye she looked away.

There was no way she could pretend he didn't know she was avoiding him.

The previous evening, although their conversation had been friendly and fairly innocuous, she'd been more than aware of a simmering sensual tension between them. Or maybe it was only on her part, and she'd imagined the intensity in the way he stared at her.

Her mouth suddenly went dry. She licked her lips. Her libido had flared back to life in the worst circumstances. But it wasn't anything serious. It was a simple bodily reaction in the presence of a handsome man. That was all it was.

She sniggered. She was doing a pretty bad job of convincing herself that was all it was. It wasn't *any* man. It was Nathan.

All the Six-Month Men were without exception gorgeous, but whenever she was near one of them—nothing. Her body remained quiet. No, her body only reacted when she was with Nathan—the man who'd broken her heart. The man who'd told her there was no future for them.

Which wasn't a problem. She wasn't looking for a future with anyone. She was looking forward to a life of independence with a fulfilling career.

'Hey, are you decent?' Nathan called out from the living room.

'Just a sec,' she called back.

She took a few calming breaths, rubbing her hands down the sides of the mini dress she'd picked out.

Act normal, she instructed herself. *He's your best friend's brother. Nothing more.*

She left the bedroom. 'Hi, Nathan. Are people waiting for me?' She faltered at his dark, intense expression as he stood staring at her. With a nervous laugh, she asked, 'What's wrong? Is there something wrong with this dress?' She performed a twirl, feeling the skirt of the dress flaring off her legs.

'That dress is perfect,' he said, swallowing. 'You look beautiful.'

Her eyes widened. Beautiful? Her heart tripped. He used to call her beautiful back when they were dating. He was probably the only person in the world who would describe her that way. Cute, pretty, maybe attractive—not beautiful. It used to fill her with happiness…she'd taken it as a sign he must have feelings for her.

She mentally rolled her eyes at her youthful naivety. She wasn't going to make that mistake again. Nathan had made it clear he didn't offer love or marriage. Calling her beautiful was a meaningless compliment which he probably used with every woman.

She decided to keep things light. 'Thank you. You scrub up quite nicely yourself.'

An understatement, of course. His pale blue shirt, open at the neck, showed off the contoured muscles of his chest. She flexed her hand. Quickly looking round, she picked up her key card, needing to hold something to stop her reaching for him.

She fumbled with her dress. 'Of course this doesn't have pockets. And I don't have an evening bag. Maybe I should change into trousers. Do I need cash or can I charge things?' She was talking too much, trying to cover her nerves. 'Oh, we never discussed how we'd sort out the charges. Presumably it will be itemised, so we can sort it out at the end. Or should I keep a tally of—?'

'Saira,' he interrupted her.

'Yes.'

'I own the place. You don't have to worry about charges.'

She frowned. 'Are the others paying for their food and drink?'

He hesitated. 'No.'

'Hmm…why don't I believe you?'

'I don't ask them to pay anything.'

'I'm sure you don't. But I can pay my own way. I'm not trying to freeload here.'

'Nobody said you are.' He raised his hand. 'Come on, the others are waiting. We can talk about this another time. I'll have my key-card, so you don't have to take yours.'

'What about if I'm ready to leave for the night and you're still having fun shaking your booty on the dance floor?' She accompanied her words with a little shimmer.

He cleared his throat. 'Shaking my booty? Yes, of course. You know me so well.'

They laughed. If they could just stay in the zone of easy-going friendship, her life would be so much easier. She suspected there was little chance of that.

Music was thumping as they were driven in a golf buggy up to the nightclub. There was a queue outside, but she followed Nathan to the side door from where they were led to a hospitality room with a large window facing the dance floor and another door leading down to it. Being in a separate room, although the music was loud, they were able to chat comfortably to the people near them.

Soon most of the group were out dancing. The only couple left besides her and Nathan were otherwise occupied. She glanced at Nathan out of the corner of her eye. Was this awkward for him too?

To break the silence, she asked him about his diving plans for the next day. He moved closer to her, bending his head as she spoke. Her breath came faster at his closeness and heat rose in her cheeks. She barely heard his answer as memories of their nights spent close together crowded her mind.

His proximity was too much. It was pointless denying she was sexually attracted to Nathan. But she needed to be independent, not starting a relationship—or restarting one. Acting on that attraction would be the worst thing she could do. Wouldn't it?

She stood up abruptly. 'I think I'll join the dancing now.'

Nathan watched Saira leave, then followed her progress through the window as she made her way to Miranda and Steve. A little rigid to begin with, she gradually relaxed and matched the rhythm of the thrumming beats. She moved with the same sensual grace he remembered from their time together.

His eyes narrowed when he saw a man move up to her, trying to get her to dance with him. He pushed forward, ready to go to her, sitting back down when she laughingly fended off the man's advances.

He left the room, taking a vantage point on the sidelines. From there he would be in a better position to intervene if Saira, or anyone else, needed him. Rahul and Bastien joined him, trying to convince him to get on the dance floor, but he resisted, telling them he didn't usually dance—didn't usually go to nightclubs. But the real reason behind his refusal was the strength of his urge to get close to Saira, hold her, move with her.

Far safer for him to keep his distance.

He walked slowly round the nightclub, making sure Saira remained in his field of vision—in case she needed his help shaking off more unwanted attention.

He smiled as he glanced at his sister, dancing close to Steve. She looked so happy. The two of them were deeply convinced they were in love. Then his gaze moved to his friends, dancing close with their current partners. Any casual observer would also think those couples adored each other, but Nathan knew all his friends would have someone else in their arms in six months' time.

They were all honest. They weren't offering a long-term relationship. Love was an illusion and the people who believed in it only ended up getting hurt in the long run.

Instinctively, his gaze went to Saira. She did look amazing in that dress.

He joined his friends on the dance floor, deliberately positioning himself away from Saira, even avoiding having her in his eyeline.

He could admit it. He was attracted to Saira—physically. It wasn't anything to be concerned about. He'd been attracted to many women and not acted on it. He was in control of his sexual appetite. He could easily ignore this attraction.

Starting anything with Saira would be a monumentally bad idea. It would be going backwards, not forwards. She was love and marriage. He was sex and commitment-free fun. He'd been called cold, callous, heartless by previous girlfriends. He couldn't deny it. He was the way he was. And the way he was would break Saira's heart—while his would remain unaffected.

After the fourth woman had come up to him, trying to get him to dance with her, he went back to the private room. He wasn't interested in them. He wasn't desperate for sex.

A few minutes later, Saira came into the room to ask for the key-card.

'I'll come back with you,' he offered.

'You don't have to do that. Stay. Enjoy yourself.' She grinned, making him catch his breath. 'Keep shaking your booty.'

Someone sniggered.

'Stop calling it that!'

She gave him an impish grin.

He smiled back. 'Come on, let's go. We can ask the concierge to order a car back to the bungalow.'

Once outside, Saira stood staring at the lights separating the hotel grounds from the beach.

'It's so lovely here, Nathan. I'm quite hot after all that dancing. I think I'll get some fresh air before I head back. I fancy a walk along the beach.'

'All right. Give me a minute. I'll come with you.' He quickly arranged for a car to meet them at the beach restaurant, giving them a ten-minute walk.

They walked to the water's edge. Saira bent to take her sandals off.

'I love feeling sand beneath my feet,' she said with a sigh.

'I'm surprised you have the energy to walk after all that dancing,' he said, forcing himself to tear his gaze away from the slender length of her legs.

She grinned. 'It was so fun. And you. You have serious moves. I forgot.' She patted his arm.

'You attracted a lot of attention yourself,' he said.

'How do you know? Were you watching?' she asked with a laugh.

He cursed internally at what he'd inadvertently revealed. 'I saw somebody try to dance with you.'

She stood still, her frown visible in the moonlight. 'I was probably one of the only single women there tonight. Unfortunate. I may not ever want to be in a relationship again, but I don't fancy the idea of hooking up with a stranger I meet in a nightclub either.'

'You don't think you'll get married again?' he asked in surprise. She was only twenty-eight. It would be unusual for her to remain single.

'Never. All I want is to get a job and find a place to live. By myself. On my own. No marriage—not even a boyfriend.'

Nathan processed her words as they were driven back to the bungalow. Did she mean what she said? She wasn't interested in a relationship? That could change things.

He'd heard her shortness of breath, her small gasps at their slight contact on the walk and in the back of the car. There was an attraction simmering between them. He felt it. He could tell from her body's reaction she did too.

The question was whether they should act on it. Earlier he'd determined it was a bad idea. But after what she'd said, was it possible Saira would accept a brief affair—no emotions, no strings?

He would make it clear that was all that was on offer. He wouldn't make the same mistake he'd made before. They'd never properly discussed the future the last time—she'd still been studying, with a year abroad to come, and he'd been building a new business. There had been no need. But it hadn't been unreasonable for her to presume there would be long-term relationship—maybe even marriage.

After his father had left Nathan knew there was no such thing as love or happily-ever-after, and he hadn't wanted to give Saira any false expectations. A brief memory of her expression when he told her flashed before him. She'd looked...stricken?

He shook his head to clear the image. He didn't want to think about it. He didn't want to think about the past and its painful memories. He meant what he'd said their first day in Malta. He wanted to put their prior relationship behind them. If Saira could do the same—forget about the past and accept a short-term sexual relationship—then perhaps they could enjoy and explore the physical attraction shimmering between them.

It was worth taking the chance to find out.

Once back in their bungalow, Saira went straight onto the deck. She needed to get away from the intensity of Nathan's presence. At the edge of the deck she rested her hands lightly against the glass railing, desperately wanting to break the charged atmosphere between them.

She took a few steadying breaths, trying to get her thoughts in order. Her efforts were in vain when he came to stand next to her, making her pulse race.

Her mouth went dry. She swallowed.

What did he want?

The gentlest of touches against her neck, his thumb stroking her nape, caused sensations to tingle through her body, turning her breasts heavy and aching. His hand moved from her nape to her shoulder, turning her to face him, and his other arm encircled her waist.

She stared deeply into his eyes, helpless to pull away from their intensity. 'What are you doing?' she whispered.

'Can't you tell?' he replied, his head moving closer. 'I'm going to kiss you. Is that all right?'

An image flashed into her mind of them, when they were teenagers, sitting on a couch watching a movie. Did he even realise he'd used exactly the same words he'd said the first time they kissed?

She licked her lips, milliseconds before his mouth covered hers. His lips were soft, gently exploring her mouth, not urging but coaxing her response. She willingly returned the pressure, rediscovering his warmth.

It could have been seconds or minutes before she pulled away, burying her face in his neck. She didn't understand what was happening. Drugged by their kisses, she forced her mind to ignore the protests of her body and tried to think rationally.

She pressed the lightest of kisses on his neck, then pushed herself out of his arms. 'I think I need to go to bed,' she said, reaching up to run a finger along his jaw.

His hand trapped hers against his mouth planting a kiss against her palm. 'Go,' he said. 'We'll talk tomorrow.'

CHAPTER FIVE

THE NEXT DAY Saira decided to look around the main hotel rather than spend time with Miranda, lying by the tranquil marble pool in the resort spa. She didn't want to avoid her best friend—Miranda was the reason she was on this holiday in the first place, and they still had catching up to do—but until she'd worked through her own thoughts she couldn't talk about them with anyone else, and Nathan's sister was, unfortunately, the last person she could use as a sounding board.

Anyway, relaxation was unlikely while her mind kept replaying that kiss from the night before.

Was this how Sleeping Beauty felt after being awakened from her slumber by an amazing kiss?

Maybe it wasn't completely unexpected that Nathan should be the one to wake up this physical response which had lain dormant since Dilip died. Nathan was her first— her first kiss, her first sexual encounter, her first love. Dilip was her second. There had never been a third.

When she was sixteen, and had first got together with Nathan, at her insistence they'd kept their relationship a secret from everyone—her parents in particular. But there had been no excuse when she was at university.

At the time she'd justified it because Miranda had been dealing poorly with the break-up from her long-term high school boyfriend, not to mention dealing with the collapse of her parents' marriage. It would have been insensitive to flaunt their new relationship in front of her.

But if anything happened between her and Nathan now—if they *wanted* something to happen—she wasn't going to hide it from her friend. Which was an added complication. If they started something there might be unintended consequences for her friendship with Miranda. Not something she was prepared to risk.

There was clearly some sexual chemistry between them. But was it just the embers of an old flame brought back to life by their forced proximity? Or was there something new burning between them?

Although their break-up had been inevitable, perhaps she wasn't as reconciled to it as she had convinced herself. Maybe there *was* unfinished business between them. They clearly had differing views on how and why it had ended. Nathan claimed she'd run away, but to her he'd been clear he didn't believe in love or long-term, so what kind of relationship could they have had?

She'd agreed to draw a line under the past so they could be comfortable with each other when people were around. Could they maintain that decision if they gave in to their attraction?

The grounds of the hotel were breath-taking. It would take her days to explore the outside alone. She walked along the traditional Maltese limestone paths towards the sounds of laughter and splashing from one of the hotel's four pools, then walked round the perimeter towards the gardens, with their mix of Mediterranean and African flora. She looked out for the small details Nathan had mentioned, designed to support conservation and wildlife without being too intrusive in the lush surroundings.

He'd accomplished so much in such a short time frame—less than ten years since he started his company. Would he have been as successful if they had stayed together? She laughed humourlessly. There was no realistic chance they would have stayed together all these years. Their relationship had been as time-bound then as all his relationships in the intervening years.

Years ago she'd dreamed of a future with Nathan—getting married, having children, growing old together. Then he'd made it clear he didn't see their future the same way. He wasn't offering marriage or children.

The irony was if they got together now they would be on exactly the same page.

She paused, arrested by the scenario forming in her head. Perhaps she'd dismissed the idea of a fling too hastily.

She'd loved Dilip, still grieved his loss. She wasn't looking for a husband or even a relationship. She had buried her dreams of having a husband and a family when Dil died.

But she was only twenty-eight. Had she assumed she would remain celibate for the rest of her life? Was it time for her to come out of her protective bubble and live a little? Perhaps a brief time-limited fling was exactly what she needed. There was no way she could deny the physical attraction between her and Nathan. She would be able to get him out of her system once and for all.

Restarting her career and finding a place to stay was her priority, so she could finally be independent. But as a modern independent woman surely she could own her sex drive. Instead of fighting the physical attraction she could give in to it, explore it. Without worrying about emotions.

She was so used to doing what was expected of her, trying not to disappoint anyone, even hiding her relationship with Nathan in case it caused problems in her family. Now, for the first time in a long time she could do what she wanted—have some fun. A short-term affair would be a perfect symbol to remind her that she was in control of her own destiny. Having an affair with Nathan would bring them full circle.

Although in the past she'd never had sex without having romantic feelings for the person, that didn't mean she couldn't try now. And it wasn't as if she was completely detached from Nathan. She admired him more than anyone else she knew, and she could acknowledge there were some lingering feelings.

But she needed to be careful. Could she maintain a sex-only relationship with him? It would be so easy to fall for him again... Although that was unlikely when they only had three days of holiday left.

The more she thought it through, the more she was convinced. If they took this physical attraction to its logical conclusion they could keep their past relationship where it belonged and find a new way to get along for Miranda's sake. These few days on holiday would be the perfect opportunity to indulge in a brief, intense fling.

Grinning at her bold decision, she hurried back to the bunglow.

The bungalow was empty when Nathan returned from diving. There were no messages from Saira. Hopefully she wasn't avoiding him.

Her reaction to him last night proved there was still something between them. There was unfinished business, but it was physical attraction only. Saira wasn't a young girl any more. If he suggested a brief sexual relationship, she might be open to it.

He should have spoken to her before they'd kissed. He'd meant to, but he hadn't been able to resist her as she stood against the railings with the moonlight reflected in her eyes.

This afternoon, though, they would have the conversation.

He grimaced. He hoped he hadn't given her the wrong impression. He didn't want to hurt her ag—

He deliberately turned his thoughts away from examining the past too closely.

They would both have to forget about whatever had happened in the past if they wanted to indulge their physical attraction and finish this thing between them once and for all.

By the time he'd showered and changed into cargo shorts and a blue polo shirt Saira had returned. If he'd expected her to be shy or awkward after their kiss, he was wrong. Her radiant smile when she saw him caused a strange pull inside his chest.

She sat down, putting her legs underneath her.

He gave her a brief account of the dive in answer to her questions, then asked, 'What about you? What have you been up to?'

'I've been having a lovely relaxing day,' she replied.

Her short sundress rode up her legs, exposing her shapely thighs as she stretched luxuriously. His gaze wandered along the length of her body. He swallowed. If everything worked out as he wanted he would be able to run his hands over the same path his eyes travelled soon, but they needed to talk first.

Cards on the table was the best policy.

'Do you have any plans now, or would you like to go for a short ride?' he asked. 'I have a beach buggy ready. There's a place I'd like to show you.'

'Sounds lovely. I'll put my bag away and be right with you.'

He drove her quickly round the main resort area, pointing out the facilities and a few areas of ecological and geographical interest, then drove the buggy to a secluded cove away from both the main hotel and the bungalows.

'This place is amazing!' she exclaimed, taking in the

view of pristine white sands as she got out of the buggy. 'I didn't read about this on the website.'

'It's my personal beach. Guests aren't permitted to come here.'

He took a beach blanket, a parasol and the picnic basket prepared by his staff out of the buggy. As Saira wandered down to the water's edge he set things up on a shady area of the beach, protected from the wind.

As she turned back to him her intake of breath was noticeable, and he gazed at the scene, trying to see it from her perspective. There was an obvious intimacy in the way the parasol had been set over the blanket, made more romantic in the light cast by the lowering afternoon sun.

'Come over here and have something to eat,' he said, patting the blanket next to him.

She gave him a weak smile and said, 'This is absolutely delightful. Thank you so much for this. I'm so grateful to you for taking the time.'

Nathan's lips twitched and he bit his lip. 'You're using that voice again.'

'What do you mean? What voice?'

'The one from a Noel Coward play.'

Saira laughed at the description, relaxing slightly. She sat down on the blanket. 'I'm a little bit nervous,' she admitted, spilling some of her drink as she reached to take a glass from him. She rolled her eyes, shook her head. 'Oops!'

He smiled, taking the glass back from her. Apart from when she was doing sports, she was so poised and graceful. She looked beautiful, sitting under the parasol with the sun casting arresting shadows across her face.

He leaned over to brush his mouth against hers.

Heat flared between them, their mouths and tongues meeting in a reciprocal thrust and parry. He covered her body as she lay down, her arms encircling his shoulders, pulling him closer.

He kissed his way along her jaw to her ear, nibbling gently before continuing his path down her neck. His hand slid along her legs to her hip, skimming the soft, smooth skin of her waist, resting briefly on her stomach, before moving to the hem of her sundress.

Suddenly he became aware of their surroundings. He moved away from her, trying to get his body under control. The attraction between them had always been strong. He'd never been able to resist her. But they had to talk first. He had to make sure she understood what the situation was—make sure that they both knew where they stood.

'Why is this happening?' she asked as she sat up.

He lay back on the blanket. 'It's simple. We're still attracted to each other,' he replied.

She nodded. 'Yes. But sex was never the problem between us.'

His body reacted under the intensity of her gaze as it travelled along his hips and chest to his face. Their eyes met, heat immediately flaring between them again.

'No, it wasn't.' There was no denying that physically they had always been in tune.

They were silent for a few moments.

'So, what do you want to do?' she asked.

'What do you mean?'

'What were you thinking would happen between us now?'

He sat up and reached out for her hand. 'You know I'm attracted to you. I want to make love with you. But I'm not going to lie and say we're together for ever from now on. I'm not offering anything more than a brief affair. I may hate being called a Six-Month Man, but it's true. I don't do long term. I don't do marriage. Even six months is probably stretching it. But I won't offer anything more. I don't want any false expectations.'

She blinked. 'So I shouldn't bother buying any bridal magazines? Well, thank you for being so frank.'

'I've learnt it's the best way,' he replied, ignoring her sarcasm. 'I don't want anyone claiming I led them on. Nobody gets hurt.'

The worst situation was when someone believed they had fallen in love with him. He usually made sure he got out before that could happen.

'Oh, don't worry. I think you've made it quite clear, on a number of occasions, there is no future here. I'm under no illusions about that.'

She pulled her hands away, hugging her legs to her chest and resting her chin on her knees.

He narrowed his eyes. Where was this bitterness coming from? Was she talking about the past? It didn't matter. It was pointless going down that path. They needed to agree on whether they would have a brief affair now—not discuss what had happened before.

He frowned. Would she expect them to rehash their past before they had an affair? It wasn't something he was prepared to do.

'I'm not going to seduce you,' he said. 'If you are happy to see where this attraction goes, that's great. If you prefer not to then that's what it is. I want to be clear up front that all I'm offering is a brief affair.'

She was silent a few moments, then she nodded. 'You're right. I'm sorry. It's good to set out the limitations from the beginning so we don't have any expectations. Like I said last night, I don't want a relationship. I'm not looking for love or romance. But I'm only twenty-eight. I don't have to be celibate for the rest of my life. I'm in control of my sex life.'

She sounded as if she was convincing herself. But if

thinking out loud was helping her decide to agree to their affair he wasn't going to interrupt.

'And you're the best person to have a fling with,' she continued. 'You'll have no expectations from me either. All you want is sex. And that's all I want too.'

They were exactly the words he wanted to hear. So why was there a sensation in his chest as if he'd lost something special?

'And what's a sun and sea holiday without sex?' she asked with a laugh.

Nathan tilted his head. He hadn't thought about how long their affair would last. He was offering her a brief affair, but he hadn't quantified what 'brief' would be—he was happy to let their relationship run its course. Because all his relationships naturally ended after a few weeks or months. Either he got bored or he began to suspect the woman was developing feelings for him. That could be the only reason he hadn't thought about an end date with Saira. But perhaps limiting the duration was something to consider.

'Do you want this to be a holiday fling? Does setting an end date make a difference?' he asked.

'It does. I never liked lying to Miranda about us. But I'm not sure if she'll understand this is just a fling. She'll probably think we're a couple, and then there's the worry we'd end the affair in a bad way, which would complicate the wedding plans.' She laughed. 'I mean, Nathan, the whole point of us drawing a line under the past is so we can get along for Miranda's sake. I think we need to agree to an end date now.'

He frowned as various scenarios went through his mind. She was right. There was a risk they could ruin any prospect of a cordial relationship in the future by indulging in an open-ended affair. It wouldn't be a problem for him. Sex was sex. It didn't matter whether he slept with someone once or thirty times—he never got emotionally involved. He wasn't capable of those big all-encompassing emotions like love. His heart was quite safe. He made sure of that.

Was Saira's? She claimed to be open to a sexual fling, but she was a loving person. Even though she'd left him behind without a backward glance all those years ago, he knew she'd cared about him then. There was a risk she would start to care about him again, want more from him than he would give. He couldn't take that chance.

Perhaps starting anything with Saira was a bad idea, given their history. Unless... Unless they agreed from the outset that their affair would end with the holiday. That way there would be no need for them to discuss the past at all.

He smiled, reaching out for her hand, running his thumb across her palm. The sharp intake of her breath confirmed his thoughts. Their attraction was strong. Better to keep their fling short and sweet. For her sake.

'I agree we should set an end date,' he said.

His eyes gazed down the length of her body. Three nights was short, but he had no doubt the time they had would be amazing.

He waggled his eyebrows in an exaggerated gesture. 'But aren't you worried? We're only here for a few days. You may not be ready for the sex to end so soon.'

'I don't know...' she teased with a wink. 'I don't remember the sex being that good.'

'I'm happy to give you a reminder.'

They'd gone from serious to light-hearted so quickly. With anyone else he would have found the changing moods frustrating, but he enjoyed Saira's unpredictability. It kept it him on his toes. He found it challenging rather than irritating.

'All right,' she said quickly.

'All right, what?'

'All right, a brief affair or fling while we're on holiday. Then we're back to real life and you're only my best friend's older brother. That works for me. Let's do it,' she said, groaning as he laughed at her unintentional double entendre.

His laughter faded as they stared at each other. She started to move her head but he cupped her chin, turning her towards him, running his hand along the soft, warm skin of her forehead, down her temple, gently moving strands of hair behind her ear before cupping her cheek, caressing her open lips with his thumb, feeling her breath warm against its tip.

He leaned in, replacing his hand with his mouth. She reached up to cup his neck, bringing him closer. Moments later he pulled back. He didn't want to make love to her on the beach. It sounded romantic, but the sand was probably uncomfortable.

'Hold that thought,' he said with a shaky breath.

Her forehead crinkled with confusion.

'Later,' he promised.

'Later,' she repeated, nodding.

She gazed out across the sea, a variety of emotions playing over her face. Then she turned to him with a wide smile.

'So what's in the picnic basket?' she asked.

The sofa bed wasn't made up when Saira entered the suite after dinner. She gulped. She was glad Nathan wasn't with her. Could he have told Housekeeping not to bother? That would have been an interesting conversation.

It was awkward, obsessing over what would happen next. Should she get into bed and lie there waiting for him? She'd never had an affair before. Was there an accepted etiquette for this situation?

Too wound up even to think about going to bed now, she walked out onto the deck. Would it be pure indulgence if she turned on the sunken hot tub? She checked her watch. It was only ten. She didn't know how long Nathan would be. He was enjoying a game of pool with the other Six-Month Men—it would have been too obvious if he'd been the only one of them to turn down a game.

She decided to change into her bikini, then enjoy a glass of wine while soaking in the hot tub, taking in the view of the starlight reflected in the Mediterranean.

Moments later, refusing to think any more about the future, Saira laid her head back, closing her eyes to indulge in the sensations as the bubbles gently burst around her. Whether it was the balmy night air against her heated cheeks or the soothing warm water lapping against her sensitive skin, images flooded through her mind of the times she and Nathan had made love in the past, making her whole body tingle and her breath come faster.

She didn't know how long it had been before her eyes opened as she heard a sharp exhalation.

Nathan stood on the deck, boldly staring at her as she lay in the water. Every nerve-ending fired into life under his intense scrutiny. She gulped, trying to take in the oxygen that had deserted her, her breasts heavy with anticipation.

As Nathan stalked towards her she slowly climbed out of the hot tub, neither of them breaking eye contact. He bent to capture her lips, one strong hand cradling her neck, angling her head for better access, while he ran warm, sensuous caresses along her spine to her rear.

The cool night air against her damp body was warmed by his strong persuasive hands, combining to cast a seductive spell she had no power to resist. As the ground moved from beneath her she instinctively wrapped her legs around his waist. He carried her as far as the outdoor seating area before sitting down with her straddling him.

'I'm getting your clothes wet,' she said, in between deep, intoxicating kisses.

'Help me out of them,' he said, leading her hands to his shirt buttons.

He kissed along her neck as her fingers explored more of his skin with every button she undid. She leaned back to enjoy the sight of his broad chest, unable to resist the urge to let her lips and tongue follow where her hands had led.

With a groan, Nathan ran his fingers through her hair, stopping her exploration so he could bring her mouth back to his. His thumbpad flicked over her hardened nipple, causing her a momentary recollection that her bikini top had been removed.

Her hands were reaching for his waistband when he covered them.

'Wait,' he gasped.

She growled. 'Please don't ask me to hold this thought again.'

'No.' He spoke in between more kisses. 'But I don't have any protection here.'

'What? At the resort?'

'Out here. But there's some in the bedroom.'

She sat back, panting, taking in their half-naked bodies. 'Let's go, then.'

CHAPTER SIX

IT HAD BEEN over a month since Saira had returned to London—the weeks had flown by.

Her short holiday had been perfect. She'd spent her days catching up with Miranda—loving the chance to reconnect with her best friend—and the evenings had usually been spent as a group, eating and chatting. But the nights had been filled with Nathan. With intoxicating kisses, long, languid explorations of each other's bodies, and deep, passionate lovemaking.

After they'd returned from Gozo they initially stuck to their decision to end the fling. A week later she had met Miranda and Steve at a bar. Nathan joined them. He offered to see her home. She invited him in for a drink.

He'd left the next morning.

They hadn't discussed what this continued affair meant. They should have been sensible and set an end date. She hadn't exactly signed up to this modern, short-term, no expectations relationship. Not that it *was* a relationship. More a series of one-night stands.

Which suited her perfectly. She didn't want any kind of real relationship. Her future didn't have to be lonely, but she didn't need a man around to make her life complete.

Their fling would end sooner or later. The only reason it hadn't yet was because they were both so busy they hardly got a chance to see each other.

Her days were filled with job hunting and flat hunting. She was ready to move out of the hotel and into a place of her own. Not that she had any complaints with the place Nathan organised for her. Far from it. She'd been expecting a standard room, but he'd arranged for her to have one of the best suites. Only the Royal and Presidential Suites in the hotel were more magnificent.

She would never get used to the breath-taking views of Green Park from her living room, or to opening her bedroom curtains to see Buckingham Palace. There was also a separate dining room, kitchenette, study and second bedroom. It was the most opulent setting she ever experienced, even after the luxury of the Haynes Malta Beach Resort.

Her lips twitched as she recalled his response to her offer to pay for the suite, when he'd quoted from Chapter Seventeen of the *Bhagavad Gita* on gift-giving without expectation at the right time in the right place to the right person, using her own words against her.

Sometimes, though, she wanted more than meals out or hotel food, no matter its Michelin star quality. The kitchenette was fine for preparing simple dishes and snacks, but designed primarily for caterers to warm meals—she couldn't cook from scratch in it. So she'd started going to her parents' flat to cook proper meals.

Saira kicked off her shoes and took the curry she'd made that afternoon at her parents' into the kitchen. She would have a long soak in the bath, followed by dinner with a movie.

Her phone pinged while she was putting the food into the fridge.

I have theatre tickets for tonight. The theatre's in Victoria. The car will collect you at six pm.

She shook her head at Nathan's text. They hadn't discussed getting together that evening. Did he expect her to be available at his whim?

In many ways it was like when she'd been at university, only back then half his texts had been cancelling on her. This time *she* would be the one changing plans. Not that it even was a plan, when it had been arranged last minute with no input from her.

She texted back.

Sorry, I'm staying in tonight. Hope the ticket doesn't go to waste.

If her days were busy, her social life was more hectic than it had ever been. On the evenings she wasn't with Nathan she was spending time with Miranda, or with her older brother Ajay, his wife and children. Occasionally she met up with people she'd lost touch with when she'd lived in the States.

With Nathan travelling a lot for work, they only had a few opportunities during the week to see each other. And when she and Nathan did get together he always wanted to be out doing something—going out for dinner, to the cinema, to plays or the opera. Always places where other people were around. It was as if the only time he could be alone with her was when they were in bed.

Spending time with Nathan in bed was always wonderful. Whether their lovemaking was soft and slow, or hard and fast, or anything in between, their bodies were perfectly in tune. So why was she not content?

Because she missed talking with Nathan—missed the old certainty that their minds were as attuned as their bodies. They didn't talk about anything deep or meaningful now. Although drawing a line under the past had been a good plan for their getting on for the sake of Miranda, or even indulging in a holiday fling, it would be hard to avoid mentioning their former relationship if they did start having proper conversations.

Until they discussed what had happened between them before she'd left for the States there would never be closure enough for them to have a future together.

She rolled her eyes. There *was* no future for them. Nathan had been clear eight years ago, and again when they were in Malta. And it was the same for her. She hadn't changed her mind. Being independent was still her priority. She didn't want a future with Nathan or anyone else.

She had to stop wondering what might have been and accept the reality she was in. Stop caring. Stop developing emotions. Steel her heart. That way she would never have to experience the pain of loss again.

With a sigh, she went to run her bath, poured herself a glass of wine, then chose a book to read while she soaked.

She was warming her curry bowl in the microwave when the bell rang. She frowned. The butler hadn't phoned to announce he was attending or sending anyone up to her suite. She glanced down at the polar-bear-covered flannel pyjamas she'd changed into after her bath and shrugged. She was comfortable and couldn't be bothered to change to answer the door.

Her eyes widened when the peephole showed Nathan standing outside. 'Didn't you get my text?' she asked as she opened the door.

Instead of replying straight away he glued his eyes to her pyjamas. 'Cute,' he said, bending to kiss her cheek. 'Yes, I got your text. Is everything okay?'

'Fine.' She walked back to the kitchen as the microwave dinged. 'Come in. I'm just about to have dinner.'

He stood near the kitchen door sniffing the aromas. 'Smells wonderful. What is it?'

'Chicken curry and saag aloo with rice.'

'From the restaurant? Or did you order a takeaway?'

'I made it.'

'You? Really?'

'Don't sound so surprised. I can cook.'

'Hmm…this I have to see. I haven't eaten yet. Is there enough for me? I could order room service if not.'

'There's enough for you, but what about the play?'

'I had my assistant return the tickets. Which reminds me…' He reached into his pocket and pulled out an envelope. 'I managed to get tickets for that Shakespeare play you mentioned.'

'The Indian adaptation of *The Tempest*?'

Saira stared at the hand holding out the ticket. She couldn't believe he'd gone to so much trouble. She'd mentioned the play in passing, as something she would have loved to watch, but performances had been sold out for months. It wasn't only his kindness and generosity in getting hold of the tickets, but also his thoughtfulness in remembering her throwaway comment. Could it mean he cared?

'Are you sure there's nothing wrong?'

Nathan's voice interrupted her thoughts. She shook her head and gave him a quick smile. 'Oh, sorry. There's nothing wrong. I'm tired and fancied a night in. I'm going to eat and watch a film.'

'All right,' he said. 'That sounds good.'

She watched as he took off his jacket and tie, then loosened the top button of his shirt. She wasn't sure about this. Only moments before she'd been complaining to herself about them always going out, but the alternative of them spending the evening in together was almost too intimate…too much like normal couple behaviour.

'Saira?'

'Sorry, what?'

'I asked if you want something to drink?'

'I already have some wine on the go. Would you like a glass?'

He efficiently prepared trays with cutlery and drinks while she plated up their meals.

'Are you sure this is okay? You don't have to stay here because I want a night at home. I don't mind if you want to leave.'

He smiled. 'And miss out on this food? Not a chance. Come on, let's watch.'

The sounds of pleasure he made as he ate were gratifying. Something about him eating a meal she'd cooked made her wish again for the kind of relationship which wasn't on offer.

She pressed play on the remote.

'Wait a minute,' he said when the film began.

'What?'

'Are you making me watch a romcom?'

'Hey! Part of the deal of you eating my food is you don't get to comment on my film choices.'

'Fine.' He grinned. 'At least the food is delicious. If I'd known you could cook like this I would have hired you for one of my restaurants.'

She rolled her eyes. 'You couldn't afford me. Now, shush, I need to concentrate.'

They ate in companionable silence. When they'd finished she scooched back to lean against the sofa, slipping off her slippers and curling her legs under her. Nathan carried the trays back to the kitchen, then returned to sit next to her, putting his arm round her shoulders. She lifted her face up to his and he dropped a kiss on her mouth, then they turned back to watch the film.

At the end of the film Saira stretched, a huge smile across her face—which faltered slightly when she met Nathan's gaze.

'What?' she asked.

'Nothing,' he replied with a shake of his head and a small smile.

Saira rolled her eyes but didn't say anything. In the past she'd often caught him looking at her rather than at the film. He'd said he loved watching her reactions as she watched.

She frowned. She should have realised memories of their time together would surface if they did the same activities. It was a big mistake, spending the evening in with Nathan. Far safer to be out on dates where there was inevitably a distance. He'd had the right idea all along.

She glanced at the time. 'It's half-nine—I suppose you have to leave now? Busy day tomorrow.'

'No, I don't have to rush,' he replied, resting his hands behind his head and leaning back. 'My first meeting tomorrow is near here. There's a documentary I'd like to watch. Do you mind?'

She shrugged, then handed him the remote control.

Nathan flipped through the channels. 'Ah, here it is,' he said.

He stretched out his legs on the footstool, then patted his lap—his old signal for her to place her legs over his as they curled up together to watch the screen.

Her breath caught. This was too much. Too evocative of their past.

Frustrated with herself for being overly emotional and contradictory, she gave herself a stern talking-to. She needed to keep their relationship strictly sexual. It was a bad idea to revive old feelings that were supposed to be dead and buried.

They'd been together only a few weeks. She didn't know how long it would be before he became tired of her and it didn't matter. Any amount of time was long enough to run the risk of her feelings growing deeper. Emotions were already surfacing. Maybe the sensible step would be to end this now.

But he had bought tickets for the play she really wanted to see, which was only a month away. It would be rude to end things before then. And the sex was great. And, overall, she was enjoying her time with him.

It was only another month. A month would go by in a flash, and they'd probably only see each other once or twice in that time. What harm could come from that?

She would be fine as long as she kept reminding herself this was a short-term sex-only thing. She was sensible— she would make sure she didn't develop deeper feelings for him. She wouldn't get hurt—not this time.

She been hurt so many times already, and experienced so much loss with Dilip's death, and then her—

She mentally shook her head. She didn't think about what had happened before. She only knew she couldn't put herself through more of that.

Nathan had the capacity to hurt her more than anyone. It had broken her heart when he'd ended things all those years ago. It had taken her a long time to move on. She had to protect herself from any future pain.

Now she was aware of the danger signs, she would proceed with caution.

Two weeks later Nathan stood in his kitchen, rinsing plates and putting them in the dishwasher. He frowned as Saira walked towards him, carrying the last of the serving dishes.

Usually he went to great lengths to avoid scenes of domesticity. His preference was to keep his relationships on a superficial level, and cooking meals together was sure to send the wrong message.

Many of his previous girlfriends had offered to cook a meal for him. He'd never accepted. It was usually a sign for him to end the relationship before they started to take things seriously. He never offered to cook for his girl-friends—never invited them to his place.

He pressed his lips together. Was he sending Saira the wrong message? Hopefully she would understand his in-vitation wasn't anything special. His offer to cook was a way of thanking her for sharing her curry. Nothing more.

This sense of belonging, of being perfectly comfort-able with her presence, wasn't unusual when he thought about it. Saira and Miranda had often baked goodies in the kitchen when they were young. It was a throwback to those times. That was all. He often forgot how long he'd known Saira. Their aborted attempts at trying a relation-ship sometimes made him think that was all their history together. Part of their history he had no intention of re-calling.

It had clearly been a mistake to invite her. She would probably read too much into the situation. Women inevi-tably did.

Staying in to make dinner for her was an aberration—like watching a film in her suite had been. The media might call him a Six-Month Man, but six months sounded like a life sentence. He preferred women who were look-ing for some company, an entertaining evening and good sex. He made it crystal-clear that was all he offered. He wasn't cut out for relationships.

Saira might have initially agreed to a physical fling, but she was a romantic at heart—a relationship person. At some point she would start thinking he'd change his mind and offer her a commitment of some sort. Offer her his heart. He would never—*could* never—do that. There was still no future for them.

It wasn't in him to love, or even to offer her long term. He knew his own limitations. Better to break it off before that happened. That way nobody got hurt. If by ending a relationship sooner rather than later he could prevent someone going through the emotional pain his mother had gone through when the man she loved walked out on her, it was worth the 'Six-Month Man' reputation.

The last thing he wanted to do was hurt Saira. He did care about her. She was his sister's best friend. She would always be part of his life. But he had to make sure she understood that from his perspective nothing had changed, and spending time cooking for her didn't mean anything.

'What?' she asked, breaking into his thoughts.

He shrugged.

'You're staring at me,' she said.

'I like looking at you. That shouldn't come as a surprise.' It was good to remind her their time together was about physical attraction.

She fluttered her eyelashes. 'Why, thank you, sir. You're not so bad yourself.'

He grabbed her, lifting her onto the counter, running his hands along her legs, slipping them under her skirt. She cradled his hips between her legs.

Their kiss was interrupted by the beep of Saira's phone. He protested when she pushed him away.

As she slid onto the floor she murmured, 'Lovely, but sex on a kitchen counter probably isn't hygienic anyway.' She read her text message. 'It's Miranda,' she said. 'She's invited us for a meal with her and Steve.'

'I see,' he said in a cold tone.

They might be on the same page about having a brief fling, but there was a risk that Miranda was reading more into the situation. When they'd continued their affair in London, Saira had insisted she couldn't hide it from Miranda. She'd told her they were having a fling, but neither of them believed Miranda would accept that explanation.

Saira frowned as she sent off a text.

'What did you say?' Nathan asked. Her reply would

be a good barometer of whether she had started thinking there was more to their affair.

'I said I'm happy to meet her and Steve, but dinner with the four of us isn't going to happen.'

Nathan's phone beeped. 'It's Miranda—asking why I won't go to dinner with you.' He rolled his eyes.

Saira laughed. 'I love your sister, but she needs to learn she won't get her own way all the time.'

'I suppose we *could* go to dinner. I've been to dinner with couples before.'

Usually on a first or second date, when there was still uncertainty about whether there would be enough conversation to last the evening. He was acting out of character this evening—was it their shared history confusing things?

'Not sure it's a good idea,' Saira said, walking out of the kitchen and putting her phone in her handbag. 'We're not a real couple. I don't want Miranda getting the wrong impression. She's already convinced I won't be able to separate my emotions from sex.'

She rolled her eyes, suggesting the idea was ludicrous.

Saira's confirmation she still viewed their relationship as only physical should have made him happy—he wouldn't hurt her when he ended it. So why was there a twinge of disappointment instead? It wasn't because *he'd* started to think there might be something more lasting between them, was it? No, that couldn't be it. He still couldn't offer a long-term commitment to anyone—not even Saira.

He gave her a curious look as she grabbed her jacket. 'Are you leaving?'

'I thought so. Unless you want to watch a film or documentary?'

He pressed his lips together. That would be a very bad idea. This evening had already been enough to show that his fling with Saira was a delicate balancing act between enjoying a short-term sexual relationship and the constant reminder she was already, and would continue to be, a part of his life.

He cared about her and she cared about him. Those feelings would continue to develop. On her part, at least. He would be safe. He wouldn't allow himself to have deeper feelings. *Allow* himself? This wasn't a choice. Was it?

Perhaps the best thing would be to end their affair immediately. Right then. Christmas was coming up quickly. He didn't want his family and Saira to become more enmeshed, which was bound to happen if their affair continued until then.

He gaze homed in on her body as she bent over to pick up her handbag. He swallowed.

Christmas was still several weeks away. There was time to end things before then. But for now he would get the affair back to its purely physical footing.

He walked towards her, taking her bag from her arm as he pressed light kisses on her cheek, then down and along her neck, quickly inflaming them both. All thoughts of dinners and home cooking and domesticity were forgotten as they gave in to their growing passion.

Much later that evening, Nathan raised his head as Saira climbed off him. He had a large comfortable bed only a few metres away, and instead they'd made love on his sofa. If they hadn't been interrupted earlier they would probably have made love on his kitchen counter.

Their sexual attraction was as strong as ever and showed no signs of diminishing. With others he started getting bored after the first couple of weeks, and he had assumed his sex drive was easily satisfied. With Saira he was almost insatiable.

It wouldn't last. It never did. This was nothing to worry

about. The sex was great—for now. Soon the rush, the immediate reaction of his body, would fade.

Saira stood up to put her panties on, smoothing down her skirt and searching for the rest of her clothes.

'What are you doing?' he asked, lying back with his arm behind his head. His hand came across her bra and he held it out silently, a broad smile on his face.

'Getting dressed.'

'Why?'

'Because I don't want to get arrested going home half-naked,' she replied with a laugh.

'You don't have to go home. You can stay over.'

Nathan sat up.

He was breaking his own rules.

He never asked someone to spend the night with him at his place—at least not since he and Saira had dated when she was at university. That was it. Again it was their past that was the explanation for his offer. He'd momentarily had a sentimental flashback.

He needed to cut it out—stop confusing the past and their current situation.

Saira scrunched up her face. 'I'm not sure. I didn't bring anything with me.'

'Why don't I call a car for you? One of our drivers is always available,' he offered.

She threw him a surprised glance. Had she expected him to try to persuade her to stay? He had to be careful about giving her mixed signals.

He purposefully checked work emails while they waited for the car to arrive. He wanted to make sure she received the message that sex was all he wanted.

He expelled a long breath after she'd left. He'd made the right decision. He would end things before Christmas.

But she was his sister's best friend. He felt a responsibility to make sure she would be all right. He'd already sorted out accommodation for her—he didn't need to worry about that. But if she had financial security he would feel better. Perhaps he could help with her job hunt. Then he would be able to end things once and for all.

CHAPTER SEVEN

A FEW WEEKS later Saira was sitting in Nathan's chauffeur-driven car resting her head against the seat, her eyes closed as she let the breeze from the partially open window refresh her.

They had initially met at the theatre, but she'd felt faint during the interval. When she admitted she hadn't eaten much, Nathan immediately suggested they leave to get her something to eat.

It was a shame to miss the play but, in reality, she hadn't been able to concentrate anyway—too busy thinking through what she'd found out that morning, mentally rehearsing what she was planning to say to Nathan once they were in private.

She frowned when the car pulled up in front of his apartment building, where they took the private lift to his penthouse flat.

'You said you were taking me home,' she said once they were inside his place.

'This is my home. It made more sense to bring you here. Now you've moved out of the hotel, there won't be anyone to check on you if you're unwell.'

She huffed. He'd made it clear he wasn't pleased she'd moved into her own flat. But what did he expect? She wanted to be independent—which was hard to do if you were living for free in accommodation provided by your sex partner.

'It was easier to arrange for food to be delivered here. Banks took it in,' he said, referring to the building's concierge. 'He said he'd put it in the oven to keep warm.' He walked towards the kitchen. 'Ah, yes. Here it is. Are you happy to eat at the breakfast bar or shall I set the table in the dining area?'

'Kitchen is fine.'

Even though the spicy aromas from the Mexican cuisine were enticing, Saira's stomach roiled. It was probably nervous agitation, or even indignation. Her shoulders slumped as she watched Nathan take out the food.

'I'm not hungry.'

'You said you haven't eaten all day. It's not good for you. Come on, take a few mouthfuls.'

If only his concern meant something. But it didn't. Concern didn't mean caring. And what he'd done about her job wasn't about caring.

'Nathan, I'm not a child,' she bit out. 'If I don't want to eat I'm not going to eat. You can't bully me into doing something I don't want to do.'

His eyes went wide. 'I'm not trying to bully you into anything. What *is* going on with you? You've been in a strange mood all evening.'

She ran her hands across her face. There was nothing to be gained from putting the conversation off. Nathan's natural inclination was to take charge and arrange things to his satisfaction. He acted the same way in business as he did in his home life. His mother and sisters relied on him to such an extent he felt as responsible for them as he did for his employees.

Well, she wasn't one of his employees.

'Now you mention it,' she began, 'an interesting thing did happen today. I told you I had an interview at Calthorpe Engineering's Birmingham location?' He nodded. 'Well, today their head of HR called, inviting me for a second interview. She asked if I would be interested in working in their London office instead.'

'Congratulations. That's good news, isn't it?'

'Sure. Only I never wanted to work in their London branch.'

He couldn't meet her eyes—a sure sign of his guilt.

'You spoke to Kent about me, didn't you?' she challenged.

He sighed. 'I mentioned your interview in passing. I may have said it would be easier if you could work in London since Miranda will need you close to help with wedding arrangements and so you can be near your family.'

'Be near my family?' she repeated. 'Are you serious?' She made no effort to keep the biting sarcasm from her tone.

'Yes. What's your issue? Kent didn't know about your application beforehand. I didn't ask him to offer. He's opposed to any indication of nepotism. He wasn't doing me a favour.'

'You had no right to discuss my job with Kent at all. The London office doesn't do the kind of engineering work I'm looking for. If I wanted to work there, I would have applied.' She took a couple of calming breaths. 'I can't believe you. This is my career you're interfering with.'

She had to make him understand what he'd tried to do was wrong. She wanted to be in charge of her life. She needed to be. When Nathan tried to interfere with that, he was taking away her control.

'It's not interfering.' His face was stone, his voice cold. 'I had a conversation with a friend. Nothing more. Now you have another option. Why are you making such a fuss about this?'

'Seriously?' she asked with a laugh. 'I can make my own decisions. I don't need you trying to control me.'

His lips thinned, and if possible his face hardened even more. 'I'm not trying to control you.'

She sighed. He didn't even recognise he was doing it.

'If you want to move to Birmingham, then move,' he continued. 'It's your choice.'

She nodded. 'I know it's my choice.'

Where she worked was one thing she could and would control. She had to make her own decisions, without any external inference. All her life she'd allowed people to make decisions for her—her parents, her brothers, Dilip. Even Nathan had made the decision that there wasn't any future for them. But no more.

She didn't want or need any help. She needed to show Nathan, make him realise she was independent and capable of standing on her two feet—making her own way.

'Remember that before you speak to any other friends about my career,' she warned him.

'Of course,' he said, shrugging.

She was sure he would be rolling his eyes if he didn't know it would inflame the situation. She sighed. At face value Nathan probably didn't think it was a big deal. He was acting out of kindness and trying to be helpful. He looked out for his family all the time—it was second nature to him. Had she overreacted?

She looked closely at him but couldn't interpret his expression. The silence was slightly unnerving. To break the tension, she began to eat. A delighted moan broke from her as the delicious spices fired her taste buds. Suddenly her appetite returned with a vengeance, and she'd finished her plate before Nathan spoke again.

'At the risk of having my head bitten off, can I ask how the job hunt is going?'

'I have a second video interview with a company near

Chicago. It's probably the best job in terms of challenge and prospects. Keep your fingers crossed.'

'I didn't realise you were applying in the States too,' he said.

She nodded cheerfully. 'Mmm-hmm. I wasn't going to, but the job market there is much better. It doesn't make sense to limit myself geographically.'

'I see.' He stood watching her for a few moments, his eyebrows furrowed.

'What now?' she asked with an annoyed sigh.

'I was thinking of Miranda. I thought you were going to be around to support her with her wedding plans. She needs her best friend now. I would expect you to realise that.'

She bristled at the implied criticism. 'I spoke to Miranda. You know she would never stand in the way of my career or what would make me happy. International communication and travel are so easy nowadays. Besides,' she added with a small smile, 'I'm sure you'd send your jet for me if there was an emergency.'

His face remained impassive.

'What?' she bit out. 'Are you going to contact the Chicago company to see whether they can offer me a job here?'

'For the last time: I don't care where you work. If Miranda's happy that's all that matters. Whether you decide to move to Birmingham or Chicago or anywhere else in the world is of no concern to me. I don't care where you live.'

Saira had forgotten how it felt to have her heart lacerated. He'd spoken the words so casually, not even thinking for a moment of their significance, not realising she still secretly harboured a dream which had disappeared in that moment.

Of course he had no interest in where she worked or lived in the future. Their relationship was time-limited.

It had already overrun its course. How had she allowed herself to believe things could be different?

Despite her intentions, her warnings, her logical rationalisations, she much suspected she had feelings for him. If she was beginning to care for him so much after only a couple of months, the pain when he finally ended things would be devastating. She didn't want to go through that. Not again.

She had to end their fling—go back to her original plan to stay single and independent. She had to end it before her feelings could grow any deeper. End it before she could get hurt again.

She glanced over at Nathan, drinking in his features. Her pulse sped up and her breath became shallow under his penetrating gaze.

One night to say goodbye. She could allow herself one more night.

Nathan woke as sunlight streamed onto the bed. The only problem with automated curtains was they didn't take into account when you wanted darkness to stay cocooned in bed with your girlfriend.

He turned his head, noticing Saira was also stirring. He frowned. She'd been acting unlike herself the previous evening. She said she accepted he wasn't trying to interfere with where she worked but at the same time she was distant—there was almost a forced lightness.

He wasn't trying to control her. He was trying to help her out. What was wrong with helping someone you cared about?

Cared? The word struck at him. He did care about Saira. He was bound to have some affection for her when she'd been part of his life for years. But it wasn't in the romantic sense. He didn't do those kinds of feelings. It wasn't a road he was prepared to travel down again.

Again?

He was distracted from what that implied by Saira's hand running along his chest and down to his hip. He halted her exploration, covering her body with his...

Afterwards, he rested his head on her chest.

'This is such a comfortable bed,' she said, stretching like a contented cat. 'I don't know how you ever leave it.'

'Neither do I at this moment.'

Saira laughed stroking his hair. 'You're not usually such a flirt.'

He made a sound of pleasure, pressing a kiss to her breast. He lay next to her in quiet contentment.

'Why six months?' she asked, moments later.

'What?' He went still, the question catching him off guard.

'Why Six-Month Men? Why not three months? Why not a year?'

Why was she bringing this up now? What bearing could it have? Was her interest in the longevity of his relationships something he should worry about? Was she hinting that she was hoping for something longer term?

Maybe that wasn't out of the question with Saira. He enjoyed spending time with her...he could relax in her company. But he still wouldn't offer her love or marriage.

He turned onto his back.

'Six months is something the tabloids came up with once they noticed the five of us at Bastien's Spring Ball, and six months later there were photographs of us on holiday,' he replied, choosing his words carefully.

'The tabloids?' She pressed her lips together, jutting her chin out, making her scepticism clear. 'Sure.'

'There's no actual calendar. I don't look at the date and say, *Sorry, your six months is up*,' he said, unable to disguise the annoyance in his tone.

'But it's not like you don't have form.'

'Form?' He sat up, folding his arms. 'Because I have a different partner when the media sees me at two different events in a year you think I have *form*?'

She closed her eyes and took a few breaths. 'I meant it was the same with me. Back when I was at uni we'd been together around six months when you started losing interest.'

He opened his eyes wide, not believing she could make that accusation. '*I* lost interest? I think that was you. One minute we were together and the next minute you'd run away to America.'

'You said that before,' she said in a puzzled tone.

She was also sitting up now, pulling the bed covers over her chest. Almost in unison, they moved along the bed, further away from each other.

'But I was always going to America. It was the third year of my course. You knew that.'

'I did know, but you didn't say goodbye. I thought we were doing good, and suddenly you were making excuses not to meet, or you didn't answer my calls or texts at all.'

There was a reason he didn't want to rehash their past. There was no way it could end well. Their previous relationship and the way it had ended was too closely tied up with thoughts of his father. One minute he was looking after his mother and sisters, after his father abandoned them. Then, within a few weeks, Saira had left him too. He couldn't think about one without the other.

'It was you who was never around,' Saira protested.

He rubbed his hands over his face. Regardless of his feelings, the moment of reckoning had arrived.

He shook his head. 'Never around? I spent as much time as I could with you.'

'Sure. Every spare moment you had between looking after your family and building up your business,' she replied, sarcasm dripping from her words.

'Do you know how selfish you sound right now? You know what my mum and sisters were going through. Dad's leaving shook them hard. I had to be there for them.'

'I didn't begrudge that.'

'It sounds like you did.'

'Of course I didn't!' she protested vehemently. 'But I didn't hear from you for days or weeks at a time.'

'I was busy with work.'

It was the one area of his life where he'd known what he was doing. Where he knew the actions he needed to take and the direction he wanted to go. At a time when everything else around him was precarious, work was the one area he was in control.

'I know,' she said. 'But it made me realise how your life was so separate from mine. We were at different stages. You were building an empire; I didn't have any clue what I'd do after I graduated.'

'I don't understand why you didn't talk to me about it instead of ignoring me,' he said.

'You were never there for me to talk to!'

He shook his head. He'd always tried to spend time with her when he could. He'd been juggling many priorities at the time. He tried to be the rock his family needed and at the same time develop his business from the ground up. He hadn't wanted to put his worries onto her shoulders.

He grimaced. But there was some truth to her accusation.

Saira already had too much on her plate at that time. She'd been busy with her second-year exams. And offering comfort to Miranda, who wasn't coping well with their parents' situation. He hadn't wanted Saira to have to be his solace too. Besides, she was going to the States for a year. With the situation at home he couldn't move abroad—and he hadn't wanted to rely on Saira when she wouldn't always be there.

So each time he'd wanted to go to her, to spend time simply being with her, he'd thrown himself into his work instead. But he'd always thought he'd been there if she asked him.

Now he was hearing it wasn't enough.

The frustration and loneliness of that time threatened to overwhelm him. He couldn't tell her that, so he turned to irritation as a defence. 'What were you expecting? Me to dance attendance on you every moment? You know, your family may treat you like a princess, but that doesn't make you one.'

'Don't bring my family into it!' She sat up even straighter.

'I don't have to; they were always there. We had to date in secret when you were at school, because your parents didn't want you to have a boyfriend until you were eighteen. Then we couldn't tell anyone about us when you were at university because you were worried your parents wouldn't like you dating a non-Indian.'

Saira made a sound, as if choking down her aggravation. 'Much as I love listening to your revisionist history, my family were not a factor once I went to university. I was ready to tell them and then—' She broke off.

'And then what?'

Her shoulders sagged. 'And then you said love was for idiots and you were never getting married. I couldn't see the point of telling my family about a fling we were having.'

He pressed his lips together. He *had* said that—straight after spending days with his mother crying on his shoulder.

'It wasn't a fling.'

'Well, it wasn't going to be anything long term, was it?' she challenged him.

'It wasn't going to be marriage, no,' he admitted. 'I

don't make any secret of that. I don't see any point in getting married. But I didn't put an end date on our relationship.'

He was too much like his father ever to risk marriage. Unless children were involved. In those circumstances he would do his duty and give them the security they deserved. But it was a moot point—he never intended to have children.

'But, you see, I didn't know that,' she said. 'When we broke up the first time we agreed we were too young. But we always spoke about being together in the future. Maybe I was immature, but in my mind that meant marriage.'

'I never made you any promises.' He'd learnt from his father that promises weren't kept.

'No, but you broke my heart anyway!' she cried out.

His body stilled, ice water running through him as she accused him of doing the one thing he swore he would never do. He refused to believe it. He was not his father.

'You broke mine too,' he said simply.

'No,' she said vehemently, shaking her head. 'No. Don't you dare say that! You cared about me, but you never loved me. Love is for idiots, remember? Your ego may have been bruised, but your heart wasn't affected.'

He puffed out a long breath, not wanting to listen to her words. She was acting as if she was the only one who'd been affected by their break-up. At the time he hadn't been one of the Six-Month Men. He was telling the truth—he hadn't put an end date to their relationship. He hadn't offered marriage, but she'd been the closest he'd ever come to long term. Until she went away and forgot about him.

'What about you? Your heartbreak didn't last long, did it?' He spat out the resentment he'd been harbouring for so many years. 'You left, and the next thing I knew Miranda told me you were getting married.' It had been a gut-punch when he heard that news.

'Come on,' she scoffed. 'That was three years later! Oh, this is a waste of time; we're going round in circles.'

She got out of bed, picked up her clothes and went into the en suite bathroom.

Nathan lay back against the pillow, covering his eyes with his arm. That had gone as well as he'd expected. He'd been right to want to avoid discussions of the past. Nothing positive ever came of it.

People always viewed the past through their own lens. She thought their relationship had been over because he hadn't been there for her. He thought she'd run away.

He glanced at the bathroom door. She was getting ready to run away again.

He debated trying to dissuade her.

There was no point. He should never have let it get this far in the first place. He'd let their strong sexual connection override his good sense. He'd meant to keep their relationship as light as all his other ones, but instead he'd constantly broken his rules and found reasons to continue it.

He frowned.

Why had he kept their relationship going? Why was he unable to walk away from Saira?

He gave himself a shake. It didn't matter. He didn't want to explore the reasons and they didn't matter anyway.

Saira might have been lashing out at him, but she'd been telling the truth. He'd broken her heart when he'd told her he didn't believe in love or marriage. She'd cared about him and he'd hurt her to the core. But nothing had changed. He still had nothing to offer her. If he didn't end things now, he would only hurt her again in the long run. If they broke up now they would be able to walk away with their hearts intact.

Saira let the water sluice over her, trying to wake herself. Her sleep had been fitful. Perhaps that was the reason she was feeling slightly nauseous.

This whole thing was a mess. They'd agreed to draw a line under the past. She'd always expected the discussion of what had happened would be the beginning of the end for their affair, but here she was, bringing it up anyway.

What was she even doing?

It wasn't as if she was looking for a long-term relationship. But it was hard being with Nathan when memories kept surfacing. They'd got on so well when they were younger. He had always been one of the most interesting people she knew. Even when they hadn't been dating she'd enjoyed spending time with him. His personality meshed with hers in a unique way. She didn't want to lose that connection with him again.

Not being in contact with him after their relationship ended had been one of the big losses of her life—not the same as losing her husband, of course, but emotionally difficult nonetheless. Now she understood why Nathan hadn't come after her—he blamed her.

She still remembered the maelstrom of feelings she'd had for Nathan when they were younger. Deep and all-encompassing. It had been difficult for her to move on from him. Move on to the safety and comfort of Dilip.

She loved Dilip, but they'd had an arranged marriage, with their love developing after they married. It had been soft and gentle, and losing him so suddenly hurt unbearably. It had taken her a long time before her grief subsided enough for her to be ready to move forward with her life.

She never wanted to feel anything as devastating as that again. And that was the risk if she carried on an affair with Nathan. She could admit that.

Physical attraction she could deal with. Ignore it if necessary. Far more dangerous was liking him again. With Nathan, liking led all too easily to love—a path she couldn't go down. Wouldn't. It almost broke her the first time.

She hadn't thought through the repercussions of their relationship when they were on holiday. Not thinking things through properly when it came to Nathan was apparently one of her major flaws.

Now she had no choice. It was far better to end their sexual relationship now, when her feelings were still nascent and could be suppressed. Then they could work on being friends, which was vital with Miranda's wedding come up.

She'd allowed herself one more night. Time was up.

Nathan was making coffee when she finally walked into the living area.

'Are you hungry?' he asked, giving her a quick glance. 'I've made some breakfast.'

His expression was completely blank—as if they hadn't argued minutes before. If she needed any reminder he didn't really care about her, he was making it very clear.

'Thanks,' she said, sitting down to a plate of waffles with berries, drizzled with maple syrup. She glanced at the mixing bowl on the dryer and the waffle maker on the counter.

They ate in silence. Occasionally she would glance his way and notice him watching her. Usually he would smile or wink whenever their eyes met, but this morning his face remained sombre.

'You're right,' she admitted, putting her cutlery down and hugging her coffee mug with both hands. 'It was me who ran away.'

He paused, then expelled a breath. 'No, you're right too. I did start to pull away from you.'

She snorted. 'Please don't start arguing with me about who's to blame again.'

'It's not about blame, though, is it, Saira? Although I have blamed you for the way it ended in the past, I should have realised you were thinking about marriage. We never defined our relationship.'

'No, we didn't.' She gave a wry smile. 'I assumed it was what I wanted it to be. I was so young, and immature for my age. I couldn't believe we could be in a relationship and having sex if we weren't going to stay together,'

'I didn't mean to lead you on. I am sorry about that,' he replied.

He was bending his head, as if hiding his guilt. But there was no emotion in his tone—he could have been reciting from a dictionary.

'I didn't think we had a future. My parents' twenty-five-year marriage got thrown in the dustbin—what chance did we have?'

She frowned. Why did he keep comparing himself to his father? Couldn't he tell he was nothing like him? But his future relationships no longer mattered to her, so instead of challenging his assertion, she nodded. 'What I don't get is why you were so aloof when I came back.'

'We didn't end it cleanly. You went silent, stopped contacting me. I had to rely on Miranda to hear any news about you. That wasn't right, Saira. After what we had, that wasn't right.'

She hung her head at the deserved condemnation in his tone. 'I'm sorry.'

She was silent for a few moments, her mind processing their conversation. Nathan had used the past tense to describe his thoughts on their future, but nothing had changed for him. He still didn't believe in love or marriage. Was still certain he couldn't make a long-term commitment.

She wished she could be the woman who showed him how wrong he was—that he cared deeply and had the capacity to have a long and happy marriage. But that wasn't her role. Too much had gone on in the past for her to be the one to convince him. He wouldn't believe her.

And too much had happened to make her believe in a happily-ever-after with him. She cared about him intensely, probably still loved him, but until he was ready to admit he could love and was ready to accept her love, nothing would change.

She couldn't carry on in a relationship where her feelings would grow stronger with every day knowing that he would never admit he even *had* feelings. It would be too painful.

She straightened her shoulders with determination. At the end of the day, this relationship was going nowhere. She was an independent, capable woman. She was in control of her future. She could live happily on her own. As she'd always intended when she returned to England. Her attraction to Nathan had derailed her for a while, but she could ignore the hormonal urges the same way she could ignore the stirrings of her foolish heart. It was safer that way. She wouldn't get hurt.

She took a deep breath. 'We both love Miranda, and she's going to need us while she plans her wedding.'

'Yes.'

'We agreed to make an effort for her, and then things got confused because we brought sex into the mix.' She raised her hand to prevent him from interrupting. 'If we keep on as we are, we will inevitably end up fighting. I would rather end it now, while we can be comfortable in each other's company. I don't want to risk us ending a few weeks down the road because we have a big argument, or because you get bored with me. That would be awkward.'

Nathan straightened, his face a mask. 'If that's what you want.'

She nodded.

It was that easy? No arguments? No attempt to convince her to change her mind?

It was over just like that.

It was strangely anti-climactic.

What had she expected? A protestation of love?

She hopped off her stool, reaching for the counter as a wave of dizziness overcame her.

Nathan was immediately by her side. 'Are you okay?'

'Yes, I'm fine. Just a bit dizzy again.'

'Are you sure?'

'Yes.' She ignored the clear concern on his face and steeled herself. 'What? Did you think I was swooning because our break-up is too much for me to take?'

He pursed his lips together. 'This is the second time you've almost fainted. Perhaps you should see a doctor.'

'Maybe you're right. I can get anaemic when I'm due my period. I'm sure that's all it is.'

He nodded, but didn't say anything, so she grabbed her things and gave him a kiss on the cheek.

This was the right decision for her. She was walking away from him again. But this time it was on her own terms. It was already hurting so much, but it was inevitable that sooner or later they would end things and say goodbye. There would always be a goodbye ahead.

The dizziness and nausea hit her again as soon as she was on the tube. Was this a physical manifestation of the utter loss she was feeling inside? What was wrong with her?

CHAPTER EIGHT

ALL THE DIFFERENT instruction leaflets scattered on her counter said the same thing—the best time to take a test was first thing in the morning. Saira knew this already. She didn't need to read the instructions to know what to do. But reading them was a good distraction from thinking about why she needed the tests...

She ran her fingers through her hair. She could be worrying about nothing. Probably was. This was a situation she was all too familiar with, and each time she was left disappointed.

Saira picked up one of the boxes. How many times had she bought one of these, full of excitement, full of joy, and then seen Dilip's crestfallen face each time she told him the negative news?

Apart from that one time. Which she didn't let herself think about. Couldn't let herself think about.

She took a couple of deep, centring breaths and focused on the boxes in front of her. After all those times when she'd yearned for a positive result, she couldn't be pregnant from a fling. Could she?

She hadn't even considered it a possibility until that morning. When Dilip died, Saira had put away her ovulation kits and thermometers and trackers, never expecting to need them again.

It was only when she saw her stock of unused sanitary

supplies and put them together with her dizzy episodes and mild morning nausea that she even entertained the thought.

The hope?

The previous times she'd taken these tests she'd been part of a loving, committed couple, for whom a child would have been a much-wanted addition to their family.

This time it couldn't be more different.

She'd returned to England to start again. Get a job. Find her own place. Be independent. Her future plans hadn't included having a child.

But those plans were based on her false assumption she would need to be in a relationship before a child could be part of the picture. Life didn't care about her assumptions. If she were pregnant she could easily adjust those plans, and would happily do so.

Pregnant.

Could it be possible?

She half-laughed, half-cried at the prospect. The fear, the worry, the doubts had already started to creep in. She held her hands over her stomach. Even a positive pregnancy test wasn't a guarantee of happiness. Those memories were getting harder to hold back. Threatening to overwhelm her.

She needed to be practical. She deliberately turned her thoughts to Nathan. To how he would react. It was bad enough trying to keep her thoughts in order, without adding the extra complication of how to involve him, the father of her possible child. She had no idea how to handle this situation. Was there some etiquette for telling someone you'd had a fling with that you might be pregnant with their baby?

How would he take the news? Not well, that was for sure. He didn't do long term. He didn't want commitment. A child was a life-long commitment. You couldn't get more long term than that. This was probably the last thing he wanted.

Her phone rang.

'Hey, Saira,' Miranda said. 'Are you in this afternoon?'

'Yes. Do you want to come over?'

'No—I meant to call you earlier, but I forgot, sorry.'

Saira's brow furrowed 'Okay. What's up?'

'Nathan was here for lunch. He offered to drop round my wedding binder and some magazines for you to look at. I told him I could post them, but he said it's on his way. He left over an hour ago, so he should be there soon.'

Ice pulsed through her body. Nathan was on his way. She hadn't seen him since she'd ended their fling three weeks ago. She wasn't prepared to see him. Not now. Not with this pile of boxes in front of her.

'Are you okay?' Miranda asked.

'Yes, of course—I'm fine. Why wouldn't I be?'

'You didn't say anything for a few minutes. Isn't this the first time you'll see him since you broke up?'

Saira resisted the urge to insist they hadn't broken up because they had never been a real couple.

'Why would that bother me? It was never a big deal between me and Nathan.'

Hopefully, she sounded believable. She changed the conversation to Operation Wedding, chatting for a few more minutes before Miranda rang off.

She leant on her elbows, pulled her cheeks down, then rubbed her face. She'd thought she'd have more time before involving Nathan. Take the test, at least. But he was on his way. Should she tell him when he came?

Perhaps she should wait to tell him until she'd entered her second trimester. She knew better than anyone how fragile new life was in the first few weeks. But what if he wanted to be at the first scan? Didn't she owe him the chance to be involved from the outset? If he even wanted to be involved...

She muffled a scream. There were too many unknowns. Instead of speculating on possibilities, she needed to concentrate on the steps she *could* control.

The doorbell rang, causing Saira to knock all the boxes off the counter. She hurriedly gathered them up, then shoved them into a drawer. Taking a couple of deep breaths, she went to answer the door.

Slightly surprised when Nathan accepted her invitation to come in rather than leaving straight after dropping off the binder and magazines, her eyes kept straying to him while she made them some tea.

His thick dark hair looked slightly longer than usual, beginning to wave in the front. Her fingers flexed with the muscle memory of running through those strands. The inky blue of his simple but expensive cashmere jumper stretched across his broad shoulders, the perfect foil to his piercing eyes. It wasn't fair. He was cover-model-gorgeous while she was the personification of Death.

At least pregnancy would explain her rollercoaster of emotions since they'd ended things. Life was a funny thing. Years ago she'd dreamt of raising a family with Nathan. Look where they were now.

She made a rueful sound.

'Are you okay?' Nathan asked.

She needed to pull herself together. Start acting naturally. 'Yes, I'm fine. Thanks.' She brought the drinks over.

'Are you sure you're okay? You don't look well,' he said.

'Well, that's flattering. Thank you.' She made a face at him.

'You know you're always beautiful. You seem a little tired, though.'

'I am a little tired,' she agreed, hoping to keep the conversation light. 'It's been a hectic couple of weeks.'

He frowned. 'Did you see the doctor about your dizzy spells?'

'No.' She waved her hand, dismissing the need. She didn't need a doctor's appointment to determine whether she was pregnant.

'How's work?' she asked. Discussions about her health were heading towards dangerous territory.

'Good—busy.'

'I read in the papers you completed that acquisition.'

'Yes, it went through a week ago.'

He was so cold and abrupt. This was worse than when they'd seen each other at Miranda's engagement party. The familiar prickling sensation at the back of her eyes energised her to stand up, excusing herself to go to the bathroom.

She sluiced water over her face. This was ridiculous. She needed to pull herself together. Concentrate on the facts. She didn't know for certain if she was pregnant. If there was a baby, Nathan was the father. She didn't know how he would react, but it was information he deserved to have.

In an ideal world she would wait until she'd taken the test before she told him, but after today she didn't know when she would see him again if it wasn't something to do with Miranda's wedding. That would not be an appropriate time to tell him the news. Wouldn't it be better to tell him in person rather than over the phone?

Did it matter how he reacted? She had always longed to have a child. She had more than enough love to raise one on her own. She was more than capable. If Nathan wanted to be involved that was a benefit, not a requirement. She could love the baby for both of them.

She straightened her shoulders, inhaled deeply, then walked back to the lounge.

'Are you sure you're all right, Saira? You weren't being sick, were you?'

Saira smiled wanly. 'I'm okay, Nathan.'

This would be a great time to segue into telling him the truth...

His brows furrowed. 'I think you should make a doctor's appointment to be on the safe side.'

'I don't need to. I—'

'I know you don't like being told what to do, but—'

'I think I'm pregnant,' she blurted out.

Nathan blinked then shook his head.

Pregnant.

Had he heard correctly? Had she said *pregnant*? Thank goodness he was already sitting down.

Pregnant.

She wasn't ill, though, which was a relief.

He'd known there was something different from her appearance. She looked beautiful, as always, but now there was a haunting quality to her beauty, a fragility he hadn't seen before. Her cheekbones were more pronounced. Had she lost weight?

He reached out to rub his thumb along her face but managed to pull his hand back before making contact.

He hadn't expected her to say she was pregnant. No, she'd said she 'thought' she was pregnant. What did she mean...*thought*?

He stood up and started to walk—from the lounge door to the window, several times, barely noticing the view of Russell Square—as he tried to process the information.

Saira was pregnant. Or she thought she could be pregnant. With his baby? Of course with his baby. If she were pregnant he would be the father.

His steps faltered. He could be a father. He never wanted to be a father. He didn't know how to be a father. What if he disappointed his child the way his father always let him down?

Saira's voice broke into his thoughts. 'Please stop pacing.'

He paused, then turned to face her. She was huddled in an armchair, her hands hugging her mug to her heart.

He nodded his head as he continued to process his thoughts while he stood still.

'Can you sit down? I don't want you looming over me.'

She looked defeated. He took a step towards her, then stopped. He needed to keep his distance until he could clear his head.

He sat down again. 'It's a lot to take in.'

'For me, too.'

He nodded. It was a lot for both of them to wrap their heads around. He needed to take control, so they could start making decisions and plans. The first step was to find out for certain.

'You said you *think* you're pregnant?'

'I haven't taken a test yet, but there have been a few signs.'

He nodded again. Keeping it formal—clinical, even— was the best course of action. 'What about your period? Have you missed it?'

'I don't know. They haven't been regular since—' She broke off, putting her mug down,then wrapping her arms round her stomach in a gesture of self-protection.

'I can buy a pregnancy test.'

'I have loads. I was planning to take one today.'

He narrowed his eyes. How long had she suspected she was pregnant? There was no way Saira would have kept her pregnancy a secret from him, but even though she already bought a test she hadn't contacted him.

'When were you planning to tell me?'

'I don't know,' she told him simply. 'It's new to me too. I only suspected I could be pregnant this morning. I don't know if I am, and I know the stats about pregnancies in the first trimester.'

Her face was a mask and her body closed in, as if she was protecting herself.

'Perhaps you should take the test while I'm here, so we know for sure.' Once he knew, he could start making plans for their future.

'It's best to take the test in the morning.'

He stared at her, unblinking. Did he sense some reluctance to get confirmation one way or another? 'You can take one now and another in the morning.'

She sighed, but made no effort to move.

'Saira?' He couldn't understand her reluctance. Wasn't it better if they knew the situation?

'Fine,' Saira said in a frustrated tone. 'I'll take the test now.'

'Good. Do you want me to come with you?' he offered, in case she was feeling nervous. He raised his eyebrows, questioning the curious expression she was giving him.

'Nate, I'm about to wee on a stick. I certainly do not want you there.'

His lips twitched. Trust Saira to bring some humour into the situation.

He resumed his pacing once she'd disappeared into the bathroom. Soon they would have their answer. What did he hope it would be?

He'd never imagined being a father. This wasn't something in his life's plan. He would have to make many adjustments and accommodations to be actively involved with his child. He wasn't going to be like his father—a phantom presence, floating in and out at his own convenience. If the test was positive, Nathan's life was going to change dramatically.

Was it usual for prospective fathers to feel this sense of overwhelm? And fear. Fear he was too much like his own father to know how to be one for his child. Fear he wouldn't be in his child's life as much as he wanted.

Saira came out the bathroom waving her phone. 'I've set the timer. Now we wait.'

She sat back in the armchair, her hands steepled together, resting against her mouth. He resisted the urge to wrap her in his arms, comfort her. She had been around when his father had waltzed in and out. She would rightly worry he was going to disappear the same way. He wanted to say something to reassure her that if she was pregnant he would be by her side.

They both started when the timer went off. They walked to the bathroom and waited for the words to appear in the small test window.

Pregnant 3+ weeks

There it was. The truth. She was pregnant. He was going to be a father.

He swallowed the lump in his throat.

How could he be a father? He didn't know the first thing about being one. His father had been the worst role model, and he never wanted to put children through what he and his sisters had gone through.

That was moot now. He was going to be a father.

Saira burst into tears, covering her face in her hands. This time without hesitation he gathered her into his arms and carried her into the lounge, settling on the sofa with her on his lap. Of course this would be overwhelming for her.

'It's fine, darling. Everything's fine.' He stroked her hair, frowning when she cried harder.

'You don't know that.' She sobbed into his chest. In a small voice she said, 'I'm so worried. Things don't work out just because you want them to.'

He closed his eyes, fearing she would mention termination. 'What do you mean?'

'I've been here before. Positive pregnancy test. We were so happy.'

It shouldn't have shocked him to learn she had been pregnant by her husband. He didn't resent her past relationship with Dilip—but at the same time he didn't want to know all the details about her marriage. Only now her past experience was causing her to worry.

He couldn't change what had happened with her previous pregnancy. Nor could he promise everything would be fine with this one. The only thing he could do was reassure her that he would be there for her. And take as much stress off her plate as he could.

'We should probably discuss what we're going to do,' he said.

'I hope to have this baby. I think that's worth saying,' she said forcefully.

'Obviously that's your decision alone, but for the record I would never suggest you shouldn't.'

'I know, but I felt you should know upfront what I plan. There's not a decision to make here. It's made.' She paused, and then added as an afterthought, 'As far as it's in my control.'

His eyes widened as deep pain flashed in her eyes. Something bad must have happened with her previous pregnancy, but asking questions at this time wouldn't ease her worries. Instead, he would concentrate on practicalities.

'In that case we should discuss what we plan to do in the future.'

'Not now—not until I'm through my first trimester.'

He nodded, not really understanding why that mattered. 'When will that be?'

Her expression was blank. 'I don't know.' She laughed without real humour. 'I don't know when I got pregnant. We used protection! It could have been any occasion—' Her voice was rising as she broke off. 'I'll arrange an appointment with a doctor and a dating scan.'

A scan. A chance to see his child. Would that make it more real?

'Will you let me know what you've arranged? I'd like to go with you.'

She nodded.

They sat in silence for a few moments, both seemingly unable to contemplate this huge, unexpected change in their future plans.

'I'm still quite tired,' Saira said after a while. 'If you don't mind, I'm going to have a nap. I'll contact you once I've got some dates.'

The urge to stay behind and take care of her warred with his instinctive sense that she wouldn't appreciate it. He wouldn't do anything to agitate her. Not now. Not when she was carrying his child.

'Good. You look after yourself…' All words were inadequate. 'Call me if you need anything. Any time.' He bent to drop a kiss on her forehead.

Once outside her apartment he expelled a breath. That was the last thing he'd expected to find out when he'd offered to take his sister's wedding binder to Saira. He hadn't thought much beyond seeing her again.

He was going to be a dad.

He might never have chosen this for himself. But now the decision had been taken from him he would be the best father he could and do right by Saira and his child. He wouldn't abandon them the way his father abandoned his family.

This might not be what he would have chosen for his life, but he would do his duty. He would make a commitment and stick with it. He would be there for his child. He would be there for Saira.

CHAPTER NINE

SAIRA BREATHED IN for a count of seven and out for a count of eleven, using the anxiety techniques she'd learnt after Dilip died while she waited for her name to be called.

This wasn't the first time she'd sat in a hospital waiting for an ultrasound, but she'd never made it to the first dating scan before. She'd purposefully kept her mind off what happened with her first pregnancy. The sorrow was always there, just beneath the surface, but she coped by grieving fully for what she'd lost and trying to look forward with hope.

She pressed a hand against her still-flat stomach. 'Please be okay, baby,' she whispered.

Nathan placed a reassuring hand on her knee. She gave him a grateful smile. His confidence and arrogant disbelief that anything bad could happen gave her the hope she was afraid to believe in herself. Earlier that morning he'd sat patiently in the waiting room while she'd had her booking appointment and his patience paid off when they were able to schedule a dating scan the same day. One of the benefits of the care offered at the most renowned private maternity hospital in London.

When Nathan first told her he'd arranged the booking appointment for her here, she'd been fuming. It was just like him to try to take charge. It was great that he was taking such an interest in the pregnancy, but he needed to recognise *she* was the one who was pregnant. *She* was the primary decision-maker.

Of course she would discuss things with him. They probably wouldn't agree on everything, so it was more important than ever she stood her ground from the outset.

The pale lilac tones of the waiting room, the pristine furniture and the top-quality equipment visible from her seat calmed her slightly, certain her baby would receive excellent care. She was prepared to give Nathan the benefit of the doubt on this call. If there was one thing they would agree on it was to have the best quality of care for their baby. And not having to wait for the appointment was a bonus.

She looked at him out of the corner of her eye. He was reading some of the pamphlets from the waiting area about tests available. She knew this situation wasn't what he wanted. He was being forced into fatherhood. Because of that he was doing what he always did—throwing himself into it, making the best outcome he could. She'd watched him to do it for his mother and sisters after his father left. She didn't want him to feel she was a responsibility. She could take care of herself.

Finally, they were called in for the scan. Because she was unsure of her due date the radiographer suggested they try an abdominal scan in the first instance. After watching her press a few buttons and make some facial expressions Saira couldn't interpret, memories of the last time she'd been in this position came flooding back. The concerned, sad look on the technician's face, her hasty exit from the room and her return with a senior doctor…

Trying to suppress the images, she turned to look up at the ceiling, using her breathing technique again.

'Would you like to see your baby for the first time?'

The radiographer turned the monitor towards them. Saira stared at the image on the screen, her eyes filling

with tears. She glanced in Nathan's direction. He was staring intently at the screen. Was that moisture in his eyes
too? She laced her fingers through his. He turned to her
with a smile, bringing her hand to his lips to press a quick
kiss to it.

She tried to concentrate as the radiographer gave them
more details, but all she could see was the pulsing image
in front of her. Her baby's heartbeat. This was their baby.
She had given up hope this would ever happen.

'From the measurements here, and the details you provided, you're around thirteen weeks. I've finished here,'
the radiographer continued, after making a few more no-
tations. 'If you go back to the waiting room someone will
come to fetch you when the consultant is ready to see you.'

'Consultant?' Nathan queried. 'Is there something
wrong?'

'My notes show Ms Dey has been referred to a consultant. You can ask for details at Reception. I'll print some
photos for you to take. At later scans we can arrange a
video too.'

During their brief wait for the consultant, Saira was
handed the scan photos. Holding them, she couldn't focus
on anything else.

Everything looked fine.

She was going to have a baby.

Once they were in the consultant's office she was
vaguely aware of Nathan speaking, saying something
about due dates, conception and consultants—but she
couldn't tear her attention away from the photos.

The consultant looked through the notes on her monitor. 'You've been referred to me because of your previous
molar pregnancy,' she said.

'I see.'

Saira glanced at Nathan. He frowned at her before he
turned back to the doctor.

'That was three years ago?' the consultant asked.

'Yes, around then.'

'And you went to all your follow-up appointments?'

'Yes.'

'For the requisite six months?'

Saira nodded.

'And there have been no other pregnancies before or since?' the doctor continued.

'No.'

The consultant typed a few notes. 'Right, then, Ms Dey. This pregnancy looks good. The baby is growing well. No signs of any problems with your uterus. I would prefer, as a precaution, to keep you under consultant supervision, but it's your choice if you want to go for midwife-led.'

'We'll go for consultant care,' Nathan said.

'Maybe we should discuss this?' Saira countered. She had to nip his control tendencies in the bud.

'No, there's no cost issue here,' he replied.

She pressed her lips together but didn't say anything. This wasn't a conversation they needed to have in public, but Nathan was going to find out being the father of her baby didn't mean he could ignore or overrule her views.

On the drive back she constantly stared at the scan pictures, reassuring herself that this wasn't a dream. She was really pregnant—and in her second trimester.

Getting past the first trimester was a major milestone—one she'd come so close to before. She scrunched her eyes tightly, still terrified at the prospect of something going wrong. She was already opening herself to more loss and hurt because she already loved her baby with all her heart—but there was nothing she could do to stop that. Loving her child was as natural and inevitable as breathing.

She glanced quickly at Nathan. He had been silent the

entire journey. What was he thinking? He'd been clear from the start he didn't believe in long-term commitments. Parenthood was as long term as you could get.

Once upon a time it would have been her dream come true to be having a baby with Nathan as the father. But so much water had passed under the bridge since then. After their tense argument the day she'd broken things off, there was too much hurt and history for them ever to find common ground. All it seemed to prove was that they couldn't make it as a couple, no matter how much she wanted to.

She'd never understood why he believed he couldn't do commitment; it was unusual for a man who was brimming over with self-confidence to be convinced he could fail at something.

She grimaced. His father's actions had a much deeper and lasting negative impact than perhaps he realised. Couldn't Nathan see what a great capacity for caring and love he had? She only needed to recall the countless ways he took care of his mother and sisters to know that. There was no doubt in her mind he would be an amazing dad.

She expelled a breath. They couldn't avoid a proper talk about the future. They had to find a way that worked for both of them. One where she kept her independence.

What chance was there for them to forge an understanding around how they would raise their child if their past issues remained unresolved? Did Nathan even recognise they needed to address it if they had any hope of coming to an arrangement?

'Are you okay?' she asked when he pulled up outside her apartment. 'I know it's a lot to take in. I can hardly believe it myself.'

'We need to talk,' he said.

She nodded. They had a lot to discuss, but she needed to get her own mind around the situation, think about what *she* wanted first.

'I know,' she replied. 'But can we do it another day? I'm tired, and I think we both need to process a bit more before we talk through things properly.'

Without waiting for his reply, she exited the car and went into her building.

Nathan stood next to the window of Saira's living room. watching the activity on the street as he tried to marshal his thoughts. Had it only been five days since they'd seen their baby on the ultrasound?

In a little over six months he was going to be a father... a dad. He might never have planned to have children, but pregnancy was always a possibility when you had sex. He knew a child was the only reason he would ever contemplate marriage.

Maybe he didn't know how to be a good father yet, but he had a great example for how *not* to be one. He would never make the same mistakes his father had. The only thing his father had done right was marry his mother when she'd found out she was pregnant with him. The least he could do for Saira was offer her the same. He would do his duty. But, unlike his father, he had no intention of leaving when he got bored. He didn't make commitments lightly—when he did, he stuck with them.

He turned as Saira walked in with mugs of tea. He grimaced, annoyed with himself—he should have thought through this moment better, brought a ring with him. But it was too late to do anything about that now. Saira would probably enjoy picking out a ring for herself. And it wasn't as if this was a romantic proposal. Was a ring even necessary?

'I think we should get married around Christmas,' he said, sitting down next to her.

A winter wedding would be the perfect way to start their future together. As soon-to-be parents, he reminded himself. This was about the baby, not him and Saira as a couple. Christmas was a time for families. He always tried to spend it with his mother and sisters. And the following Christmas he would have his own family to spend the time with. He smiled inwardly as he imagined Saira and his child in front of a large, brightly decorated tree.

He glanced at Saira when he realised she hadn't responded.

She was looking at him blankly, then she made a choking sound. 'Sorry, what?' she asked, shaking her head and smiling.

His eyes narrowed. He had been quite clear. He sighed and with great patience said, 'It would be good if we were married around Christmas. I was planning to spend a few days with my mother and sisters over the holidays, so my family will be around. I can send my plane for your parents.'

Saira covered her mouth with her fingers for a moment, as if she were holding back a laugh. Humour wasn't the reaction he was expecting.

'I'm sorry. Are you being serious?' she asked.

'Of course. I'm asking you to marry me.'

'Well, you're not actually *asking*,' she muttered.

He frowned. Had she been expecting him to go down on one knee? 'Getting married is the right thing to do,' he insisted.

At that she did burst out laughing. 'Right thing?' she exclaimed. She placed a hand on her chest, widening her eyes and fluttering her eyelashes. 'That's truly so romantic.'

He pursed his lips. He could do without her mockery when they had serious matters to discuss. 'We need to be practical right now.'

'Yes. By all means let's be practical.' She sighed. 'But getting married isn't about practicality. Or at least it shouldn't be.'

He closed his eyes, gathering his patience. He should have anticipated she would be difficult about this. She was going to fight him all the way if he didn't get a handle on the situation. Perhaps she didn't believe he was prepared to offer her commitment—offer their child the security it deserved. He had to find the right argument, the right words to persuade her.

'It will be best for our child if we're married,' he said.

'Says who?'

He definitely should have come better prepared. 'I'm sure there are studies. I can get my assistant to send you some research.'

Saira rolled her eyes. 'This would be so funny if you weren't being serious right now. I don't care what *research* says. I'm not marrying you.'

'Would you care to tell me why?'

'I don't plan on getting married again.'

'Did you plan on having a child?' he challenged.

'Maybe not.'

'Plans change and we need to adapt. I'm prepared to adapt. I'm offering to do the right thing and marry you.' He rubbed the back of his neck. 'I don't understand why you're being difficult.'

'Difficult?' Her voice's pitch went an octave higher. 'Disagreeing with you doesn't make me "difficult".'

'I'm not going to abandon my child.'

He would be part of his child's life. He was offering them security, protection—he could meet their every need. What more did she want?

'I don't think you would. Marriage isn't the solution, though. It would be different if we were in love, or even in a relationship.'

He raised an eyebrow. He was offering marriage. He wasn't offering love. He couldn't. She knew that. He'd never made a secret about that.

'You never even wanted a long-term commitment,' she continued. 'And I'm not going to trap you into one.'

'I want to get married,' he protested, although he couldn't deny the accuracy of her statement. He'd never thought he would have children or get married. But that didn't matter any more. They had a baby on the way. He could and would be there for his child. Now he'd made the conscious decision to be part of his baby's life he wasn't going anywhere—he would never rip his child's heart apart the way his father had done. And Saira would finally be a part of his life as well. They would be together the way he'd always...

He refused to let his thoughts continue down that path. 'It's not a trap if I'm asking you.'

'It really is. People don't have to get married because they're having a baby. My dad's not going to be there holding a shotgun.' She paused for a few moments. 'Be sensible, Nathan. You can't marry every woman you get pregnant.'

His mouth slackened. He closed his eyes briefly, pinching the bridge of his nose. 'I haven't got any other woman pregnant.'

'That you know of.'

'I know,' he insisted.

How could she even suggest he wouldn't know about it?

He inhaled slowly, rubbing his hand over his face. 'None of my exes are pregnant or have had my secret baby. And I'm not going to argue with you about an unrealistic hypothetical situation.'

'Okay, but you don't marry someone because they're pregnant. At least, I don't think you should. I know you think you're doing the honourable thing here, but it isn't necessary. There has to be more to marriage. Believe me, I know. How can you even think about spending your life with someone when they can't even hold your interest for six months? The rest of your life! How is that rational?'

He was silent. He would have done his duty whatever the circumstances. Wouldn't he? Marriage was always the correct step. There was no point speculating on whether he would have done his duty if someone else had been pregnant. Saira was the one who was pregnant. And he couldn't imagine anyone else being the mother of his child. Everything else was irrelevant.

'It makes sense for us to be married. You know it's the right thing.'

She shook her head. 'Stop saying that. It's not the right thing for me,' she said with a shrug. 'I don't believe it would be the right thing for our child in our circumstances. You more than anyone should know that.'

'What does that mean?'

'You told me your dad stayed with your mum for the children. It made your dad miserable.'

His narrowed his eyes. It always came back to his father—to comparisons with him. 'My father was a selfish man who abandoned his family. He cheated on my mother constantly. Did I ever tell you that?'

'Your parents should never have married. They were miserable. I'm not going to put you through the same thing.'

'I would never cheat on you.'

'I know. Instead, you would be stuck with me for the rest of your life, like some kind of punishment. You would resent me and be unhappy.'

He shook his head. He could make it work. If he put his mind to it, he could be a good husband and father. It wouldn't be a punishment being in his son or daughter's life. He would be happy being married to Saira.

'What's more, *I* would be unhappy,' Saira continued.

His shoulders slumped. He would never want that. 'I want to be involved with my child,' he said. 'I want to be a good father. I want to be there for her or him. The best way for me to do that is if I'm married to you. I don't promise to love you. I'm not capable of that emotion. We have a strong basis for marriage without bringing emotions into it. You should consider my proposition seriously.'

'I've already told you it's not happening. We barely know each other anymore! And I'm not going to force you into a marriage you don't want.'

Nathan sighed. 'I wouldn't be asking if I didn't want this.'

She shook her head.

What could he say that would convince her marriage was not only the best thing for their child, it was the best thing for him too? Without marriage, Saira could run away again—leave him, taking his child with her. He would never let that happen.

'Can't we take marriage off the table for now?' she pleaded. 'We'll never get anywhere if our discussions stall arguing about something that's never going to happen. There must be lots of options other than marriage. Of course you'll have all your parental rights, and I'm sure we can work out generous visitation.'

That wasn't enough. He didn't want to be a part-time father. He wanted a proper family.

'Think about what I'm offering, Saira. I can give you and our child a great life. You don't even have a job. I can give you financial security. Neither of you will want for anything.'

'Money isn't everything,' she said, in a neutral tone that caused a knot in his stomach.

'Money has its advantages.'

'You're right. It does. Maybe I'm not a billionaire, but I have more than enough money to take care of my child and raise them comfortably even without a job.'

'Really?' He raised his eyebrows. 'How do you propose to do that?'

'The thing is, Nathan, money has always been a tool for you to get your own way. But this time it's not going to work.'

Nathan narrowed his eyes. He had a sinking sensation he'd made a serious strategical error. 'What do you mean?'

'I've been a millionaire since I was twenty-two.'

He stared at her, trying to absorb this disclosure. A disclosure which could change everything for their future relationship. 'How?'

'I engineered a component and now I own the international patents. I sold the licence for a lump sum, and I also get a small pay-out for each component sold. It brings in a fair amount annually. I never used the money during my marriage; Dilip didn't want me to. I've left my annual income in the hands of some financial investment companies, and the initial licence capital has been sitting in savings accounts gathering interest for six years. I think I'll have enough resources to bring my child up adequately. Even if I don't have a job.'

The disdain dripping in those last sentences was palpable. Nathan was silent. He warred between intense admiration and pride in her accomplishment and shock. 'Why didn't you ever tell me?'

She shrugged. 'It didn't seem important.'

He blinked, trying to reassess the situation. If she didn't need him for financial security, what else could he use to convince her they should be married. He expelled a breath. He should have anticipated this wasn't going to be a quick, easy discussion. They needed to spend some more time together, so they could talk uninterrupted.

He ran a hand over his face. Work was hectic for the next few weeks and it would be Christmas soon. But Saira was right. They needed time to get to know each other again.

CHAPTER TEN

FOUR WEEKS LATER, Saira looked around her as she deboarded Nathan's plane at a private airstrip in the Alps.

Snow. He'd brought her to snow. Snow always held a magical quality for her. It had been years since she'd seen real snow. She'd missed it so much while living in Texas. His kindness warmed her heart.

She'd been hesitant when Nathan first suggested they take a getaway in the New Year to make decisions about the baby. Part of her had worried it was too early to be making decisions—but she knew she couldn't let her anxiety about the pregnancy prevent her from moving forward and making plans. She was trying her best not to let her worries about what could go wrong stop her from experiencing the joy of pregnancy.

'The roads to my chalet are clear,' Nathan said, resting his hand in the curve of her back to direct her. 'My SUV should be waiting outside. We can head there now, unless you want to get something to eat first.'

She shook her head. 'Chalet? So you don't have a Haynes resort here?'

'No. I did a feasibility study at one stage, but I think the ski industry is already well serviced in Europe. Ultimately I went in a different direction.'

Her excitement mounted as Nathan drove along the

cleared roads edged by mounds of snow. He had large warm overcoats and fur-lined boots in her size in the boot.

She bit her lip. She wasn't going to well up at his thoughtfulness. She needed to keep her emotions under control for the difficult conversations they would inevitably have. But that was later. For now she would concentrate on what she'd do once she was outside, crunching in the snowfall.

The chalet was set back in the side of the mountain, but even with Saira's untrained eye she could see its position still allowed easy access to the slopes. There were fifteen other chalets in the area, but there was enough distance between them for privacy.

'Let me show you around,' Nathan said as he helped her down the from the car.

The chalet had a traditional Alpine design, with exposed beams and rustic stone features throughout. Almost every window provided a breath-taking view of the magnificent mountainous vista. The furnishings in the main living area were contemporary, as were the kitchen appliances, but the two en suite bedrooms had the rustic, chic charm she'd imagined for chalet living.

He put her suitcases in what was clearly the master bedroom, and carried his luggage to the smaller room.

Saira sat on a comfy sofa in her favourite area—a cosy snug off the main living room, with a log fire. It was a place where she could curl up with a mug of hot chocolate and a good book...

Although she wasn't here for indulgence but for a difficult and tense conversation.

She ran her hand across the slight swell of her stomach. She smiled. Each day the baby was growing a little bigger, a little stronger. And the need to make some decisions grew bigger too.

'What are you thinking?' Nathan asked, bringing her a cup of tea.

'Thinking about what your lawyers said.'

All of it seemed practical and sensible. Would Nathan accept one of the options offered instead since they would give him the same legal protection as if they were married. What would he get out of marriage that he wouldn't get from these other options?

She tried to see it from his perspective. The only difference was that he wouldn't live with the child. Why was marriage his preferred option when he would be spending so much time working anyway?

She realised she'd asked the question out loud when he replied, 'I want to be around whenever I'm not working. I'd prefer not to juggle my work travel and visitation dates. Marriage is the best solution. It also provides financial security and protection. It's a convenient arrangement.'

Saira heroically refrained from rolling her eyes. He wasn't answering the fundamental question—just concentrating on the work issue. Had she really expected anything different? 'Thanks, but I've already had one arranged marriage. I don't feel the need to have another one.'

He sat back. 'Your marriage to Dilip was arranged?'

'Yes.' She looked at him in surprise. 'I assumed you knew. I mean, it was the modern kind of arrangement. We were introduced by an aunty.'

'I didn't know you had an aunty.'

She grinned. 'An Indian aunty—no actual relation at all.'

'It wasn't love, then?'

'Not at first, but I knew I *could* love him when I agreed to the marriage, and I did grow to love him,' Saira said.

If she hadn't loved Dilip his death wouldn't have broken her. She didn't want to think about losing him. She wrapped her arms across her stomach. She didn't want to think about loss at all.

'What do you care anyway? You don't believe in love.'

'If you had an arranged marriage with Dilip, what's so different about marrying me?' Confusion was clear in his tone.

'Because Dilip wanted to get married. We were both actively looking for a lasting future. We believed we would grow to love each other, and we did. You don't think that's possible, do you?'

He dropped his head, obviously unable to meet her eye.

'So what you're suggesting is worse than an arranged marriage. With you, there's not even the possibility of feelings growing between us. What you're offering is cold and emotionless, and that's not what a marriage should be—definitely not when there's a child involved.'

She paused. She had assumed he was offering a real marriage, but perhaps that wasn't the case.

'Or are you suggesting we have a marriage of convenience only?'

'Marriage *would* be convenient. I've already said that.'

Saira sighed. 'I mean are you thinking we would have a marriage in name only?'

He raised his eyebrows. 'Name only?'

'Yes. Marriage for you to get your legal rights but with no relationship between the two of us.' She spelt it out for him. 'No sex.'

'No!'

She laughed at his emphatic response. Their physical attraction hadn't gone away. If they could have a relationship based on sex alone, she had no doubt it would be successful. But she already knew that wasn't possible. Her feelings for Nathan were too strong.

She sighed as she looked through the large window at the lights from the neighbouring windows, far enough away for them to have absolute privacy, but close enough to cast a magical haze over the scenery.

'What's wrong?' Nathan asked.

'It feels strange.'

He raised his eyebrows in silent question.

'We're in this beautiful place. I'm surrounded by snow.' She gestured widely with her hand. 'And we're here to discuss the future. We'll probably disagree a lot, because that's all we've done so far.' She laughed humourlessly. 'It's a shame I…we…won't get to enjoy it.'

He was silent for a few moments. She sighed. Had she already spoilt the moment by voicing her thoughts?

He came to stand next to her, putting his hand on her shoulder. 'We're here for a week, Saira. We don't have to start the serious discussions straight away. If you want to take a few days to enjoy the area that's not a bad idea. Maybe it will help us feel comfortable in each other's company again. I'm happy with that. Come on, let's take a walk round the chalets into the forest. There's a café on the other side which does excellent cheesy fries. Tomorrow perhaps we can wander round the village. They may still have the Christmas market stalls up, but there are plenty of shops there if not.' He paused. 'Unless you'd prefer to rest?'

Saira shook her head vehemently, desperate to get out into the white wonderland.

After visiting the café, where they shared a bowl of the most delicious fries Saira had ever eaten, they tramped through the snow around the chalets. Nathan looked on with an indulgent smile while she made a rudimentary snowman, giving her confidence to voice her secret wish.

'Really?' he asked, raising an eyebrow. 'You want to make a snow angel?'

'I haven't made one in years,' she replied, staring yearn-

ingly at the snow. It was so hard to resist the temptation
to fling herself down.

'That's because you're an adult.'

In response, she stuck out her tongue and threw a snowball at him.

'That's not fair. I'm a gentleman. I can't retaliate.'

'A gentleman? Or are you being sexist?' She grinned
as she spoke her challenge.

'I'm not going to throw snowballs at a pregnant lady.'

'Is that right?' She bent to gather more snow. 'Good
to know.'

She threw snowballs in quick succession.

'Stop,' he protested with a laugh.

'Make a snow angel for me and I will.'

'*For* you? You want me to make the snow angel?'

'I'm pregnant.' She pressed a hand to her stomach. 'I
don't want to risk hurting the baby if I fall backwards onto
the snow. But I really want to see one.'

She opened her eyes and gave him her most pleading
expression.

'You're doing this to see how far you can push me.'

'Not at all,' she protested, with a lack of conviction.
'One day our child will want to make snow angels. I'll be
the cool, fun mum, right there, playing in the snow with
them. Do you want to be the boring, humourless dad?'

'If that occasion ever happens I promise I will be in
the snow too.'

He turned to head back inside, only stopping when another snowball hit him. She raised her hands in front of
her face in the classic gesture of innocence.

'Come on, Nate. Just one snow angel. I think you should
practise. You don't want to be a huge disappointment to
your kid in the making snow angels department, do you?'
She scrunched her nose. 'I'm only trying to help you.'

Her heart leapt as he laughed, the deep sound reverberating in her soul. He was far too serious at times. She could spend all her days trying to make him laugh.

She turned away to gather her thoughts. She needed to remember their relationship was because they were having a baby, not because of their feelings.

She turned back as he called her name—in time to see him fall back, then wave his arms and legs up and down.

Again, the tears welled up. Why did this kind, generous person believe he had nothing to give in a relationship? If only he would open himself up to the possibility love might develop between them they could have a chance at a real future. She wished she knew how to break through to him—she wished she had the right words.

To stem the flood of emotion, she took out her phone and snapped a picture. 'This one's going on social media.'

She grinned, stretching out a hand. He grabbed it, gently pulling her forward onto her knees.

She laughed. 'I should have expected that.'

He sat up, staring at her but saying nothing. Their gazes locked. She couldn't break away, didn't want to do anything other than drown in those blue depths.

She licked her lips. The flare of awareness was an unwelcome intrusion. The rational part of her brain kept trying to remind her she needed to keep her distance, physically and emotionally, but every other part of her wanted to fling herself into his arms and bury herself in the warmth and security of his embrace.

If she was merely experiencing the old sexual attraction it wouldn't be such a problem; she could resist it. But the lid kept rising on the Pandora's box of her feelings and it was out of her control.

Vaguely she was aware of a cold, wet sensation in her knees. One of them needed to act—do something to release the charged atmosphere. Finally, she moved.

Throwing herself into his arms, she pushed him back in the snow as her lips covered his.

Nathan already had the fire going when Saira came into the snug. She gave him a quick smile before taking a seat.

She hadn't said anything after their kiss. After he'd broken their connection they'd come inside, and she'd gone straight to her bedroom to change out of her wet snowsuit. He almost regretted ending the kiss, but it had flared quickly into desire and he had been moments away from making love to her right there in the snow.

Her expression was inscrutable as she thanked him for the hot chocolate, but at least there were no obvious signs of embarrassment.

'That shouldn't have happened,' she said. 'But it did.' She paused, drawing in a deep breath. 'And, let's be frank, we're still attracted to each other. It will probably keep happening.'

He grinned. Typical Saira—upfront and honest. It was refreshing how she owned her desire.

'What do you think we should do?' she asked.

His brows furrowed. He couldn't pretend the confirmation their sexual attraction was as strong as ever wasn't a huge advantage in his plan to convince her to marry him. But he was prepared to take this slowly, to bank down his sexual needs and give her the space to come round to his way of thinking.

He sat down next to her, turning slightly so he could look at her. Sex with Saira was wonderful, but the last thing he wanted was any resentment on her part. Not if they were going to have a real, true relationship together.

He went still at the thought. Was that what he wanted? A real relationship? Of course he did—but he meant sexually, not emotionally, particularly after what she'd suggested earlier.

'We need to decide this together,' he said.

She nodded in acknowledgement. 'I know, but it's not a simple decision of whether we have an affair or not. Not this time. We have more than Miranda's wedding to think about.'

He nodded too. 'We're going to be parents soon. We're going to be part of each other's lives for the rest of our lives.'

She gave a harsh laugh. 'That's a grim prospect.'

He pursed his lips. If that was how she felt, he had his work cut out for him. 'It's reality. What we need to decide on is what else we'll be to each other.'

It wouldn't be a hardship to be married to Saira. And if he was getting married he wanted a physical relationship with his wife. He would be making a commitment to stay with her. He wasn't going to leave his family looking for sex outside the relationship. He wasn't his father.

His brow furrowed. Was that why she was so adamant she wouldn't marry him? Was she worried he would treat her like his father had treated his mother, ultimately abandoning her after a few years? He didn't blame her if those were her concerns. All he could do was prove to her he was a better man than his father.

Growing up, he had been proud when people compared him to his father, too young to notice all his flaws. Now he tried to distance himself from those comparisons. Even his preference for short-term relationships, ending them before they could get serious, was a reaction to his father, who had been constantly unfaithful during his marriage. It was better to end a relationship early rather than risk hurting someone, risk breaking their heart.

Nathan could promise Saira he wouldn't do the same. Marriage might not have been in his plans, but once he took his vows he would keep them. He needed to convince Saira of that.

He deliberately adopted a matter-of-fact tone. 'You know my preference.' He held up his hand as she opened her mouth to protest. 'But that's a separate discussion for another day.'

'It shouldn't be this hard,' she said with a rueful smile. 'All I wanted was a brief affair with an attractive man I really liked. And now look where we are. I don't want to rush into anything.'

She placed her hand across her stomach in a protective gesture. He might worry about whether he would be a good father after the baby was born, but she was worrying constantly already. It wasn't only about the future. She was anxious for this pregnancy. He understood why, based on her previous experience. He wished he could take her worry away. All he could do was be supportive while remaining positive—and make sure he didn't add to her worries.

'Part of the problem is you overthink things,' he said, reaching out to shake her knee gently. His hand rested there of its own accord.

On cue, she laughed in disbelief. 'Me? You do too.'

He shrugged casually. The best course of action was to keep things light between them. Sex didn't have to be a big deal. Not if they agreed boundaries. It had worked after they'd had the discussion in Gozo. There was no reason they couldn't come to a mutually satisfactory agreement this time too.

Although of course their initial agreement to keep their fling to their time on the island had gone out of the window once they'd continued their affair in London. Their physical attraction was special. He had never experienced the same with anyone else.

His mouth went dry as Saira reached out to put her mug on the low coffee table, the action tautening her jeans along her thighs, stretching her jumper across her full breasts.

Hopefully that agreement would find her in his arms and in his bed.

'How about we let things happen for the time being?' he said. 'We've already agreed we'll spend a few days enjoying the area before we have a serious talk. Why don't we decide how we factor in our attraction then?'

'So, ignore it until then?'

'No, that's not what I meant at all.'

The warmth from the simple touch of his hand on her knee was spreading through him, providing a sense of ease and comfort rather than anything sexual at that moment.

'Why don't we enjoy this time together for the next few days, indulge this attraction? Later, when we discuss the baby, we can talk about whether we end it then, or continue for a limited time, or see how it plays out.'

'Go with the flow?' She quirked an eyebrow. 'That doesn't sound like you at all.'

'I'm not going to pretend I like this uncertainty, but you need to relax. Let's enjoy a few days without any talk of future plans, enjoy each other's company and see where our attraction takes us.'

He stared intently into her eyes, willing her to agree with his suggestion.

CHAPTER ELEVEN

SAIRA SAT CLOSE to the fire in the living room, sad that their brief holiday was already half over. Nathan was in the kitchen, preparing dinner, as he had every night so far.

He wasn't being subtle. He hadn't given up on the idea of them getting married, and there wasn't much he wouldn't do to get what he wanted. And she had to admit if she could make her decision based on his domestic skills alone they'd be in front of the registrar signing the marriage certificate as soon as they landed in London.

He hadn't argued with her decision to keep their relationship platonic. Tempted as she was to indulge their attraction, she wanted a clear head when they had their talk. She didn't want to be clouded by a sexual fug.

It hadn't stopped him flirting with her constantly. Which was fine. She was flirting outrageously back, and both of them were sneaking in quick kisses.

It was light and fun—like being a comfortable married couple.

She sighed. If they were a married couple it would be anything but comfortable. Much as she hated to end this idyllic time, they couldn't put off having their serious discussion much longer. The last couple of days had been a brief glimpse into what her world would be like if all her dreams could come true. But reality was always lurking, ready to intrude.

In an effort to distract herself she scrolled through messages and emails on her phone, smiling at an email from her mother with Indian wives' remedies for growing a healthy baby.

When she'd told her parents about her pregnancy over Christmas their reaction had taken her aback. Rather than being disappointed or concerned they'd both been overjoyed she was happy. She hadn't appreciated how worried they were about her since she'd lost her pregnancy and then Dilip died.

When they asked about the baby's father, it had been tempting to lie and pretend she and Nathan were together. In the end she wanted an honest relationship with her parents. She was strong enough to deal with the consequences of her actions and follow through on her decisions. They'd have to respect her independence.

They hadn't even blinked an eye when she explained the situation. They didn't know Nathan well, but they already loved Miranda, and were prepared to extend that love to her brother if he made their daughter happy.

She sighed. Sometimes it was hard to see that her parents' overprotective and disciplined approach to her upbringing was their way of loving her—a product of their own upbringing, not an attempt to assert control. She was learning there were many aspects of her past that she'd interpreted from an immature perspective. Including her relationship with Nathan.

Looking back from his point of view, she could see how her leaving him so soon after his father had abandoned the family contributed to his belief love and relationships were not meant to last.

She'd promised herself to stop dwelling on the past. She had to concentrate on the future—which included finding somewhere else to live.

After sending a quick reply to her mother, she checked

her emails from estate agents. At the end of December her landlord had told her he was selling the flat and she needed to leave. So now she had to add house hunting on top of everything else she had to do to prepare for the baby.

Her hand cupped her slight but growing bump as she tried to download a file without success.

She walked through to the kitchen. Her glance took in the table setting, with flowers and candles, and she grimaced. If only she could make Nathan understand romantic gestures meant little unless there was true sentiment behind them. He cared about her. And because of that he would always look after her. But she wasn't interested in being taken care of. She was strong enough to take care of herself.

'What's up?' he asked.

'Can I use your laptop, please? Some estate agents have sent through a few particulars but I can't see them properly on my phone. I want to make appointments for viewings for when we get back home.'

He nodded. 'You mentioned you have to leave your flat soon.'

'Yes. But to be honest once I found out about the pregnancy I decided I want to buy a house. Somewhere with a garden, ideally.'

'Then you're staying in England? What about those job opportunities abroad?'

She pressed her lips together. It was curiosity, she reminded herself. He wasn't telling her where to live. It was irrelevant anyway.

'I'm putting my job hunt on the back burner for now. I don't know what the future holds, but I do know I want to be with our child while they're young. I feel blessed I have the choice. I put some feelers out about voluntary positions, so I can still contribute. We'll see,' she finished with a shrug.

'Any ideas where you'll live?'

'I was thinking, perhaps, looking in Buckinghamshire. I loved growing up there. And it's near your mum, and not too far from Ajay. It would be nice to be close to family. In an ideal world I would be able to buy before I have to move out, but there's such a shortage of houses available so who knows?' she said, flinging her hands up in the air. 'At least I don't have to worry about getting a mortgage, so I'm not going to complain about my first world problems.'

'You could stay at my place until you find somewhere.'

She reared her head. 'Really?'

'Of course. And we ought to discuss together where our child lives.'

Saira nodded slowly. 'I guess that makes sense... You'll want us to live close to London, so you don't have to travel too far for visits.'

'It's more than that. I meant what I said before. I would rather not have restrictions on when I can spend time with my kid. That's one of the reasons it would be best if we're married. I'm sure you don't want to be apart from the baby while he or she is with me, particularly if you're breast-feeding.'

Her mouth opened and she furrowed her brows. 'I hadn't really thought about it.' How had she not thought about that before? Deep anguish filled her at the realisation that unless she lived with Nathan her baby would regularly be away from her.

When she'd thought about Nathan seeing their baby, for some reason she'd imagined him in her house, spending time there. She hadn't for one moment thought the baby would be away overnight with him. How could she have been so naïve?

But now the reality of her future flooded through her mind. Periods of separation from her child. How many moments, how many milestones would she miss?

Nathan tilted her chin up with a questioning expression. 'Is something wrong?' he asked.

She shook her head giving him a wan smile.

'Dinner's almost ready. Do you want to use my laptop first?'

'No, it can wait,' she replied, taking a seat at the table.

Her thoughts were whirling, but until she had time to put them in order she didn't want to discuss them with anyone.

She took a mouthful of tender chunks of beef with perfectly cooked vegetables and groaned. 'This is delicious, Nate. Thank you.'

'You're welcome. How about a kiss for the chef?' he asked, bending towards her, his lips puckered.

She laughed before giving him a quick peck, then pushed his head away. She loved this light-hearted side of him. Why couldn't he admit he had feelings? Or allow the possibility that they could grow?

He did care about her—she could tell. If he would just try to give their relationship a chance to be loving and real—the way she had when she'd married Dilip—then they would both get what they wanted. But unless he admitted there was a chance he could love her it was hopeless.

And that was the crux of the matter. The real reason she didn't want to marry Nathan.

If he wasn't open to love growing between them he would feel trapped in their marriage. She would have to stand by every day knowing he desperately wanted to be free but was bound to her by his strong sense of honour and his need to prove he wasn't like his father.

He would come to resent her, and then, perversely, she would lose what mattered most. She would lose any chance of being loved, any chance at lasting happiness.

But if she didn't marry him she faced the idea of being

separated from her baby for days and weeks at a time. The mere notion tore at her heartstrings. How had she been so foolish that she hadn't considered the reality of her child spending part of their time in a different house? For the first time she could understand why women married men they barely knew to ensure they would always be in their child's life.

She would consider all options if it meant not being separated from her baby. It didn't matter what the risk to her heart was. She sighed heavily. Why couldn't she have both?

Nathan sprayed whipped cream on the mug of hot chocolate, then added some marshmallows. He placed the mug on a tray next to a glass of orange juice and some breakfast pastries.

The previous evening Saira had been quiet over dinner and had then retired to her room. The discussions they needed to have were clearly weighing on her mind.

'Morning,' Saira said, coming into the kitchen area. 'Can I use your laptop later, please? I still need to email the estate agents.'

'Sure. I was about to bring you up some breakfast.' He gave her a bright smile which she didn't return.

She glanced quickly at the tray. 'Thanks, but I'm not hungry.'

'You didn't have much dinner last night either. It's not good for the baby if you don't eat properly.'

'Fine,' she said, perching on one of the kitchen bar stools and pulling the tray towards her. Irritation crossed her face.

What had he said wrong now? Wasn't he supposed to be concerned for his child's wellbeing? He wasn't accusing her of anything.

Perhaps she was in a mood because she hadn't slept well. He thought he'd heard her pacing during the night.

She ate without speaking, deliberately concentrating on her phone.

'Ugh,' she groaned.

'What's up?' he asked.

'My mobile's reception here is terrible. Do you get a good signal? Can I use yours, please? I need to speak to Bastien.'

'Sure,' he said handing over his mobile.

Bastien? Why was she speaking to him?

She walked over to the window, where he couldn't hear her, but it was clear she was laughing. It wasn't jealousy he was experiencing, but her body language was completely relaxed as she chatted to Bastien. So different from the slight tension which was now present in their conversations.

'Is everything all right?' he asked when she returned.

Her smile dropped when she faced him. 'Yes. He says hello and he'll be in touch with you soon.'

'I didn't realise you and Bastien knew each other.'

Her eyebrows rose. 'We met on the holiday, remember?'

'I know. I meant I didn't realise you kept in touch.' It shouldn't bother him. He hoped it didn't sound as if he was bothered.

Saira frowned. 'I'm in touch with most of the people I met on holiday.'

'Why?'

'Why not? I liked them. I've met up with some of them individually a couple of times since we've been back. I'm surprised they didn't mention it, since you and I were together at the time. I haven't seen them since I found out about the pregnancy, though. I'm looking forward to seeing them at the Spring Ball. I should probably tell them about the baby, otherwise the big belly could come as a bit of a shock,' she said, giving him the first smile he'd seen from her that morning.

'The Spring Ball? I didn't know you were going to it.'

'I'm helping Bastien and his family with their foundation. They want to add a STEM element, so they've been liaising with Kent and me. I cannot believe Bastien's brother is an earl. I mean an honest to goodness peer of the realm. I almost curtseyed when we were introduced. No wonder Bastien sometimes hams up playing the part of the feckless spare to the heir so well.' She was silent for a moment. 'What is it? Have I done something wrong?'

'No, I wasn't aware you were in touch with my friends. That's all.'

How had he not known his friends had kept in contact with Saira? They never bothered to keep in touch with his other former girlfriends, thankfully.

'Don't worry. It's not going to interfere with your Six-Month Men Club. I'm their friend in my own right, not as your ex-girlfriend. I hope you don't have a problem with that,' she said, and then he caught the mumble under her breath. 'Not that it would matter to me if you *did* have a problem.'

His lips twitched. What a relief. The sass was back. His friends enjoyed wit and intelligent banter. Saira was exactly the kind of woman they'd like as a friend. And it would make their semi-annual get-togethers much better if they all got on well.

He tilted his head. The baby would only be a couple of months old in September. Perhaps Saira wouldn't want to travel.

He grinned. He was sure his friends would understand his reason for being the first one of them not to show up at their annual holiday. Hopefully, it would only be that first year, and after that Saira would be happy to join them with the baby. Then there would be family holidays with the three of them, or maybe four or more in the future…

An image of him in a swimming pool surrounded by Saira and their children came to mind. He was getting ahead of himself. He and Saira would have a practical marriage—it wasn't going to be like some romanticised family travel advert.

They still hadn't made any decisions.

'Would you like some coffee?' he asked holding up the pot. 'It's decaf.'

He grimaced. He hadn't realised how much he relied on caffeine to fuel him before he'd gone cold turkey in solidarity with Saira's pregnancy.

'No, thanks. The hot chocolate and orange juice are already more than enough for my bladder to handle.'

He glanced at her stomach, marvelling at the slight swell—a visible sign of his growing child. Ever since his father had left he never thought he would be a father himself, scared he was genetically incapable of being around for his children. But watching his baby grow a little each week was an experience he wouldn't want to miss.

The truth was his father hadn't been a presence in their lives for most of his childhood. His final abandonment had been more difficult for his mother and sisters to handle than it had for him. He would never do the same thing.

He frowned. Marrying Saira made the most sense to him in this situation, but the reality was he had no concern she would restrict his time with his child. He had no doubts she would be generous with visitation and give him the same legal rights he would have if they were married.

And she had made it clear she was staying in the country. She wasn't planning to run away this time.

Could he honestly say he would have offered marriage to any woman who came to him with an unexpected pregnancy? He would have done the right thing, of course, so if any of his exes had become pregnant and wanted marriage he would have complied, but it wouldn't have been something he would insist on if he could have the necessary legal protections without it.

Why was he being so insistent with Saira? It wasn't simply because she was his sister's friend.

'We should talk,' he said abruptly.

'I know. I'm ready. Shall we go into the other room? We may as well be comfortable, and it will seem too formal if we talk over the table.'

They moved into the snug, sitting on separate sofas. The intimacy had already disappeared.

'We may as well dive in,' he said. 'You know my opinion. We get on well. I think we could have a successful marriage.'

'Based on what?' She raised her hands, shaking her head. 'I don't get this complete one-eighty you've done. You made it clear over and over that there was no future. You were adamant you don't do long-term commitment.'

'Things are different now.'

'Because there's a baby?'

'What other reason would there be?'

It wasn't a one-eighty. He still didn't believe marriages based on the romantic fiction of everlasting love would work. But a marriage based on raising a child, where there was also mutual respect and attraction, could be successful. He would work hard to make sure of it.

She rubbed her eyes. 'It doesn't matter what kind of marriage you're suggesting. I don't want to get married again. Not now, not ever. For me, having a child doesn't change the way I feel.'

He ran his hand over his face. For someone who claimed she'd once dreamed of a long-term future with him, getting married and having children together, she was showing great reluctance at the possibility of her dreams coming true.

He grimaced. He wasn't making her dreams come true, though—not really. She was a romantic at heart. She might have had an arranged marriage, but by her own words she had grown to love her husband. Her dream had never been for a loveless marriage—he couldn't offer her anything else.

He couldn't offer her love, or even pretend there was the possibility love would grow between them. Emotions were a weakness. Romantic love was a hormonal-induced illusion which didn't last.

He could try saying the words, if they would persuade her to marry him, but she would see through his deception which would make the situation worse.

He still had to make his case for a chance to have a real family.

'I think marriage is the best option for us.' He raised his hand before she could protest. 'I promise I'll keep an open mind while we talk about other options. As long as you promise to do the same about marriage.'

Saira furrowed her brows. He could see her wrestling with her thoughts before she gave a brief nod.

'At work, when we're trying to decide what action to take, we keep nothing off the table,' she said. 'All ideas are up for debate, nothing is too stupid. The only rule is we don't argue for or against until we've run out of ideas. Then we go to the evaluation phase. Perhaps we should approach this like that.'

'All ideas are on the table?'

'Everything—no matter how stupid.'

His lips twitched. If it kept marriage as an option he'd go with whatever method she proposed. How would she react if he suggested they use a SWOT analysis for their evaluation?

'Fine,' he said.

'Okay, then.'

Saira's smile warmed his heart.

She looked around, then walked away, coming back a few moments later with a paper and pens.

'The first option is to stay as we are. Stay separate, with a legal agreement to outline our arrangements.'

'Or we could get married.'

Saira rolled her eyes, but wrote on the paper. 'Perhaps we should outline what kind of marriage. We've already talked about having a platonic marriage of convenience.'

Nathan inhaled. He'd already discarded that notion, but he'd agreed nothing was off the table. 'That's one possibility. Or we could have a real marriage—with sex.'

'Well, I did say no idea was stupid at this stage,' she replied, writing it down.

He cleared his throat, trying to cover his laugh. 'Is that it, then? Some kind of marriage or continuing the way we are?'

Frankly, he didn't have much hope of them coming to an agreement during the holiday if those were the only options.

'We could have a time-limited marriage of convenience, so you could get your legal rights, and then we separate.'

'That is a possibility,' he said.

Not one he would agree to. If he got married he would be making a commitment and he would be staying married. He wouldn't be another Haynes male who couldn't make his marriage last. Like father, like son.

'I suppose my concern now is not being with the baby when it's your visitation time,' Saira said.

Marriage would take care of that. He nodded encouragingly.

'We could buy a place together,' she continued.

That was an unexpected suggestion. He turned the idea over in his mind. 'Live together, you mean?'

'Yes. Like housemates. I'm sure we could find a place big enough for us to live separate lives under the same roof. You could have the east wing and I could have the west wing.'

She giggled, and something intense flared through him.

'Or we could live together as a couple,' he suggested.

'You mean with sex?'

'Yes.'

'I don't know—'

'No stupid ideas, remember? Write it down.' He smiled watching her chew her lips as she wrote. 'Unless we have any more options, why don't I make us a drink and we can move on to evaluation,' he said, standing.

If he could convince her to live together as a couple it wouldn't be a far stretch to convince her to marry him. Then he would be able to do his duty to Saira and his child. And prove he wasn't like his father.

CHAPTER TWELVE

'I DON'T THINK we'll be able to buy a place before I need to move out of my flat,' Saira said, her dejection obvious. 'I guess I shouldn't complain. At least I have options. I can find somewhere to rent or move into my parents' place.'

They'd been back in England for almost a month. At the end of their Alpine holiday they'd agreed to buy a place together—live together but not as a couple. It was the solution she had hoped for. The only one that meant she wouldn't be separated from her child but Nathan wouldn't feel trapped, and she could remain hopeful that a real, loving relationship between the two of them might develop.

Since her return home, she'd spent every day she could going on house viewings. Nathan accompanied her when he was in town, but he'd been travelling most of the time.

There was one house she had fallen in love with immediately on viewing. It ticked all her boxes, and also included the non-essential extras Nathan had mentioned, with its basement leisure and entertainment suite. But the extras took it out of her budgeted price. She'd only agreed to the viewing because Nathan wanted to get an idea of what was available at different price points. Which was a mistake—it set the bar too high for any other properties they'd seen since.

'Your mother also suggested I move in with her,' she said, glancing in his direction, wondering whether he would suggest she move in with him while they continued the search.

He was looking straight ahead, with a strange smile on his face.

She narrowed her eyes. 'What?'

He shook his head, pressing his lips together. 'I have a surprise for you.'

They were on their way to have lunch with Nathan's mother and sisters, taking the opportunity to show them the picture of their baby from the twenty-week scan the previous week. It was still unbelievable to her how clear the image of their daughter was.

She grinned. *Daughter.* They were having a girl. And if the scan was anything to go by she'd inherited her father's nose.

How was she already halfway through her pregnancy?

She rubbed a hand across her stomach. Her growing bump and the fluttering movements she was beginning to feel were a welcome sign her baby was growing and getting stronger. Part of her would always worry about this pregnancy, but every milestone she passed was a celebration for her.

There was still four months before the baby was due, but she felt unprepared. Did she even know how to be a mother to a girl? Loving her daughter and taking the best care of her weren't in question. But she wanted to be more.

Their daughter would love and admire her father—there was no doubt about that. But could she be a guide for her daughter? Someone she would look up to and be proud of?

She had to stop second-guessing herself. But this unknown territory terrified her.

She glanced over at Nathan, who still had a Cheshire Cat grin on his face. She'd missed him so much while he'd been travelling. But he wanted to take at least a month off once the baby was born; she couldn't fault him for that.

When they'd agreed to buy a place together it had sounded rational. She'd congratulated herself for getting Nathan to agree to her practical, if unorthodox, solution. But was it really a solution or was she being naive? Wasn't she risking more hurt and loss if Nathan did decide to leave her one day?

She'd asked herself the same questions over and over again and would probably continue to do so.

She wasn't sure how far she believed in Nathan's promise to keep marriage off the table—she suspected it might make a reappearance at any time.

She understood his need for the security of knowing he would be a real part of his child's life. She'd watched how he and Miranda had suffered the first time their father had left—even as a teenager he had a deep-seated desire not to be seen as like his father. She could even understand his need to create a family of his own—although she suspected he hadn't even admitted that was one of his reasons for asking her to marry him.

Was she even correct in thinking if Nathan was forced to marry her he would feel trapped and never learn to love her? Were his feelings more likely to grow if they stayed unmarried? She'd taken a chance with Dilip that he would come to love her—couldn't she do it again?

She mentally shook her head. No, that could only happen if Nathan was open to the idea that love and happily-ever-after existed. He hadn't said anything to show he had changed his mind about that.

They'd also come to a more formal agreement on the future arrangements for their daughter, including contingencies if things didn't work out.

And that was what her marriage to Nathan would be—a relationship with contingencies. She didn't want that. She wanted a true relationship in which she could love openly, with all her heart. And be loved in return.

Nathan wasn't offering her that.

In all their discussions they'd concentrated on what would happen in the future. They still weren't talking about the past, about the problems that had driven them apart—although it was clear the resentment, the blame, was still a sore point for him. For both of them. Until they did talk about that, any real future together wasn't a possibility.

The sudden quiet stillness made her realise the car had stopped and the engine was turned off. He turned to face her, reaching across the gearstick to cover her hands.

'Well,' he said. 'Here we are.'

They were in front of her dream house. Her smile faltered. 'Why are we here? We've already viewed this house.'

'You loved it—be honest.'

'Of course. It's perfect, except it's too expensive. We already discussed this.'

What was he thinking? Why did he look so pleased?

He shrugged. 'Come on,' he said, getting out of the car and coming round to open her door. 'Come with me.'

He took a set of keys from his jacket pocket and opened the front door.

'Surprise!' he said, with a large smile on his face as he threw his arms wide.

Saira gave a smaller smile, looking round the hall in bewilderment.

'I don't understand,' she said. 'What's the surprise?'

'This,' he replied, gesturing round.

'This house?'

He nodded, beaming.

'You bought it?' she asked in disbelief.

Nathan laughed. 'No, of course not. I know you have this ridiculously strange desire to be involved in the conveyancing process. I wasn't going to deprive you of that joy.' He tapped her nose affectionately. 'No. I rented it.'

She shook her head. 'I need to sit down.'

She walked into the lounge area, noticing the furniture in place. When they'd viewed the property it had been empty, the owners having moved out already.

'What's happened? Where did all this come from?' she asked, pointing to the furniture.

'I rented that too. If you don't like anything we can easily replace it. Either buy new stuff or rent something different. Up to you. I didn't want you to come into an empty house.'

The last thing she'd expected this morning was for Nathan to have rented the house she loved.

'How did this happen? I didn't know it was available for rent.'

He gave her a pointed look.

'Oh, I see,' she said with dawning understanding. 'Money talks.'

'I made them an offer they couldn't refuse.' He waggled his eyebrows. 'I've rented it for a year with an option to buy.'

She laughed at his playfulness. 'Why? Why would you go to that trouble?' she asked.

'Because you love this house. And you were getting stressed about not having somewhere to move to. I know you're worried about tempting fate by doing things too early for the baby. Renting was the perfect solution to all those issues.'

Saira covered her mouth. How had he known? The first time she'd voiced her concern about not finding a place had been in the car earlier. And she *had* been reluctant to commit to large purchases or finalise things for the baby. How had he picked up on that?

She would do anything to keep this Nathan around—

not the stern, serious man he often presented to the rest of the world. This Nathan, with his generous heart and cheerful, carefree manner. She wanted a relationship with this Nathan.

'Saira...' His voice broke softly into her thoughts. 'Is everything all right?'

Saira gulped. 'Everything's perfect. This is perfect.' She stood up, walked over to him, and threw her arms round his waist—or as far as she could reach with her protruding bump getting between them. 'Thank you.'

'You're welcome,' he replied, kissing the top of her head. 'I'd do anything for you and our baby—you know that.'

Saira was unable to say anything, reluctant to break away from his enveloping warmth.

After a few moments he gently pulled away. 'Come on, my mum's expecting us. We should head off.'

They arrived at his mother's house within half an hour and went straight into the dining room for their meal.

Lunch with Nathan, his mother and his sisters was always an entertaining occasion. Miranda and Steve had also come up for the day. Naturally, most of the focus was on the baby, the scan photos, and Nathan's surprise house rental.

Saira had a broad smile perpetually on her face as she watched the family interact. Her baby was lucky to be a part of this close-knit group. She studied Nathan's profile as he listened intently to his sisters. His expression was soft and there was an indulgent half-smile about his lips.

There was no doubt in her mind he would make a loving, involved, if somewhat overprotective, father. He was the kindest, most caring, most thoughtful person she knew.

It was one part of the complex tapestry that made up the man she was in love with.

She inhaled sharply, her eyes widening.

She was in love with him. Of course she was. Why else had she been worried about a loveless marriage?

She didn't *want* to love him. Had tried to stop herself. Convince herself she wanted to be independent. Love meant losing control. Love meant loss, and she'd already lost so much—her baby, Dil… She'd even lost Nathan once before.

But it didn't matter. She loved Nathan.

They were having a baby together. They were going to live together. If she reached out and told him how she felt, perhaps he would start believing that long-lasting love was possible. Perhaps they could work through the past. Perhaps he would be open to the idea that he might come to love her. And perhaps they could have a real future together.

The possibility was terrifying.

She tuned back in to the conversation in the middle of Beatrice telling them a story about something that had happened to her on the internet.

'I think you need to be careful,' Nathan said to his sister when she'd finished her story. 'It all sounds a bit fishy to me.'

'Yeah, that's what Dad said too,' Beatrice replied.

Nathan reared back, his entire torso stiffening. Keeping his voice quiet and steady, he asked, 'What did you say?'

Beatrice stared at him defiantly—an expression he hadn't seen on his sister since her rebellious teen years.

'Dad got in touch with us,' Beatrice explained. 'He wanted to meet with us and we wanted to meet with him. So we did. He wants to be back in our lives.'

Back in their lives. Just like that. After eight years his father had waltzed back into his sisters' lives. Probably not caring about the damage he would do.

He clenched his fist. A warm hand covered it, giving it a gentle squeeze. He looked at Saira while he tried to gather his whirling thoughts.

Why was his father back? What did he want?

And his sisters didn't seem to have any problem in agreeing to meet him. Had they forgotten how he'd abandoned them when they were younger? Didn't they remember the nights they spent crying in Nathan's arms, asking him why their daddy didn't love them any more?

'Why?'

A simple question, but he needed answers to many different whys.

Why had his father returned? Why now? Why was he disrupting their carefully rebuilt lives after so many years? Why were his sisters letting their father back in their lives? Why weren't they worried his father would turn his backs on them again? Why didn't they care how Nathan felt—after everything he tried to do for them? Why didn't they care how much meeting their father would hurt Nathan? *Why?*

'He wants to get to know us,' Beatrice said.

'He hasn't cared about that for years.'

'That's not true, Nathan,' his mother said.

He turned to focus his attention on her. 'What do you mean?' he asked.

'He tried to keep in touch after he went to Australia, but he knew it upset me so he didn't push it. And I honestly believed it was better for the girls not to be torn between us. But he's asked a few times every year. He told me he's tried to contact you and Miranda on a number of occasions, but you've rebuffed him.'

'Did he expect me to welcome him with open arms?'

His mother glanced at her plate, her hand playing with the stem of her wine glass. 'When Juliet turned eighteen

I said it was her choice, and she and Beatrice both decided to see him.'

'I see. It doesn't bother you he's back?' he asked his mother.

'I'm fine with it—honestly, Nathan,' his mother replied. 'What about you? Do you think you'll meet your father while he's in the country?'

'I don't think so.'

He had nothing to say to the man. Juliet and Beatrice might be ready for a relationship with their father, but he knew better. His father was fickle—his love for his family nothing but a transient emotion. Nathan suspected any warnings he tried to give would fall on deaf ears.

He sighed internally. If he couldn't protect his sisters from hurt, then he would have to be ready to comfort them when his father walked away again.

He turned to Miranda, who hadn't said much so far. 'Has Dad been in contact with you?'

His sister's inability to meet his eyes gave him her answer. He closed his eyes, lowering his head. She'd lied to him too.

He took a deep breath, looking round the table at his family. 'I'm sorry I made you feel you couldn't tell me you were meeting with him.'

'I didn't know how I would feel until I did.' Miranda took a deep breath, grasping Steve's hand. 'I know it was hard when Dad left. The last time particularly. You were there for us—you stepped in as a father figure even though you were barely an adult yourself. I understand why you don't want to be in contact with Dad. But over the last few years I've been thinking about Dad a lot. Especially after I started falling for Steve. I've wanted to meet Dad for a while. I hope you understand, Nathan.'

He was trying hard to understand, but out of his whole

family keeping their father's return from him, Miranda's secrecy felt the most like betrayal.

He loved all his sisters—would do anything for them. But he and Miranda had always been particularly close. There was a large age gap between them and Beatrice and Juliet. Miranda had been only ten when their dad had left the first time. Nathan looked after her when their mother was unable to, trying to make up for his father's absence.

Now she had hidden this meeting from him.

'Nathan,' Miranda said. 'I want to invite Dad to my wedding.'

He took a forceful breath, trying to calm the blood rushing through his head. He pasted on a smile. 'It's your wedding, Miranda. You should invite whoever you want to invite. You don't need to check with me.'

They discussed the wedding arrangements for a while, with talk of their father seemingly forgotten, until Juliet said with a grin, 'Maybe Dad can walk you down the aisle, Miranda.'

Miranda laughed, but didn't say anything to contradict her. Nathan hoped his face didn't show his shock. Perhaps it made sense that a daughter wanted her father to perform the traditional role. But his sense of betrayal was stronger than ever.

'It's odd you don't want to meet Dad,' Beatrice said. 'Particularly now you're going to be a father yourself. I think you'd get along well. You're exactly like him.'

Although he'd heard people say that for years, the comparison was a bitter pill that day, Finding out his mother and sisters had been lying, keeping secrets from him—excluding him from their lives. Hearing they were ready to welcome a man who'd walked out on them before. A man who'd already proved he couldn't be trusted. A man who had never been there when they'd needed him. A man they couldn't depend on.

Was that really how his family saw him too? Like that man?

He'd given up so much for his family. Changed his plans so he could stay around for them. Lost his relationship with Saira. And they thought he was exactly like the man who'd abandoned his family without a backward glance.

A small squeak from Saira brought him back to the present. He loosened his grip on her hand. He took a deep, shuddering breath and tried to concentrate on the ongoing conversation.

The drive back to Saira's apartment was made in silence. He ignored Saira's efforts to initiate a conversation. He didn't want her pity—or, worse, her justifications for his family's decision to hide their meetings with his father. In the end she dozed off.

He'd never expected to be a father, and his instinct to be there for this child had been so strong it had overpowered his rational common sense. For a brief moment he'd thought he could be the kind of parent his father never was. But past was prologue. He couldn't do long term and he would be a fool to convince himself otherwise.

He *was* like his father. Everyone said it. As much as he would like to deny it, he had to accept it was true. Like his father, he didn't know how to commit. He couldn't take a chance on hurting his child the way his sisters had been hurt.

He would hurt Saira too. Perhaps she didn't care for him yet, but she would eventually—particularly if he persuaded her to restart their physical relationship. It was in her nature to care, to love wholeheartedly. He would inevitably hurt her the way he had before.

He could finally admit it to himself—the reality he'd been refusing to acknowledge for years. Despite their youth, Saira had developed strong feelings for him in the past. She'd loved him then. He'd pulled away and it had broken her heart. Despite his best intentions, in trying to spare her feelings and not wanting to give her false expectations he'd ended up doing the one thing he never wanted to do.

He'd hurt her deeply.

Maybe as deeply as his father had hurt his mother.

Wasn't he about to repeat the same behaviour? Promising Saira something based on the best intentions but knowing it wasn't something he could truly deliver. What if he really was like his father and would walk out on his family some time in the future. He wanted to commit to them, but he could he, from the bottom of his heart, make that promise?

He could potentially hurt Saira much more in the future if he tried to stay a part of her life. And, worse, this time he would also hurt their daughter. He couldn't put them through that. He wanted to believe he was a better man, but he wouldn't risk hurting Saira or his daughter. He wouldn't risk breaking their hearts when he couldn't live up to their expectations.

Far better not to be there at all than to break their hearts somewhere down the line. Far better to do it now, before he caused her more pain.

Something shifted inside him as he closed the doors around the possibility of raising the daughter he already loved. It was the hardest decision he would ever have to make. But walking away now was the best thing for her— and for Saira.

He parked outside Saira's place, then shook her gently awake. She gave him a sweet smile which twisted his heart.

'Saira, we need to talk.'

She blinked a couple of times, as if trying to clear the sleep away. 'Sure, do you want to come up?'

He shook his head. 'I think you and the baby will be better off if I'm not part of your lives.'

'What?' she asked with a disbelieving laugh.

'I'm only going to hurt you and her in the long run. I'll provide financial support, naturally. But I don't think we should live together. I don't think it's sensible for me to be part of her life while she's growing up. It's too big a risk. Perhaps when she's older she can decide whether she wants to know me.'

Saira scrunched her forehead. 'I don't understand. What risk? We shouldn't talk about this in the car. Why don't you come up and we can discuss this properly?'

'There's nothing to discuss. I won't be responsible for breaking her heart.'

'I don't understand,' Saira repeated. 'Where is all this coming from? You're not making sense. The whole point of all this, and us looking for a house together, is so you can be there for your child. So that we can both be.'

'I thought that was the best solution, but I was wrong. Our girl will be better off without me in her life at all rather than have me float in and out when I have time for her. I saw what that did to my sisters and my mother.'

Saira turned to him, shock in her eyes, 'You would never do that.'

'I wish that was true, but I can't guarantee it. I'm too much like my father. As much as I hate it, it's true. I understand now why you don't want to marry me. I'm a bad risk. I hurt you in the past, and you're rightly worried I'm going to hurt you both by abandoning you and the baby.'

'That's not it at all. Look, Nathan… I get the news of your father has come as a huge shock, but there's no need to overreact. Of course it would be better if our daughter grows up with you in her life.'

He stiffened at her implication he was overreacting. He was doing the best thing for his daughter and for Saira.

'You're wrong. Miranda, Juliet and Beatrice, even my mother, were all better off when my father left once and for all.'

Saira opened her mouth, but then closed it. He swallowed under her intense scrutiny and turned to face forward, concentrating heavily on the car parked in front. She sighed deeply. He sensed her nodding a couple of times before she opened the car door. He turned to the side as he felt cold air come through the open door.

She leaned in. 'I don't think you're going to listen to anything I have to say at the moment. But I know you will be there for us. I trust you. I hope you change your mind, Nathan. I hope it for your sake and our baby's.'

She closed the door.

Why did she trust him? All the evidence showed to the contrary. He was his father's son. She was wrong to trust him.

He watched as she walked to her apartment building, resisting the temptation to go after her. As she entered the code she rested her other hand on her growing bump. He sucked in a breath. It would kill him not to be able to watch his daughter grow up. It would kill him to stay away from Saira—not to talk to her, not to hear her laugh, not to hold her in his arms.

But he was doing the right thing. For them—if not for him. He had to walk away before anyone else got hurt.

CHAPTER THIRTEEN

IT HAD BEEN two weeks since Nathan had dropped his bombshell announcement. Saira waited for him to contact her, tell her he'd made a mistake, changed his mind. Nothing.

With no scans or doctor's appointments on the horizon, in the end she'd messaged him, asking for the keys to the rental house. Now she was standing outside the property, waiting for them to be brought round.

She was trying to empathise with his situation. It must have been devastating to find out from his sisters that his father was back in their lives. Worse to realise they'd kept it from him. She didn't blame him for his reaction. She was sure once he'd had the chance to process things he would see there was no comparison between his father and himself, and he would want to carry on with their plans to move in together.

Why couldn't he talk about how he was feeling with her instead of closing himself off and shutting her out? Every time she wanted him to turn to her, to show her he needed her, he turned away instead.

Her heart literally hurt as her dreams of the future crashed before her.

It didn't even make any sense. Nathan couldn't simply drop out of their lives. She was his sister's best friend. They would always be seeing each other.

She couldn't believe he really meant to stay away. She didn't want to believe it.

Perhaps she was fooling herself, but the fact that Nathan had spoken impulsively, that he hadn't had time to process or think things through rationally, so this wasn't the most level-headed decision, perversely gave her a glimmer of hope that there was still a way forward for them together.

Or perhaps she needed to accept they weren't meant to be together. They'd already tried so many times, and each one of those times had created a ghost that haunted their interactions in the present.

She'd bounced between extreme emotions countless times over the past couple of weeks. She had to know one way or another. She couldn't carry on living in this limbo land of half-hope, half-despair.

Each time they said goodbye she never really believed it was the final time. Even when she'd left for the States, thinking her relationship with Nathan was over, she hadn't been able to imagine feeling strongly for another man. She never wanted to experience those lows again. Initially relationships of any kind weren't on her agenda. Her total focus had been on her work and studies.

Looking back at that time through the lens of maturity, pursuing an arranged marriage had only become an attractive proposition after she'd read a gossip article about Nathan and the women he was dating. The realisation he had moved on had been the final sign that she needed to move on as well.

Calm, quiet Dilip had been the perfect antidote after the intensity of her relationship with Nathan. She'd cared for him when they'd married and truly believed love would develop over time. Her devastation when Dilip had died was a clear sign she had grown to love him, making her more determined never to expose herself to that kind of loss again.

Her need to be independent and stand on her own two feet was a way to protect herself. Closing her heart to love and romance was meant to close her heart to pain. Unfortunately, she was learning the hard way that when it came to love, in a war between head and heart, the head rarely won.

She loved Nathan—deeply, completely, enduringly.

She could be independent and raise her daughter on her own if she needed to. It wouldn't change the way she felt about Nathan. Even though loving him meant opening herself up to the possibility of loss.

And she needed to accept part of the blame. Had her refusal to marry him contributed to his belief he was untrustworthy?

He didn't believe in love or lasting commitments because of the way his father had walked out on his family. Hadn't she exacerbated his belief when she'd gone to the States? Run away when he needed her the most? If she had spoken to him before she left—explained how she felt, what she hoped for their future—might there have been a different outcome?

Didn't she owe it to him—and to herself—to be honest now? Instead of hiding her true feelings she needed to tell him what she wanted—a real, loving relationship. Or at least the chance of one in the future. She'd taken that chance before, when she had her arranged marriage, she could do it again.

If only she could convince him to open his heart to the possibility of love growing between them. That would be enough for her. She didn't expect him to love her now. That was fine—she had enough love for all of them. All she needed was the mere possibility they could have a loving relationship in the future.

Her head turned as she heard a car pulling into the driveway. She didn't recognise the vehicle, but there was no doubt Nathan was driving.

He'd come.

He didn't have to come. He could have sent a courier with the keys. His presence had to mean something.

Maybe she was going to go down in flames. She didn't care. She wasn't scared of demanding what she wanted any more. She had nothing to lose and the chance of gaining something wonderful.

Her heart sank when Nathan walked towards her. Stiff. Grim. Unyielding.

He let them into the house, then deactivated the alarm. 'Keys,' he said as he handed them over.

'Thank you.'

'A car's coming to take me to the airport soon. Is it all right if I wait here until it arrives?'

'Of course,' she replied as they walked through to the open plan kitchen-living area. 'But what's going to happen to the car you came in?'

'Oh, yes.' He reached into his pocket. 'I've leased that car for you. I didn't want you staying here without any transportation and I know you can't borrow a family car. Again, if you don't like it you can lease something else.'

Tears pricked behind her eyes. He was always trying to find ways to make things easier for her. Was it any wonder she loved him?

'Oh, I nearly forgot.' He walked out of the house, then came back with a couple of grocery bags. 'I picked up a few things. I didn't know whether you would have time to shop before you got here.'

She bit her lip, blinking rapidly as she fought against her instinct to hug him. Any child would be lucky to have this wonderful, caring man as their father. He cherished the people he cared about.

She loved him. She had to let him know—even though she would be exposing herself to more hurt. It would be worth it for the chance of the future she wanted. She had to lay everything on the line.

Could she do it? Would he turn away? Would he reject her? Would he break her heart again?

She stood up straight, her shoulders back. She was strong enough to deal with that if it happened.

'Me not wanting to get married was never about you. It was about me,' she blurted out.

He stiffened 'It's okay. You have every reason to think I won't be a good husband.'

'No. That's not it. I wanted to be independent. To prove I could bring up a child on my own if I had to. I've already lost so much in my life—Dilip, a baby, even you. I didn't want to risk getting hurt again.'

'I understand. I've hurt you so many times before and I would only hurt you both in the long run. You deserve better.'

She tutted with frustration. She was saying this all wrong. 'That's not true. You wouldn't hurt us.'

He walked over to the windows, staring out at the garden. 'You don't know that.'

'I *do* know,' she said with complete conviction. She needed to make him believe he was capable of commitment—that he was trustworthy.

He turned suddenly, a questioning look on his face.

'You're always there for the people you care about,' she began. 'You've always been there for your mother and your sisters. I can see how much you love them. You can't have any doubts about how much they love you. That's probably why your sisters are so open to knowing your dad.'

His brows creased. 'What do you mean?'

'You gave them everything they needed. You did everything for your family. You looked after them. You supported them. You protected them.'

Was anything she said getting through to him? She couldn't stop now.

'They never lacked for a father figure growing up because of you. They have no reason to resent your dad for not being there because *you* were instead. That's why I know you're going to be the most amazing dad.'

When he didn't respond, she continued.

'Look at what you've already done for us. You rented this place. You leased a car. You made sure we would be safe. You even brought food.'

'That's nothing.'

'That's not nothing. You didn't have to do that. Your father would never have done that—it wouldn't even cross his mind. Your father was a selfish man. The only person he cared about was himself. With every action you show how different the two of you are. You are nothing like him.'

She swallowed when he shook his head. The scars of his father's actions ran deep within Nathan. Her heart ached at his mistaken belief they were in any way similar.

'You know, I've been worrying a lot recently,' she said. 'Not only about the house or our living arrangements. I worry about the pregnancy. I worry about looking after the baby when she's born. I worry about whether I'll make a good mother. And it's not going to stop. I'm going to be a mum. I know I'm going to worry about my child for the rest of my life. But I've never—not for a moment—worried about you leaving us.'

There was still no obvious reaction from him. He just stood there, watching her.

'I'm not worried you will abandon me or our daughter. I have never once thought that. I have always known you will do everything you can to be part of our child's life. I don't believe there is any risk of you leaving us. I trust you, and if it takes marriage to convince you then we can get married.' She inhaled deeply. 'I love you, Nate.'

She held her breath, willing him to speak.

His phone beeped. 'The car's here. I have to go,' he said.

Her jaw dropped. That was all he had to say.

She'd done everything she could. All she could do was watch him walk out the door. Her shoulders slumped. She put herself out there, risking her heart, and now she was left alone with her dashed hopes.

Nathan glanced out of the window of the hospitality facilities in the private hangar where his plane was sitting on the Tarmac. He was due to board within fifteen minutes, then he'd be in New York for three or four days at least.

He tried to concentrate on the legal papers in front of him. If he couldn't get his act together it was pointless him even going to this meeting. The last thing he needed to deal with was a potential hostile management issue when there was something more important to sort out back at home.

Some*one* more important.

He frowned. When had Saira become the most important person in his life?

He admired her forthright attitude. He was fascinated by how her mind worked. He respected her opinions. He trusted her.

He inhaled sharply. If that was the case—if he trusted her—why was he finding it hard to believe what she was telling him now?

She'd always believed in him. Believed he would be there for the baby. For her. In her mind there had never been any shadow of a doubt he could be a good father and a stable presence in his child's life. How did she have so much faith in him?

He replayed their conversation. She was right. He loved his mother and his sisters. Even though he was hurt, felt betrayed when he heard they were in contact with his father, he was and always would be there for them. He already loved his daughter and would always be there for her. He would never abandon them. He wasn't like his father.

Saira was right and he would always be there for her too. Because he loved her.

Saira was his priority. She always would be. Not because of the baby but because she was Saira.

He was an idiot. Too blind to see what was patently obvious.

In his early twenties, his father's abandonment had caused him to doubt love existed. He dealt with that by pushing away people he cared about, not trusting that forever was possible.

When Saira had run away soon afterwards—when he pushed her away—he'd become convinced he wasn't capable of loving anyone. But that wasn't true. Far from being someone who didn't believe in love, he'd loved once and it lasted a lifetime.

The media dubbed him one of the Six-Month Men because he didn't have any relationship lasting longer than six months. But they'd got one major thing wrong. It wasn't because he was incapable of commitment that none of his relationships were long term. It was because nobody could come close to the woman he'd given his heart to years before.

He loved Saira. Had always loved her. He'd loved her years ago with the passion of youth. He loved her now with a depth borne of time, distance and maturity. Even after all these years he'd never stopped loving her. He never would.

And she loved him.

They would always be in each other's lives. Tied to each other not only because of the baby but because they loved each other.

He laughed at the simplicity of his realisation, eager to return to her—to tell her how he felt.

If it wasn't too late.

He'd almost let it all slip away by not believing in himself. By walking away before he could cause pain to the people he loved. The legacy of his father had burrowed deep.

He would need to have an open and honest conversation with his family about his father's return. His father's actions had far-reaching consequences beyond the pain he'd inflicted on his family. It almost cost Nathan the love of his life.

Perhaps he would arrange to meet his dad—there were clearly things that needed to be said. But right now his priority was to get back to Saira.

With his usual efficiency and determination he rearranged his flight, discussed the complex issues which would need to be resolved at the New York meeting with the employees who would cover his absence, and called his driver back.

Perhaps he should send a text to Saira? He got out his phone, then hesitated. What would he write? If he told her he was on his way back she would worry about the reasons. He didn't want her to worry. But he couldn't give her an explanation yet. What he wanted to say was too important for a text message.

He paced around the hangar until he was finally in his car, heading out of London. If his driver was giving him curious glances, unused to his employer changing his mind about anything, Nathan didn't care. He leaned against the car seat, closing his eyes, mentally rehearsing what he was going to say.

Abruptly he opened his eyes again.

There was no planning this. If he wanted to tell her what was in his heart, he could only speak from his heart.

No matter how it went today, the baby was a connection between them, and he would reassure her his devotion to the baby wouldn't alter even if she told him she never wanted to see him again.

He already loved their daughter, but at first he'd grasped at the pregnancy as an excuse to stay in Saira's life.

If only he hadn't proposed to her in such a pragmatic fashion. No wonder she believed the reason he'd asked her to marry him was because he wanted to do the right thing for their child. The baby had nothing to do with his insistence on marriage anyway. Their child was a tie binding them together irrevocably—marriage wouldn't change that.

Despite what he rationalised, the simple fact was he'd proposed because he wanted to spend the rest of his life with Saira. He needed her; she was the missing piece which made him whole.

Marriage was too important for her to agree to it for the sake of the baby. She would never treat it as a legal tool the way he'd suggested. It was in her nature to put her heart and soul into her family, and he couldn't offer anything less than the same. Her offer to marry him earlier showed how much faith she had in him.

His driver made good progress and they were soon driving up the road to the house.

Nathan ran a business empire. Thousands of people relied on him for their livelihoods. He liaised regularly with royalty and politicians. But nothing was more nerve-racking than the moment the car pulled in through the gates of the house.

'Is something wrong? Aren't you flying to New York?' Saira asked as he entered the house. Her hand reached out, but she brought it down and gathered the fabric at the side of her dress.

That was a good sign, wasn't it? She was concerned about him. That had to mean he hadn't ruined everything by leaving.

'I am. I will be. They can handle things without me for a few days,' he replied.

'Okay. Would you like a drink?' she asked, leading the way to the living area.

He shook his head. 'I'm fine.'

Now he was in front of her he didn't know where to start. He took a deep breath. These were probably the most important words he would ever say.

CHAPTER FOURTEEN

SAIRA BRACED HERSELF, hoping her face wasn't showing the signs of her tears. Why was he here? Why was he back? Why was he looking so nervous?

'Saira.' He cleared his throat.

'Nathan.'

'I'll always be here for you.'

'I know, Nathan.'

She smiled weakly. He didn't have to come all the way back here to tell her, although it was reassuring—if not a little surprising.

'I've never doubted you would be here for the baby. I'm glad you believe it yourself now,' she said.

'Not only for the baby. Of course I want to be part of our child's life. Of course I do. But it's more than that. I'll always be there for you too.'

She took a sharp intake of breath. What did he mean, he would always be there for her? She was trying not to read too much into his words.

He shrugged. 'We were too young to start dating when we were at school. I think we both knew that. But there was still something between us. When you started university I moved to London so I could be there too. I wanted us to be together when you were in your first year, but I waited until you had at least a year to experience university life before I contacted you.'

Her eyes widened. She hadn't known he'd planned that. When she'd started university she'd hoped Nathan would contact her—keeping tabs on what he was doing through Miranda. Even entering her second year, no man could hold her interest. She'd thought her dreams were coming true when he finally asked her to meet him. She hadn't realised he'd waited to give her space to experience university life—putting her needs above his.

He continued, 'I knew you would be spending a year abroad in the States. My plan was to open a satellite office in the same area, so I could still be there with you.'

She opened her mouth but no words came out. She blinked heavily, trying not to let her emotions run wild. Trying not to interrupt. He needed to get this off his chest.

'When we argued, and you left, I was going to follow but my family needed me. I had to stay here. Then you got married. Although I would still have been there if you ever needed me, I knew there wasn't any realistic chance of that—so I put my effort into growing a successful business. I convinced myself I wasn't capable of caring for somebody enough to make a commitment.' He shrugged. 'Somehow I knew there would never be anyone else for me. That's why no other relationship had any chance of lasting. When you came back, I couldn't believe we had another chance. I'm sorry I blew it. I'm sorry I turned my back on you after lunch with my mum and sisters. I didn't trust myself—didn't trust that I could be there for you. But I trust you. And you trust me.'

His tense expression faded as his mouth widened in a grin.

A cocktail of jumbled thoughts mingled with the avalanche of emotions rooting Saira to the spot. She stared at him, her knees giving way as she stumbled for the sofa. He could have warned her she would need to sit down for his declaration.

For someone who measured every word and never spoke more than necessary, Nathan's hastily spoken speech, tripping over the words to get them out, showed her the depth of his feelings more clearly than what he hadn't quite got round to saying.

'Saira?' he said, his voice low and uncertain.

'You said you'll always be there for the people you love,' she said in a soft tone.

He nodded. 'Yes.'

'And you said you'll always be there for me.'

'Always.'

'That sounds like you might love me,' she suggested hesitantly.

'Of course I love you. I always have.'

The simplicity of his words opened the floodgates, and she convulsed with the emotional impact of the declaration she'd longed for so long to hear. He took a step towards her, then stopped. She looked up, giving him a tremulous smile. He smiled as he gathered her in his arms, holding her close while she tried to compose herself.

Finally she met his gaze fully, unflinchingly. 'Why have you never told me before?'

'I thought actions spoke louder than words,' he replied, wiping the tears off her cheeks.

She laughed, and sniffed. 'I need the words too.'

He rubbed his chin. 'I love you.'

The words were stark. Simple. There was no doubting their sincerity.

With a startled exclamation she put her hand over her stomach.

'What's the matter? Are you in pain?' he asked with immediate concern.

'No,' she replied, with wonder in her voice. 'I definitely felt the baby move that time. I think your daughter likes hearing the words as well.'

She took her hand in his and placed it where she'd felt the movement. They sat close together in perfect harmony, experiencing the faintly discernible movements of their child.

Without saying a word they let their lips meet—tender, loving, with an undercurrent of the passion that inevitably flowed between them.

'Does that mean you still love me?' he asked.

'I will never stop loving you.'

'It's the same for me. I've loved you for so long now it's a part of me,' he said. 'I can't believe I almost didn't recognise it until it was too late. Now I know it can never be too late for us.'

Her heart skittered. She would never get tired of hearing that.

'It's painful to think about,' Nathan said in between kisses. 'If I hadn't been such a fool when my dad left, and spouted that nonsense about love and marriage, we could have been together all this time.'

'Perhaps,' Saira acknowledged. 'But maybe it's better this way. You were my whole world and I was too young and naive to keep my feelings in proportion. They were all-consuming. But our past and what we've gone through has shaped us. A deep and passionate love doesn't have to burn out any more than a slow, soft love is going to last for ever. I needed to learn so I could appreciate all the many aspects of the way I feel about you. I've grown in the last few years—definitely in the last couple of months. You've challenged me and supported me to become the woman I am now.'

'"Past is prologue,"' he said with a smile, repeating the phrase she'd used all those months ago.

'Finally, you realise I'm always right,' she said, laughing.

Nathan couldn't stop thinking of how close he'd come to losing all this because of his fears.

'Saira...?' he said.

She murmured, indicating that she'd heard him.

'I was thinking about meeting my dad. Do you think that's a good idea?'

'I think maybe that's exactly what you need.'

'Would you go with me?'

She was silent. Then, 'If you need or want me to, of course I will. But it may be something you need to do on your own the first time.'

'And what if I decide I don't want to stay in contact? That I don't want our daughter to know him?'

'Then I'll know that will be the best decision for our daughter.' She spoke without hesitation, and in a matter-of-fact way, making it clear her love was unconditional.

He was usually the one who supported other people. It humbled him to recognise that Saira would always be there to support him.

He bent his face to kiss her, before drawing her back to rest her head against his shoulder, fully content and secure in their future.

She giggled suddenly.

'What's so funny?' he asked.

'I'm thinking you'll have to leave your club. I'm not sure you'll qualify as a Six-Month Man much longer.'

'I never qualified for that club,' he said pressing a kiss to her temple. 'I've been in love with you for much longer than six months.'

'Oh...' she said, her eyes sparkling with unshed tears.

She drew his face into her hands, leaning up to give him a deep, passionate kiss.

After they broke for air, he interlaced his fingers through hers. 'Much as I hate to spoil the mood, we still need to make a few decisions. Do you want to carry on house-hunting now, or are you happy to stay here until after the baby's born?'

'I like this house. It's an amazing gesture you made, Nate. We can wait until after the baby's born to buy a place, but maybe we should continue to look at houses. Not that I expect we'll find a place that suits us better. But I insist I pay my share of the rent.'

He grinned. His independent woman. He knew better than to argue.

'Agreed.'

He bent forward to cover her mouth, felt their kiss deepening, flaring into passion. It was only when he sensed they were slipping off the couch that he broke apart.

'Enough. We still have things to discuss. You can't distract me with sex.'

'I'm willing to bet otherwise,' she said with a grin, running her fingers down his chest.

'If you don't behave, you're going to have to sit at the other end of the couch,' he replied, drawing her closer again.

'Okay, you win,' she said, snuggling into him. What do you want to talk about?'

'We agreed I would move in in a few weeks before the baby's due. Do you still want to keep to that plan?'

He knew she loved him, but she was still worried about the pregnancy. If she thought his moving in earlier would tempt fate he wouldn't do it.

She tilted her head, as if appraising him. What was going through her mind?

'It's a big house,' she said. 'I imagine it could be scary if I was here on my own all the time.'

He grinned. 'I see. Do you think if I move in with you it would be less scary?'

'Well, you'll still be travelling a lot for business before the baby's due, won't you? I don't want you under my feet all the time.'

They both laughed at the idea that was even a possibility with the amount of space in the house.

'I'd like you to move in whenever you can,' Saira said, 'but I know it's easier for you to be in London for work, so don't come before you planned to if it's less convenient.'

'If you're happy for me to be here, I can move in this weekend.'

He wasn't his father. He wouldn't put his business over his family. He would find a way to make it work.

She burrowed into his chest, fitting him perfectly, as always. He couldn't remember a time when he'd been happier. There was only one thing that could make it more perfect.

'Saira,' he began softly, 'does this mean you'll marry me?'

He cursed under his breath when she pulled away from him, straightened up, then put her legs back on the floor. 'No, it doesn't,' she answered with a slight laugh.

'Why not?' he asked, surprise in his voice.

She reached up to cup his face. 'I don't feel the need to get married at the moment.'

'But—'

'Nate, I love you. I'm not going to leave you and I know you're always going to be there for me. With the baby, we're committed to each other in every way possible. We don't need to be married to prove that,' she said, staring deeply into his eyes.

'You said earlier you would marry me.' She wouldn't have lied to him. What had changed her mind?

'And maybe one day I will. Nate, I'm not saying never. I'm saying not now. We don't want to steal Miranda's thunder. There's no rush.'

'One day, though?' he asked, needing reassurance.

'Nate, you're not going to get rid of me—ever. I'm not going anywhere. You have to believe that. You have to trust me. And, more importantly, you have to trust yourself.'

'I do trust you.'

It was as simple as that. He trusted her, and because she believed in him, he believed too. Because she was Saira.

'I'll have to wait until you ask me, then?'

She winked. 'That sounds right to me.'

He could be patient. He'd waited for her before—he could do it again.

'Marriage doesn't give us any guarantees,' she said, staring deeply into his eyes. There was no hiding the sincerity in them. 'Forever, happily-ever-after... Those take a leap of faith.'

'I know,' he replied. 'I've never taken that leap before, though.'

'That's all right,' she said, taking his hands in hers. 'You're not doing it alone. I'll be leaping with you.'

EPILOGUE

A year later

STANDING IN THE kitchenette of the hotel suite at Haynes Mayfair, overlooking the living area, Saira clasped her hands to her heart. Everyone she cared about was in one place. Her parents had broken their stay in India to be here, as well as her brothers, their families and Nathan's family.

His sisters were still in touch with his father, who'd attended Miranda's wedding but hadn't been asked to give the bride away. Over the past year Nathan had met with his father on a few occasions. He hadn't invited his father to today's ceremony, but they were continuing to work on their relationship. Saira supported Nathan's decisions regarding when and how his father might be welcomed into their lives, knowing that Nathan was open to giving his father a chance, and believed his father wanted to and was capable of change.

The Six-Month Men were there too, breaking off from their habitual half-yearly get-together to support Nathan.

All were gathered around Jaan, her and Nate's seven-month-old daughter, watching her having her first solids ceremony. She was gurgling and in her element, lapping up the attention while sitting safe and secure on Nathan's lap. He paid no attention to the tiny food-covered hand gripping his tie, or the globs of rice over his suit.

The past few months had been practically perfect. Apart from being a couple of weeks overdue, Jaan's birth had gone smoothly, and she was generally a content child. Nathan had taken a few weeks off after the birth, adapting to fatherhood as easily as he did anything else he turned his mind to.

Now he travelled less frequently and worked from home regularly. As he often told her, he used to enjoy travelling because he had nothing to stay home for. Now he had something more important waiting for him than work.

In a few weeks she would be working from home too. She'd accepted a position with Bastien's family foundation to encourage a learning initiative to empower girls. She was doing it on a voluntary basis, but it would provide the intellectual challenge she wanted.

Who would have thought that in the space of eighteen months she would have changed from being someone convinced independence and having a career were her only focus in life, and relationships were an unnecessary distraction, to being the person she was now, content to be a mother, working as a volunteer and deeply in love with an amazing man.

Nathan came into the kitchen and wrapped his arm around her waist. He pressed a kiss against her temple before turning to look at Jaan. She drank in every detail of the expression of pure adoration and devotion on his face as he watched his daughter. She took in a deep, shaky breath, burying her head in his chest as emotions engulfed her.

'Hey, what's this?' Nathan asked, running a thumb under her eye to catch the teardrops.

'I'm so happy right now,' she whispered.

'Me too.'

They stood peacefully wrapped in each other for a few moments before turning to their guests.

'Everyone's here,' Nathan said. 'It's time.' He stared deeply into her eyes. 'Are you sure you want to do this?'

'Never been more sure of anything in my life.'

The smile he gave on hearing her reply was so full of love and close to complete joy. She hoped it would never change.

'I love you.'

'I love *you*.'

He bent to kiss her fully on the mouth before taking her hand as they walked to the centre of the room, taking their daughter from his mother.

'Saira and I are so happy and grateful you're here today, celebrating Jaan's Mukhe Bhaat.'

Saira's family cheered at Nathan's perfect pronunciation of the Bengali name for the ceremony.

He continued. 'I know some of you are wondering why we decided to have Jaan's ceremony at this hotel rather than our house. It's because her first solids isn't the only event we're celebrating today.'

Saira smiled at the various expressions of their family and friends, some of them already guessing what was about to happen.

Nathan clasped her hand in his and brought it to his lips. 'Saira and Jaan fill my world completely. I am already the luckiest, happiest man on the planet. But after many, many, many, *many...*' He grimaced as Saira nudged him playfully with her elbow. 'Many months,' he reiterated, giving her a mock stern look, 'On New Year's Eve Saira finally asked me to marry her. And naturally I said yes. I didn't want to give her time to change her mind, so we're getting married today—downstairs in the Regent Ballroom—in an hour.'

The next sixty minutes passed in a haze of activity as their guests got ready—either freshening up or picking out new outfits from the designer boutiques in the hotel. Miranda, the only person they'd let in on their plans, kept Saira steady and calm—the same way Saira had done for her on her wedding day.

Saira had chosen to wear a lengha in traditional red, with ornate gold embroidery—exactly the kind of dress she'd dreamed of wearing on the day of her wedding to Nathan when she was a nineteen-year-old, first learning what love was.

Her vision blurred as she walked towards where Nathan was waiting for her in front of the registrar. Dreams could come true, and in only a few more breaths hers were about to be fully realised.

She was barely aware of repeating the words which would unite her with Nathan before the registrar pronounced them husband and wife.

'At last,' Nathan whispered, before meeting her lips with his in a kiss sealing their future together.

* * * * *

COMING SOON!

We really hope you enjoyed reading this book.
If you're looking for more romance, be sure to
head to the shops when new books are
available on

Thursday 3rd March

To see which titles are coming soon, please visit

millsandboon.co.uk/nextmonth

MILLS & BOON®

Coming soon

FINDING FOREVER ON THEIR ISLAND PARADISE
Therese Beharrie

'Everything about this feels real. Too real,' he said with a frown.

A piece of her hair fluttered over her forehead. He focused on that. The slight curl of it; the tiniest fuzz around its edges. Slowly, he lifted his hand, gripped the strands in his index finger and thumb, and gently put it back behind her head. It promptly flew to the front again. He smiled.

'When you say things like that…when you do things like this…' She nodded her head so he'd know she was talking about his actions with her hair. 'You take my breath away.' Her hands gripped the front of his t-shirt. 'I don't like feeling vulnerable either. The last time a man made me feel that way, I almost lost…' Her voice faded. Her fingers tightened.

'I don't want you to lose anything,' he whispered.

'I know.' Her gaze met his. 'Maybe that's why I feel like I'm gaining something with you instead.'

His heart filled. Overflowed. With what, he didn't know. Wasn't sure he wanted to find out. But he knew that honesty had brought them here. Vulnerability. Things he'd viewed as enemies since they'd done nothing but hurt him when he'd tried them with his family.

But now they'd brought him this closeness with Morgan.

Literally and figuratively; both seemed of the utmost importance. Although literal took precedence now that he could see the faint dusting of freckles on her right cheek. There was nothing on her left, and it fascinated him. As did the sparkle in her eyes. Every time he looked at them he came up with a better description for their colour. Today, they looked mahogany. Full, deep, rich; the colour would make the most beautiful piece of furniture. A desk, he thought. He'd make a desk of this exact colour so that he could be reminded of her eyes, of her, whenever he sat down to work.

'What are you thinking about?' she asked quietly.

His eyes dipped to her lips. They were somewhere between pink and red, reminding him of a tart fruit, and their creases formed a pattern he wanted to memorise. An impossible task. An illogical task. He wanted to take it on nevertheless.

'I'm thinking I'd...I'd like to kiss you.'

She smiled. 'What are you waiting for?'

Continue reading
FINDING FOREVER ON THEIR ISLAND PARADISE
Therese Beharrie

Available next month
www.millsandboon.co.uk

MILLS & BOON

Desire

Indulge in secrets and scandal, intense drama and plenty of sizzling hot action with powerful and passionate heroes who have it all: wealth, status, good looks…everything but the right woman.